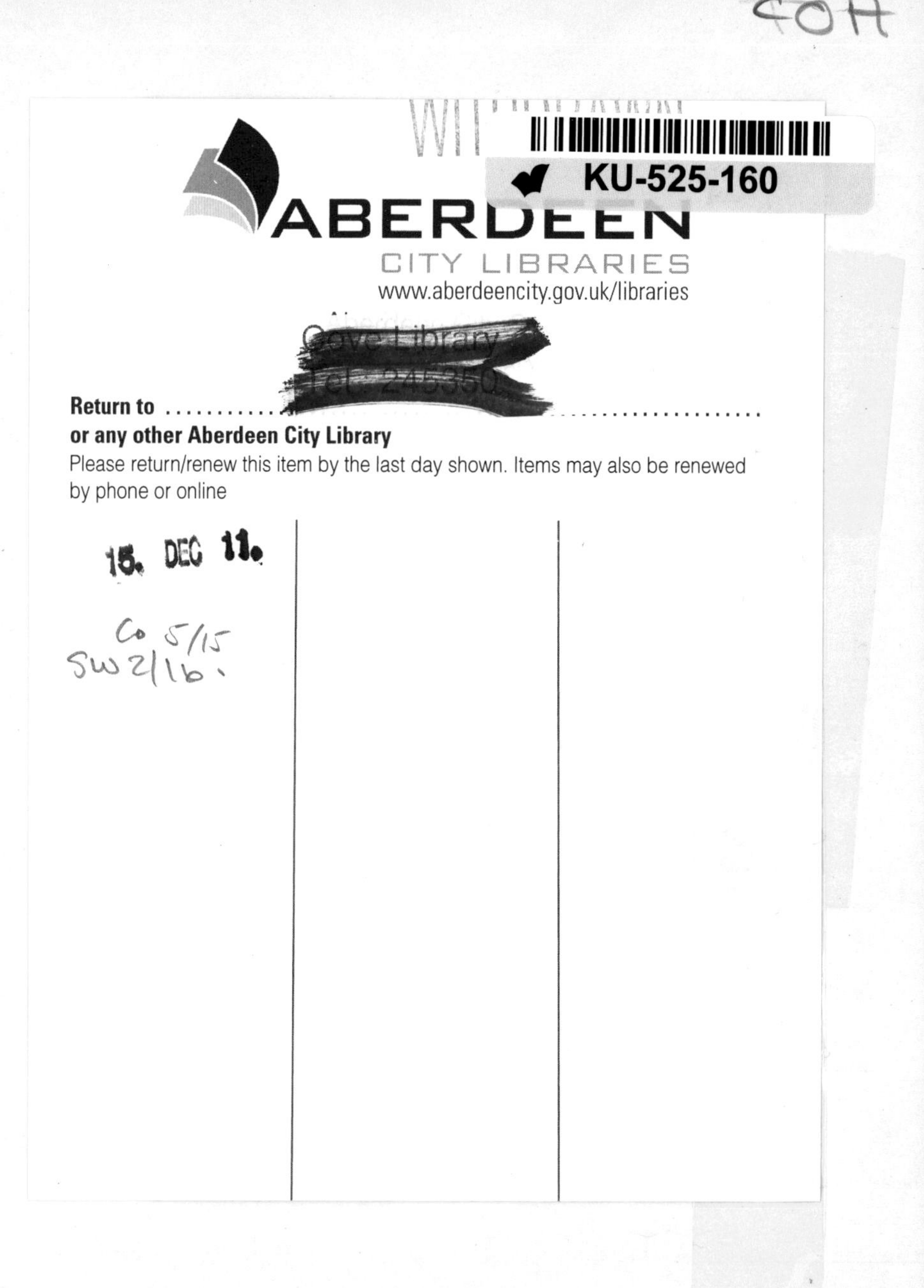
ABERDEEN
CITY LIBRARIES
www.aberdeencity.gov.uk/libraries
KU-525-160
Return to
or any other Aberdeen City Library
Please return/renew this item by the last day shown. Items may also be renewed by phone or online
15. DEC 11.

ABERDEEN CITY LIBRARIES

ALSO BY JANE LOVERING
FROM CLIPPER LARGE PRINT

Please Don't Stop the Music

Star Struck

Jane Lovering

W F HOWES LTD

This large print edition published in 2011 by
W F Howes Ltd
Unit 4, Rearsby Business Park, Gaddesby Lane,
Rearsby, Leicester LE7 4YH

1 3 5 7 9 10 8 6 4 2

First published in the United Kingdom in 2011
by Choc Lit Limited

A CIP catalogue record for this book is available
from the British Library

ISBN 978 1 40749 118 9

Typeset by Palimpsest Book Production Limited,
Falkirk, Stirlingshire
Printed and bound in Great Britain
by MPG Books Ltd, Bodmin, Cornwall

PROLOGUE

Long ago, in a galaxy far, far away . . .

The huge, helmet-headed alien moved forward, gas hissing slightly from the respiration packs on its back, but the man in the ripped shirt stood unmoving under the glare of the desert sun. He barely even blinked as the lumbering form came closer, merely held out his arms; one hand hovered close to his blaster rifle, and his trigger finger twitched ominously.

Behind them both, out of sight, out of range, Jack watched, bleary-eyed, feeling as though the back of his skull had been unscrewed and inexpertly replaced. All his muscles ached in the kind of concerted unity that meant things had been very, very bad recently and, although he vaguely understood what was going on, he couldn't for the life of him remember what he was supposed to be doing about it.

Suddenly the alien stumbled, lurched forward under the weight of the gas tanks, and its momentum carried it onwards and downwards until it hit the ground at the feet of the armed man, where it sprawled, helmet askew, grunting with the force of the impact.

The armed man threw his head back and laughed at the sky.

There was a sudden cry of 'Cut! For fuck's sake!' and a third man burst onto the scene, large and angry in a worn T-shirt. 'Christ! Gethryn, you could at least help the poor bastard to stand up!' But Gethryn just put both hands out in a helpless gesture, bending forward under the weight of his laughter and the now helmetless alien, revealed as a skinny guy with an encroaching bald spot, was forced to scramble to his feet via his knees, finally being helped to stand by two flustered girls who had to let go of their clipboards to assist him.

Jack watched warily, half a moment from helping. Behind his eyes pinpricks of light swung; gravity had no meaning other than to give 'down' and 'up' some kind of notional value, which his stomach was ignoring, and his ears registered a vague thrumming from some seriously heavy-duty engines somewhere off to his left. *This isn't good. In fact, this is so far out the other side of good that it's probably circling hell.*

'Hey, Iceman!'

That's me, thought Jack. *Yeah. Fairly sure that's me. What does he want me to do? God, my head hurts.*

Angry-man walked over to him, clearly suffering a serious case of artistic strop. 'You're gonna have to do something about him, Ice. We can't keep shooting the show like this, and, you know, he was four hours late onto set today. I had to shoot the battle scene first and that's kinda thrown the timing out for tomorrow. Ice? You listening?'

Urgh. 'Yeah, yeah, I'm listening. Look . . . um . . . Scotty . . .' *Please let that be his name* . . . 'I'll deal with it, okay?'

A pause. Angry-man . . . Scotty (probably) stared into his eyes for a second, then dropped his gaze to the dusty desert beneath his feet. 'Okay, boss, if you say so. Just, you know, make it soon, eh? Before we get cancelled?'

Cancelled. That's bad, I know that much. God, wish I could think straight. He squinted into the sunlight at the team of people behind Angry . . . Scotty's shoulder. Bustling, busy, all moving with the precision of a machine, and here he stood like a loose cog. This was *his* machine, and it was going to break down if he didn't fix it.

I'm a waste of a watch-strap. A hopeless, guilt-ridden drunk – I'm being offered everything that could mean something to me and if I don't sort myself out I'm going to lose it all.

CHAPTER 1

'What do you want most in all the world?'

Usually my answer to this is 'to wake up gradually', but this clearly wasn't the answer Felix had in mind. He's one of those congenitally cheerful people, full of energy and enthusiasm, like a spaniel. That talks. On amphetamines.

'Right now, Felix, I want you to go away. To Australia, preferably, but anywhere a long way away will do. Somewhere where they punish people who are jolly in the mornings. Close the door behind you.' I turned over and pulled the duvet higher around my ears. He might be my best friend, but jolting me out of blissful sleep was no way to go about showing it. 'I mean it.'

'Ha. Come on, Skye. Really. The thing that you most want, *ever*.' He bounced around a bit. At least, I think he was bouncing; I still had my eyes closed, but the furniture was clunking and ornaments kept falling over.

'Still you, to go away.' I humphed myself around in the bed and winched open my eyes. 'You are contravening the Geneva Convention, you know, breaking into my house and waking me up.'

'Darling, you are no fun.' He sat on the edge of the bed, which made me feel like a hospital patient, and a rattling sound told me he'd picked up the little brown bottle from my cabinet. 'I've told you about these sleepers – emergencies only.'

'I had bad dreams,' I muttered.

'The doctor said occasional use only.'

'Yeah, well, I've got an occasional table and I use that pretty much all the time.'

Felix gave me a hard stare. 'But still . . . Anyway, why aren't you working? I thought you'd got a load of people wanting your – ' he coughed pointedly – 'research skills.'

'Research is a real job you know. It's not like I'm running some kind of porn hotline, anyway my Internet is still down. Five days and counting, I'm going to ring them today and . . .'

'And what? Be ineffectual at them? Skye, you need to . . .'

'You know about those people who suddenly turn on their best friends?'

A pause. 'Yes?'

'I was being subtle. I'm sort of waiting for you to take the hint. Look, just say what you came to say, Fe, then go, all right?' I was beginning to regret giving him a key now. It was supposed to be on the understanding that he only used it if it was *absolutely vital*, but he'd developed a very loose interpretation of *absolutely vital* lately. It had apparently been *absolutely vital* that he came in last week while I was hanging out the washing; when I got in from the garden he'd been half-way through my toast and marmalade and had made me jump so hard I'd nearly wet myself.

'Here goes then . . .' I couldn't see him past the shoulder of duvet, but the mattress wobbled as he breathed heavily in a useless attempt at suspense. 'I've got tickets to the *Fallen Skies* convention.'

I'd been so sure he was going to tell me that he'd finally, *finally* got a long-term part in one of the soap operas he was continually auditioning for, that I'd got the words 'That's terrific' already lined up on my tongue. 'That's terrific,' I said, so as not to waste them, and then, '*what?*' I sat up so suddenly that my head sang, and was confronted by Felix in a bright red velvet jacket and luminous green trousers. 'Ow. Can you not have some sort of warning device for when you're being trendy? You look like someone cut the middle out of a set of traffic lights.'

'Is that all you can say?' Felix huffed. He leaned forward and stared at me, his hazel eyes a bit wild in his boyish face. Combined with his punky haircut and unshaved cheeks he looked like a Botticelli angel after an all-night party and a lost hairdressing bet. '"*That's terrific*?" I'm telling you that I've got,' and he pulled two cardboard oblongs from his overly tight pocket, 'tickets to the convention for your favourite TV programme *in the world*, which features the deliciously bad Gethryn Tudor-

Morgan and, by the way, this outfit is *designer*, totally on-trend, and you just tell me it's *terrific?*'

My heart was pounding, not just from the exertion of disentangling myself from the bedcovers, and my lips were stuck to my teeth. Was he suggesting what I thought he was suggesting? But he *knew*, he of all people *understood* how it was for me . . . 'You smell of perfume,' was all I could come out with, nearly non-sequituring myself to death. 'Into girls again, are we?'

Felix stood up, the dimness of the room making his skinny shape appear to loom over me. 'Oh, come on.' He tapped the tickets against one long leg. 'Just think, if my metronome stuck at hetero fifty per cent of the gorgeous people out there would be disappointed.'

'More relieved I'd have thought,' I muttered. He was acting normally. Well, as normally as was normal for Felix, which wasn't very. I must have misread his intentions. He was . . . boasting. Yes, just boasting. My eyes followed the tickets, which unfortunately meant staring at Felix's thigh. I was afraid if I looked away the tickets might vanish, disappear back into his pocket never to be seen again. 'Where did you get those from? I thought all convention tickets sold out the day after release? I know *Fallen Skies* isn't exactly *Doctor Who*, but, even so Fe . . .'

Felix grinned a Machiavellian grin and tapped the side of his nose. 'Aha. Ask no questions. Suffice it to say, I met a man who knows a man.'

'You meet lots of men,' I said sarcastically. Not really believing, I held out a hand. Slowly, obviously relishing the moment, Felix laid one of the tickets on my palm. 'Bloody hell. Fe.' The blue-tinted card bore the *Fallen Skies* logo of a single jagged peak and a low horizon and looked genuine. I rubbed my thumb over the embossing which didn't, as had memorably once been the case with tickets Fe had 'obtained', smear off onto my skin.

'It's in October. Three months to prep yourself if you want to go?'

My heart skipped and then double-timed like an overwound clock. Did I? Well, of course I *wanted* to, but, you know, I wanted to win the lottery and paint the kitchen and maybe, finally, do something about my terrible hair but . . . 'I can't. You know I can't. I mean, I would . . . if I could, but . . .' Was he doing this to taunt me? To try to force some kind of reaction from a body only recently weaned off so many anti-depressants that it had been a wonder I could even cry at *Bambi*? I'd watched it with Fe last week, just to check. 'Anyway, it's a long way away, isn't it?'

'It's only in America, Skye. They won't let them hold it on Mars. Health and Safety or something. It's five days of *Fallen Skies* – just think about that. Five *days*. Total immersion.'

I thought about it. About leaving my lovely little Edwardian terraced house, with its view over the ridged mound of grassy earth which led to the base of York's city wall. Where, from my bedroom window, I could see all the various strata of building, starting with the Roman and passing through the Anglo-Saxon and fourteenth century to a block of Victorian repair work squidged on the top like a bit of incompetent icing. Comforting. Permanent.

And then I thought about Gethryn Tudor-Morgan. Captain Lucas James of the Galactic Fleet, the best pilot in the B'Ha sector, hero of the recent Shadow War, and wearer of the least number of clothes in any given episode. Tall, golden-blond, rangy and *sinfully* good looking. I'd fallen for him before the first ad break of the series, and had remained faithful ever since. But. Even so . . .

I looked over at the poster on my bedroom wall where Captain Lucas James stood, one hand shading his eyes from the glare of a CGI double sun, the other hand clasped around the grip of a blaster rifle. His hair rippled behind him in the wake of a fixed-wing jet blasting up into the star-strewn sky, his mouth half-curved into a grin of happy anarchy and all visible muscles bulging. My insides, as ever, liquidised.

Felix watched me with his eyes narrowed. This made his cheeks even pudgier; now he looked like a choirboy having impure thoughts. 'He *is* gorgeous,' he said, as if noticing the poster for the first time.

'Yeah, well.' I swung my legs over the edge of the bed and stood up, my oversized nightshirt flapping around me. 'I know my limitations, Fe.' *Ugly, ugly Skye . . .*

'Ah, Skye.' Felix put his hands on my shoulders. 'You're not *that* bad, y'know. I'd do you. If you weren't my friend, obviously,' he added quickly, as I glared.

'Fe, you'd do *toads* if they didn't keep getting away.' I raked a hand through my hair. It too was suffering this morning, scrubby and tousled at the back and lank at the front and yet it was the least of my appearance-related worries. 'Oh. And you're still here. I'm going to call the UN. Have you crated up and locked away.' The smell of drugged sleep hung heavy around me, sweet and fuggy. I rubbed at my face with numb fingers and felt the creases and folds of my skin. 'I might even make that NATO, if you're not gone in ten seconds.'

'Mmmm, men in uniform.'

'Bugger off.'

'Okay, well, I'm not hanging around to be insulted, not at,' Felix glanced at the luminous bedside clock, 'eight o'clock on a Wednesday morning.' He looked around at the walls of my little room, where they could be seen between my grandmother's amateur watercolours of bluebell woods and strained-looking kittens. 'Suppose you're going to need room for another poster, once the new guy starts. Where are you going to put it? Or, you could take down some of those godawful paintings, although, knowing your grandmother, she probably glued them to the walls.'

I looked around as well. None of my late relative's paintings were *that* terrible, but I had to confess that I'd stopped noticing them years ago. 'What do you mean, the new guy?' I stretched and made to lift my nightshirt over my head in the hope that my imminent nakedness would scare Felix from the room.

'When the T-M leaves. They're replacing him with some Yank, used to be in one of those American soaps where everyone's banging their sister.'

My head went suddenly fuzzy. 'What?' I let the hem drop and sat suddenly on the bed. The brass frame creaked in sympathy. 'Why? How? I mean . . . the whole show revolves around him.' And what would I do without my weekly glimpse of the man who'd helped save my sanity?

'Yeah, he's quitting his contract at the end of the current series. So I guess they'll be writing him out.'

Carefully I breathed. In, out. Remember what they told you, manage the panic, don't let it get away from you. 'How do you know?'

'Read it online. You've really got to get that Internet connection sorted, you know. You're missing all kinds of interesting gossip, the Beckhams have . . . oh, never mind, guess you're not interested enough.'

'I *am*. I mean in the other stuff, not the Victoria and David thing. It's just . . . yes, I miss my Internet, but . . . all that dealing with people . . .

I'm not so good these days, Felix, you know that. You *understand.*' I'd half-hoped that he'd offer to make the calls for me, but he'd insisted that it was better for me to do it, that it would be a step towards recovery for me. Yeah, right, and I could have signed up for *Come Dine with Me* while I was at it, a TV appearance and my inadequate cooking would get me the full set of humiliating experiences in one go. 'And it's all confirmed? Gethryn's really leaving? You know what *Fallen Skies* is like for rumours.'

'Yep. And this one's true. Means that this convention is going to be his last.' Felix squinted out of the window and shifted himself from foot to foot, then turned to give me a manic grin. 'So? How about it? Your last chance to actually meet the guy. Or you could, y'know, stay in your room, just absorb the atmosphere. Maybe see him out of the window.'

The house throbbed around me, one second too big, the next too small and pushing half my furniture onto the pavement. That poster shot into full focus, Gethryn becoming huge, those deep brown eyes seeming to smile straight into mine. There was a small worn patch over his mouth where I kissed the poster before bed every night, and I prayed that Felix didn't know about that.

'I need to think.'

'Well, you've got until seven. I'll drop by after work, and if the answer's no then I'm putting these on eBay.' Felix rotated once more then headed for the door, still standing open from his earlier entrance. He was just about to step out when he came back and yanked the ticket from my hand. It needed considerable force, and I think, in my shaken and shocked state, that I might have bitten him. 'Want anything while I'm at the shop?'

'When I'm short of oversized jeans and funky belts I'm sure you'll be the first to tell me.'

'Maybe. Maybe I'll just let you fester in last year's fashion.' A short pause, and then he said, with his back to me. 'It would be good for you, Skye, change of scenery and all that. You never know, it might help.'

A second of clamour in my head again, and then I touched the wall, the lovely, comforting, solid brick wall. 'It won't, Felix. You know it won't.'

'All right, maybe "help" was the wrong word. But getting away might give you a break from everything. Put things in a different perspective.' A moment while he swayed his skinny body in the doorway, waiting for me to shoot him down, and then, 'Okay, lover, I'm off then. See you tonight, yeah?' There was the tap and slide of his boots on the stairs and then the definite bang of the front door.

The wall felt dusty under my fingers. My grandmother, who'd left me the place 'to take care of', must be absolutely rotating in her grave. I blew, and the dust motes took off, lazily swirled around and then resettled on different surfaces. I ought to clean, I knew. But somehow I didn't have the energy; there were always other things to be done, other claims on my time. Like work. Even with the Internet down there was reading to do and notes to make.

My job these days was not as high-profile as Felix's, which, as he worked in a shop at the sharp end of the gay clothing industry, involved the movement of more leather than a cattle drive. In fact, my work was so low-profile as to hardly stick up at all. But it paid and I didn't have to mix with people who would stare, which was all I really asked of work these days. Gone were the hours spent poring over *The Stage* for open auditions, obsessing over whether I was too tall, too skinny, whether my nose needed trimming. Now I was a freelance research consultant – basically a fancy name for someone who looked up things that other people couldn't be bothered to. Currently I was working on researching the life of an infamous pirate, the history of knitting patterns and had two outstanding commissions for a mustard company. No water-cooler gossip, no chance of a selection for stardom, but it was the only job I'd ever had where clothing was optional.

I sorted out my pile of books and prepared to continue work for the author who wrote piracy-porn, taking notes and making sketches of sixteenth-century fashion. I'd stuck Post-Its on the relevant texts and was poised to start skim reading when a new message pinged into my phone, with the characteristic chime that made me want to hide my mobile under something big and wet.

From: Fe Brand
Come on Skye, u no u want 2.

I typed straight back.

From: Skye
I told you I'm thinking about it. And stop using text speak, you're not twelve.

From: Fe Brand
Yeh, yeh. Cme on, don't u thnk its tme u got out of tht wheelchair?

From: Skye
You've got predictive text stuck on again. Wheelchair?!

From: Fe Brand
It's a <u>metaphorical</u> wheelchair you pilchard. An emotional one. You don't have the monopoly on grieving and all that crap, and if I can get on with my life after what happened, then so should you. So, what the fuck, let's go to America!

Serious stuff. So serious that he'd abandoned his jokey, half-text-speak, and mentioned things we didn't talk about in real life. Things so raw and overwhelming that we pretended they'd never happened. I dropped the phone and my fingers began twisting around one another, plucking at my nails. The skin around them was nearly healed, but ugly white scars streaked each fingertip.

From: Fe Brand
And stop doing that shit with your fingers.

I smiled without meaning to. Felix knew me so well. But then, we'd known each other for . . . how many years? Ten? More, maybe, by now, but I'd stopped counting. Stopped even thinking about him as a person, as a man. He was just Fe, irritating as an itchy bum. So much like Faith that I hadn't been able to look at him for the first six months after the accident without seeing her looking back from behind those hazel eyes. I'd become so accustomed to the feeling that it had worn away without my noticing, until one day he was just Felix again.

From: Skye
Whereabouts in America?

CHAPTER 2

I awoke from disturbing dreams to grit between my teeth, a sun blazing through a windscreen and a seemingly endless rank of telephone poles marching beside the road. My feet were cold but my back prickled with dried sweat and I had never regretted letting Felix talk me into anything quite so much. Surely even Gethryn wasn't worth this much discomfort? 'Where are we?' I twisted my head against the uncomfortable upholstery of the hired car.

Felix looked over his shoulder at me. He was concentrating ferociously on staying the right side of the road whilst juggling the map across his lap. 'Bloody hell, Valium worn off already?'

I licked my lips. The sedative had left my mouth feeling as though it had been unscrupulously carpeted and my tongue was as heavy as a corpse. ''S okay. I feel . . . okay.' This was a lie. Through the layer of Valium I felt displaced, anxious. The car was confining and yet not safe. Outside I could see a landscape scrolling past in a backdrop of dust; bare hills sketched against a white sky and some buildings that looked like aircraft hangars.

There was nothing familiar to pin myself onto. 'Fe –'

'Nearly there, apparently. God, I wish you hadn't talked me out of that GPS, there's places here, actual *places*. They weren't on the map.' *I'd* wanted to hire a car with GPS, but he'd raised his eyebrows and pointed out that this was Nevada; once we got on the right road the motel was virtually the only thing of note in 200 miles, and that an extra seventy-five dollars for pin-point accuracy probably wasn't necessary unless I wanted to nuke it. He was paying and I was hot and confused so I'd shut up. But I wasn't going to be sympathetic if we were lost. Felix was driving without looking at the road, staring out of the window as we passed through a town that looked as though a missile strike would probably improve it. 'Not a single Gap for miles – how do these people *manage*? Honestly, it's just a patch of desert with two office blocks, ridiculously oversized houses, a school and a hospital . . . Where's the fashion?'

I stuck my head out from under the blanket which covered me as I lay sprawled across the whole back seat, half-drugged. Felix insisted on running the air-con full blast despite the fact that this was pushing the fuel costs into the 'ridiculous' bracket, and yet he wouldn't pay extra for the GPS. I suppose that's men for you. 'Maybe they don't need fashion out here.'

'Skye, this is America! Land of the free, or at least, the reasonably priced. Everyone needs fashion. Particularly that chap over there . . . that is the *ugliest* shirt I've ever seen. Anyway. Soon be there, the Broken Hill Motel, Nevada. Sounds exotic, doesn't it?'

'No, it sounds tacky. Who holds conventions in Nevada? Apart from *CSI* fans.' I clutched the blanket closer to me for the fake sense of security. 'I want to go home.' The panic was building, knocking against my temples like an old friend wanting to come in.

'No, you don't. I didn't go through all that business getting you onto the plane and force-feeding you tranquilisers just for you to dip out on me.' Felix swung the car's weight into a minor curve. I rocked against the door and had to half-sit to balance myself. As I did, I caught his eye in the rearview mirror, and the next thing I knew we were stationary, with the car slewed across the edge of the road, and Fe was half-in, half-out of the back seat, hanging through from the driver's side to flap his hands in my face, encouraging a sluggish current of air to puff against my cheek.

'What . . .' I drew a breath. My throat ached and my eyes felt like they'd been thumbed.

'Oh good, you're back with me. I was a bit worried there, your eyes rolled right back in your head, which is not a good look, let me tell you. Nearly as hideous as Mr Shirt and his incredible diamante buttons back there.' A half-sighed breath wobbled his words and made him sound more concerned than I'd ever heard him. 'Skye, look, I'm sorry, I didn't know you'd be this bad, I just thought it would be good for you, a break from . . . everything, you know? I thought, away from York, from the memories of it all, you might . . .' He flopped back into his seat, a passing motorcyclist distracting his attention.

I forced my fists to uncurl, and laid my head carefully back on the seat. 'It's okay. Really. No, you were right, Fe, I had to start living again sometime and if it took something like this to make it happen, then that's a good thing, isn't it?' *Isn't it*? 'Besides, I *am* getting better, look, I got that Internet problem fixed, didn't I? Talked to a strange man for *ages* to sort it out, and I was getting a bit sick of the same old places – home, library, supermarket . . . It will be *good* to see some new sights. Like . . .' I waved a hand at the window, 'that.'

'It's a chemist's.'

I sighed, the tension in my shoulders barely allowing any air in. 'But it's not Boots. That's what I mean, it's different. A change of scenery, like you said.' The slight wobble in my voice gave the lie to the words.

'Just say the word and I'll drive straight back to Vegas, we'll get on a plane and you'll never have to leave town again.'

I looked through the gap between the seats. His knuckles were a bluish-grey where his hands were clenched around the steering wheel, and his back was pressed right into the seat, as though he was somehow nervous about my reply. *That's right,*

Skye, run away when it gets difficult . . . 'We'll go on.' My voice was so quiet he didn't hear and I had to repeat myself. 'To the motel.' A half-hysterical laugh bubbled out with the words. 'Might as well, since we've come this far.'

His body slumped a little in . . . what? Relief? 'All right, if you say so. Better get going before the cops arrive, anyhow. Hey, do you think they wear those uniforms, like when they rock up on *CSI*? With the really tight trousers? Maybe we should hang around. Look, pop another Valium, that should tide you over till we get there.' He flipped the glove box open and passed back the brown prescription container and a bottle of water. 'Here. Take two.'

'Two? Are you sure?'

'Darling, I take more than that when I'm getting my feet done, you'll be fine.' He kept his head turned, watching me swallow. 'There. You'll be nice and calm for our arrival now.'

'Thanks.'

'Don't mention. What set you off, if you don't mind me asking, and now that you've got a neck full of calmdown? You were doing so well up 'til now.'

'Just . . . for one second it was . . . I haven't been in a car since.'

Felix's face seemed to ripple as various emotions struggled for expression. 'Like a flashback? Yeah.'

We sat quietly for a moment, while my brain shuffled through the blankness that was all that was left where so many memories had once been, until it was caught in the soft edging between sleep and wakefulness. 'Do you think we'll ever get over it?' I let the words trickle from my mouth, muffled by the blanket, and heard Felix's reply likewise sieved through the wool.

'I hope not. I really hope not. Now, go to sleep, we'll be there very soon.'

CHAPTER 3

In an untidy room at the front of the motel, an equally untidy Jack fired up his laptop, waited until the *Fallen Skies* logo appeared and then began to work.

'INT. SPACESHIP – DAY he typed, then leaned back and chewed his lip. *Hell's teeth, it never used to be this hard. Maybe I've lost it, maybe I'm not meant to do this any more.* His fingers roamed the surface of the desk, subconsciously searching for the pack of cigarettes he knew he'd carefully hidden from his writing self, found a pencil sitting blamelessly on top of a sheaf of papers, and deliberately snapped it in half. The noise made him jump. *Bugger. Must stop doing this, running out of pencils.*

As he turned his attention back to the screen, which throbbed accusingly before him, his hand continued its unconscious movement, and the next thing he realised he was sucking on the broken pencil end, filling his mouth with the boxy taste of wood and tiny granules of graphite. He snatched the stub from between his teeth, spat ferociously, and hurled it onto the floor, where it sat damply between his bare feet.

I want to go home. The thought took him by surprise and he pulled a face at his reflection in the screen, where the words shone through his hair and INT and DAY formed double images on the lenses of his glasses. *I wake up dreaming that I can smell the moors, that the heather is flowering and the ground is damp and clingy underfoot. I'm walking out under the high sky with the birds like little full stops up between the clouds and there's nothing for miles but me and the sky and those little purple bells of flower which smell like honey on toast.* The expression which stared back at him twisted its mouth. *Yeah, right. And Enid Blyton used to pop over for tea with Beatrix Potter and her talking bloody rabbits. Pull yourself together, you nutter. That was then, this is now, Iceman, and you've got work to do. Bills to pay, things to hold together and one hell of a lot of forgetting to do.*

He blanked his mind and went back to the script, not even noticing when the other half of the pencil found its way between his lips, and he sucked on it with oblivious contentment.

CHAPTER 4

I jerked into a loose kind of wakefulness as the car drew up under a tree, dusty with leaves and ornamented with some kind of bird I didn't recognise. My limbs were dull and unresponsive, my attempts to sit up made me look like a cadaver being poked. 'Wha'?'

'This is it.' Felix's voice was edgy, excited. 'This is the convention. Look at it, Skye, all the cars! And there's one of those great big van things, whatchacallems . . .'

'Horse box.'

'Winnebagos. Wow. How American. And look, there's one of the Shadow Fighter craft.'

Sleepily I turned my head until I could see the black triangular ship, parked incongruously on a trailer behind a Volkswagen Beetle. Its swept-back wings looked a little the worse for wear in the white sunlight and part of the paintwork had peeled off near the pilot's section, but that just added to the glamour in my eyes. It was *real*, it was *used*. It looked as though it genuinely had flown through the B'Ha sector with a Skeel warrior on its tail. Despite the Valium my heart beat a tiny bit faster.

Felix turned in his seat. 'Okay, we're going to have to get out now, Skye. Take a deep breath, lover, it's not a long trip, I can see the foyer from here.'

I slumped back against the seat, unable even to rally the sense of terror I knew I should be feeling at the prospect of that overarching sky pressing onto my head. Felix opened the door and helped me to manoeuvre myself out onto the sandy concourse. 'Here we go.'

The light burst upon me as the hot air hit. Air rattled into my lungs and yet the feeling of suffocation grew.

'Look, I know you're Valiumed up to the hilt, but is there *any* chance that you can walk?' Felix panted, lugging my unresponsive body along the length of the car, propping me against the hot metalwork with blatant disregard for the potential for third-degree burns.

'Can't . . . feel my . . . feet,' I mumbled, through numb lips. Life streamed past, dreamlike.

'Oh, this is just bloody great. What am I going to do now, leave you here and hope that everyone thinks you're a really convincing special effect?'

The air blew across my face, incendiary-hot and laced with grit. I could barely summon the strength to blink. Slowly and inevitably my legs gave way and I slithered down the car's bodywork in a sweat-lubricated collapse, landing with my skirt bunched under my buttocks and my shirt rucked over my bare midriff. The smell of hot tyres made me feel slightly sick.

Footsteps approached, soft in the dust and I saw a pair of feet surrounded by the trailing hems of what looked like pyjama bottoms. 'Hey. What's up?' The voice was unfamiliar. British. Northern English to be exact, the flat vowels reminding me of home. I tried to look up but could only waggle my head.

'Just a little hitch, nothing to worry about.' Felix bent his head to my ear. 'Skye, you might want to get up here, this guy is a definite twelve on the ten-point scale.'

'She looks pretty out of it,' the considering voice went on. 'You might have to carry her.'

'What, with my back?' Felix stood up again. 'We'll wait a minute; the drugs should be wearing off by now.'

'Oh, right.' The voice softened, not quite as far as sympathy but definitely less brusque. 'Not a good traveller then, your girlfriend?'

'Girlfriend? Seriously?' Felix threw me a look. 'Well, she's a friend, she's definitely a girl, but my God, if there was a wrong end of the stick award, you just took it.' Felix went into full camp mode. 'I've had this all the way from England, d'you know she can't even *pee* unaided when she's like this?'

Er, hello, I wanted to say, you insisted that the tranquillisers would help . . . I didn't need them at home any more. Much.

'Look, I'll give you a hand; it's too hot to leave her here.' And the next thing I knew I was being lifted and hurled across a bony shoulder, with my skirt pinging free from my buttocks to fall up around my waist leaving my knickers on display. If I'd been half-way capable I would have kicked and screamed, but the Valium was still jamming my system like an unfriendly radio-wave; I knew I was the subject of some indignity but couldn't do a damn thing about it.

As my head lolled onto the chest of my carrier I registered a rib cage under a thin T-shirt, lots of dark hair brushing against me, and I must have been hallucinating a little, because it looked to my slightly unfocused eyes as though there was half a broken pencil sticking out of his mouth.

'This is very kind of you.' Felix was trotting along-side. I hoped it was his hand that pulled my skirt down to conceal my cheap chain-store briefs. 'Very impressive, throwing her over your shoulder too. Very butch. I know she looks like there's nothing to her but, phew, she's got really dense bones, our Skye.'

Thanks, Fe, I thought, as the man dropped me unceremoniously into what felt like a leather armchair.

''S okay. She looked a bit uncomfortable out there on the ground.' A pause during which I tried to look up again, but couldn't get much more than an impressionistic view of various limbs and a patch of wall covering which gave the initial impression that Nevada motels were decorated by the state's trainee graffiti artists. 'Anyhow. If you're here for the convention, I'll see you around.'

There was a short pause, during which my rescuer left and Felix took in our surroundings. I felt contained in the armchair and my breathing slowed. Fe started to giggle.

'Wow, trust you to find the yummiest guy around to get carried by. Stay there, I'll check us in.'

I didn't enquire into the alternative to staying, bearing in mind that I had almost no control over my arms and my legs seemed to be made of fuzzy felt. I sprawled against the leather, head hanging over an arm and my hair pendulous in the heat. An upside-down view through the huge tinted window showed me a vast brown sky, overtopped by a vast brown plain. A couple of spectral mountains in the far distance looked like an enormous sway-backed old horse sketched against the sky and served to emphasise the immediate flatness. In my head Nevada = Las Vegas glitz, not that bottom-of-a-pond flat beigeness.

There were people moving around me, a general feeling of swirling humanity. Voices collided, accents clashed. All I could see though, from my position in the chair, was feet, and my drug-padded brain did its best to match intonation to shoe-culture. The drawl of the southern states seemed to marry up to several pairs of Kicker boots and one pair of flip-flop sandals standing near the window. The brittle English tones belonged to some polished brogues and high heels walking towards the door. Two pairs of bare Scandinavian-designate feet paddled briefly into vision and then out again, and an immaculate set of New York loafers hesitated beside me for an instant before meeting another, similar pair and disappearing from my field of view.

'Okay, I got our key.'

Drugged as I was, I registered this. 'One room?'

Felix's face swung into sharp focus. 'By the time I'd got the tickets, this was all that was left. Don't sweat it, we can always take it in turns to use the bed. And –' he looked around and then lowered his voice – 'hopes are that I'm going to get part-shares on a few other rooms, if you get my drift.' His voice went down another notch. '*Seriously tasty*. Bloody hell, Skye, why did we never come to the States sooner?'

'Have you seen Gethryn?' Despite the brain-numbing, I was still conscious of why we'd come. Of why I'd left my comfort-zone so far behind that it wasn't even visible with binoculars. 'Is he here?'

'That's most likely his Winnebago out front there. But it doesn't look like he's hanging round the check-in, no.'

'Oh.' I slumped further into the chair and my eyes closed. 'Pro'ly should sleep.'

Felix sighed. 'All right.' He jerked me upright and bundled me physically into a lift. After several goes the doors managed to close, everything jolted and jangled for a few moments and then the doors opened onto a grey-floored corridor, along which Felix half-dragged me by my elbows with my heels kicking little static sparks off the floor covering as I shuffled along beside him. We must have looked like room service for a shy serial killer. There was a moment of juggling as Felix tried to cope with my drooping form and the room key, which involved my being propped against the wall by my forehead like a roll of unwanted carpet, then we were in. As we entered I thought I heard Fe mutter quietly, 'Got to get you fit for Friday.'

Fit? For what? But I hardly even had enough wakefulness for curiosity, and the feel of pliancy beneath my back as I dropped onto the bed drove any questions out of my head altogether.

CHAPTER 5

Wakefulness came suddenly. The room was awash with garish daylight, which streamed through the too-thin curtains and bounced off every surface like a toddler full of additives. The place seemed to be made of mirrors and edges. Judging by the silence and the immobility of the blanket-wrapped floor-blob that was Felix, it was early in the morning, but I'd even slept off the jet-lag and was now spread out under the remaining covers in the vast bed, wide awake. Not just awake either; there was an almost unrecognised tingling in my middle, a vague tugging sensation near my heart. I was actually *excited.* I lay still for a moment, realising how much I'd missed these everyday feelings then, careful not to wake Fe, I padded over to the window and threw open the flimsy curtains, alert for my first real view of Nevada desert beyond the windows.

Alas, this last available room in the motel had still been available for a reason. The view from our first-floor window was a small yard, bounded on three sides by off-shoots of the motel and partially haunted by a rangy yellow dog which wandered in and out of vision, nosing the dusty ground. Tucked behind what was obviously the kitchen wing I could see the tops of a couple of dumpsters, and the slumped landscape I'd noticed the night before was reduced by the buildings to a taupe hillside. Even so I felt the fizz of anticipation rise. I was here, I'd done it – this was America! Somewhere, out there, beyond those bins and dog turds, was Gethryn Tudor-Morgan, and beyond that . . . I gave a little shudder. Since the accident I'd lost my love for boundless horizons; those things that had once seemed full of promise and exhilaration now held the unknown and unfamiliar and the possibility of sudden screaming.

Cautiously I opened the window and pushed my head out. The air smelled strange. Not badly strange, just different. At home the air smelled of diesel fumes from the ring-road, the zippy scent of pine from the trees opposite the window and sometimes, when the wind was coming from the north, of heather and wildness from the moors. Here the air smelled dry, spicy. And slightly 'off', but that was probably the dumpsters.

Two Hispanic boys came arguing out from a doorway, aprons tied around slim waists. I watched eagerly. It made a change from ogling Mr Harrison next-door-but-one coming home from his teaching job with his jacket off. These two were shouting Spanish obscenities, all waving fists and sleek hair, until they'd fought their way into the shade of the wall under my window, where they made up with a deep kiss and went back inside, arm-in-arm and laughing. I pushed down the inevitable needle of pain that wormed its way under my ribs. *Michael and I had been like that, once. Fighting and making up, loving and laughing. Michael* . . . A sudden image flowed into my head, a man, tall and blond standing in a doorway. It was so much like a memory that, for a second, I almost thought . . . but then I realised I was thinking of a photograph that Felix had shown me. A second-hand memory. All there was. All that was left of our love.

Tears kissed against my cheek and I swiped them away angrily. Except for the brain damage and stress-related panic attacks, I'd got over the whole thing marvellously. Everyone said so. Even as their eyes traced the scars, they agreed that I'd done amazingly well . . .

'Leave your fingers alone.' The sleepy voice rose from the middle of the rolled-up bedcover.

'Sorry.'

'What are you doing anyway, hanging out of the window and thinking about the past?' Fe snuffled his way forward to grab his phone. 'Jesus Christ, it's six a.m., Skye! Get some more sleep.' There was a waft of fusty sleep-warmed air as he turned over. 'Things'll kick off soon enough.'

'Mm, maybe.' But I had no intention of sleeping. The curiously gold sky beyond the window enthralled me, the warm scents in the air were shouting to me of exotic life going on where I couldn't see it. There was a weird unreality about this pebble-dashed dawn. Like this whole trip was a vision or a play, that the world outside was just a stage set. Nevada, with its completely fantastical landscape, beckoned to me like a carnival stallholder and, for the first time since the accident, I actually wanted to see what was happening outside.

I dressed in the little bathroom. Felix must have brought the cases up after undressing me last night, which I knew I hadn't done myself because I wouldn't have left my bra on. Thank heavens he still had some sense of decency left. Then, cautiously aware that it had been a long time since I'd ventured anywhere strange alone, I took a deep breath and tiptoed out of the room. I found my way down a flight of stairs and out of an unlocked side-door into the emptiness of the day.

The air hit me like a missile. All my pride at my new confidence evaporated and I crouched as the hugeness of the outdoors crashed against me, raging and worrying its way inside my head, making my heart knock against my ribs and my breath sting inside my mouth. *This wasn't home.* Everything was new, and the newness threw itself against me, filled with unpredictability, like a dog that appeared friendly but might at any time turn and bite, and I knew I couldn't do it. Couldn't face this new strangeness; I'd been stupid even to think that I might. *Stupid, stupid Skye* . . . As I began backing my way towards the safety of the building, the door behind me swung open again, catching me with its leading edge and sending me flying down into the gravelly dust of the pathway.

'Oh, bollocks!' The voice of the person who had so carelessly flung open the door sounded annoyed rather than apologetic. 'What the hell is anyone doing out here at this time in the morning?'

The shock and indignation counteracted the panic, drove back the stress-demons and shrank the world to a manageable size. The sky stopped its assault and I could breathe properly, so I made the most of it and scrambled to my feet, brushing my knees with my hands ostentatiously. 'Don't mention it,' I said, wheezing slightly as the panic abated. 'No, really, I'm fine. Hardly any arteries severed.'

I was unsurprised, given the English accent, to find myself grinding my teeth at yesterday's rescuer, a man who had had a closer view of my knickers than any man I wasn't sleeping with. Now I was finally getting a proper look at him, I suspected that my knickers were the closest he'd ever come to female underwear, unless he was a secret transvestite. He didn't, to put it plainly, look like a man who got on with women.

He didn't look like a man who got on with *people*.

It wasn't as though he was ugly. Oh no. Not ugly at all. In fact, on first glance you might even call him obliquely handsome. Hair slightly too long, eyes very dark in a lean, frowning face, shoulders which stooped as though his nose was somehow invisibly connected to the floor; he looked like a beautiful man that someone had rubbed with worry until his edges blurred. It was his expression that made him look so disagreeable. As well as pyjama bottoms and a long shirt, he wore a scowl that instantly made the infinity of outdoors seem not enough space to get away from him in. He was scowling so hard that his eyes were down to slits and his mouth was twisted *and* pursed in a feat of gurning I'd never seen bettered.

He surprised me by muttering 'yeah, sorry', but then went right back to reinforcing my prejudice against him by flopping down onto a raised planter and extending his scowl to include it. The bed contained a desiccated-looking bush and some brittle earth, and his expression was so irritable that I was slightly surprised nothing burst into flames. He stretched out his legs in front of him, revealing a grubby pair of bare feet, and fumbled in a pocket, relaxing his mouth enough to clamp the resultant cigarette between his lips and then swearing around it until he found a lighter.

The presence of another body helped me feel less like the scenery was on some personal attack mission. My muscles began to slacken and my breathing eased into a regular rhythm as I took a large lungful of the desert air. It smelled primarily of tarmac from the road that ran about fifty yards from us, occupied only by the occasional sticky swish of overheated rubber as a car passed or turned into one of the parking spaces that were ranged along the white painted sides of the hotel. Great. All the way to Nevada and it smelled like a warm afternoon on the York by-pass. I sneaked a sidelong look at the man lounging against the planter and found that he was looking at me.

'What's the story?' He blew a ribbon of smoke from the corner of his mouth and chewed at his lip. 'You part of this circus?' A filter-tip waved to indicate the banner stretched taut across the front entrance 'Broken Hill Motel welcomes Fallen Skis Fans!!'

I stared. 'Spelling mistake *and* dodgy punctuation?'

A grudging inclination of the head. 'Guess we'd better watch out for those fallen skis. Could be bloody dangerous.'

The first hint of a sense of humour encouraged me. 'I came because . . . well, Felix made me.'

'You're not a fan then.' Another stream of smoke billowed out like a speech bubble.

'Oh, no, I am! A huge fan, I mean, I've got all the DVDs and the books and I'm a member of the forum and everything. I even –' half-embarrassed I looked down at my feet kicking little piles of stones into order – 'I'm teaching myself to speak B'Ha.'

'Good for you.' Whether or not he meant to be condescending I couldn't tell, his face refused to reveal anything. But at least he'd stopped frowning. 'What was all that, yesterday? Not being able to walk?'

'Oh, nothing. Just – stupid. Valium. I . . . I have these weird panic attacks sometimes. When I'm stressed.' I felt myself blushing, as though I was admitting to something perverted. 'Felix thought . . .

I don't take it much any more,' and even I heard the words as justification. 'Stupid,' I repeated.

He turned those dark eyes my way. 'Hey.' The glowing cigarette tip described a series of tiny circles as his gaze flickered from me to it and back again. 'We all have our crutches.'

'I'm not an addict,' I found myself forced to add. 'It was just to help with the travelling and being in strange places and everything.'

'Okay.'

'How about you?' I was getting no sense that he was enjoying our staccato conversation but I wanted to keep it going, for some reason which escaped me. Perhaps I just wanted him to distract me from the fact that I was thousands of miles from home. His long Yorkshire vowels could have come from next-door. 'Are you with the show?'

Now he wasn't looking at me any more, his eyes had found the distant horizon beyond the car park and were scanning up and down the pencil-lines of the mountains as though he was waiting for some kind of sign. 'Me? Oh, yeah, I'm "with the show".' A deep sigh that made the smoke trail stutter. 'But, hey, it pays the bills.' Then his gaze came back, scanning my face. I watched his eyes trace the line that vanished up under my, necessarily over-long, fringe. 'What happened?'

'What do you mean?' My mouth had gone dry. I should have been used to it by now, but nowadays fewer people mentioned it and I'd managed to kid myself that it wasn't as noticeable.

'The scar. On your face.'

My hand came up and I slid a fingertip along the raised weal which ran from the top of my cheekbone, around my eye, through the brow to hide beneath my hair. It was an unconscious movement; I was only aware I was doing it when I saw him make a twisted-mouth face again. 'I was in a car smash.'

His eyes darkened. 'How long ago?'

'Eighteen months. Well, nearly two years now.' I dropped my hand. Watched him reach out, almost as though he was going to touch my face, but instead he wove his hand through his own hair, hooking swathes of it back.

'Anyone hurt?'

I raised an eyebrow. 'Uh, yes. Me.' I pointed again at my forehead.

A half-smile around the cigarette. 'I meant, anyone else.'

I closed my eyes. Felt the ghosts. 'My best friend. And my fiancé. They died.'

I kept my eyes shut, waiting for the platitudes, but none came. The man said nothing. From the sounds of it he was lighting another cigarette. When I finally pushed the most overwhelming of the emotions back underground and opened my eyes again, he was staring at the dust. The still-glowing tip of his previous smoke lay beside his bare feet, but he didn't seem to be looking at that, instead his eyes flickered as though he was reading his own thoughts. After a few seconds he shook his head, glanced at me quickly, and rolled up the sleeve of his shirt. Held out his forearm to me. It was criss-crossed with pin-prick scars regularly spaced around the elbow, as though his arm was attached with flesh nails.

'Snap,' he said.

CHAPTER 6

W*ow.* He sat suddenly on the edge of the unmade bed, the nicotine still swimming through his bloodstream. Something which might have been pity swam along with it, but he pushed it away with long-practised ease. *That was weird. Strange kid. Wonder how she gets by with that scar? Maybe she's used to people staring, maybe that's why she didn't once look me in the face. Well she ain't gonna see sympathy here.* The momentary need to bolster the cigarettes with a glass of something tickled his spine and he jumped up, began firing up the laptop. Early morning was best for writing, the sun hadn't yet reached full baking potential; even in October it could still burn through metal at midday, but just now the air still held the silver edge of last night's chill and he could pretend that he was at home. Sitting in the little office in the farmhouse, fire blazing to keep the long shadows at bay; watching the scenery stretching back into the centuries where nothing changed except the positions of the sheep that dotted the moorland like clouds that had shed all their rain.

The *Fallen Skies* logo pinged up onto the screen and he stared at it for a moment, trying to remember. *Before all this. When space and time were new, when I wasn't carrying this weight of guilt and regret. How far back would I have to go to lose it all? How far?* A deep breath shook his shoulders, another attempt at emotion made it nearly as far as his heart before he stopped it, ruthlessly reaching inside himself and dragging it out half-born, killing it with his neglect.

Yeah. Too far back. But you don't go back, do you? Back is defeat, despair; all those things you swore you'd never feel again. Course, you won't feel anything else either, but that's the price you pay for being the Iceman.

But it's funny how one little thing can force you to remember. Today it was a voice, an accent. A couple of words and a girl with a scarred face and it was like I was sixteen again, back in Leeds, skinny little runt dragging the tail-end of his adolescence for fear of growing up. Back then, scars were badges of courage, like tattoos but with a better back-story.

Before everything went evil. Before everything I am was ruined.

He closed his eyes and let images fill his mind. Huge ships ponderously crossing galaxies, planets of water and fire, shadows which hid in plain sight. A fight for freedom. And then he started to write.

CHAPTER 7

Felix was irritably awake when I got back to our room, squatting against the small bedside cupboard, doing tricep dips.

'Bloody jet lag,' he puffed. 'It's the middle of the *night* as far as my brain is concerned. Been anywhere exciting?'

'Outside,' I muttered. I didn't mention the man with the scars. There had been something in our brief communion under the bronze sky that had gone beyond mere comparison of physical hurts. Something raw. I couldn't talk about it to Felix. 'It's already warm out there.'

'Hey.' He sat on the bed and wiped his face with a towel. 'Sounds like this trip was just what you needed to make you realise there's more to life than supermarkets and bookshops.' I watched him dab under his arms and then pull a pure white T-shirt over his head. Felix had an almost perfect body, about which he was horribly vain, and he was already working hard at beating a middle age which wouldn't come knocking for at least twenty years. 'So, shall we go look for breakfast, or are you just going to stand there staring at the back of your eyeballs?'

'I was looking at you. Actually.'

'Hey!' He struck a pose. 'Still got it. Damn, I'm *hot.*' A momentary pause. 'Hotter with sausages, though. You reckon the Americans know about sausages? And bacon?'

'I think they might have a few ideas. Where do we go for food?'

There was a diner built onto the back of the motel. One wall was made of a series of huge glass doors which looked out over the unimpressive view whilst the rest of it looked as though it had been formed by tunnelling away part of the original building. Doors from the main motel led into it at either end, making it more of a giant corridor than an aesthetic addition; it looked as though someone had seen a picture of a conservatory and tried to recreate one on an industrial scale. 'Architectural design really passed Nevada by, didn't it?' Felix, arbiter of all things tasteful, remarked as we stood in the doorway, watching the movement of people within. Smells wafted from the kitchen, which looked like an afterthought, tucked away behind double doors.

'It's busy. Let's come back later.' I pressed myself against the wall.

'Aw, come on Skye, don't bottle on me now. I want to know whether they serve grits. Always wondered what the hell *they* are, I mean, come on, who names food after stuff you shovel?' Felix grabbed my elbow but I pulled back.

'You go. I'm not really hungry; I'll just go back to the room and . . .'

But my words were cut off by a commotion at the far end of the diner, where a door gave entry to the other end of the motel. What could only be described as an entourage came sweeping through, two girls with such smooth hair that I could only imagine that they never slept on it, followed by a burly man carrying a clipboard, followed by –

I gave a small moan.

'That's Gethryn Tudor-Morgan over there,' Felix hissed unnecessarily in my ear. 'Just coming in! He's up early, maybe they have to hose him down before they put him in front of us.'

'He doesn't need anything doing to him from where I'm standing.' I moaned. 'Oh God.'

In the middle of his thrusting crowd, Gethryn looked smaller than he did in my head. I knew his height, of course I did, five foot nine, half an inch shorter than Felix, but there was something about real life which seemed to diminish him a touch and add a layer or two of flesh to his jaw and cheekbones. He'd grown his hair out of the ragged, streaked untidiness that he'd had in last year's publicity photos into a tidy version of a surfer-cut, gained a Californian tan and stubble and glowed with stardom. And, oh, what a star! Even with all the pictures and the posters and the frame-grabs, I'd never managed to conjure the reality of the man, the full-on, slender-hipped, broad-chested reality. The reality which was standing by a table on the far side of the diner, looking slightly hung-over.

I found myself trying to tidy my hair with my fingers. 'Great.' I groaned in the back of my throat. 'I could have put a skirt on.' I pulled the tucked-in shirt from the waistband of my jeans so that I didn't look so much like Disco Dad. 'And maybe had some kind of hot-wax treatment.' My frizz of hair sprang back from between my hands into its customary pubic bush impersonation.

'Well, it's hardly my fault you can't dress yourself! Come on, I want to see what they do when I order gravel.'

'Grits.'

Felix gave me a Look, but the proximity of Gethryn had wiped any trace of my sense of humour away. All I could see, all I could think, all I could feel, was sitting himself down only a score of tables away from me, propping his chin on his hands and gazing, dark-eyed, at the breeze-block walls. There was a brief scuffle as Felix and I fought to take the seat facing towards him and his party, but I won and Felix had to collapse gasping into the opposite chair.

'That, my darling, was below the belt.' He rubbed himself under the table. 'You didn't need to pinch my nadgers *quite* so hard; a simple 'please' would have done the job.'

A waitress approached to take our order, spotted Felix's furtive sub-counter massaging and wheeled away smartly. I hid behind the menu and stared out from behind some mouth-watering waffle pictures. 'Oh. My. God.'

'Well, he's all *right* I suppose, if you like that taut and rippling thing. Which, I have to admit, is growing on me. I wouldn't mind some action backstage with him, if you get my drift.'

'I think the natives of Alaska got your drift. Whisper, Fe, please.'

'My parents didn't send me to drama school to learn to whisper, lover. Projection, it's what gets you noticed.' Several of Gethryn's collection of people were glancing our way, a forest of frowns springing up amid the ruthless busyness and chatter. 'See?' Felix projected at me. 'They're noticing us already.'

'Through laser-sights, I should think.'

A different waitress, rather older, approached our table. Just as I was about to order toast and coffee, she spoke. 'I'm afraid I'm gonna have to ask you to leave.'

'But . . . breakfast . . .' Felix began.

'Yeah, well, y'see, we don't allow lewd behaviour in this diner, and that's how it is. If you can learn to keep your hands to yourself, then we might reconsider, but for today –' She jerked her head at the door behind us.

'But I . . .'

'I don't wanna have to call the boys.'

Dejectedly Felix stood up. 'I was only rubbing my crotch,' he said, compounding matters still further. 'It's Skye's fault. She grabbed me.'

'Sir. Ma' am.'

We found ourselves hustled over the threshold, but with the tiny advantage that Gethryn's party had all stopped ordering to watch. A couple of walkie-talkie radios were laid upon the table looking like potential trouble.

'And that was your fault.' Felix marched crossly away towards the reception area. 'If you hadn't tweaked my underparts like that, we'd be stuffing our faces with egg and bacon right now. I'm bloody starving.'

'Then why are we heading this way? There's a vending machine on the corridor near our room, get some crisps or chips or whatever they call them.' I stomped after him.

'Checking on the programme for today. See if there've been any changes. Don't suppose your ruthless studies of all things *Fallen Skies* told you anything about the timetable of events?' Felix chewed the side of a thumbnail and then held his fingers away from him, examining his hands.

'Well, sort of, but it did say that everything is subject to change. I guess they're never quite sure exactly who is going to turn up, after all the actors can't commit for definite and one of the writers had to cry off because she had a baby. So I know there's all kinds of things going on but I never read a complete timetable. There's all sorts of stuff . . .' My voice fell away at the end of the sentence and I really hoped that Felix was adept enough to understand the dropping tone. Even until I'd got on the plane I'd been wavering. Could I do it? *Really*? Leave my safety nets, my carefully cultivated self-protection to step out into a world that had shown itself capable of turning and savaging me? I'd not truly *believed* that I'd ever get here, which had meant that my presence on the *Fallen Skies* forum had been nebulous and my convention studies had held a certain edge of 'yeah, right. Great stuff, but not for you, Skye. Seriously, not for you.' *Yeah, Skye, you look away, you avoid the subject . . .*

'Never mind.' There was a curious tone to his voice, one I didn't recognise, but sounded as though it was almost relief. 'It'll all be here somewhere.' And sure enough, there in the middle of the reception area stood a peg board. In white pegs against a black dotty background, and with an almost life-threatening disregard for punctuation, it announced:

'THURSDAY.
AUTOGRAPH SIGNING IN MEETING ROOM,
ONE ELEVEN AM.
SALES MEETING ROOM TWO FIGURE'S; PICTURE'S DVD'S.
TONIGHT DINNER – YOU'RE CHANCE TO RELAX
WITH FALLEN SKY'S STARS'

'I think I just fell into hell,' I moaned. 'A "Meet the Stars" dinner? In a place that now thinks you wank under tables and I'm some kind of flop-bodied drug taker?'

'Well, you are.'

'Only when it's necessary.'

'Well, I only . . .'

'No! Let's keep some mystery. Look, I need some breakfast; shall we go get some disposable food from the machine?'

He huffed but followed me, and we took several packets of assorted convenience foods to our room. I lay on the bed while Felix ripped open unfamiliar packaging and spread the potato- and corn-related products over the table.

'Okay. You want the greasy orange things or these flat white ones?'

I chose a fistful and munched as I lay. Felix sprawled himself at my feet and dipped idly between crisps. 'Skye.'

'Mmmm?'

'You're really into *Fallen Skies*, aren't you?'

'What do you mean?' I'd found something that tasted exactly like *Wotsits* and was sucking the coating off.

'I mean, you've been a fan since the beginning, but the series started just after the accident, right?'

'Six weeks after I came out of hospital.'

'Yeah. So, you know, with the surgery and all that . . . how much do you really remember about the early stuff? I mean, you had quite a bit of brain damage, didn't you?'

'That was the operation.'

'Yeah, but how much memory did you *really* lose?'

I stared at him. 'Fe, you know all this.'

I got a single raised-eyebrow comment. 'Humour me.'

I found that I was rubbing my scar, feeling the warped skin on my fingertips against its puckered surface. 'My childhood is more or less intact. Everything from my teens onward is . . . fuzzy. I can remember bits and pieces but nothing really clearly, and I've lost the whole of the year leading up to the accident completely.' I shrugged. 'Everything I remember about Michael, about us, comes from photographs.'

'So when you say you remember the early *Fallen Skies* stuff, are you really remembering, or half-remembering what people have told you about it?' By 'people' Felix meant him. No-one else had my obsessive interest, although one of the library assistants and I had exchanged some speculation on the new series, but even he had gone a bit glazed-over when I'd launched into my theories about the alien Skeel race and their motivations. Perhaps, on reflection, the queue at the counter should have been my clue that I'd gone on a bit.

I used a finger to knock oily crumbs from my top lip. 'No. I remember.' The programme had saved my sanity, how could I have forgotten a single episode? My life had changed beyond recognition; I'd lost Faith, Michael, all my hopes for the future, and along had come a science-fiction drama that had made me suspend everything, even the grieving, for the brief hour it lasted. Gethryn Tudor-Morgan had stormed into my Wednesday evenings and taken me over. 'All of it. Everything.'

'Okay. Just curious.' Felix dipped a moistened finger into a nearly empty packet. 'Would you . . . you know, if things had been different, would you have wanted to come over to the States and audition?'

I shook my head. 'I dunno. Think my hair has always been a bit too much for American TV.' I smiled, but inside my heart had clenched into a ball. I'd joke and I'd smile and Felix would never know how I felt about my new life. How, deep down in the core of myself, in the place where I allowed introspection, I hated myself for losing any skills I'd ever had, any looks, any confidence. 'And I'd never get a part now, even if I wanted one.'

'It's really not that bad.' Fe's eyes ran over my scar. 'Better than it was, anyway.'

'Not televisual-friendly though, you have to admit. I could probably try out for War of the Killer Zombies, if anyone's casting for that.'

'Yeah. No make-up needed.' Fe smirked, until I hit him with a pillow. 'Right then, just for my own personal satisfaction, a little test. What was the name of the first ship that Lucas James flew?'

The answer was there, as soon as he'd finished speaking, as though my new post-operative recall system was all on some instant-access Rolodex. 'Everyone thinks it was the *Medusa*, because that was the one he was flying across the Ice Nebula, but it was the *B'Ha Virgin*. It was only in the pilot episode, which never got commercially screened . . . think they showed it to advertisers to check the revenue-earning response . . . but it counts. Not many people know about it, but someone on the show once sneaked an illicit clip out – put it up on YouTube. Why?'

'Just checking, darling, just checking.'

I'd swear I only closed my eyes for a couple of seconds. Just to allow my stomach to get to work on all that saturated fat. But when I opened them the room was empty and all the crisp wrappers had been balled up into the bin, from where they occasionally crackled and spat like plastic flames.

'Fe?'

I already knew he wasn't there; it wasn't in Felix's nature to sit quietly in a corner – he'd have been banging around the bathroom swearing and covering himself in expensive sprays or trying his hand with the dubious fake tanning lotion he'd bought at the airport. Instead the room was full of muffled sounds from outside and a smell of elderly fried food filtering up from the dumpsters through the slightly open window. It was twenty past eleven.

I shuffled myself back up against the pillows. The room felt secure, promoted from too small to cosy, particularly when compared to the boom and thump of all those voices travelling up the stairwells. I could stay here. It was safe.

But.

Autographs. The signing began at eleven. Gethryn would be there, in Meeting Room One, wherever that was. I could be there too, a mere table away. *I could speak to him!*

Even as I thought it, my heart sped up and the sweat burst onto the palms of my hands. Yes, Gethryn would be there, but so would just about everyone else who'd come to the convention – that was kind of the point, wasn't it? To mingle. After all, this godforsaken little motel in the middle of the Nevada desert wasn't exactly offering any alternative entertainment, was it? You came to see and be seen. To mix with other like-minded folks, to chat and compare and pull apart episodes until your lips bled. To talk about characters who were as fixed in your mind as your own family. To have strangers stare . . .

Breathe.

Or. I could stay in my room. Safe. After all, Gethryn was *here*, wasn't he? I'd probably got closer to him during our aborted attempt at breakfast than I would heading downstairs any time soon, where I'd have to queue and compete and I'd still be no more than a face across a table, shoving his own picture in front of him and probably too shy to even tell him my name. I'd wait. Go down later. Yes. Later. And, in the meantime,

I'd pop a Valium. That way, it would have time to work, to blunt the impact of the looks, the nudges, the comments made behind raised hands, as though I'd been struck deaf rather than scarred. With a little chemical help I could pretend I didn't care, pretend that the whispers didn't touch me.

I swallowed one capsule with half a glass of water, listened briefly to the continued sounds of activity from downstairs and then swilled down another capsule to keep the first one company. Pulled a pillow to myself and cuddled it against me, exploring the cheesy soreness of my mouth cautiously with my tongue. Pined, briefly, for my laptop and tried to ignore my stomach's cries for solid food, whilst I listened to the tidal noises travelling along the corridors.

There was a large TV in the corner, its standby light an alluring red wink, but I couldn't find the remote. My search did turn up a Gideon Bible in a bedside cupboard and two sachets of instant coffee, although the kettle was long gone. I remade the bed, pulling the nylon sheets taut and then spent ten minutes staring out of the window at the people in the yard.

It wasn't what I'd imagined conventions to be like. In my head any collection of sci-fi people was a mass of bespectacled, T-shirted, skinny guys who communicated in quotes and in-jokes and took one another's picture posing with hardware and props. Which wasn't me, of course, but I was different. I wasn't just a fan, I was a FAN, and not for the space ships and the shiny rifles but for the stories, the characters, the knowledge that good would always win. The sometimes painfully beautiful speeches that Gethryn delivered, some of which had made me cry, while others had made me think hard about the nature of my life.

But here, outside my window there were few stereotypes in evidence. Instead, large motherly women chatted to model-gorgeous girls, two guys wearing Skeel costumes from the series – enormous cylinders strapped to their backs, full-face helmets and full-body Lycra suits – posed for pictures alongside a trio of small children playing tag in the dust. The air was loud with greetings and sharp with promise. I could almost cut myself on my own potential, and yet here I was, hanging onto the window frame like a child waiting for Mummy. I hated myself for my weakness, ground my teeth with the desire to walk downstairs but somehow I couldn't persuade my fingers to let go.

A door opened. I could hear distinct voices from a room further up the corridor, arguing their way to their open doorway, then a pause. It gave me just long enough to scoot across to my own door and open it the crack necessary to peep out.

'All you ever give a *fuck* about is your *work*,' a roundly American voice was scolding. It had the Californian intonation that I recognised from TV, a voice with the carrying power and destructiveness of a razor-edged Frisbee. 'Do you really not care about anything else at all? Like, say, meeting your adoring public?'

Out came a slim tanned arm. It hooked itself around the doorframe and dug its nails into the plasterwork, as if anchoring itself against the unpleasantness inside the room. I watched, fascinated. A true American domestic! Like Jerry Springer!

Inside the room, a dull, inaudible tone answered her and she snapped back.

'Yeah, well, that's just great. I'm your *agent*, it's kinda in the job description for you to need to hang around with me! Unless, you know, you never want to work again, and that's just fucking ungrateful, Jack, you know that? It's okay, you being some big-shot writer-guy in the UK, but the network brought you over here to write TV and in the good old US of A they like to see your face, know what I'm saying here? Hermits is for crabs!'

I had to close the door right up to a little sliver to avoid being seen when the arm was joined by the rest of the body outside the room. This gave me the narrowest of views of my welcome distraction, but it was enough to ascertain that she was very thin, wore a tiny white vest over powder-pink jeans and had hair which obeyed the laws of physics that mine broke on a regular basis. Her face matched her arms by being brown, thin and angular. Pretty in the same way that a Wheaten Terrier is; soft and silky but with a mouth capable of inflicting great damage.

I watched the slice of corridor as she swept along past me, then I opened the door a little further as her slender back disappeared towards the lift. I only just managed to withdraw into the room in time to avoid being seen when she stopped and turned. She was so beautifully framed by the window at the head of the stairs that it had to be deliberate, the hard Nevada light giving her a golden aura. 'I'm tired of it,' she directed back along the landing. 'How can I sell an emotionally frigid pig?'

I had to squint through the hinges in order to eyeball the pig in question. Felt a short stab of surprise at realising it was the dark-haired man I'd already run into twice and then a sense of inevitability that if he actually *had* a girlfriend she would be gorgeous and feisty. I could see how her blonde fragile beauty would complement his saturnine looks, and she'd need to be feisty to put up with his moody self-contemplation for very long. In fact, sod feisty, she'd have to have passed sainthood and been heading towards deification if this morning was anything to go by.

'Hey, I'm sorry, Lissa. But you've always known what I'm like! You of all people . . . But you didn't have to come, I did. And, yeah, I know I owe them, the fans . . . I know it's important to them. I know I have to show that I'm grateful for what they've done for *Fallen Skies* but . . . it's hard for me.' He lowered his voice to a still-audible-if-I-put-my-ear-to-the-crack mumble. 'And I know what you're going through, Liss, honestly. I appreciate it, I really do, but . . . You and him, what happened, it's history now.'

'Huh! History for you, maybe,' came from the direction of the lift. It was annoying, I could only look in one direction once I'd established my position by the door, and the hinges only showed me the man – Jack, she'd called him – standing half-outside the room in pyjama bottoms and a different top from the one he'd worn earlier; this was a faded T-shirt. His hair was wild as though he'd been running his hands through it. Or she had.

'I can't help the way I am.'

'And how come this fucking lift is broken again?'

'Ah, whatever else you're pinning on me, *that* is not my fault.'

There was another 'huh', and the expression on his face changed, indicating that the woman had moved to the staircase next to the lifts and started a picturesque descent. It relaxed, further and further, until, by the time she must have reached ground level, he was almost smiling.

I stayed totally still. Watched him walk leisurely along the corridor towards the stairs, bare feet sticky on the functional grey flooring, until he was opposite me, when he turned round and stared directly at the point where I was standing, peering between the door and the wall.

'Hey.' And the single, flat syllable sounded like home. 'One little tip I picked up here from one of the camera guys, if you want to stay invisible, watch your shadow. By the way, nice work this morning. Takes something to get chucked out of a diner the calibre of the Broken Hill Motel. What happened, they find crack in your luggage?'

I was so astonished at being addressed through a hole in the wall that I answered. 'They thought Felix was . . . y'know, well, under the table.'

A broken stutter of a laugh. I could only see half his face but it looked genuine. 'Genius. I presume he wasn't?'

'Oh, no. Misunderstanding, that's all.' A pause. 'Why aren't you downstairs?'

Another laugh. 'No-one wants *my* autograph. I'm not one of the pretty boys in front of camera. What's your excuse?'

I could just feel the very faint Valium-induced haze pulling down across my mind. Nothing much, a whisper of net-curtain between me and the prurient world. 'I was . . . tired. Early morning, y'see, oh, of course, you were there. Fell asleep and Felix went down without me.'

He moved, shifting his weight, but suddenly I couldn't see his face any more. 'You could go down now, you won't have missed much.'

I shrugged, hoping it made me look as though I wasn't really bothered, rather than vulnerable and pathetic, which was what I felt. 'Maybe in a bit.'

His face creased into something that wasn't a smile. 'Look. This morning. You took off so suddenly . . . listen, I didn't mean to upset you, I only – I could see something had happened; when you said it was an RTA I thought, hey, point of contact. Guess it hit you badly, yes?'

'No, I was in the back of the car.'

'I meant, my asking. Stirred you up. The way you shot inside, I thought I'd said something stupid, something that made you think things that you'd rather forget. I'm always doing that, talk first, think later. It's because most of the people I talk to don't really exist.'

I stared for a moment. What kind of person talks to people who don't exist? And then I remembered my late-night 'conversations' with Captain Lucas James. 'No. It's all right. *I'm* all right.'

'Well. Sorry anyway.' The door swung slowly open as he pushed it until I was forced out from the narrowing angle between it and the wall and faced him across the threshold. He tugged at the hem of his T-shirt, easing out the creases, and rubbed one hand around the back of his neck, mouth beginning an uncertain grin. 'Since we both seem to be at a loose end, do you fancy popping along the landing?' He jerked his head in the direction of his room, then had to scrape untidy hair away from his face in order to look at me again. 'As the only two Brits left sober, I reckon we should stick together.'

The double-bass beat which was my heart was steady. 'I'm not sure.'

'Come on, this is a convention! You're contractually obliged to relax and enjoy yourself and to mingle with the fan-boys. Besides, I need a fag to calm me down after that little episode.' He inclined his head towards the stairs. 'Bloody Lissa.'

'Smoking is bad for you.'

I got an arch look for that. 'Right. I'll bear it in mind. So, you up for it?'

How come I could contemplate going to a strange man's hotel room without a qualm when the mere thought of walking downstairs into a group of people who were fans of the same programme that I revered made the Valium work overtime? I turned the question over in my head. But the thought of spending the rest of the day alone in a room had nothing to recommend it. And there was something ineptly appealing about this shaggy-haired stranger.

'Okay. But I'll have to be quick, in case Felix comes back and misses me.'

Another head-jerk. 'Is he likely to? I mean, I don't know what you two are to each other, but he did imply you weren't lovers, and when I saw him earlier he looked like a man on a mission.'

'He's my friend.'

'Just "a friend"?'

'Oh, yes. That's as close as it's wise to get to a man who thinks monogamy is something you make tables out of.'

For that I got a proper grin. 'Great line. Might nick that one. Anyway, you coming, 'cos I'm about to gnaw off the last of my fingernails.'

I pulled the door closed behind me and followed his barefoot and pyjama'd shape up past two doors, to the room I'd seen his girlfriend erupt from.

He swiped his key-card. 'You've not got your key?'

'Think Felix took it. He wouldn't want to disturb me by knocking to come in and, anyway, where on *earth* would I ever want to go?'

'He's in for a shock then.' He held the door wide. 'It's a bit messy, but you don't look like you'd mind that,' he said, standing aside to let me pass. 'Liss has done her usual trick of making the place look like she's exploded in it. Came in to talk work, next thing I know she's using my shower 'cos *hers* isn't working properly or something. It's eighty degrees out there in the daytime and she wants a hot shower? I told her to go down and ask housekeeping to fix the one in her room, but apparently it's just easier for her to come prancing over here to use mine. And why couldn't she take the clothes away afterwards, or at least carry them downstairs with her – some kind of hold-all might be in order, but that's a bit too much like forward planning for Lissa – what is it with you women and clothes that you have to change every five minutes? Always with the showering and the changing . . . I'm talking too much, aren't I?'

'A bit.'

'Sorry.' An unabashed grin. 'Spent too long at the keyboard again, always makes me a bit . . . I forget real people need gaps to reply.'

'Real people?'

A one-shoulder shrug. 'I'm a writer. Which, weirdly, doesn't make for great communication skills. Obviously. Words on paper, yep, that's my forte, I can do that, no problems, oh God, shut up Jack.'

Gosh. I'm here with one of the writers. Even the Valium couldn't quite stop my eyes widening with a flash of hero-worship, quickly stilled in the face of those tatty pyjamas and unbrushed hair.

The room smelled of her perfume. Sweet and pink, like overblown roses. The bed was rumpled and I had to work hard not to imagine this dark man and his preciously blonde Lissa busy rumpling it. 'Won't your girlfriend mind you having me in here?'

The click and flare of a lighter. 'I'm not intending to have you.'

A horribly disfiguring blush rose up my cheeks and neck. I knew from experience that this would make my scar stand out even more, a jagged white against the dull red skin. Fortunately he wasn't looking at me, but was desperately trying to get a bent remnant of cigarette into conjunction with the flame of the lighter, sucking at it until it squeaked.

'Besides, Lissa isn't my girlfriend. She *was*, once upon a time, and that's not any kind of fairy-tale you'd want to hear. But, yeah, I guess you're right, she probably wouldn't like it all that much, so, would you mind standing out in the corridor?'

I balanced awkwardly on one leg, not sure whether he was being serious or not. 'It's just, you know, I don't want to upset anyone.'

'Lissa is a big girl. She can cope with a few upsets.' He smiled, and it was a nice smile, a proper smile. His eyes creased under the weight of it and it took away some of that look he wore that said the world had disappointed him in some way. 'Stop worrying. Hey, what about a drink?' He crouched down to look under the bed and I tried really hard not to stare at his pyjama bottoms, which were baggy and striped and almost cartoonishly loose, held up with a piece of frayed cord. 'I'm not supposed to smoke in here, but sometimes . . . ah. White do you?'

'Do I what?'

He straightened up and I had to drag my eyes from their natural resting place which happened to be directly level with his flappy crotch. 'Would you like a glass of white wine?'

'It's a bit early.'

'Convention, remember? They'll all be on the Southern Comfort downstairs and no-one will be sober until Monday. What are we now, Thursday? Can you really stand the idea of being the only person sober for five days? Might as well join them.' A pause and his eyes looked inward for a moment, fingertips flicked in a kind of low-level mini shrug. 'At least . . .' He spun away, leaving a smoke trail like a low-flying aircraft and now I was free to stare at his back view, a crumpled picture of Mighty Boosh and a sagging pair of pyjama bottoms which managed not to make his backside look wrinkly and enormous by some fluke of tailoring. The T-shirt did nothing to cover his scarred arm but he didn't seem to care. 'Right. Not especially well-chilled, but still better than downstairs' Tequila Slammers.' He leaned forward, glass in hand. 'Oh. My name's Jack, by the way. And you're . . . ?'

'Skye. Skye Threppel.'

'Well, Skye. Here's to hiding from the world.' Jack picked up another glass from next to the laptop and raised it, seeming to toast the screen-saver picture of purple-heathered moorland, as though he was blocking out the Nevada desert with a picture of home. Then he plonked himself on the floor, knees drawn up. The only chair in the room was in front of the laptop and covered in papers, so for want of anywhere else available, I sat on the bed.

'Are you? Hiding from the world?' I asked, jiggling my wine between my fingers.

'Ah, now there's the question.'

'I know. That's why my voice did that going up at the end thing,' I replied a little sharply. I was nervous and being nervous made me edgy these days, and defensive. 'Maybe I should write the conversation down for you.' Jack seemed nice, a little tense perhaps, but the raw feeling of connection that we'd shared earlier had ebbed and I was concerned that maybe I'd imagined it. I couldn't always trust the way I felt, when those feelings were built on memories or associations I could no longer recall. It was as though my body reacted in certain situations without my mind having any kind of control and I was very conscious that this made me easy to take advantage of.

He made an appeasing gesture, holding his hands out and spilling some of his drink on the T-shirt. 'Point to you. I'm struggling with the lack of dramatic convention.' He sipped and looked at me over the rim of the glass.

I felt the blush start again and the edgy sensation that my nerves had all been driven to the surface.

'Maybe I should go. Rather than sit here and force you to make conversation.'

'Maybe.' Jack rested his glass on his knees and looked up at me. It might have been my imagination but I was fairly certain that what was in his glass wasn't wine. It was too clear, too transparent. 'But I'd quite like it if you didn't.'

Despite the Valium I could feel my skin growing clammy and my hands had moistened as though beads of blood were seeping through the palms. 'I ought . . .' My voice sounded croaky and about a hundred years old. I cleared my throat but it didn't help, just made the air thicken around me so that I had to concentrate on breathing.

'What is it you're frightened of, Skye? You look terrified right now, and no-one's ever found me that scary before – arrogant and self-righteous, yes, scary, no.' His head tilted to one side. 'Panic attacks worse when there're lots of people about, yes? And yet being alone, closed in, scares you, too. Am I getting warm?'

Suddenly uneasy at the intensity with which he was looking at me, I drained my glass in one gulp. 'I'm not scared. It's stress related. I get . . . when I'm a bit . . . when things are *different*, when I don't know what's going to happen next, sometimes I get panicky. But it's not that, I'm just worried that Felix will wonder where I am.'

Jack stood up and refilled my glass. 'Do you want me to leave the door open? Will that help?' He was looking at me with an expression that seemed partly compassion and partly curiosity and I hated myself suddenly, which surprised me. Hated this pathetic, helpless Skye with her inabilities and her carefully modified behaviour. He tilted his head to one side, stubbing out his nearly completely smoked cigarette without taking his eyes off me. 'You might feel better if you know you can run whenever you want. A bit more in control of the situation. And if Felix comes back, you'll be able to hear him.'

I gave a short, tight nod and he snicked the door off its latch, propping it open with a lone trainer. 'Thank you.' I could feel my airways relaxing. 'It isn't you, I'm sorry, they think it's something to do with the accident, the head injury, it's been over a year-and-a-half and I still can't . . .'

'Oh, and there was me feeling special.' Jack

grinned and his face was suddenly attractive. 'Okay then, let's talk neutral subjects, shall we? So, what's so great about *Fallen Skies*?'

I wanted to sound erudite and literary, as though I analysed the metaphorical allegories of today's political situation and enjoyed the complex interplay of meta-media. 'I like all of it,' was what I found my mouth going ahead with. 'Really.'

Jack nodded over his glass. 'Gethryn. Am I right?'

My blush answered for me.

'Is that why you came? Chance to meet him?'

This time I just shrugged and managed to mutter, 'I like the storylines too.'

'Glad to hear it.' He sounded a bit terse, and I didn't miss the sidelong glance at the open laptop, now displaying a screensaver picture of random swirls of colour. 'Glad we're doing something right.'

'Sorry, yes, you said you're one of the writers, didn't you? Because, what I meant to say was, you know, it's the scripting, isn't it, that makes the whole show. And the character arcs, and the way that the Shadow War has implications for all the planets across the galaxy.'

'Too late, Skye, far too late. But, nice recovery.' Jack stood up to top up my glass. 'Don't worry about fancying Gethryn, you're not the only one.'

'I didn't mean . . .'

But he cut me off by turning away. 'Doesn't matter.'

I drained my second glass of wine out of embarrassment. Jack was rummaging through the pockets of a jacket hanging on the back of a chair, triumphantly pulling forth an unopened packet of cigarettes and dragging off the cellophane like an addict. When he finally turned back to me he was blowing smoke like a dragon and the air had turned chilly. 'Do you want another?' He gestured towards my glass. 'Or had you better be going?'

Feeling dismissed I went to stand up, at which point two things happened. Drunkenness fell, breaking over my head like an enormous egg, and I lurched, staggered and grabbed out for any solid object, the nearest of which happened to be Jack. My wavering hand secured a fistful of his T-shirt, pulling him with me as I toppled back onto the bed.

And there was the sound of someone pushing the door open from outside.

'Oh, bloody hell.' Jack managed not to suffocate me by propping himself clear of my prone body, which caused the T-shirt to stretch obscenely. 'This is really *not* my day.'

And into the room, bouncing on the balls of her feet, walked the skinny girl in the pink jeans. 'Oh, right,' she drawled, seeing us in our state of near-collapse on the bed. 'I know the Nevada call-girls ain't up to much but, brother, you should ask for your money back.'

'Hey, Liss.' Jack walked backwards, dragging his shirt off over his head and leaving me with two handfuls of fabric. 'This is Skye. I think she's had a bit too much to drink.'

'Great. If she throws up on me, I shall *so* sue her ass.'

'She's not well, Lissa. Help me.'

I tried to look up into their faces but everything spun, then jumped, as though milliseconds were being cut out of the morning. 'Did you . . . spike my drink?'

Lissa gave a hollow little laugh. 'Lady, look at him. He doesn't need to spike drinks to get laid.'

'Shut *up*.' Jack walked around the bed, looking down on me, nervously fiddling with a leather necklace around his throat. It hung black and stark against his bare skin. 'She's only had two glasses; it's more than just the alcohol.' His face unfocused then pirouetted around the top of his body. 'Shall I get your friend?'

I shook my head, which turned out to be a terrible mistake. The whole room wheeled and split and I felt myself flying through the air, which was an illusion caused by Jack picking me up and thrusting me at light speed in the direction of the toilet, which we managed to reach before Catastrophe came calling at *Wotsit*-ville.

It took far, far longer than it should have, to bring up two packets of cheesy puffs. Between noisy heaves I could hear Jack on the phone, calling downstairs, and in a few minutes Felix arrived in the bathroom, overheated and with a lipstick mark on the side of his neck.

'Whoa!' He looked down on me for a moment as I drooled bile into the toilet bowl. 'You look crappy, darling.'

I rolled a bloodshot eye up at him and heaved a few more intestines closer to the waterline. To his credit, Jack brought me a glass of water, although I couldn't steady my hand enough to take it and he ended up feeding me sips, crouched next to the nasty-smelling toilet with me.

'And you missed such a fantastic outing.' Felix patted my back ineffectually as another burst of retching caught up with me. 'Gethryn is down there, chatting. You could have had your moment with him, if you hadn't been –' he cast an eye over Jack – 'making friends up here.' And then, impatiently, 'Surely there can't be anything *else* to bring up.'

A commotion in the bedroom, and both men turned. My already rock-bottom self-esteem managed a feat of geology to become even lower as Lissa's penetratingly nasal voice asked, 'What are you all *doing* in there?'

Jack straightened up beside me. 'We're looking after Skye.'

'Well, fuck *you*.'

I managed to sit away from the toilet bowl for long enough to clock Lissa's expression of revulsion peering into the bathroom.

'Jeez, Jack, you do pick them. Surely it doesn't take two of you. Felix, you could come back downstairs with me.'

'Lissa and I met earlier,' Felix explained, and the way his eyes traced the contours of those very tight pink jeans spoke an absolute library. 'So. You and Jack been together long?' He spoke to her without meeting her eye, which said even more.

'Way, *way* too long. How about you, you two . . . ?'

'Oh, no, we're – look, it's a long story.'

All this was going on over my shoulder as the final crisps exited my system in the most undignified and, possibly, loudest, way imaginable. My eyes streamed from the effort, my nose trailed vomit and my head hurt. I just wanted to lie, very still, on the cool floor of the bathroom. Instead I had an audience.

'Does she have a very low tolerance for alcohol?' Jack asked. 'I only gave her a couple of glasses. What? Don't look at me like that, Lissa.'

'Here we go again . . .'

'No! No, this isn't like that, Liss.'

I could feel the blonde's eyes on me. They didn't seem particularly angry, as I would have expected from a girl finding her boyfriend, however 'ex' the nature of the relationship, embroiled with another woman. She looked more sad. 'If you say so. But if you'd rather chat to some whacked-out, beat-up English chick than *me*, man, you have your priorities *way* wrong.'

'Lissa, you didn't want to talk, you wanted to harangue me about some director you've met that I need to know, nothing that's going to help me, just some bunch of *auteur* fuckwits who want cheap labour and a British accent to give credibility to their pseudo-porn.'

As I dribbled the remnants of my pathetic breakfast down my chin, Felix grinned at me. 'Aren't other people's lives *fun*? You see what you miss when you've got your face in someone else's flusher?'

'I didn't exactly choose this position,' I said, round the drool.

Jack and Lissa had moved back into the bedroom to continue their argument. Felix grabbed my elbow and dragged me to my feet, keeping up the momentum so that we staggered through into the next room, with me still hunched forward over an invisible toilet. 'Chucker-upper coming through, don't mind us, keep chatting amongst yourselves and thanks for the most *wonderful* insights into coupledom. Remind me to stay single forever, would you? Rather sand off my own nipples than go through this, okay, ready to make a dash to our room? And *here* we go.'

We shot out, down the corridor to our room, where Felix propped me against the wall. 'Key?'

'I don't have it. I thought . . .' A threatening belch erupted, 'I thought you'd got it.'

'Why would *I* take the key, when you were in the room?' He dropped his head into his hands in a moment of despair. 'Thought you'd be there all morning, catching up on your beauty sleep. Oh, this is buggering *terrific*. And you – just breathe, my days of the mop and bucket are long behind me.'

I took a deep breath. 'Won't the reception desk have a pass key?'

'Suppose.' Felix turned to head towards the lift.

'Don't leave me! Fe, please . . .'

With a dramatic sigh and a turn that was more flouncy than Cinderella's party frock, Felix came back and grabbed my elbow again. 'All right. We'll both go down, but I am warning you now, any more vomit and you can spend the rest of the convention sitting outside in the yard with the kitchen boys Miguel and Carlo – cute, but put it this way, they're not much good to you.'

'I'm sorry.' I tried to explain as we got into the lift, which was apparently working again, but now bore a sign in very large letters saying 'three persons maximum'. 'I really only had two glasses of wine . . . thought it would be fun, the Valium was stopping me feeling scared, it was boring being on my own and he asked me –'

'And he was so cute you couldn't resist.' Felix looked sour. 'Yeah, all right, ten out of ten for lusty thoughts, lover, but Jesus H-in-a-catsuit, you never, *never* drink on Valium, you got that?'

'An hour ago that would have been good advice.'

'I thought you knew.' The lift arrived on the ground floor and the doors sprang open to reveal that the foyer was packed with people coming and going, mingling, queuing out of the door of one room and round into another. Felix and I dropped into this crowd like a shovel full of shit in church.

I caught my breath and my hands sprang closed into defensive fists, even though our arrival went largely unnoticed. Everyone was too busy circulating, greeting, loud hails overhead trumpeted triumphant names as successfully autographed pictures waved. Toddlers chased one another through the forest of legs, and an occasional costumed figure progressed between the crowds in its own space.

I froze until Felix poked me in the back, prodding me towards the reception desk. I moved alongside him, hoping that no-one would register the stink of alcohol and vomit, until I could rest my elbows on the desk and drop my head into my hands. I stayed there, very, very still. I could hear Felix talking to someone but my brain had shut down and wouldn't even contemplate trying to make out actual words. It was enough of an effort to keep breathing.

'Okay, babe. Antonio here says he'll come and open up for us.' I straightened up as Felix turned to me, momentarily forced to stand so close that he almost brushed my chin as a tight knot of people surged forward from one of the meeting rooms. They were all heading for the main doors, moving through a gap in the crowd caused by –

'Shoot me, Fe. Please.'

If I'd thought being seen by Gethryn with a tucked-in top was the height of embarrassment, then being seen by Gethryn whilst smeared in my own sick was the depth and breadth of it. I wanted to close my eyes but didn't dare, since the dark brought back the swinging unsteadiness, and the acid-burn was already far too close to my tonsils for comfort.

Gethryn's voice travelled across the space between us and my ears quivered at the sound. 'Look, I'm only going to stretch my legs. Sitting in that chair is playing havoc with my quads, you know? I'm not going to do a runner, if you stay in the line I'll be back signing in just a minute . . .' Oh, that deep Welsh accent. It poured into my ears like a molten love letter. I wanted to hug every word to my chest, to memorise every intonation, but I didn't even dare to raise my gaze from the ghastly reception-area carpet. Out of the corner of my eye I could see Gethryn marching his way through the crowd, preceded by several large clipboard-carrying men who wore headsets and luminous Security vests. As he drew level with where Felix and I cowered, the crowd in front was as thick as the crowd behind and one of the guards had to go on ahead to forge a path, leaving Gethryn stationary opposite us.

He turned his head and met my eye.

In that second there was no crowd. No guards, no walkie-talkies, no shouting. Just Gethryn Tudor-Morgan, a stray wisp of hair fluttering in an unfelt breeze, gazing at me with his pure white shirt open at the neck to show a silver chain against his smooth skin. He was beautiful. From the soft expression in his amber eyes to the artful highlights in his flicked hair, he was poster-perfect. I was frozen with longing for him, until a sly burp rippled up to scald my back teeth with a wave of acidic saliva, which made my eyes water.

Sound rushed in, followed by movement and Gethryn being hustled on towards the doors. Just before the crowd filled the space between us again, he half-turned in my direction and dropped me the tiniest, cheekiest little wink you have ever seen, and my knickers would have erupted if I hadn't been feeling like a pile of second-hand crap.

Oh, and so embarrassed about the whole vomit-stained thing that I wanted to die.

'I think he fancy you.' Antonio, a burly Hispanic guy with a receding hairline which was about to meet an increasing neckline, nudged me. 'You be good girl and he maybe buy you drink.'

The retch that this thought engendered sent another dribble to join the stains already ornamenting my front, but at least we were moving towards the lift by then.

CHAPTER 8

'Well, that was fun. No, not fun, what's that other thing? Yeah, *pathetic*.' Lissa stomped around the room and Jack thought how much she resembled an angry stick insect. She turned her back on him and rested her hands on her hips, her shoulder-blades sticking out behind her like spines, her whole body all angles. 'And why are you laughing? This ain't no laughing matter, Jackie, 'cos if she decides to take this to the press . . .'

'What, getting sick-drunk in my room? Hardly headline material is it, even out here.' And anyway he hadn't been laughing at that, he'd been laughing at the thought that making love to Lissa had been like shagging a set-square. He shook his head, wondering why he'd ever done it, why he'd ever found that underfed-rabbit look attractive. The humour died as he remembered why, remembered all the things that had come associated with dating Lissa, all those things that had almost cut through his famed detachment. Fear, of the world, of *himself*, trying to forget who he was and what he'd done and the running, the endless *fucking* running. And then the pain. 'Mind you, in this place it probably makes the papers when a cow craps.'

'You would be surprised.' Lissa rummaged in her bag for her phone and checked it quickly for messages. 'You wanna know why I *really* came schlepping over to this God-forsaken corner that's got more dust than my Aunt Effie's shelving unit? I came 'cos I'm worried about you. That last meet we had, you were wound tighter than I've ever seen you and this last little while you've been kinda weird, twitchy – and you're smoking more. And the one thing I *do* understand about you is that you smoke when you're stressed.'

Jack turned back to his laptop, using his interest in it as an excuse to keep his face averted. Whatever else she might be, Liss had always been good at reading his expressions, at knowing what he was thinking and at times like these he wasn't sure that staying friends had been such a good idea. 'I'm fine. What about you? How're you doing these days, Liss?'

He could hear her careful breathing behind him. When she spoke again her voice was different, softer and without the top-note of complaint. 'Hey. It's okay, I'm not blaming you. Some chick got drunk, not your fault. I've never blamed you, Jack, not for any of it.'

'What about Geth? Does he come under this 'blame moratorium' that you've got going? He's done a bloody good job of bringing both of us to our knees in his own, inimitable way.' And all Jack could see then was Skye's face, her wide blue eyes as she tried to hide her desperate crush, the little flush that broke out on her cheeks when she said Gethryn's name. 'Please don't tell me that you're prepared to forgive and forget, Liss, you know how he operates – the moment you weaken he's in there like a dog with a new leg to hump.'

'All I'm saying is, he's got his reasons. We're not all as strong as you.' He heard the soft step as she came across the carpet, and smelled that scent she used, so floral that it was surprising she wasn't mugged by bees every time she went outdoors. Her fingers closed on his elbow. '*I'm* not as strong as you.'

Another laugh broke from his throat, this one hollow and heavy. 'Yeah, but it was all my fault in the first place, wasn't it? And now Gethryn's making me pay for it; just seeing his face every day is like having my nose rubbed in what I've done. Every day, Liss. Well, every day he can be bothered to get his starry arse out of bed and come to work, that is.'

Lissa said nothing, just stood, keeping one hand on his arm. Jack looked around the room but it wasn't the tacky wallpaper, the grim works of so-called art that hung askew, that he was seeing. His body might be nailed to Nevada but his mind was running free on the moors, and he suddenly felt the lack of huge grey skies and the solid ranks of hills like a pain. He pulled a face. *Okay, you miss the place. Now lock it away.*

Lissa did that short sighing thing that drove him round the bend. 'You can't blame me for thinking something's up though, Ice. I mean, here you are, up to your ass in talent and deadlines, and I find you shut up in here with some Limey chick throwing up like there's no tomorrow.'

'Working well, Liss, I actually understood the majority of the words in that sentence. The actual order they appear in is a bit more problematic.' He twisted away from her hand back to his screen and tapped a few keys in a lackadaisical way. 'Look, you're right, I feel . . . I dunno. I need some time. Why don't you head back downstairs, or, better still, go to your own room? Let me do what I have to here.'

'And is part of what you have to do that spaced-out honey?' Lissa tucked some hair behind her ear, leaving the side of her face bare. It made her look vulnerable and Jack felt a pang in his chest. Sometimes the shadow cast by what had gone before hung long and low over his life, like a sundial at evening.

'No.' He typed randomly, hoping she'd take the hint and leave. 'You know me, Liss. Strictly hands-off policy. She's a Brit, I heard the accent, fancied talking to someone who doesn't think Stonehenge is a theme park.' There was no point in being more specific; Liss thought Dick-Van-Dyke-cockney was an accurate representation. 'I get homesick,

Liss, you know that.' Type, type. The quick brown fox jumped feverishly over the lazy dog, and then back again. Eventually Lissa's reflection dropped the scowl and gave a quick smile he wasn't sure he was supposed to have seen.

'Homesick, huh. Nice that you admit to feeling anything, Iceman. I'll head back down then. See how the signings are going. Gauge interest for Sunday night, that kinda thing.'

'You do that.' Type, type and it was only when the door swung closed behind her that Jack allowed himself to relax and look at what he'd written.

'Why isn't anything ever *simple*?'

CHAPTER 9

'Skye, you *have* to come!' Felix was almost on his knees. 'What was the point in coming all the way out here if you're going to spend the whole convention hiding in your fucking *room*?'

I pulled another pillow in front of me. 'All those people, Fe. They've all seen me dribbling and vomiting and all gakky and disgusting *and* most of them have seen us being chucked out of the diner. Why, in God's name, would you think I'd *want* to be seen again by any of them, in any state? I can only imagine what might happen next; my knickers fall to my knees, perhaps? My boobs roll out of my top and settle on the table just as the waiters bring in a bowl of melons?'

'You are over-reacting, darling.'

'Believe me, refusing to go to this dinner is *under*-reacting on a scale you can't imagine.'

'But wouldn't you like Gethryn to see you all done up properly? Give him a chance to check you out when you've got your make-up on and you're dressed up? After all,' Felix lowered his voice, 'he *did* wink at you earlier on. *And* that was when you were totally scuzzy. See what he thinks of the delicious Skye Threppel when she's got up like a Scissor Sisters concert.'

'Not helping.' But I had to admit my morning run-in with Gethryn had given a new edge to the possibility of going out in public. 'Besides, look at my hair. I can't appear in public with hair like this, they'll think Sasquatch is making a guest appearance.' To illustrate my point I raked my hands over my scalp and they jammed half-way through, making my hair jut at odd angles.

'Oh, that is *easily* sorted.' He dragged his phone from his pocket and tapped in a quick text. The answer beeped back almost immediately. 'Wait there.' And he leapt up and ran out of the door.

I stared at myself in the mirror across the room. A lengthy shower and sleep had removed the evidence of my morning's activities, leaving me looking at the real me. All frizzy hair and skinny shoulders, in a vest top that made my chest look like two poached eggs on a plank. And scars. I lifted my fringe and traced the scar downwards, through my eyebrow, round my eye socket where it had thankfully not affected my sight, and down to the top of my cheekbone, where it split into two before fading out in a little radius of tiny lines, like a sunburst. I'd seen out 2008 as a whole, unblemished actress and only hours later my entire life had revolved around an unknown degree of brain damage and scars. Passing time had seen this one blur and whiten, from an evil incision-red, marked with the dashes of staples, to a pale pink, stammering over half-healed sections which continually peeled away in patches of renewed redness. It was healing. Cleanly and without infection. And this made me *lucky*.

Part of me could appreciate the irony. I was lucky not to be dead. Of course I was. But not being dead meant living with scars which marked me so resolutely, so absolutely, that it had stopped my career as dead as I wasn't. Casting directors didn't want a girl with a huge brand down one side of her face. I was too noticeable. Maybe, in a few years . . .

Yeah. Maybe.

'Fingers!' Felix barked as he walked back in, and I untwisted my hands, stopped picking. 'I got you some hair gunk. What'cha think?' With a flourish, he pulled out a bottle I didn't recognise and passed it to me. 'Some kind of Yank stuff. Reckon it makes your hair smooth. Want to try?'

Despite myself I found I was tipping hair-smoother into my palm. Curious. 'Where did you get this from?' Stroked a tiny amount through a few strands and was amazed. 'It actually works.'

'Lissa.'

'Oh. Okay. Are you sure she gave it to you? Only I know that you sometimes have a very loose interpretation of "borrowing" things.'

He shrugged. 'I asked if I could have it and she said yes. She didn't mention returning it, all right? Anyway, come on, I want to get you out of here and downstairs asap, sweetie.'

'And she's all right about my having it?' Felix said nothing. 'So that would be, why?'

He avoided meeting my eye. 'Lissa and I, we got talking, she's very . . . amusing.'

I pulled back to look at him, all buffed up and wearing black. 'Right. I know. *That* kind of amusing.'

'Come on, Skye, you've seen her, would *you* turn it down? I mean, really?'

I shrugged. 'It's up to you. But do you really want Jack looking over your shoulder all the time?' I finished rubbing serum-covered fingers through my hair and let it lie, unaccustomedly slick, on my shoulders; dabbed mascara at my eyes and applied my usual cover-up make-up, adding an extra layer for luck and Gethryn-potential.

'Nah, they're long over. And even then it was just a thing, she says. Between you and me, I think there was some serious shit going on with this show. You know the online chat, come on, give.'

I shrugged, stared at my reflection and wondered what people would see if I ventured downstairs. A scarred girl trying too hard? 'First series ran into trouble and nearly got cancelled, but there was an online campaign to keep it going and it got picked up again. They do that sometimes over here, if there's enough advertising revenue coming in.' I shook my head and my hair amazed me by following the movement. Usually it flared out and surrounded my face, leaving me peeping out like the aftermath of a cartoon explosion.

'And talking of picking things up . . .' Felix

handed me my smart white top. 'You and Jack, eh? Mind you, *I* wouldn't throw him out of bed for eating oysters.'

'We've yet to find *anyone* you'd throw out of bed; you're not exactly discriminating, are you? And it's not like that. He's nice. He's kind. But that's all.'

'Holding out for the big guy are you?' Felix was looking at me with an expression I couldn't read.

'Hardly! And anyway . . .' I dropped my hand away from my face, 'I can't do it. I mean, who am I trying to kid, dressing up like this and doing my hair and everything? I'm a failed actress with a stonking great scar, not the kind of person you want me to be. This whole thing . . . it's not that I'm not grateful, Fe, and it's fantastic that I'm here and I've met new people . . .' well, one new person, and all that, but . . . a *dinner*? With people standing around talking?' All my insides took a little step sideways. 'I'll stay up here.' *Useless, useless Skye.*

'But you *can't*. You can't spend the whole convention up here!' As though he'd scared himself, Fe stopped, ran a hand through his hair and cleared his throat. 'Just . . .' look. You came to get a chance to meet Gethryn Tudor-Morgan, right?'

I scrunched up my face, but didn't reply.

'All right. And down there, it's not like it's a top-hat-and-tails do. It's a buffet, meet-the-stars kind of thing. You're looking gorgeous – believe it, sweetie – and you've already broken the ice, so to speak, downstairs earlier. Come on, you want Gethryn to see you in a good light, don't you?'

My fingers went again to my scar. 'I'd actually prefer him to see me in total darkness.'

'Mmmmm . . .' Felix ran his hands up and down his body, suggestively. 'Gethryn, by Braille. Bet he's a fluent body-reader.'

'He'd hear nothing from mine.'

'Do you want some of the Valium? It would help . . . take the edge off.'

I thought about it. 'No. I don't really *need* it, I just panicked. After all, even with the make-up people are going to see the scar, they're going to think whatever they think whether I've taken Valium or not. I'm tired of being dependent, on you, on drugs, on the doctors.'

He stared at me. 'Grief, one drunken episode with a gorgeous man and you're swearing off pharmaceuticals? They should put him on the NHS.'

'I'm *tired* of feeling out of control. I want a life, Fe. I know it won't be the old one back again, and I know I'm going to have to work at it, but, now I'm here I think I should try.' I sat down on the bed. 'Except . . . I'm not sure trying involves being in a crowded place.'

Felix gave me one of his Looks, and handed me my black trousers. 'Even if a *very* large part of that crowd is Gethryn? You want him, you know it. And don't try to tell me otherwise, when your nipples are sticking up like a couple of brass door handles at the thought of meeting him. Look, if you can't do it for yourself, do it for me.' Another unreadable look. 'For Faith. You know if she was here she'd be *so* excited; she'd have you in one of your old tarty frocks, flaunting it from here to Arkansas. Wouldn't she? *Wouldn't she, Skye?*'

I felt the shiver I always felt when he talked about Faith. As though my skin was trying to get my attention. 'Yes, she would.'

'So?' Felix did a little dance on the spot. 'Can you at least try? For my sister?'

For Faith. For my beautiful best friend. Could I? 'Don't leave me, will you, Fe?'

Felix stood up and held out his arm. 'I will be stapled to your side all evening. As long as you don't end up heaving in the Ladies', of course.' Cautiously I hooked my arm through his. 'Right. Let's get laid!' Then, seeing my look, 'Figure of speech, sweetheart, figure of speech.'

The party was restricted to those convention-goers who were actually staying in the motel, the day-visitors being bussed in from the town an hour's drive away every morning, so the numbers were far lower than had flooded around in reception earlier. A brave few had come in costume and there was something oddly unsettling about watching a Shadow pilot juggle a plate of nibbles and a glass of red wine alongside his blaster rifle. The two lads dressed as Skeel were labouring around the room under the weight of their cylinders, unable to eat because of the full-face helmets their outfits dictated, playing their parts to the max, while the rest of us who wore street clothes hung around the walls like kids at a school disco, waiting for the Big Boys to arrive. The diner was stripped out, tables stacked to the sides and the buffet laid down the centre on trestles. A projector showed a constant stream of images from the show on a huge screen made by closing off the door at the end furthest from reception and putting a board across it but despite the organisers' best efforts it still felt like a canteen in fancy dress.

But Felix was right. Having already been faced with most of these people, and particularly when I'd been at my physical lowest, had broken the ice for me a little. Although I felt as though I was travelling inside an egg-shell which might shatter into a million shards at any moment, no-one looked, no-one stared or nudged their neighbour, no-one whispered.

As Felix and I made as unobtrusive an entrance as possible, we were overtaken by two of Gethryn's co-stars, who immediately started milling around and chatting to people.

'Who're they?' Felix nudged me.

I pointed at the pale, blond lad in the tight blue sari-style costume. 'Jared White, who plays Defries, Lucas James's second-in-command, and the girl is Martha Cohen. She's Defries's wife. B'Ha, but she's on their side because her family were wiped out in the war.'

'*Verrrry* nice.' He hustled me up to the tables, picked up a paper plate and began scouting, knowing Felix, for the most phallic-shaped food on offer.

I looked at Martha again. 'She's almost impossible

to recognise, out of make-up. Wouldn't have known who she was, except . . .'

'I meant, *him*.' Felix picked up a carrot baton and nibbled the end, suggestively. Left it a moment, then smiled across the room. To my amazement, he got a smile in return.

'Wheyhey, looks like I've still got it, babe.'

'Felix.'

He jabbed the plate at me, until I took it. 'Just popping over to introduce myself.'

Don't leave me, I was too late to say. He was gone, crossing the room, armed with nothing but a smile and a root vegetable. I watched, envying his physical ease and his wit, his absolute certainty that life wouldn't let him down. I'd been like that once. *Hadn't I?* The room rocked with the sudden doubt. *What had I been like?* I had to search through scrambled memories just to try to pin myself down – a floating collection of thoughts and doubts with islands of complete remembrance jutting from them like little gold nuggets in a coal seam. And that missing year hadn't even left a smear of memory behind; it had been stolen from me completely. No-one ever really talked about the time before the accident, not Felix, not my briefly visiting parents, nor the occasional passing friend. Maybe they didn't want to upset me by reminding me of everything I'd lost, maybe they were upset on their own behalves that I couldn't remember them, or that I'd lost so many memories that they thought I should have treasured. But it meant that my whole identity had to be assumed, I had nothing of my past adult self to build upon. All I had was those typically distant memories of childhood, my fuzzed-over adolescence and then nothing but fragments which could have been dreams. I was like a huge newborn baby, learning everything for the first time.

I looked down at the plate and concentrated on the creases in its cardboard. I felt okay as long as I didn't think about how full the room was, and I was eating, well, snacking, looking interested – *just like a real person*. No-one could tell that I couldn't even remember if I'd grown to like pickles; and if I didn't think about how many people there were, milling about in that small space, where I couldn't touch the walls, I'd be fine. Fine, yes, if I didn't think about the people breathing my air, holding me in place so I couldn't run, couldn't get out, *get out* . . .

I found myself standing in the dusty yard, plate still in hand, unable to remember how I'd got through the crowd and slightly surprised, because I hadn't consciously *felt* stressed, until I'd run. And yet, here I was, gasping, dragging the hot air down into my lungs, feeling it scritch and swirl down my throat, knowing that I couldn't be dying because I was breathing. My heart chiselled away at my ribs and I had to drop the plate because my hands were shaking so much.

It was caught before it hit the ground. 'Careful, girl. They're valuable, these plates. Ten dollars per hundred, see?'

Clenching my toes to prevent the incipient faint, I looked up. Gethryn stood beside me, his own plate in his hand and his face wrapped in a smile that I wasn't sure was for me. I looked over my shoulder, but there was nothing there apart from the scrubby cactuses which had been planted all along the wall. He couldn't be smiling at a cactus, could he? Cautiously I smiled back.

'That's better. Pretty girl like you shouldn't be frowning. You'll give yourself wrinkles.' A hand extended my way. 'Name's Gethryn. Unless you knew that, in which case just call me Mr Moron.'

'I . . . did know.' Almost afraid to make contact in case he disseminated into a stream of atoms, I touched his hand. Cool and sure it closed around mine. 'I'm Skye.' Still trembling.

He didn't seem to notice the vibration of my fingers. Gave my hand a firm shake. 'Jesus, I'm glad to meet someone who's not completely barking.' A confidentially lowered voice. 'Most of the women in there? They'd have the boxers off my arse if I stopped moving long enough. Christ, fans are bad when they're at a distance, never mind being trapped in a room with a hundred of the buggers.' He tipped his head towards the people standing at the doors to the diner or sitting on the steps that led down, out into the desert, chatting to one another and pretending not to know who he was.

'Actually, I'm a fan,' I managed to stammer out. 'I'm here for the convention.'

Gorgeous tawny eyes met mine and a firm hand

under my elbow guided me further from the pretending-not-to-be-listening crowd. 'Ah, but you're not barking though, are you? Haven't noticed you lifting your top to get your boobs signed, or sitting outside my trailer all night in a tiny little dress and no knickers.'

I couldn't force my eyes away from his face. Gethryn must have thought I had some kind of staring disorder. 'I . . . like . . . the programme.'

Yeah, that's kind of the definition of 'fan', I berated myself from inside my head, but Gethryn was gracious. 'Thanks, *bach*. If only I could have stayed on . . . I had plans for Lucas James – oh, never mind.'

Now I could only nod. I felt much as I should think a toddler feels on being quizzed by a department-store Santa, as though I was in the presence of a representative of God. Every millimetre of his face was familiar to me, yet I still couldn't stop my eyes from blazing all over it, seeing the raised lines of stubble around his mouth and the way his lips pouted around his Welsh accent. In the show he spoke with a generic English inflection; there was something erotic beyond words at the dips and swoops of the Brecon intonation. There was something about the way he said *bach* that made it sound far more intimate and sexy than the English equivalent 'dear'. And *he was still holding my hand*. I was afraid to move and draw attention to the fact, so I just stood. My mouth was open slightly, I didn't dare lick my lips, he might think I was drooling, so I just gaped at half-mast and hoped that I didn't look like the village idiot.

'You looked a bit panicked in there.' Gethryn spoke again; his voice was quieter now, for me only. 'Not like crowds then, *cariad*?'

Cariad? Had he just called me *darling*?

'I'm not good with lots of people, no.' He didn't need to know about the stress thing that caused the anxiety attacks; it might make him revise his opinion of me up to Grade Two Bonkers.

Gethryn moved closer, half a step, a full step. Now he was right beside me and I could feel him breathing, the weight of his pale linen suit brushing against my wrist. 'Something we have in common, lovely, I don't like the crowds so much either. It's a stupid profession that I'm in for someone who hates gatherings like this, but, hey, you do what you're good at, don't you?'

I gave a hard, slow blink to stop myself wondering exactly what *else* he was good at. 'Where's your . . . every time I've seen you there's been . . . security men?'

'Ah, Bill and Ben the Flowerpot Men. Given them the slip for a moment.' He gestured towards a bottle of Scotch and a single, full glass balanced on the wall near the steps. 'Just wanted some fresh air and a drink of something that doesn't taste like mule's piss.' The voice dropped to that whisper again and I had to lean in close to catch his words. 'You won't give me away, will you, *bach?*' He shook his head, comically scuffing a toe in the sand like a child.

Suddenly there was a presence at my other shoulder.

'Geth? You're wanted inside. They're going to announce the arrangements for tomorrow's Big Competition, you have to be there.'

'Oh, what? Why? Can't they get on without me?'

'You're the *star*.' Jack's voice was bitter. 'Of course they can't do it without you.'

'But . . .'

'Geth.' Warning, now.

'Oh, fuck. All right, boy, I'll be there. Keep your shirt on.' Gethryn turned to me. 'Rain check on this then, *bach*, yes?' And before I could answer he'd headed back up the steps into the diner.

I stayed where he'd left me, stunned. Half-consciously rubbing my scar with the back of my hand and making a mental note to always *always* use this brand of cover-up. Mouth still open.

'And you, pull yourself together.' Jack spoke from between clenched teeth. 'Mr Fantastic has gone now.'

'I can't believe . . .' I was staring into space. 'He spoke to me. He actually *spoke* to me!'

'Whoopee doo.' Jack sounded sardonic now. 'Is that his drink?' He gestured towards the bottle and glass on the wall.

'No.' I wanted Jack to give me the bottle. It was something Gethryn had touched. I would keep it forever. And I was never going to wash this hand again.

'Okay. If you say so.' Jack gave me an odd look.

A sudden renegade breeze startled his hair over his face and, as he brushed it back, I noticed his eyes looked worried. Unsettled. 'Just . . . Skye. Gethryn isn't . . . He's sometimes a bit . . . difficult, you know?'

'You don't have to worry about me,' I said tightly. 'I'm capable of looking out for myself.'

All I got for that was an ironically raised eyebrow which, bearing in mind this morning's little fiasco, had a point. 'I realise that I'm shouting prayers in the Church of Satan here but just . . . be careful. That's all.'

He was more smartly dressed than I'd seen him before, I noticed now. A proper shirt, and jeans that were if not exactly dressy, then at least clean. He wore a narrow-framed pair of glasses and for one tiny second I felt a tickle of familiarity. *I've seen you somewhere before. A long time ago* . . . Before the accident? Possibly, but this had the feeling of not being part of the memory loss, simply something I couldn't immediately recall. Perfectly normal not-remembering of *something* . . . Something that came associated with . . . trouble?

'Oh, *there* you are.' Felix came fussing across the yard like a hen whose chicks have become dispersed. 'Fancy a stroll?'

Jack stared at him. 'Are you not going to listen to the announcement about tomorrow's qu –'

Felix cut him off. 'Are you feeling all right, Skye? You're a bit pink . . . Did it all get a bit much?'

'She's been having a téte-à-téte with Mr Tudor-Morgan.' Jack's voice was dry.

'I'd actually quite like to go inside now.' I tried to disengage myself from Felix's arm but he had a surprisingly strong grip on my elbow.

'Oh, it's nothing important. I shouldn't think,' he added hastily. 'But shouldn't you be . . . ?' A nod to Jack and an indication of the head towards the rapidly filling diner, where I could see Gethryn being hustled towards an empty square of flooring, being kept free from people by more of the jacketed security men. 'Don't they need you?'

Jack shrugged and he blew out as though he had another lit cigarette between his lips. 'Not really. I'm just one of the team, that's all. And, let's face it, I could be standing beside Geth with my dick out and no-one would notice.'

'*I* would,' Felix said gamely. 'I'd be looking.'

'Cheers. I think.'

'What have you got against Gethryn?' My anger was rising at his cavalier way of dispatching a man who had been flirting so ego-boostingly with me.

Jack fixed me with a suddenly very serious brown-eyed gaze. 'Skye. I wouldn't hold *anything* against Gethryn Tudor-Morgan that wasn't made of asbestos, and even then it would have to be reinforced.' I watched his eyes move, taking in my scar. 'But you're right. I'd better go. Someone who knows what's going on should be there with him.' And he was gone, slipping his shadowy body up the three shallow steps and back inside, where the crowd moved to allow him entrance.

I twitched to follow, but Felix pulled me back.

'Come on. I want to know where you vanished to. I'd just got across to Mr Jared White in there, who, I might add has the scrummiest set of abs under that get-up and he needn't try to pretend otherwise, and when I turned round, you'd gone.'

'I had a bit of a panic, went outside and Gethryn and I got talking. That's all, nothing scandalous.' We started walking. Dusk was gathering overhead and the cicadas' thrumming noise was all around us like tiny razors being stropped. 'Jack came and interrupted before it got interesting.'

Felix looked up, checking our position. We were out of sight of the diner now, heading around the motel towards the main doors . . . 'So, was Gethryn chatting you up? Go on, lover, tell me everything.'

I recounted as much of the conversation as I thought repeatable. I wanted to hold some of the words secret, not spread them out and make them public property but keep them only for myself, to take out and think over when I was alone. And besides, what really remained of the conversation boiled down to the memory of Gethryn's studied stubble and his hair moving in the breeze; the feel of his fingers holding my hand and those leonine eyes watching my soul.

'Darling, I'm surprised your underwear hasn't spontaneously combusted – do you know how many women here would pay *any money* to have Gethryn Tudor-Morgan get them alone? And a fair few men as well; at least, I'm hoping.'

'It was . . . nice, yes.'

'*Nice? How* long have you been lusting after that man? A year-and-a-half? Two series' worth of *Fallen Skies*; what, nearly fifty episodes? I seriously fear for your attitude sometimes, Skye. Next time he chats you up – and yes, I am *certain* there will be a next time – then you just follow along anywhere he wants to lead, *tout de suite* and I shan't have a glass to the wall, all right?'

I gave a kind of sideways nod which could have meant anything, but Felix took it as agreement. He always thought I agreed with him. We stood in the softly encroaching dark for a while, Felix leaning against the wall of the motel while I crossed my arms over my chest.

'You thinking about the accident?' Felix's voice was surprisingly gentle. 'Your fingers.'

I tucked my hands into the pockets of my jeans. 'Faith, actually.' Felix gave an almost inaudible sigh. 'She wanted to go to America, didn't she?'

'Yeah.' He bent to examine the toe of his shoe. 'Never got the chance.'

'I miss her.' Inside my pockets my thumbs were running along the fingertip scars, tracing them. Inside my head the colours of the accident raged, the blue flames, the red-hot metal. Not memories, something older, harder and more primitive.

'You and me both, babe. You and me both.'

Another silence. A loved-up couple who'd been strolling around outside under the almost unnaturally clear desert sky came towards us, hand in hand. As they passed, I saw the girl's eyes, dark in the moonlight, flick to my face and I felt the almost pre-emptive embarrassment rise into my throat. 'I think . . . Can we go up to the room now?'

'Sure.' But Fe didn't move; he seemed lost inside his thoughts, scuffing his feet in the dust. I felt a little burst of fondness for him, he looked so young with his tousled hair and his face all scrunched up. So unaware of how people looked at me, and, by extension, him.

'I am glad we came, Fe.'

Then his head came up and that choirboy smile folded his cheeks. 'That's really good, Skye. I mean, this whole thing, it's been good for you, yeah? Even if you never get inside the supremely tight pants of the T-M, you're having a great time, aren't you? And then there's our Jack –'

'He's weird.'

'Whatever. Just you remember, darling, *who* saw him first.' Felix pushed himself away from the wall. 'C'mon.'

But the motel had erupted into noise and light. With the coming dark, even those not attending Gethryn's little address-the-masses moment had crowded inside and I could hear the voices bursting through every wall. 'I think I might just stay out here for a bit longer, actually. If that's okay.'

He nodded. 'The T-M isn't likely to strike twice in one night, though, lover.'

'I'm just enjoying the peace and quiet.'

'Two shakes then.' He leapt inside and was back in a couple of minutes with a large glass of something amber. 'Here. Drink that down and you'll be fit for an early night.'

I sniffed it. 'Wow. Smells like paint stripper.'

'That, darling, is a Broken Hill Special.'

'Smells like it. Broken something, anyway.' I sniffed again. 'Intestines, possibly.'

'Chug-a-lug, there's a good girl.'

I took a cautious first sip. The warmth rode down my throat like a roping cowboy, captured my tonsils and begged for backup. 'It's not bad. It's a bit like . . . tequila?'

'Mm, *mostly* tequila.' Felix watched me drain the glass, then took the empty and sat next to me on the edge of the little raised wall that circled the entire motel, as though it marked some kind of border. 'Ever thought about moving out here? To the States?'

'No.'

'You could sell the house, make enough to move. Might do you good. I'm sure you talked about moving to the States, you know.'

I frowned. Trying to find the memories was like staring into a black maelstrom and made my forehead ache. 'Did I?'

'That's what you told me.'

I shook my head. 'I wish I could remember. Sometimes I feel like one of those pod aliens –

everything you tell me about the past sounds so weird and so unlike me, as though I was someone different before. Like I'm a new soul in a body you think you know.'

Felix shrugged an elegant shoulder and stared off into the desert. There was an expression on his face that was close to pain and I touched his hand. 'I'm sorry. I don't mean to remind you of . . . back then. It makes me feel so strange when I think that there's a life that we had that I can't remember, stuff that we did, stuff I can't share in any more. I mean, I can do that whole "remember that time?" thing, but only up to a certain point, and that makes me feel stupid. Like I'm not really trying. I know I can't help it, but I am sorry, all the same.'

He turned, his expression too complicated to read. 'I guess you are,' he said, his eyes tracing the outline of my scar. 'Right. Feeling better now?'

I wanted to say that I hadn't been feeling bad to start with, but, although my eyebrows seemed to be fully functioning, the rest of my face had been hit with a kind of palsy which made my lips go numb and my nose start to run. ''S a bit . . . bloopy.' The desert began to melt and I stood up, panicked.

'Bloopy?'

'Y'know, when you're all kind of . . . woooo.' I took a step forward and the ground spiralled.

'Whoops, here we go.' Felix caught hold of me and pulled me against him. 'That was quick.'

'What's happening?' I had to force the words out past an unco-operative tongue which felt like a lump of Spam squatting in my mouth. 'Oh. Tired now.'

'Okay.' With one arm wrapped around my waist, Felix began towing me towards the motel entrance. 'You'll be fine by the morning. It's only half a tablet, just to make sure you get a good night's sleep.'

His words floated into my brain, almost without meaning. 'A wha'?' I asked drowsily.

'Sleepers.' Felix spoke into my ear. 'I brought them just in case. You'll be fine,' he repeated. 'Wouldn't give you anything that would do you any harm, even with alcohol. *Some* of us know what we're doing, drugwise.'

'Skye?' Another voice, sounding annoyed. 'What's up now?'

'It's all right.' Felix changed his hold on me but I felt another hand move my hair away from my face. 'She's just off to bed.'

'Skye?' It was Jack. I knew he was talking to me but I couldn't raise the energy to answer. 'Are you okay?'

'Bed,' I echoed Fe sleepily.

Jack's face came into sudden focus; he must have crouched down in front of me. 'I'd have to know you a lot better first,' he said, quietly and, despite the alcohol and sleeping tablet, I felt a little shiver kick at my stomach. 'I'll probably see you in the morning, before it all starts off. If you need anything, you know where I am.'

'What time do we have to be there?' Felix tightened his grip on my waist. It almost hurt.

'If you'd been in the diner, you'd have heard.' Jack sounded sharp.

'Skye needed some fresh air.'

'Mmm.' Not altogether accepting. 'Starts at eleven. Entrants need to be seated by half-ten, so they can be checked over for any cheat sheets.' A cool hand on my forehead. 'Why? Are you entering?'

'Skye is.'

I'm what? I thought, but nothing inside me would respond. Not curiosity, not nerves, nothing. It was worse than Valium, at least that just deadened the world. Whatever Felix had given me had killed it.

'Better get her to bed then.'

'Off now.' Then, cheekily, 'Don't suppose you want to join us?'

A half-laugh, fading into the night. 'Wrong guy.'

I think I might have passed out, because the next thing I knew was Felix rolling me up in the duvet and switching out the light. 'I'll see you in the morning.'

'Bu' . . .' I managed to get one eye open. 'Where . . . ?'

Silhouetted in the doorway, Felix grinned. 'You'll sleep 'til morning, don't worry. And while you are sleeping, Mr White is, shall we say, going to be gaining a certain grubbiness.'

CHAPTER 10

He couldn't sleep. There were still people wandering around the motel, singles looking for a chat, a drinking partner, a bedmate, and a few couples and groups talking in the earnest way that told him they were discussing the show rather than current affairs or last night's TV.

Jack didn't particularly want to be alone, but keeping company with a bottle of Jack Daniels was out of the question and any kind of human company would come with questions he wasn't willing to answer; to distract himself he fetched his keys and let himself into the prop store which was a posh name for a tin shed at the side of the motel. From the looks of it the kitchen staff used it to store jars and bottled goods, which had been shoved into a chaotic, rolling mass at the back of the shed to make way for the Shadow Fighter and some random articles from the set – a rack of costumes, some blaster rifles and a trunk which had the words Marketing Dept stencilled on the side.

He leaned back against the sun-warmed wall of

the shed and breathed in the smell of acrylic paint and hot plastic from the props, overlaid with a vinegar smell from a spilled jar of pickles. *The smell of Fallen Skies. Artificial substance and sour preservation, in a room that a four-year old could break the lock off. And this is what I've done with my life.*

His mind drifted, aided by the medicinal tang of so much vinegar in a confined space, until it landed on the thought of Skye and he felt his skin prickle into goosebumps. *Cute girl. Weird friendship she seems to have . . . with a guy that's way too controlling for it to be good.* Two steps into the shed and he could run his hand over the reassuring solidity of the Shadow Fighter, another step and he had his hand on the sleeve of the costume of a refugee from one of the frozen planets. *And why am I even thinking about her? I've got enough problems, don't need a girl with self-esteem issues to add to the collection of Great Fuck-Ups of Our Time, and if she needs help . . . I am so far from the person she should have anywhere near her.*

A sudden burst of laughter from somewhere outside. Jack straightened up, took his hand away from the costume, and gritted his teeth. *It's all pretend. This, Fallen Skies, who I am, who I've become, it's all pretend. So, this whole Iceman thing I've got going on, the person people believe me to be, the stone-cold writer-man – the thing that stops me from wanting . . . needing someone . . . how real is* <u>*that*</u>*?*

CHAPTER 11

I was woken by the sounds of a Spanish argument and the banging of pans. Felix must have left the window open. I huddled down and turned over but the noise continued and then the dog joined in, shrill yelps that rattled and echoed around the yard until I had to get up.

My mouth was dry and I was thirsty. Couldn't work out why. Little, half-remembered snippets from last night kept drifting through my head; the firmness of Felix's hold on me as he carried me to bed, Jack pushing my hair away from my face. And Gethryn, always back to Gethryn, talking to me outside the diner, taking my hand, looking in my eyes.

I swallowed water and rinsed my face. How much of last night had been real, and how much had been some complicated form of hallucination? The whole of the last twelve hours flowed together in one confused image: drinks, Jack's smile, Felix's touch. And still, Gethryn. My one, huge, dream-come-true moment and I was kicking myself for my gaucheness, my cautious reactions, when what I *should* have done was entrance him with my wit and sophistication. Shouldn't I?

I dressed. Still no Felix; he was probably sleeping in. A quick shard of jealousy cut a curl from my heart and I imagined myself lying sprawled in someone's arms, or involved in a bed-bouncingly enthusiastic leave-taking, but when I tried to imagine the man concerned all I could conjure were memories of Michael dragged from photographs. It made me shudder, and I didn't know why.

The corridors were quiet at this time in the morning as I wandered down the stairs, in case Fe had found his way to the diner without me. But the place was still locked up, although I could see girls inside, tying on aprons and turning on coffee machines, so I went back to reception, where I found Antonio earnestly pushing letter pegs into today's Board of Events.

I read it as he prodded the letters into place. When he finally stepped back to admire the overall effect, I was so close behind him that he nearly broke my nose.

'Miss! Why you read so close?' He eyed me cautiously.

'You all right?'

'This . . . this is today?'

'Yes. Much excitement. Much competition, I think.'

Even knowing Felix, even knowing that he was so self-centred he had his own gravitational field,

I *still* had trouble believing it. 'The bastard.' But even given all that . . . why? What was in it for him?

Leaving Antonio standing baffled, I chased back up the stairs to find Felix still conspicuously not in our room. I wondered now if it was deliberate, if he was going to avoid me until the last possible minute, and if he did – how the *hell* did he think he was going to get me to go along with it? I slammed around the room, hoping that he'd come in just so I could throw things at him, but he continued not to arrive. Bastard! He'd spent the night jumping on some gorgeous guy, leaving me sleeping off the effects of – what, something to keep me out of trouble? To keep me from asking questions? *Well, think again, Felix, my old mate, because I'm good at questions. But then, who could I ask, who did I know out here who'd even answer?* Jack.

I hammered on his door until he opened up, looking rumpled but unsleepy. He was wearing the pyjama bottoms again, and this time they were topped with a Metallica T-shirt that looked as if it had belonged to several other men previously, all of them bigger.

'What? Oh, it's you.'

'You told me to come to you if I needed anything, didn't you? I mean, last night, I didn't dream that, did I?'

'No, but I'm impressed that you remember. You were pretty out of things.'

'Felix doped me.'

'He *what*?' Jack waved me inside and cleared his laptop off the bed, where he'd obviously been working. The screen had the *Fallen Skies* logo in one corner. 'That's a bit . . . immoral, isn't it?' He sat where the laptop had been, tucking his legs up in front of him in a kind of half-yoga pose which made the pyjama bottoms gape revealingly around the fly, giving me flashes of pale blue lycra. 'Sit down and tell me.'

'I can't. I can't sit down. I'm so *angry*, I want to hit someone.' I paced up and down the floor around the bed, Jack's head swivelling to keep me in view. 'I just went down to reception, found out that the activity of today is a quiz, yes?'

'Yeah. Big thing. Main reason for the whole convention.'

'Yes. I remember reading about last year's.' I wasn't going to confess to the all-consuming fire of jealous hatred I'd felt, flicking through magazines to see pictures of the winner, a self-possessed girl, draping herself all over the cast and crew. 'I knew there'd be one this year, but . . .' I stopped short of revealing that I may have been intrigued, but my lack of self-confidence would never in a million years have let me enter. 'Last night, Felix said that I was taking part in something? I didn't dream that either?'

He blew a long breath. 'He entered you. And you didn't *know*?'

I began slapping the wall. 'I should have. I should

have realised that Felix thinks altruism is some kind of learning disorder, that he'd never bring me all the way out here just to – just to cheer me up. He's been planning this!' I rounded on Jack. 'How the hell can he have entered me without my knowing? Don't you have to sign things or something?'

A shrug, and Metallica threatened to abandon his skinny shoulders. 'Course.' He swept his hair back from his face and frowned at me. 'It's all done properly you know, we're not some fly-by-night, single-series merchants. Could he forge your signature? I mean, we try to keep it all watertight but there's only so much we can do.'

'Yes.' My fists were tight. I'd got handfuls of my shirt on each side and was twisting, feeling my scars catch on the fabric. 'When I was first out of hospital I used to give him my bank card to get money out of the cash machine and to get shopping. I . . . I wasn't coping very well, I just didn't *think* . . . He must have learned to copy my signature from that.'

'Wow. He's like immorality Ground Zero, isn't he? Does he . . . I mean, he doesn't . . . you're all right, aren't you? He's not . . . God, what am I trying to say here?'

'Fe has a very loose interpretation of what's right. Anything that benefits him is a good thing and he can't see any reason not to do it. I'm just so *angry* that he didn't come out and tell me! I thought we were coming over here to meet . . .

I mean, to socialise, to get away from York, to help me stop dwelling on things. All wide-eyed innocence and "it will be good for you", you know? When what he should have been saying was "let me drug you up, drag you to the middle of nowhere and then force you to enter a competition"!'

'And he's your *friend*? Bloody hell, I'd hate to meet your enemies.'

'I'm sure in Felix's head it all makes sense. But the question is, why? What good is it going to do him if I enter?'

Jack stood up and grabbed my arms, pulling them forward. I saw his scar stretch and flex as he reached out and wondered if mine looked like that under tension. 'The quiz, it's really tough. I mean *I* don't know the answers and I wrote most of the *series*. How much do you really know about *Fallen Skies*? I mean, really? Are you an obsessive fan? Watch it, sit on the forum, read up on everything?'

My arms went limp in his grasp. His hands were cold. 'Yes.' That was me, obsessive.

'First prize, y'see, is a part in the next series. Nothing big, a walk-on probably, not really thought about it much, we tailor the part to the winner.' His eyes were looking somewhere inside, not at me. 'Probably this one guy I'm writing, veteran of the Shadow War . . . yeah, could be Seran Vye . . .'

'Shut up. What is it with everyone's obsession with men in uniform? So, Felix wants me to win . . .' That was why he'd asked all those questions about me trying out for a part. *If things had been different*, he'd said. Different enough that I'd still have the confidence to stand in front of a camera? Knowing all along that I wouldn't, *couldn't*.

And then the whole plan snapped into focus. I knew *exactly* why Felix had brought me here. 'He wants me to win the part for him,' I said, almost breathless with the audacity. 'He entered me knowing I wouldn't take the prize if I won it – and then, there he'd be, stepping into the breach.' I half-laughed. 'I can just picture him now, combing through the tiny print to make sure it would be allowed. Wow. You have got to admire his deviousness.'

Jack seemed to realise he was still holding my arms. Slowly, one finger at a time, he released his grip. 'If he'd asked you nicely, told you what he wanted, would you have come here?'

'I don't know. Maybe.' But I knew that if Felix had asked me to fly to America just to try to win him a part in a series, I'd have refused. Would have chosen my cosy little house, my safe, established little life over everything. But the way he'd put it – that it would be good for me, and then, once I was here, that I could take things at my own pace, stay in the room all the time if I wanted to – lying bastard.

'So, will you do it?'

I shrugged this time. 'I might, just to get every answer wrong. That'd show him.'

Jack grinned. 'Yeah, go for the booby prize, it's a series of Scratch-n-Sniff cards. Somehow I don't see Felix as a Scratch-n-Sniff kind of guy. Not of cards, at any rate.' The grin fell away and he was left looking darkly serious. 'You care a lot about him, don't you?'

'Of course I do. Felix's sister Faith was my best friend. We went through drama school together, got our first jobs in theatre together, I even moved in with her family for a while. Fe was just her brother, just this bloke tomcatting around at the edge of our circle – he's two years younger than Faith, two years behind at drama school.' I found myself twisting my fingers again, picking at the scars. Questions about the past always did that to me. I answered by rote now. Practised. 'And then, when I got together with Michael, and he was Fe's friend, we were a bit of a foursome.' Now my hand went up to my face. 'But . . . I don't know. Everything to do with Michael is stuff Felix has told me, the gaps he's filled in for me, you can't understand if you haven't been there. Not knowing is . . . Fe is all I have left. He's the only person who remembers . . .'

'You mean you don't?'

I stared at him for a second then tapped my head. 'Brain damage. I was thrown through the windscreen, back of my head got crushed, there was a blood clot on my brain and they had to operate . . . My memory got . . .' I waved my fingers in the air as though playing an invisible harp.

'So, Felix is like your professional rememberer? That's actually quite cool, there's a whole sci-fi concept in there.' He tailed off. 'You don't remember the accident?'

'Only what Felix has told me. We were on our way home from a New Year party, Faith and Michael were in the front, Felix and I were in the back, and we crashed at high speed.' The words were empty of any emotion; I might as well have been reporting the plot of an EastEnders episode.

Jack tipped his head back and looked at me from under a heavy overhang of hair. It made him look remote somehow. 'You weren't in the front?'

'No. It probably saved my life.'

'Your . . . best friend was sitting next to your fiancé?'

My breath caught. Raked down my throat like a mis-swallow. 'Yes.' I gulped, couldn't get air down fast enough and began to panic. Sweat broke out on my forehead, my breathing began to race and yet I still couldn't fill my lungs. Sickness rose, but I couldn't throw up, didn't dare, how could I breathe if I was vomiting?

'Skye.' Jack spoke suddenly close, right by my ear. 'It's all right. Relax. Just breathe.' I could feel a cautious hand stroking my hair. 'Don't think about it; let your body do the work for you. Trust me, it wants to breathe, when you fight you're stopping it from doing its job.'

I tried to push him away; he was crowding my air, breathing my oxygen. But gradually his slow words and the rhythm of his stroking took over the irregular gasping of my inhalation and I felt my heart rate begin to settle. 'Sorry.' I was exhausted. 'Stupid.' Couldn't even stop to think *why* I'd got so stressed at the thought of the accident. Maybe I wasn't as over it as I thought.

He was still standing very close and I felt him shake his head. 'Nah. Perfectly reasonable. We all handle the trauma in our own ways. After my accident I didn't speak for six months, some kind of shock, they said. Drove everyone completely insane, lot of them thought I was faking it for the attention.' A high grunt of derision. 'Yeah, 'cos everyone wants doctors and psychiatrists buzzing round them all hours.'

'What happened?'

Jack flopped down onto the bed, drew his knees up against his chest and wrapped his arms around them. 'Like you, car crash. I was sixteen. Ryan, my best friend, was killed; I got my arm nearly ripped off.' Thoughtfully he flexed his muscles, pulling his hand up to his face and away again. 'They reattached it, eight hours of microsurgery, and it's pretty nearly as good as it was.' He wiggled his fingers in my direction. 'I'm a bit clumsy sometimes, don't grip as well as I should, but it's okay.' He stared at his palm as though for the first time. 'Yeah,' he repeated. 'It's okay. Right. Now, you're going to come to breakfast with me. Couple of cups of coffee and a plate of eggs, you'll feel better. Then you can decide what you're doing about this quiz.' Long legs unfolded onto the carpet. 'But reckon I'd better get dressed. This is my writing gear and not every restaurant appreciates genius out of its jeans.'

'I'll go and . . .'

'No, stay there. I'll just be a minute.' He dragged open a couple of drawers, withdrew the contents of one of them and headed into the bathroom, half-closing the door behind him. 'Where's Felix now?' His voice was muffled, the T-shirt coming off, probably.

'Shagging Jared White, I think.'

'*Really*?' A head came round the door and I tried not to notice the exposed chest under it. 'Good luck to him then.' There was a thin white scar along the side of his rib cage that I hadn't been in a fit state to notice last time I'd seen him topless, fading as it curved into the hair scattered down his stomach. He still wore the leather lace; it contrasted with his pale skin like a slash.

'Oh, I think Felix is up to it.'

Another manic grin and the torso vanished. I could hear the rustling sounds of clothing removal, and desperately tried not to say anything which might call for an appearance. 'What are the other prizes then? For the quiz, I mean.'

A momentary hiatus behind the door, then Jack emerged buttoning his fly. His chest was still bare, revealing that the scar tore across a nipple before angling down towards his diaphragm. 'You really want to know? Okay. First is the part in the show.

Second is a dinner date with Geth. Third . . . I think it's some kind of memorabilia – one of the flight cruiser cockpits maybe, we've not really settled yet, depends what's needed next series.' He opened another drawer and pulled out a white shirt, sniffed it and held it out to me. 'Reckon this'll do another day?'

'Looks fine,' I said idly, thinking about that second-prize dinner date with Gethryn. If I could win that . . .

'Hmm. You're not fussy, I'll add that to the list. Okay. You coming?' And he yanked the shirt on, did up two middle buttons to hold it across his chest and opened the door, barefoot, pulling a pair of wire-framed glasses from his bedside table and poking them onto his nose as he went.

'You call that dressed?' I followed him into the corridor. 'Don't you ever wear shoes?'

'Only if I have to.' He closed the bedroom door, pausing to check his pockets for his key card. As he patted himself down, I saw Felix heading up the corridor towards our room. His jaunty walk stammered for a second when he caught sight of me and the partly clad Jack and he held a theatrical hand to his forehead.

'Skye, Skye, Skye, I take my eyes off you for one night and you're bonking the workforce; what *am* I going to do with you?'

'I think it's more what *I'm* going to do with *you* that you ought to be worrying about.'

'Steady, darling, after last night I'm not sure I

can take much more. I think I might be broken, actually. Certainly feels like it. Can I have the key, please? Or have you locked us out again for the dubious pleasure of having to invoke Antonio's wrath?'

I held it out at arm's length. '*Felix*.'

'Ah. So. Ah. I think we might need to have a little chat.' Felix took the key card, his eyes flicking from Jack to me and back again but, I must admit, mostly resting on Jack's half-naked chest where his shirt barely managed to make contact.

'Later.' Jack said, firmly. He half-turned and gave me a gentle shove. 'I'm taking Skye for something to eat. You can discuss this when she's got something inside her.'

There was a looooong pause. Felix was bursting to add the obvious rejoinder but my expression must have put him off his stroke, as I didn't think Jack looked in the mood for Fe's speculation into our collective love-lives. 'All right,' Felix said, cautiously, after a second or two, obviously reluctant to let the double entendre go unentendred. 'I need some sleep anyhoo. Catch you on the flipside?'

'No.' I must have sounded unlike myself, because both men raised their eyebrows. 'I'll catch you in about half-an-hour. I am *not* just going to fall in line with your plans, Felix.'

Felix bit his lip, hard. I saw the skin split and wondered what he was trying to stop himself from saying, as he waved a casual hand in agreement, pushing his way into our room and falling on the bed with a groan which was audible as we headed towards the lift.

Jack and I ate eggs and drank coffee in the now open but still-deserted diner. There wasn't much conversation between us; he seemed to have slipped into deep thought and I was more concerned with what I was going to say to Felix. *Had* he really brought me all the way out here just to try to win him a part? It seemed a bit of a long-shot, but then he wasn't exactly meeting with huge success in Britain; maybe he saw this as his one chance. And I . . . was I happy to go along with it? To finally admit the death of my own ambitions?

I watched Jack's long fingers fiddle with the toothpick container on the table while he ate his eggs one-handed. He pulled the lid off the box and, as soon as the eggs were finished, he put a toothpick between his lips, not even seeming to notice what he'd done.

'You'll never get it to light.' I ate my last piece of bacon.

'What?' As he spoke he noticed the wood, pulled a face and shuffled it to one corner of his mouth. 'Oh, bugger.'

'Why don't you try giving up? There's all those nicotine patches and everything now, supposed to make it easy.' I drained my coffee and a hovering waitress pounced with a refill.

'Have you ever given anything up, Skye?' Jack

pulled the chewed end from between his teeth. 'Because, let me tell you, it's not a bundle of laughs. In fact, it's not even one small giggle. I smoke because . . . well, because everyone needs a vice, a crutch, something to hang onto, and that's mine.' He wasn't looking at me; he kept his eyes on the scratched tabletop. 'And unless you can talk from a position of experience . . .' now he raised his eyes and his gaze met mine, something like a flare of anger shone deep inside it, 'then don't moralise, okay?'

I opened my mouth to ask how he could talk when he obviously *hadn't* given up, but then it suddenly struck me that I was sitting in a diner in America eating breakfast with a writer from my favourite TV series and the oddest urge to start giggling swept over me. My lips must have twitched because Jack raised his eyebrows. 'This is just so weird,' I tried to explain. 'A few weeks ago the high spot of my life was watching *Fallen Skies* on TV, and now . . .' I waved an arm, 'here I am!'

Jack gave an answering grin and I had another jolt of realisation that he was quite a good-looking man, under all that dark, scowling facade. 'Yeah. Moving and shaking with the movers and shakers. Not that I can get my head around myself as either a mover or a shaker. I'm a bit more of the slight oscillator.' He wiggled his head from side to side. 'We're not as popular.'

The moment opened up, stretched somehow,

and enclosed both of us in a little bubble of time. Jack was still smiling and I was still grinning like a mad person, fighting the urge to burst out laughing at the absurdity of actually *being* here. Our eyes met, something moved between us, a recognition, an acknowledgement that we saw a piece of ourselves in the other, and then the moment moved past and was gone like a lighthouse beam that had picked us out for a fleeting second.

I cleared my throat and stared down into my unwanted refill. 'I'd better go and talk to Felix. He's got so much explaining to do . . .'

'You want me to come? Is there likely to be violence done, or is it all going to be tedious hugging and forgiveness?' Jack swallowed a last mouthful of coffee. ''Cos if it is, I'm gonna stay right here and get another refill. I can watch *Friends* re-runs anytime.' His eyes were back on the table, as though he was ashamed of letting me see a glimmer of what lay underneath his grouchy persona.

'There may be shouting. But you stay, I'll be fine.'

He reached out without looking, and grasped my wrist. 'Need me, I'll come. Okay?' He was still focusing on the dregs in the bottom of his cup, looking serious.

'Understood. But Fe's not likely to do me any damage.' I pushed away from the table and stood up. Jack still didn't look at me.

'I'm kinda in charge of the quiz, so . . . if you decide to take part, I'll be there.'

I couldn't help myself, I looked back over my shoulder as I left the diner. Jack was sitting, still alone at the table despite the comings and goings surrounding him as the diner began to fill up. He looked like an island in a constantly moving sea. People would glance at him, at the empty three seats tucked in around his table, then quietly move away as though they didn't want to disturb him. He wasn't exactly looking open to contact, leaning back in his chair, hands embracing a coffee cup, eyes partly closed behind his slim glasses with his hair dancing an untidy fandango in the breeze from the open doors, but why were people giving him such deference, such a wide berth? What the hell was he thinking, this dark man, hidden behind those heavy lids?

What the hell am I thinking? Jack tipped his head back and felt the tension in his neck. *Why am I even getting involved*? The wash of conversation became so much white noise and static as he let his thoughts roam, falling into the writer's zone of what-if and what-could-be.

What if Skye got herself caught up with Gethryn? That was what lay behind it all, he knew that. This was where having an imagination was not a good thing – extrapolating the real and happening and pushing it into the place of what-could-be – and in this case it was worryingly easy.

She was obviously completely swept away by Geth, beyond the point of any rational words getting through. He could warn her, he could even lay it on the line, tell her exactly what Geth was like, and she'd smile, nod, accept his words and then go right out and let herself get taken in by the charm, that almost supernatural ability the man had to form a connection.

Bugger. Jack drained another cup and felt the caffeine give his system a good kicking, the nervous twang of a brain in overdrive. Why hadn't *he* got it, that easy smile, the charisma that enabled Geth to chat, flirt, draw the girls in? Why did talking to Skye make him feel that urge to withdraw, like he was indulging in something that was eventually going to hurt? As if he didn't know.

Did he want to save her? And if so, what from? She was clearly an adult . . . he let the memory of her slim body in the really quite see-through T-shirt she'd worn yesterday flow through him . . . clearly adult, oh yes. She could make her own decisions, reach her own conclusions. He had a life, a complicated one that needed no more help to get even more problematical. Two perfectly good reasons for him to shrug his shoulders and get back upstairs to the next episode. Easy.

He put the cup down but didn't move.

CHAPTER 12

Felix was flat out on the bed, wearing underpants and with his head wrapped in a towel. When he woke up he was going to have scary hair, I thought happily. Then I bounced on him.

'Ow! Sod! Oh, it's you, how was your breakfast with Mr Luscious? You know, if you decide you don't want him then I think it's only fair that you let me have a go; did you see that body? Oh, sorry, of course you did, in great and glorious Technicolor close-up. Is he really huge? Looks like he's a big boy in those jeans, but then, denim can be so . . . oooof.'

I kept my hand over his mouth. 'Why didn't you just tell me? About the quiz.'

'Mmmmmffffff.'

'Sorry.' I removed my palm and wiped it on the sheet.

'I didn't know how to. I knew you wouldn't go for it. But, Skye, think about it, *please,* you're brilliant at anything to do with *Fallen Skies,* and you might just decide you *did* want the part, and if not . . . well . . . I could do with the break,' he finished, sounding unFelixly downbeat.

‘It’s all about *you*, isn’t it? You drug me up, drag me out here, and all so that I can be your patsy in some scheme to get a job! Why couldn’t you just audition like everyone else?’

He unwound the towel from his hair and began to rub, spreading his spiky locks around and mopping at them, thinking. ‘It was Faith’s idea.’ He nearly whispered it.

‘Oh come on! Faith . . . it . . . the accident happened before *Fallen Skies* ever started.’ But the mention of her name made my heart rate rise again. ‘Don’t put this onto her.’

‘Honestly. We used to . . . when we were kids, we’d do these competitions. Like the ones you get in the paper, win a year’s supply of chocolate, win a bike, you know.’ His eyes were serious, the twinkle had faded and his dimples were nowhere in evidence. ‘When we’d both come out of drama school we’d watch those stupid “Choose a Leading Lady for Broadway” shows and say that it would be better if they chose people with a passion for the *show*, not just a talent for singing and dancing. Faith used to pretend it was all beneath her. I can still see her sitting there, making like she was reading a magazine and then jumping up to yell at the screen. And she said . . .’ His eyes swam for a moment, then he sniffed and gave a pathetic smile, ‘Faith said that if anything like that came up, we’d go for it. You remember, when Faith auditioned for Nancy? I know it was just before the accident, but you *must* remember *that*. Most exciting thing to happen in York since the railways came.'

'Felix.' I swallowed. 'Why didn't you just tell me?' I scrubbed a slightly eggy hand over my eyes, pretending I wasn't crying. 'Why?'

'Because you don't remember! You don't remember how it was, being driven, being hungry for the part you knew was so *right*, so *you*. You felt it, we all did. And I feel it now, about this, about *Fallen Skies*. I don't even care what the part is, I just know that being in this series would be the making of my career.' There was a single tear running picturesquely down his cheek and his eyes looked huge. 'But I don't think you really want to remember what it was like. You don't even want to try to remember.'

'That's not true!' Now my nose had started to run as well as my eyes and I gave up trying to hide it, just let the emotion come. 'I want to remember, but I *can't*. I wish I could. And I hate it, I *hate* that I have a whole year missing; everything I learned, all the experiences and all the familiarity from then have vanished! Everything is new and you'd think that would be a good thing, but it's not, Fe, it's really not. But I do remember this, Faith was my friend.'

'But you've forgotten everything she did for you in that last year . . . everything my family did to help you; it's all just wiped out, isn't it? Like none of it ever existed.' His tear was joined by another, a mirror image on his other cheek. He just sat, towel around his shoulders, tight black underwear on display, and the tears fell onto the duvet tucked around him. 'It's gone from your head, Skye. Just . . . poof!' He flicked his fingers as though conjuring stars.

'Fe . . .' I was almost pleading. 'It's not my fault. It was the accident, the head injury.'

'But deep down, Skye, deep down, don't you think it was because you *wanted* to forget? This is your big chance to build yourself a new life, to remake yourself into the person you've always wanted to be – like being a kid but with enough knowledge to change yourself. Wipe out your background, forget the past, start again from scratch?'

'No!' I almost wailed. 'I didn't want to forget! I want to remember, but it's like this big black hole where it all should be, and it's all gone and nothing left and it means I don't even know who I *am* any more . . .'

He touched my face. Stroked away the tears with a thumb, looking into my eyes. 'You've got me, Skye. You've still got me. If you win this . . . you win it for all three of us: me, you and Faith.' He brought his face closer, rested his forehead against mine. 'I'd do anything for you, you know that,' he whispered. 'I look out for you, keep you safe . . . will you do this one thing for me?' He was barely breathing the words, all I could see were his immense hazel eyes reddening around the lids as his tears mixed with mine. 'Skye?'

My shoulders shook as I pushed the sobs down into my body. Felix put a careful arm around me and pulled me against him. I could feel the strength of his muscles under his skin as he held me tightly. His body was more compact than Jack's, more strung with muscle, and he smelled familiar under the faintly foreign scent of someone else's shower gel. Tears salted our skins for a while longer, then by mutual consent we pulled away. There was much blowing of noses and covert wiping of faces; Felix tried without noticeable results to tidy his hair and I combed a layer of mascara onto my lashes. 'So? Have you decided?'

Somewhere among all the emotion, I had decided what to do. 'I'll do it. Just this once, for Faith, for you.' I felt a tremor of disloyalty but pushed the feeling away. After all, I was entering, wasn't I? The chances of winning first prize had to be remote, but *second* prize now . . .

'And how about for Jack?'

'Jack? Why would I do anything for him? I didn't sleep with him last night, Fe; I only went to him to find out what was going on. It's not my fault the man has a very odd idea of "dressed".'

'Yeah, so I noticed, coming out with his shirt down to here.' Felix demonstrated. 'He wants to have you, you can tell. And as for you, missy . . . it's been a long time. A good pipe-opener, that's what you need, a run up the slope. And Mr Whitaker there, he'd take you nice and slow.'

'You are horrible.' Then, 'What? Hold on, back

up a bit . . . Whitaker? *Jack* is Jay Whitaker?' I scrubbed both hands over my face. *'Really?'*

Felix stared. 'I thought you knew! I thought that was why you were all over the guy!'

'But he . . .' I groped for something suitable to say, 'he's *clean!* And wearing . . . you know, shirts and jeans instead of raggy shorts and, okay, so his hair is a bit long where's the beard?'

Jay Whitaker, the reclusive, anti-publicity show-runner, the man in charge of the whole *Fallen Skies* shebang. Chief writer, main storyliner, hirer-and-firer, the man rumoured to be a drunken shambles? *Jack??* 'The last pictures I saw of Jay Whitaker, he had a beard down to here and a fringe you could lose a baby in. He was so hairy that I thought it must be some kind of disguise!' I tried to match that year-old image with the slightly shabby, quiet man who'd bought me breakfast. That scruffy, half-dressed brooder was the man who put those sexy phrases in Lucas James's mouth? Things slotted into place – Jay Whitaker, British guy, one of the team of writers for the huge sci-fi hit *Two Turns North*. Jack. Of course. Now I felt stupid.

'Hmm. Half-an-hour before you have to be there, Skye. You've got thirty minutes to pull out.'

'Oh my God. I've seen him with no shirt on! He's like . . . as famous as Joss Whedon, and I've vomited in his toilet!'

'Who?'

'Joss Whedon! The guy who ran the whole Buffy show! Felix, you do *watch* television, don't you?'

'Yeah, all right, don't get carried away. The quiz . . . ?'

'Good Lord. I've eaten eggs with the Iceman. Wow.' I tried to slot the two images one over the other, the few, blurry, backstage pictures of someone that made Bigfoot look well turned-out and the real-life barefoot man who chewed pencils. 'He's from Leeds, you know.'

'Er, yeah. Calm down, Mastermind, what about . . . ?'

'I've said I'll do it.' I began to yank a brush through my hair, which resisted with everything it had. The thought of sitting in a room full of people made my knees shake, but I was committed now. I'd do it. If I knew half as much about *Fallen Skies* as I thought – I was heading for a dinner date with Gethryn.

CHAPTER 13

A chunky girl with pink hair and a T-shirt which said 'Mrs Lucas James' stood in the queue to get into Meeting Room One right in front of me. As I slipped into place, breathing carefully, she turned and gave me a grin.

'Great turn out.'

'Mmm.' I felt the urge to rush upstairs and help myself to a Valium. It would soothe me, calm this terrible feeling that there wasn't going to be enough oxygen once we were shut in a room together, and stop my fingertips tingling with the panic and the overbreathing as I subconsciously tried to store up the air. *Stress. That's all it is, doing new stuff, making me feel as though I can't cope.* I forced myself not to run. *Dinner date,* my secret inner-self whispered. *Just think about that. Sitting opposite Gethryn. Watching him eat. Stay sharp.* I relaxed my shoulders and forced my legs to step forward through the crowd, focusing hard on not thinking about the number of people who surrounded me. Further ahead, in the room itself, I could see Jack and two guys wearing official *Fallen Skies* T-shirts, shuffling papers. It made me feel better.

'You nervous? I'm nervous as hell, really in this to win the date with Gethryn Tudor-Morgan but, hey, take it as it comes. You on the forum?' She pulled the front of her shirt out to show the message. 'This is me. My forum name. Come true, I wish.' She gave a shrug and the queue moved forward a few steps as some more people joined behind me.

'I'm Blue Sky.'

'Oh. Hey, yeah, you started the thread on why Defries couldn't really call himself Prince of Skeldar, way to go, girl, that was some serious political argument there. My real name's Ruth.'

'Skye.'

'Cool.' Ruth leaned across me to address the man behind. 'Hey, B'Ha-man, this is Blue Sky.'

The man bent forward. He looked like an accountant. 'Hi.' Carefully ironed shirt, neatly pressed jeans and shiny shoes were out of place here, where loose T-shirts covered in *Fallen Skies* related slogans seemed *de rigueur.* 'This is just so exciting.'

My breathing had steadied. With Ruth in front and B'Ha-man behind I had acquired a degree of security and the rest of the convention crowd was being filtered off to Meeting Room Two, where I understood another signing session would shortly be underway, where Felix would be pretending to pay attention whilst, no doubt, twitching. This left only us quiz-participants standing in line and, as the numbers dwindled, I felt better.

Up front Jack was levering open the doors. 'Everyone take a seat. We'll be coming around to check you don't have any crib sheets or phones set up, okay?'

I sat in one of the evenly spaced chairs, between Ruth, who was bouncing around with excitement, and B'Ha-man who sat rigidly, feet together. Each of us was handed a clipboard with logoed sheets of paper and a *Fallen Skies* biro attached. Adrenaline surged, leaving me feeling slightly light-headed as one of the T-shirted men looked me over quickly, patted my pockets and moved onto Ruth. This was *serious*.

'We're closing the room now.' Jack, up front, was standing on a makeshift stage, put together from some enormous wooden blocks, wearing a microphone headset. I was glad to see he had put shoes on and buttoned up the shirt. He was still wearing his glasses, which made him look particularly writerly. 'Don't want any accusations of anyone getting answers from the crowd.'

And now I knew why he'd looked familiar. The beard was gone, replaced by an untidy brush of stubble, his hair was much shorter and he'd lost a little weight but . . . yes. I could see it now. *Jay Whitaker. A huge change, a huge improvement. What made you pull yourself back?*

The wondering shook me. Why the hell was I so concerned about Jack? Okay, he'd undergone a radical make-over . . . well, judging by the persistent jeans and bare feet it hadn't been *that* radical, but he was certainly a long way from the drunken writer who'd been the subject of the sci-fi community's more lurid speculations. I watched him check the mic connection, ignoring the bantering exchanges of the back-stage crew as he did so, and felt again the cool touch of his hand on my forehead last night, the firmness of his fingers around my wrist earlier this morning. For all his cantankerous posturing, he was secretly a really nice guy.

And then, throwing Jack into sudden shadow, Gethryn was there. He climbed up onto the stage, circling like a wild animal, eyes on the crowd. He looked burnished, polished by fame to a golden perfection and dressed in cool tans and natural mossy greens like a force of nature personified.

I think my mouth fell open a little. He was just . . . *gorgeous*.

I followed his gaze as he looked around the room. There must have been nearly a hundred people; if this room got blown up the world's knowledge of *Fallen Skies* trivia would probably drop to near zero. I breathed carefully. Didn't want to scare myself by thinking about all these people, all in the same space. Talked myself down: there was nothing to stress over. If I won, terrific, if I lost, well, at least I'd tried. All the same, my heart raced and the sweat broke out between my shoulder blades. Gethryn stood a moment longer, staring out over the heads of the hopefuls, then pursed his mouth and turned away, jumping down and vanishing off the back of the stage. My heart gave a little moan of protest.

'All done?' Jack looked towards the officials, then

did another quick mic check. As he counted down from ten, to make sure the people in the back could hear and that feedback wasn't an issue, he caught my eye and smiled.

'Wow.' Ruth bent towards me. The chairs were so far apart, to prevent collaborative cheating I suppose, that she had to push most of her torso off her chair. 'That's Jay Whitaker. No wonder they keep *him* under wraps. Isn't he just one sexy mother of a writer?' She gazed up at the stage again. 'I recognise him from those pics on BackStageSpy's blog. They call him the Iceman, isn't that just the *coolest* name ever? Wrote 'Behind Evil', voted best TV episode in *Scene* magazine last year. Made an entire nation cry.'

'Yeah. And they say that he came up with the idea for the series when he was waterskiing – isn't that just too *cool*?' B'Ha-man came in from the other side.

I wondered if they were trying to intimidate me with their knowledge. They needn't have bothered, I knew about the magazine award, who presented it and which clip they'd played at the ceremony. And I didn't think Jack was a waterskiing kind of bloke. I was still trying to get my head around his being one of the driving forces behind all this.

'Okay. Each of your chairs has a number underneath.' Jack's voice crackled over the speakers. 'Write that number at the top of your paper. When you leave the room, you'll be asked for your name and seat number and that information won't be revealed until the results are announced. All papers will be marked anonymously.' We dutifully crouched down and wrote our seat numbers, then sat, pens sweaty in hands. 'Block capitals only, yeah? My eyesight's not what it was.' Jack indicated his glasses and the crowd gave a dutiful giggle. 'Here we go. Question one. What prevents the pilot of the fighter craft D'liss from landing on Skeldar?'

And the questions went on. Fifty of them, to be precise, getting harder and harder. I found myself oddly excited, feeling the challenge in every planet name asked for, every piece of observation needed, had to stop myself from groaning 'oh, that's *easy*', or muttering under my breath as I calculated the load weight of a Shadow craft. Beside me Ruth was frowning, scrunching her face up; almost every question past fifteen made her sigh and her scribbled answers grew fewer, the pauses longer. B'Ha-man was writing furiously in answer to every question, even one-word answers seemed to draw forth a frenzied stream of penmanship. I wondered whether he was answering the questions or putting forward a script of his own.

Between questions twenty-five and twenty-six, there was a short break for Jack to take a swig from a bottle of water. He removed the headset and his glasses to do so, throwing his head back to stretch out his spine and I heard Ruth give a stifled moan in her chair. He did look good, I had to admit, all lanky and dark and in charge as he was, although from the way he was twisting his water bottle around on the table and sucking on the end of his biro I could tell he was dying for a cigarette.

Then we started again and I almost forgot to get it wrong. I'd just written my answer to question forty, 'What was the *real* name of Defries's mother?' (It was Lauria, but the name was only mentioned once, during the title sequence of episode 13, *Sleeping with the Enemy*) when I realised that I was finding this too easy. I crossed out my answer and wrote 'Mary' neatly beside it. Two more answers got deliberately sabotaged, that should be enough; this crowd looked seriously fanatical. Ah well, at worst I'd get a series of Scratch-n-Sniffs, and at best . . . ah, at best I'd get my date with Gethryn.

Who was now lounging on the stage. I hadn't seen him come back, I'd been so intent on my answer sheet, but Ruth's eyes were fixed on him and her robust bosom was definitely heaving in his direction as we dutifully answered question fifty and the officials came round to collect our papers. My eyes joined Ruth's.

'He looks like a vampire,' Ruth whispered, once the papers were all in. 'All kinda pent-up and dangerous, like he's got a whole secret life. Jeez, I really hope I did enough to win that dinner with him. If I don't, I think I might just curl up and die.'

Gethryn moved over and spoke to Jack, who was co-ordinating the careful sealing of the answer papers into envelopes. His question was inaudible, but Jack's reply hissed over his microphone, 'Just stay out of the way!' before he pulled off the headset to engage in a furious debate at the back of the stage. Gethryn looked relaxed, unflustered, making soothing hand-gestures, but Jack seemed wound-up and angry, pacing around with his head down.

We were hustled out in two lines, officials on the door waiting to take our names and seat numbers as we passed through. Out in the reception area Felix was waiting for me, hopping up and down. 'Well?' he tried to whisper as soon as I was out. 'How did it go? Stupid question, you know everything there is to know about *Fallen Skies* . . . No, but really. How did it go?'

Ruth gave me a daggers look as she passed us, and linked her arm through B'Ha-man's. 'Let's go to the forum meet,' she said to him, deliberately cutting me. 'Everyone's going to be there.'

'What's up with her?' Felix watched the unlikely pair go towards the bar. 'And what's with *him*? They look like a Munsters out-take.'

'I think, maybe, she didn't know as much as she thought.' A brief flurry of activity and Gethryn was leaving Meeting Room One, surrounded by a bevy of girls, all talking and swooping around him, urging him to this event and that, giving him schedules and itinerary run-downs until the poor guy must have felt dizzy with it all. Felix's hand tightened on my arm.

'I'm beginning to see your point about him,' he said. 'Totally *amazing*.'

'I really don't think Gethryn is into guys, Fe.'

'You don't know.' Felix's gaze followed Gethryn's progress. 'He might be bi-curious.' He gave a quiet whistle. 'Oh, now look at that arse. You can't tell me that's not a waste, an arse like that has definitely *got* to have leanings.'

'Looks pretty straight-up to me.'

As if he'd heard, Gethryn turned a wide arc across the floor and approached us, preceded by his multi-coloured harem, like a crow chasing down a flock of parrots. 'Skye! Hey there, you been taking part in the quiz?' The expression on his face told me that he knew damn well I had. 'And I hope you've not been taking too much notice of old disaster-knickers there, Mr Whitaker. Bit of an old woman, he is.'

'No, I . . .'

For a second Gethryn pressed close. 'Hope you get second prize, my lovely,' he whispered, directly in my ear. 'Think I'd rather have you as a dinner date than some of the things I saw in there.' Then he dropped another one of his patent winks my way and was gone again, back into the middle of his flock, all still talking non-stop.

Felix fanned himself. 'Oh, my Lord.'

'Hey, Felix.' We both jumped. It was Lissa, now wearing a tiny little skirt from which her legs protruded, shiny and brown. 'Wanna go for a ride? I got the car out front, nowhere to go, nothing to do, so I thought you might be up for an adventure.' Her eyes were suspiciously wide and she was weaving from foot to foot as though undergoing some kind of personal earthquake.

'Sure. I'll just . . .' He made some kind of meaningless hand movement.

'I'll see you in ten. Little pink convertible, yeah?'

'That's no way to talk about you,' I giggled as she sashayed outside, walking carefully and swinging car keys from one finger.

'Hey, too right, no-one's *ever* called me little. But I was hoping to hang around for the results of the quiz, find out if I . . . I mean, if *you've* done well.'

'Oh, those won't be released until later. Go off and make use of all that sexual energy you've got burning a hole in your underwear. After all, if you've even started to contemplate doing the lusty thing with Mr I'm-so-hetero-it-hurts Tudor-Morgan, you need to calm it all down or you are going to get into *so* much trouble.'

'Well, yeah, but I kind of told Jared that I'm up for a rematch tonight, and that is a man you do *not* want to disappoint. You would not *believe* . . .'

'Fe. Just go.'

'Will you be okay here on your own?'

'I'll manage.' I flicked a finger at him and headed away. It probably looked as though I was going towards Meeting Room Two, with its queue still snaking in an orderly way out through the doors and half-way across reception, but at the last minute I diverted and headed up the stairs back to our room. At the bottom of the staircase I peeped back. Felix was draining a furtive scotch at the bar as though fortifying himself for the afternoon and I really hoped Lissa knew what she was letting herself in for, hanging around with him.

Once alone in the room, I felt a brief burst of self-pity which I tried to squash down. After all, Gethryn seemed to like me, didn't he? I lifted my shirt and looked down my body at the intricate web of scars and stitch marks left by the accident, marks like cracks in droughty earth, and wondered what he'd say if he could see these. There had been an episode late in Series Two, where Lucas James had rescued a badly burned woman from a downed Shadow craft. He'd spoken such words of consolation and acceptance that I'd watched the DVD over and over until it started sticking on that scene. He'd talked about how no-one should be defined by the way they looked, that it was *who they truly were* that defined them; their memories and their actions. She'd died, of course; all Lucas' women had a tendency to keel over before the end of the series – it was a high-risk job being the chosen partner of a man who fought such battles for justice and understanding for other races.

I traced a finger over the scars. *Nothing in life is truly perfect, and those who pretend to be are covering up something nastier than these.* I could hear his voice as my lips mouthed the words that were etched on my brain, along with the image of Lucas James holding his lover, gazing down on her damaged body. Words I'd clutched for the comfort they brought when I was at my absolute lowest.

No-one was perfect. No-one. You could see my imperfections, that was all. And they could be overlooked too, by the right man.

There was a bang on the door and I let the shirt fall. 'What?'

'Skye? You in there?' It was Jack. 'Have you seen Lissa?' He was inside the room, panting and dishevelled, as soon as I opened the door, scanning the floor as though I'd got her hidden under the boards. 'She's been drinking, gone off with her car keys. We'll be pulling her from the wreckage . . .' My face must have gone rigid, because he added, more gently, 'Metaphorically speaking, obviously.'

I told him about Lissa and Felix heading off to get the car and he swore inventively for a minute. You could tell he was a writer. 'We could go after them.'

'Can't. I don't drive.' He paced up and down for a bit. 'And I can't call the cops, she'll get done for drunk driving, and the last thing I need is more of that kind of thing hanging over the show.' He paused. 'Not that the show is the really important thing, obviously.'

'We could take Felix's car.' The keys were sitting on the little bedside cupboard. 'It's not great but . . .'

'I just want to find them, to know that she's safe. Get her back. Everyone knows she's my agent, I don't want rumours flying around about her . . . about *me*, I mean, I know we need press coverage, we *need* them, pull in the advertisers, but . . .' He stopped pacing and rubbed the back of his neck. 'Oh God, I'm doing the talking thing again, just punch me in the mouth, Skye, for the good of us all.' His hands came round and he hid his face in them. 'I need sleep.'

'Jack?'

A quick head shake. 'No, nothing. Sorry, Skye. Don't even know why I'm here to tell the truth, I just sort of panicked and . . .' He shrugged and chewed a nail.

I made a huge, a monumental, decision. Jack would probably never know how big. 'I can drive.'

Maybe he did know. Or guessed. 'And have you driven lately?'

'Not *lately*. As such. But I can.'

'Skye, have you driven *anywhere* since the accident?'

'I . . .' *You're such a crap driver. Useless, Skye. Pathetic.*

He gave me a long, dark look. 'I can't ask you to do this.'

'But Felix is my friend. Let's go.' I picked up the keys and almost ran from the room. I didn't want to give myself a chance to change my mind, to feel the terror that I knew was going to come flooding in somewhere. It was bad enough being a passenger, how much worse was it going to be getting behind the wheel?

I found out, when I sat in the hired Ford, with the seat burning through my trousers, my hand shaking so hard that I couldn't start the bloody thing.

'Skye. Look. Maybe I panicked too soon. I'm sure they'll be fine.' Jack was hunched up on the other side of the car, legs too long for the pathetic footwell.

'No. I can do this.' I gritted my teeth so hard I could hear grating inside my head. 'I have to stop letting the accident rule my life. I drove before, there's absolutely no reason why I shouldn't drive now.'

'It's been a long time for you, hasn't it?'

I thought back over all the things I couldn't now do. Of all the things I *didn't* do. 'Yeah, but you don't forget.' The key shook, chiming against the keyhole as my nerveless fingers tried to turn it again. 'You don't forget,' I repeated.

Jack gave a strange kind of laugh. 'The roads are dead straight though. Boringly straight. Even smashed out of her tiny, Liss can drive these roads.'

The engine caught, and my shaky leg eased off the brake. 'Do you want to do this or not?' I had to push down on my knee to stop the shaking. 'Because I'm going to find Felix. If you want to find Lissa, then stop whining and come with me.'

'My God, you're bolshy, aren't you? Don't know how Felix puts up with it.' Jack half-smiled at me. 'All right. If you're sure. But take it easy.'

The car juddered as I tried to pull away in 'Park'. I'd never driven an automatic before and I kept pulling at the non-existent gears when we started moving. Jack remained manfully silent while I swore and raged and used the anger to stopper the fear and prevent its escape. The car was too small for terror *and* the two of us. Finally I got the measure of it, practicalities meaning that I had to focus on driving, not my fear of driving, and we headed up the highway, cutting slowly through the dust and the heat. For some reason having Jack next to me calmed some of my more immediate nerves; his quiet presence had a reassuring air about it, despite his occasional muttered swearing. The little air-conditioning unit groaned and emitted high-pitched squeals at heart-stopping moments – it was like driving a television studio audience.

'There.' Jack suddenly grabbed my arm and I nearly drove off the road. 'They just turned down that track.'

'Are you sure?' Everything was dust-coloured, even the sky, occasional little scrubby bushes beside the road, and one lone cow who watched us zigzag slowly past her, with sad, dust-coloured eyes.

'Well, there *could* be more than one pink convertible out here but somehow I doubt it. Turn left, here.'

He reached across me and pulled the wheel so that the car swung out across the non-existent oncoming traffic and bumped onto the rutted side-road which led, apparently, nowhere. We jolted along it for about a quarter of a mile and then, in a dip, we found them.

I couldn't go near. Couldn't even drive past. I pulled up a hundred yards back and sat with the window down in case I was sick, watching Jack cautiously approaching the other car, which stood, with the roof up, at an angle to the roadway. *Felix. Felix could be dead in there. Don't be stupid, the car hasn't hit anything, hasn't rolled. It's just standing there. No-one can be dead in a car that's just parked . . .*

A couple of minutes later Jack was back. He climbed back into the passenger seat without a word, slumped down with his head in his hands and gave a huge sigh.

'Well? Is she okay? And Fe?'

'Skye.' Jack didn't look up. 'They are in that car, banging like rabbits. You want to go and ask him how he is, you be my guest, because I am not going to interrupt.'

We sat silently for a moment. 'Are you all right?' I asked eventually, when my eyes had grown tired of fixating on the slowly rocking pink car in front of us. 'I know you said you and she weren't . . . well, you know . . . any more but you did seem really worried about her.'

He stopped rubbing his hands through his hair and stared out too. 'She's my agent, she does all my paperwork and besides I . . . ah, never mind. So, yeah, I worry about her. Especially if she's going to go off on one with the best part of a bottle of vodka inside her.'

We sat a while longer, watching the pink car, waves of heat coming off it in all directions. The rocking subsided, returned and then stopped.

'We'd better wait, follow them back. Make sure nothing happens.'

'Jack, there's absolutely nothing on these roads apart from squashed . . . whatever those grey things are. She's not going to hit anything bigger than a pebble.'

He gave me a hard stare. 'But if she does? It's not just Liss and Felix on the line here, Skye, it's the whole reputation of the show. My show. Something I've pulled back from the brink, and there are journos out there all agog for the details, all wanting to poke around and find things out and pull us all down into their own particular version of hell, and it's all I've fucking got, right now, so please don't start telling me that everything will be fine, that it's all okay, all right?' A shaky hand pushed his hair away from his face and he looked down at the floor. 'Sorry. I'm sorry, none of this is your fault; you've done nothing but try to help. I shouldn't be such a miserable bastard to you.' Then he surprised me by giving me a small, sheepish grin. 'Should I?'

'They're moving,' was all the response I could come up with. His shamefaced vulnerability gave me a curious, achy feeling.

We waited until Lissa and Felix had driven a large loop around us and regained the main road before we followed. They were driving at about fifteen miles an hour, we had to match speed, and so the slowest car-chase in the world began.

'They'll be sobering up around now.' Jack had lit a cigarette and was puffing out of the window, letting the heat in but at least considerate enough not to force me to breathe his smoke. 'Listen carefully and you might be able to hear the sounds of terrible embarrassment.'

'Don't tell me you've never had stupid drunken sex with someone you didn't really fancy?' I managed to tear my eyes away from the road for long enough to give him a thin grin.

'You look like the type of guy . . .'

His eyes were sudden and black on me. 'Do I?' Smoke formed a veil between us. 'Are you sure about that, Skye?'

It was suddenly hard to lift my eyes from the steering wheel. 'I don't know, do I? I know nothing about you at all, Jack. Even your Wiki page just has some sketchy stuff about you being born in Leeds and being a bit . . . reclusive.'

'A bit reclusive. Yeah. You don't get phrases like solipsistic intoxication psychosis on Wikipedia.' Jack turned away and stared out of the window at the unfascinating landscape beyond. 'And I have no idea why I'm talking to you about it.'

'Because I'm here?'

He turned back, his eyes immense. His gaze moved over my face, slowly, not lingering on the scar as people usually did but travelling from my eyes to my mouth and back up again. 'Yeah,' he said, and his voice was a bit croaky. 'Yeah, that'll be it.'

Silence fell, broken only by my occasional swearing, as we inched along behind Felix and Lissa, with our engine complaining at the slow speed all the way. If Lissa's tyres had had markers on they would have described a series of 33s, as the car covered almost the entire road's surface in its attempts to go straight. At last we both reached the motel car park and the pink car slewed into two-and-a-half spaces, parked at an angle. The driver's door flew open and Lissa stuck her head out to puke on the gravel.

'She's not much of an advert for recreational alcohol abuse, is she?' Jack stayed sitting beside me, despite the fact that the little car was now as airless and hot as a bread oven. Felix clambered out and grabbed Lissa by the arm. He waited, like a prison warder, while she locked the car door – taking several stabs to hit the right button – and then half-dragged her towards the motel. Lissa had one hand over her eyes and vomit on her skirt but that was normal for Felix's girlfriends.

'Skye.' Jack put a hand on my arm to prevent me from opening my door. 'Can I just . . . you're interested in Gethryn, aren't you?'

I was so relieved that the driving was over I had a system throbbing with endorphins. 'Well, I'm female, I've got a pulse.' My eyes followed Felix and Lissa, hoping that he wasn't going to take her to our room, as I was looking forward to a shower and a change of clothes, and a drunken Lissa wasn't my first choice of bathroom accessories.

'He looks like he's got his eye on you.'

My heart did a little swipe around my chest. *Gethryn fancied me!* Me, little Skye Threppel from Nowhereville, with her scarred face and aborted acting career and her scuzzy hair. Me! 'Does he?' I asked, trying to sound cool but remembering the soft touch of Gethryn's fingers on mine last night, the way his leonine eyes had held my stare. 'Gosh. Did you put in a word for me?'

'Me? Quite the reverse. Look, Skye, Gethryn's got . . . problems. What you see on screen, it's not him.'

'It's all right, Jack, I might have some brain damage but I can still separate fantasy from reality just like everyone else.'

'And it's Lucas James that you want, isn't it? I mean, you don't know Gethryn at all, would you normally contemplate . . . whatever it is that you're contemplating, with a man you don't know?'

Now I turned to look at him. He had *very* dark eyes, I noticed for the first time, almost black, and his hair snagged on the uneven stubble which peppered his cheeks. 'You don't know *what* I'm contemplating.'

'Okay, tell me it's a Scrabble match.' Jack leaned in closer and put his hands on my shoulders. I could see my reflection in his eyes. 'I just don't think that someone like you should be anywhere near Gethryn at the moment, that's all.'

I screwed my eyes up. Why the hell should he care? '"Someone like me"? What's that supposed to mean? What do you think I'm like, then? And who died and made you Freud?'

'I'm a writer. It kind of goes with the territory that we understand people, and I'm good at getting inside people's heads, at least I think I am. And I think you're too fragile for Gethryn.'

My eyes were dragged away from him, back to the accident-waiting-to-happen which was Lissa and Felix at the front of the motel. They appeared to be having a very shouty argument. 'Are you calling me pathetic?'

'No! Not at all. It's more that you've been damaged so badly the last thing you need is some bloke with issues getting his hands on you.'

'Look.' This time he didn't try to stop me opening the car door. 'I might have been injured but I'm over it. I'm learning to cope with the memory loss, I'm even getting over the whole stress panic attack thing, and if Gethryn wants – well, anything with me, then I can use my own judgement about the situation. I'm twenty-nine, Jack, and I didn't get to be twenty-nine by not having any critical faculties, you know.'

His head turned. Hell-black eyes moved over my face, lingering on the scar this time. 'I'm sure you didn't. I just think that they might be overridden sometimes.' A slow, almost reluctant hand caught my chin and turned my face towards his. 'It's when you think you're okay, when you think you're doing well; that's when life can rise up and shake you by the throat, you know that?'

I could see his eyelashes, the tiny fragments of green that lifted the colour of his eyes. I could smell the recent smoke on his skin, feel his fingers on my jawbone. I sat there, rigid, not knowing what was coming, or even what I *wanted* to come; there was something very powerful about Jack Whitaker in that second. As though his words were aimed at me but contained something of himself, something he wanted me to know.

'Still. None of my business, eh?' His voice was suddenly flat, the northern vowels dropping like stones and he released his grip on my face. 'Guess I'll see you at the Q and A tonight?'

'What's the Q and A about?' My voice was slightly shaky as the sudden change of subject left me winded.

'Everyone's chance to ask anything they want about the making of the show. Strictly back-room stuff. I'm on the panel with make-up and costume people. Wouldn't have done it, wouldn't even be here, but the writer who likes to turn out for these things has just had a baby. She was booked to come but the baby was premature and the network bosses thought it was time I put my face out in front of people; therefore, well, here I am.'

'Juliette Coles. She had a little boy three weeks ago.' I couldn't help myself. It was a kind of hang-over from the quiz.

'Yeah. Sorry, forgot that I was talking to the *Fallen Skies* Brain of Britain.' He flipped the door open and unfolded himself into the air, then bent to look at me through the window. 'Want to take bets on how many times I get asked where I get my ideas from?' He leaned a little closer. 'Want to take bets on how many people ask me what

Gethryn's *really* like?' A stretch of his lanky body as though his back was hurting him. 'Want to take bets on what I say?'

The silence went on for a few seconds longer than was comfortable. I didn't want to get out of the car with him standing there. The hugeness of the world, the indefinite boundaries, the uncontainedness of it, all were suddenly nothing compared to the scary closeness of the man leaning against the car. I found my fingers were moving without my permission, picking and twisting around each other, snakelike. Scar to scar.

Without another word Jack walked off, heading not towards the motel but out into the grilling heat. His head was bent and his shoulders forward, hands deep into the back pockets of his jeans, drawing attention to the perfect nature of his backside. I didn't know whether he knew I was looking or not.

I let out a breath, then another. There was relief in feeling the air flood out of me, taking a little more tension with it every time. Sweat was rolling between my shoulder blades and pooling in the small of my back; I felt itchy and hot. And annoyed with Jack, and the annoyance managed to push me out of the car when the heat couldn't; into the motel and up to the room with the lure of a cool shower.

CHAPTER 14

Jack ignored the sun burning a tattoo on the top of his head through his hair. Ignored the heat eating up through the soles of his tatty trainers, ignored everything physical. Walked and let his mind run free, let the ideas and scenarios play themselves out on the screen behind his eyes. Not for the first time he found himself thinking about home, not the apartment in LA but real home. The farm on the moors, the acres of rain, the sound of water racing. His head spun with the urge to go back. *Go home. Is it really that simple? Just . . . leave here and go back? Leave all this fame and fortune shit way behind and go back to the quiet life? And why do I even want to?* But he knew why. It was all because of Skye. Skye who reminded him that life could be simple and calm, that it didn't have to contain these high-octane, high maintenance lifestyles. A scarred girl with a gentle smile, who hated the manic and the overblown – everything that his life had become.

But Skye wanted Gethryn. She believed she knew him, understood him, although all she really knew were the words that Jack had given him. Which meant all she really wanted was the body. Which, Jack had to admit, was pretty spectacular. He'd seen Geth striding about in the buff more times than he cared to remember and he knew it was the kind of muscular, toned thing that the girls went for. A butt like two footballs and a six-pack you could have got a tune out of if you'd hit it with a stick.

Not like me. For the first time in a very long while Jack wished he'd inherited his da's ability to talk to women, not just his spare frame and a way with words. Really *talk*, about the things that meant something, the things that hurt and the things that healed. The ability to have a relationship that didn't just skate along the icy surface, but smashed it and explored the depths beneath. Or even to have that twinkle that had so enthralled his mum, kept her giggly and girlish until the day she died. He'd got none of it. And now, for the first time, *it mattered.*

He'll ruin her. He'll take that lovely naivety and strip it back until she's chilly and hard. He'll play on her insecurities, make her feel worthless and unlovable, he'll take her to bed and . . . Jack stopped suddenly. *Am I jealous? Is that it?* He played the thought of Skye touching Gethryn, stopped and rewound it, let it play out again, but every time it got as far as her taking her clothes off Gethryn would disappear and be replaced by a shadowy figure and the POV would switch until he was watching her strip through his own eyes. *So. It's not that I want to save her. I want her to want me.*

He pushed his hands into his pockets to distract himself from the loop, which now had Skye tugging off the last of her clothes with an inviting smile, and shook his head. Knowing now that it wasn't saving Skye that was really on his mind, that keeping her from Geth wasn't about preventing a tragedy. This was all about saving himself. Jack Whitaker, the heartless, the emotionally invincible, was actually beginning to feel something. *And it hurt.*

CHAPTER 15

Doused and damp, I lay on the bed, thinking about Jack.

Well, less thinking and more wondering. Why was he so . . . so . . . cut off? I'd always expected the crew of *Fallen Skies* to be a rollicking bunch, full of in-jokes and private feuds, a tight-knit group who worked hard together for months on end. And, the others *were*. Felix had told me they crowded into the bar at night with the punters, joking and punching shoulders and telling elaborate stories about set-ups and on-screen mistakes.

But not Jack. I'd hardly seen him speak to a soul, apart from Gethryn and Lissa. Except for this Q and A panel he didn't seem to mix with the others, neither actors nor crew; he just sat in his room and typed on his laptop rather than carouse and party the night away. All the magazine articles I'd read about *Fallen Skies* had the show-runner down as a loner; lured away from writing his best-selling sci-fi series of novels by the network's head honcho to work on the now defunct *Two Turns North*, then going on to mastermind his own show. So why did he come across as someone who kept himself a deliberate outsider? Why not enjoy his position, even exploit it a little? Why did he behave as though he was somehow ashamed of being successful? And why, in the name of all that was fashionable, did he go practically everywhere barefoot and put anything which even slightly resembled a cigarette into his mouth?

But he's more than just a little bit cute, too, eh Skye? All those moody looks, those eyes like something out of a Poe novel . . . come on, admit it to yourself, you quite fancy that serious thing he's got going on, don't you?

Michael had been reckless, apparently. Hell bent on success, on living life fast and long. Never sleeping while there was mischief to be made. *That* was my type of man, the fun-grabbing madcap sort, not the shy, retiring type. Previous boyfriends had all verged on the illegally wild side, or at least the ones I could remember had. Maybe my tastes had changed? Or maybe I had . . . I rubbed the rough edges of my fingertips over my scar again and shook my head, troubled by the feeling that my life had become one huge stammer, disconnected ends that never met, a dotted line. Those gaps, they contained all the things that made me *me*, and I couldn't get them to join up, as hard as I tried.

I finally twisted my thoughts away from the shadowy writer and back towards where I wanted them. *Gethryn*. That head-singing moment of absolute bliss when Gethryn had talked to me last night. That almost-promise of further talking. I rolled gleefully on the bed – it wasn't my imagination, Jack had seen it too – Gethryn *wanted me*.

There was a knock at the door. I opened it. Felix stood there radiating a negatively attractive aura. He was horribly pale, his pupils were oscillating crazily and he seemed to have acquired a facial tic which caused his upper lip to wrinkle every few seconds. He had sand in his hair which fell like solid dandruff every time he moved, and either his eyes were extremely bloodshot or he'd been possessed by the devil.

'Don't,' he said. 'Just *don't*.'

Then he staggered into the bathroom and, without closing the door or taking off any clothes, turned on the shower and stood under it, eyes so wide open that his lids seemed to have been pulled up like blinds.

'Fe?'

'Is there any Valium left?' he slurred through rigid lips. 'And, please God, let the answer be yes.'

I fumbled two tablets from the little brown bottle and took them into the bathroom where he swallowed them, tipping his head back to let the water from the shower carry them down his throat. 'Oh God. Oh God. I am *wrecked*.'

'But you've been drinking . . .'

One solitary, counter-rotating eye glared at me. 'Lover, you are looking at the walking image of habituation here. I'd have to swallow the entire bottle before I felt even a little bit peaky.' He slowly closed his eyes, letting the water pound down on the top of his head, slicking his hair flat until he looked like a Brylcreem advert. 'Oh, my Lord. How did Jack stand it? He must be made of fucking *iron.*' One eye opened again. 'And if you have any information on that, lover, then give it up. Don't think I didn't notice the two of you dogging it behind us.'

'We were worried.'

'Quite right, too. She is crazy. Christ, she's got some serious issues and she is not afraid to take them out on innocent bystanders.' He winced. 'I really need to sleep. Seriously.'

'Oh, *Fe.* I thought you'd come with me to the Q and A session.'

'Sorry, darling.' Felix flopped out of the shower and started pulling off his soaking clothes. 'All I'm fit for now is to sleep it off. Q and A is at seven, that's . . .' he waved his watch in front of his eyes but was obviously focus-impaired at the moment, '*hours* away. I'll try and fit it in before I get busy. Okay, lover?' Stark naked he stood in front of me, swaying.

'You're a mess.'

'Yeah. Trashed.' A quick, glorious smile. 'That's how you know you're on holiday.' Then he took a few, faltering steps into the bedroom and collapsed, still soaking wet from the shower, face down on the bed. 'Thank God for Valium,' he muttered into the duvet, and either passed out or fell asleep.

* * *

At five past seven I was hovering around inside the main doors to the motel. A few hardy fans were drinking in the bar behind me but the Q and A event and an impromptu Karaoke session, which had broken out in the diner, had soaked up most of the crowd. Felix was still out for the count on the bed and Jack was on the stage in Meeting Room One. A quick glance through the doors had seen him safely seated between a bearded special-effects wizard and a girl from the wardrobe department, holding forth in enormous detail on story-arc plotting.

Any other time I would have been entranced by just such a talk. To be honest, I'd have listened to Jack Whitaker reading from the phone book, under normal conditions. But, this was my only chance to get a glimpse of Gethryn, without Jack stomping around muttering psychological rubbish, or Felix's hair-tossing attempts to be noticed. I'd got my breathing under control, slicked my hair with that miracle serum, covered my scar with a careful layer of make-up, and here I stood. Staring out through the tinted plate glass at the wide-stretched ridged brownness that was Nevada, heaped foothills on the horizon and air that smelled of boiled dust.

But there was no sign of Gethryn. I'd been hoping that he'd come to hang around the bar like so many of the other *Fallen Skies* crew members were doing, lounging around in their logoed T-shirts drinking cold beer and occasionally becoming involved in deep discussions with earnest fans. I knew he hadn't dropped in on the Q and A; maybe he'd decided on an early night and was tucked up in the Winnebago with a whisky and a detective novel.

I'd give it another five minutes. I stood near the windows, my palms sweating, trying to look as though gazing out over the desert was my preferred way of spending time and hoping that Gethryn might at least choose to waft through with his posse once tonight. Thanks to the open-plan reception area with the bar at the back, I could look as though I was lost in thought and Nevada scenery whilst keeping my entire body on alert for his appearance in the reflections in the window. Just a little *peep*, I thought, longingly, just let me *see* him, and I promise I'll go to bed without a fuss. Just a sight of those well-muscled hips striding through reception, maybe another of those saucy winks thrown my way? Was that too much to ask?

And then, suddenly, there he was.

I watched his reflection saunter across the carpet, unacknowledged. He was wearing jeans with interesting slashes down the thighs revealing toned muscles and tanned skin, and a white shirt with the sleeves rolled up to elbow height. A few of the drinkers greeted him, I saw his transparent self raise a hand in acceptance, but he remained unaccompanied as he approached the bar. Ordered a glass of something, then turned around.

I carefully kept my eyes front, still appearing to

gaze out on the rapidly darkening landscape, but in reality unable to focus on anything other than Gethryn, who was staring at my back view in a very considered way. The expanse of tinted glass, silvered with night, was a perfect reflective surface and I could see every nuance of expression on his face, the slightly raised eyebrows and the half-grin that curled his mouth as he watched me. When I saw him ignore his glass and push off from the bar, I hastily wiped my hands down my skirt and made sure that I had a far-away look on my face.

'All alone?' He spoke behind my left shoulder, and now I allowed my eyes to refocus, seeing his reflection embossed on mine. 'You not wanting to hear all the backstage slander then, *bach*?'

Play it cool, Skye. I didn't turn around, but spoke to him whilst keeping my eyes on the desert. 'It's more interesting here, listening to everyone chat.'

'Ah, they're all talking bollocks, girl. We both know there's more to the world than *Fallen Skies,* don't we?' His ghostly self stretched its arms wide and I felt the brief, thrilling press of his chest against my back.

My heart scuttered and my voice had to work to get past it. 'But they're here because *Fallen Skies* means something to them. It's touched them in some way.'

I felt Gethryn's hands come down from their stretch and lightly rest on my shoulders. Our reflections kept their eyes front. 'Oh, our Jack is one fine writer, I'll give him that. He gave me speeches that have stayed in my head; that one about "the horizons of all worlds are reachable by all races –", not a pair of eyes without tears on set when we recorded that. But . . .' he lowered his voice and his accent became stronger and thicker like good coffee, 'at the end of the day, *bach*, it's just a TV show.'

I turned around. Over at the far side of the bar a small knot of women had realised Gethryn was in the room and a fumbling search for cameras and autograph books was underway. 'Whoo-hoo, Gethryn honey!' One of the women held up a pen. 'Could you come over a minute, my friend Dorinda here wants to get your picture?'

Gethryn still had his hands on my shoulders. 'Uh oh,' he said lightly, close to my ear. 'Bunch of menopausal matriarchs want some cuddle-shots. Better go, lovely.' The hands ran away down my arms, skimming lightly over the skin and raising hairs as they went. 'But, look. You go outside, I'll get rid of the sci-fi Saga girls, and I'll meet you out there. There's this tree, out beyond the car park, wait by there.' Then, as if he hadn't just arranged an assignation that was making my skin heat up all over, he sauntered nonchalantly across to the bar where waiting hands seized him and pulled him into the centre of attention.

Oh God. Gethryn wanted me *alone*. Nevada, despite the perpetual brownness and heat, was now officially Paradise. A real-life, tawny-headed, lion-eyed bona fide TV star wanted to talk to me!

Alone! Surreptitiously I watched him pressing flesh with the good ladies in the corner, and there was, despite their collective age, quite a lot of flesh on display. Low necklines, high hemlines and some well-preserved tanned skin on the peripheries, hair colours that could surely never be natural, and mountainous heels. Coral lips offered up kisses he couldn't turn down and I had to grin. He turned, in the midst of it all, saw me watching and gave a heart-melting smile, raising his eyebrows to indicate the ridiculousness of it all.

I dashed outside and headed out across the car park. There, just beyond the ranks of cars, stood one of the few trees in the area, a species I didn't recognise with scrubby, brush-like leaves. In fact, it didn't so much stand as squat, as though the heat and dust had beaten a perfectly normal tree down over decades. I went and sat beside it. The heat pushed my head down onto my chest, and my breathing felt like artificial respiration by hairdryer.

I sat for a while, during which I lost track of time. Darkness thickened around me and there were weird noises floating through the air, but, to be honest, I was more worried about being discovered by Jack than I was about being eaten by wolves. His utter condemnation of Gethryn was so inexplicable and profound that I wondered if it was a form of jealousy. Perhaps he was tired of losing out to Gethryn's burnished perfection, tired of his scratchy nature and persistent smoking habit being compared to Gethryn's easy temperament.

I shook my head. Jack was attractive with all that dark hair and those intense eyes: I'd seen plenty of the women at the convention watching him. He could have taken his pick of a bunch of the hangers-on, wannabe writers and TV groupies. But he clearly wasn't a groupie kind of guy. A little voice whispered in the back of my head '*and you really want to find out just what kind of guy he is, Skye, don't you*?'

'Hey, lovely.' I shook my head again and raised my eyes to the skyline. 'Sorry to take so long, got caught up. And the girls wanted to buy me a drink, would have been rude to refuse, wouldn't it?' The rise and fall of his accent was almost edible, like chocolate drizzled over cream, blunted just a touch by alcohol. He was carrying a bottle. 'Fancy joining me in another?'

'Well . . .' *Gethryn Tudor-Morgan is offering you a drink*! 'Just a bit, maybe.'

'Good girl.' The bottle swung my way, dark liquid slopping at the neck. 'Haven't got a glass though, *bach*, we'll have to drink it out of the bottle.'

It was sharp, whatever it was, and rolled down my throat like a razor blade. As I drank, Gethryn came and crouched beside me, leaning his back against the trunk of the tree. I watched as his eyes traced the line of my scar under the make-up down to my cheekbone, didn't stop but wandered across the neckline of my shirt and halted at the depths of the V formed by the open buttons. Then his gaze moved up to my face again and his eyes were molten. 'So,' he said, taking the bottle back, 'what's a nice girl like you doing in a place like this?' I'd only managed to sip at the liquor. He gulped it as though it was water.

'Oh, you know. Felix got tickets, thought I'd like to come.' I wasn't going to go into Felix's treachery, my stupidity at believing him. Not with this sensational man leaning companionably close in the shelter of the little tree, passing me the bottle again and brushing my fingers with his as he did so. I managed a bit more alcohol this time; the sharpness was gone and the fire that replaced it was welcome. Gethryn's touch had made me shiver.

'Thought you might have been a friend of Jack's.' He watched me drink. 'Has he warned you off me yet?' My mouth was full so all I could do was shake my head. 'Fucking Jack.' His voice was sour now, accent hard. 'Thinks he's so fucking clever, and what is he? Just a jumped-up storyteller, that's what.' The hand that grabbed the bottle back had white knuckles showing. 'If they really knew what he was . . . Well, who is he to dictate what we can and can't do?'

Nearly all of the bottle's contents had disappeared. I pinched my leg hard to keep concentrating. I was *here* sharing a drink with *Gethryn Tudor-Morgan*. It was like my own personal heaven. 'What's Jack got against you, anyway?' My tongue felt heavy in my mouth and the words were imprecise.

Gethryn looked sideways at me. 'He doesn't like

it that I'm a star, that's what it is, *cariad.* I'm heading up his precious show, while all he can do is scribble away in the dark and smoke his fucking fags. And he hates it that I get the girls, oh yes, he *hates* that. Hates that all he can do is ruin 'em, when *I* know how to love 'em proper, like.' A finger extended, ran down my throat towards the neck-line of my shirt and when I looked up into his face I saw the heat in his eyes. 'Skye,' he whis-pered. 'You are beautiful. Is it all right if I kiss you?'

Whoa. Oh . . . no, I mean . . . *what? Gethryn* wanted to kiss me? Captain Lucas James, hero of the Shadow War wanted to kiss me . . . 'I'm not sure.' The words came out as a whisper, but he'd already moved in for the clinch, both hands wound into my hair holding my head steady.

'It's fine, *bach.*' His breath smelled of alcohol and felt hot against my lips. 'Nothing to be afraid of, just a little kiss, yes?' And then, before I could answer, he fastened his mouth onto mine in a bruising, hard kiss that battered against my lips. I stood up, trying to loosen his mouth but he rose with me, keeping his lips locked onto mine and dropping his hands to grip my shoulders. His tongue slipped between my teeth and licked the roof of my mouth and as a current of night air became more intrusive it dawned on me that he'd moved his hands, his fingers were unbuttoning my shirt, one hand hooking itself around the cup of my best bra. I was in a sweat of gratitude that I'd at least thought to put on my decent underwear, but disturbed that he was actually going to see it with so little preamble.

I struggled back and jerked my head away. Felt his tongue slide down my cheek as he aimed at my mouth again and missed. 'I'm sorry, but I don't know . . .' My heart was beating faster and I could hear a high drone inside my head. Lust or fear? Couldn't be sure.

'Oh, come on now.' Gethryn moved in again and his grip tightened. 'I'm not gonna hurt you, am I? Let's just . . . see how it goes.' And the hand was on my bra again, fingers fumbling at the cup, until the tiny embroidered flowers that I'd thought so pretty began cutting into my skin. 'No-one's watching, you don't need to worry.'

I could feel the rise of the panic now. *Was I misreading this? Was he being flirty – a little over-forceful maybe but that could be my fault – or was this going further than I wanted?* He was blocking my airway, his mouth not allowing enough space for breathing and the passage of his hands over my skin was getting dangerously close to needing a passport. But this was *Gethryn Tudor-Morgan! Captain Lucas James . . .*

'Geth?' Jack's voice sounded like a klaxon above the noise of my pulse. 'What's going on?'

'Oh, *fuck*.' Fingers unwound from my underwire and the air came as a relief against my skin. There was suddenly a much larger gap between us and a hastened attempt to pull my shirt straight. 'What's up?'

'Skye?' I could see him now, silhouetted against the flickering neon of the motel sign, fingers flicking ash from a glowing stub. 'Are you all right?' He was moving towards me at the same rate that Gethryn was moving away; it was like standing in the middle of a weather-house. 'Hey.' The calmness of his tone steadied me and I breathed carefully, feeling the panic balance itself somewhere in the centre of my chest, pivoting on the moment. 'Skye.'

'I'm . . .' A sudden flare of pain as the wind reached the scoring along my cheek that I hadn't realised was there. Gethryn's picturesque stubble had rubbed my skin raw. 'I . . .'

'Get away from her.' Jack's voice was harsh now, sounding as though he needed a drink. 'Geth. I'm warning you.' A quick, angry movement of one hand. 'Get inside.'

'Or what?' Gethryn had stopped moving now. I could see the shadow the moonlight gave him, stretching long and dark towards me from where he stood behind my left shoulder. 'Eh, Iceman? What's the bottom line here? What can you do that you've not already done?'

Jack stopped walking too. He was near enough for me to smell the smoke on him, to see the individual strands of his hair as they blew, reaching for me across the sand, as though they wanted to wrap around me. 'Nothing. That's the point, no threats, nothing. Just Leave. Her. Alone.' And the words were like weapons in their own right.

The shadow moved and there was the sloshing sound of liquid moving on glass, a swallow. 'Yeah, yeah, I get it. Scared that you'll lose another one, are you, Ice? You know you've got nothing. Tell you this, Skye can see sense, she can see who's got something to offer, who's the fucking Hollywood star and who's the punk loser.' The shadow dwindled and his voice was more distant. 'She'll find out about you, boy. Sooner or later, she'll know. And then . . . I'll be waiting. But I will tell you this, Ice . . .' There was a temporary strength in his words as though he'd turned back to face Jack or raised his voice, 'She's got a fantastic pair of tits.'

I didn't move and neither did Jack, although I saw his fists twitch, just once. A few seconds passed and then Jack held out a hand. 'Did he hurt you?'

'No.' I still stood. 'He . . . kissed me.'

'Did you want him to?'

'I don't know.' *Did I? Had I? How was I supposed to feel?*

'Oh.' The hand lowered. 'And the . . . ?' Fingers made vague motions at the chest region of his shirt. 'You might want to do up some buttons, by the way.'

Without taking my eyes from him I fumbled my shirt closed. Shrugged once.

'Skye.'

'It's all right, I don't want to cause any trouble, we were having a drink that's all, I think I got a bit carried away.' I ran out of breath and stopped speaking on an inward sob of air.

Jack moved closer until he could put a hand on my arm. Stroked my shoulder for a moment, then shook his head slowly, not dropping his hand. I could feel the weight of his fingers, but no warmth; and a slight tremor, as though he was fighting the urge to grab at me. 'I should have asked the security guys to keep a closer eye. I know what he's like, Skye, I should have . . .'

'Like I said. I'm twenty-nine. I can look out for myself, Jack, don't beat yourself up about it.' My voice sounded surprisingly strong. 'Nothing terrible happened, nothing was *going* to happen, Geth and I are capable of understanding the word "no".' Moonlight hit us both. Made Jack look haunted. As I already felt pale and stretched, it probably made me look like a movie version of some kind of ghoul.

There was suddenly too much sky.

'Come inside.' It wasn't the sharp order that Gethryn had got, it was a gentle suggestion, accompanied by half an arm across my shoulder. 'Come on. I'll take you back to your room.' The calm words and his even tone stopped the panic before it could rise, and the pull of his arm tugged me against his body as he started to move. It was protection against the wideness of the world and I found that I could keep everything scary at bay as long as I concentrated on the simple business of walking and the slightly swaying body of the man walking next to me.

We walked back to the main doors and immediately into Felix who was drinking Southern Comfort at the bar.

'Well, look what the cat dragged in.' Felix squinted at me. 'You're a bit pink. So, how've you been?' He wagged eyebrows unsubtly. 'Sorry I dipped out on you earlier but . . . well.'

'Yes, I saw. I've been okay.' My body shivered. 'Well. Yes. Okay.'

Jack had dropped his arm from my shoulders and shoved both hands in his pockets. 'Have you eaten, Skye?'

'Eaten?' I stared at him.

'Yes, eaten. Food in, mouth move, num num. Eaten.'

I couldn't see his eyes; he'd dropped his head so that his hair hung over his face, but his voice was tight. 'No.'

'Come on then.' Jack put a hand on my forearm and closed his fingers around it. 'I'll get you some food.'

'But I –'

Felix gave me a stern look and then rolled his eyes. 'Go on, lover. You're too skinny already. You need to eat.'

'There's no such thing as too skinny.' I tried an uppish defence, even though I knew he was right. For my shape, I *was* too thin. I looked like a skeleton someone had thrown clothes at. 'Oh, all right.'

'So gracious.' Jack headed away, not, as I'd thought, towards the diner but towards the stairs.

'Sorry.' I followed him. 'I'm feeling a bit . . . odd.'

'Bit pissed you mean. What were you and Geth drinking out there?' He'd stopped on a stair, back to me but rigid. Waiting.

'Did I say we were drinking?'

'You didn't need to. But you didn't admit to it – interesting. Did he tell you not to talk to me?'

We walked along the corridor to his room and I stopped to think while he unlocked the door. 'No.'

Jack ushered me past him, but stopped me before I could get inside by putting both hands on my shoulders and pulling me around to face him. 'Skye, look –'

'Oh, don't start again with all the "stay away from Gethryn" bullshit, please. I'm sorry if you two have problems and I'm sorry you've both got all this machismo shit going on, but I'm not your little sister, and I bloody well don't have a virginity to lose, so just stop all these dire warnings and leave me alone. What happened out there tonight was – well, it was under control.'

He held both hands up in the air. 'Under control. Okay. You're right, you're a big girl, you can decide for yourself who you see.'

'All right,' I said, dubiously.

'But whatever you think of me, I don't make a practice of riding in every time I see a couple in a clinch, you know. I'm not some big killjoy who can't bear anyone to be happy. I saw your *face*, Skye, and happy was not on the agenda there.'

'So you were watching because it was *me?*'

Jack shook his head and moved inside the room. 'You . . . you've just hurled in from home and I guess the accent and all, it's making me feel a bit homesick. A bit . . .' He tailed off, his eyes lost focus and he stared out of the window, hands working their way deep into the pockets of his black jeans. 'Yeah. So. Food. These places are always rubbish at producing anything that's actually good for you, so I brought some things along.'

'Okay.' What was he playing at? He seemed nervous, he'd lost that whole lone-hunter edge he'd had when we'd come in from the desert. Maybe he just needed a smoke.

'Fine.' He turned to the tiny fridge in the corner under the laptop and pulled out some fruit and a bar of chocolate, then plopped a pile of apples and oranges on the bed beside me and suddenly his words were coming in a breathless rush. 'The fancy dress ball, Sunday night. Would you come with me?'

I let the apple I'd picked up drop back onto the duvet. 'What, you mean like . . . a date?'

'Well, I suppose . . . kind of.'

'But you . . . this isn't . . . that's just *weird.*'

Jack sat down and stared at me over an orange he was peeling with his teeth. 'What's weird? Asking you to the ball?' He tipped his head on one side. 'I like you. And I know that I'm a miserable old bastard who smokes under stress and has a variable sense of humour, and sometimes I don't know when I'm talking to real people and when I'm talking to the people in my head, but I can be fun, too. I think we could have a good time together. Now tell me, in what way is that weird?'

'Is this just to stop me from seeing Gethryn?' I felt the strangest urge to giggle like a schoolgirl.

'No.' Jack cupped the orange in his hand, pulled a segment away and looked at it closely. 'I'm crediting you with some good sense on that one.' His expression was dark. 'I'm just a writer, a nobody and he's the star.' Shadowed eyes met mine and he let the orange fall onto his lap. 'Gethryn will go with Martha,' he said, quietly. 'They're both part of the cast and we like them to appear at these things together. Come with me.' Long fingers elegantly excised a pip from the flesh and flicked it accurately into an ashtray on the table.

'Can you dance?' Stupid question.

'Only one way to find out.'

'Can I think about it?' I could see the individual lashes of his eyes, the unconscious twitch of his lips, and all of a sudden I knew if he kissed my mouth it would be gentle, and I found myself wondering how he would taste; what he looked like, naked.

He stood up abruptly and went to the fridge. Took a can out, popped it open and drank. 'I guess so. Although I'm already disappointed that you need to.'

'You fancy yourself a bit, don't you?'

A quick smile and his saturnine looks lifted as

his eyes gleamed. 'I've already had offers. Ruth, girl who was sitting next you to at the quiz, she cornered me in the bar and asked me to go with her.'

'The cow!'

'She said she wanted to dance with me at the ball, and if I played my cards right she'd show me a few tricks later on in her room.' Jack went back to concentrating hard on segmenting the orange.

'You're making it up.'

Another smile. 'Maybe. Maybe not.'

'You bastard.'

'Now, eat something. There's some bread. Or there's some chocolate, if you're going to come over all female on me.'

Listlessly I picked up the apple I'd dropped. Jack licked his fingers clean of orange juice and wiped them down his jeans, then poked his laptop into life and tapped away at a few keys, sucking orange segments in a way that made the juice spurt into his hair and down over his chin in an unwarrantedly lascivious way; I suspected on purpose. I refused to comment, kept my eyes down and bit the apple down to the core. A sudden flashback to earlier that evening caught me in the throat, *Gethryn, fingers eager. Would he have stopped if I'd asked?*

A loud bang at the door made me gasp in shock. An apple pip shot into my windpipe and I began to cough and choke. Jack opened the door and then came over and started slapping me between the shoulder blades. Lissa stomped into the room, took one look at me and rolled her eyes.

'Is she doing it again?'

'Choking.' Jack banged me hard again on my spine, and with one loud cough the pip flew from my mouth and curled away across the room.

'You really are quite accident-prone, aren't you?' Lissa sat beside me on the bed. 'Perhaps you should stick to soft foods.'

'Perhaps *you* should stop drink-driving.' Jack stopped thumping me and looked at her.

'Hey, cut me a little slack, Jackie-boy.' Lissa glanced at my face and wrinkled her nose. 'Sheesh. You Brits.' Unexpectedly she reached into her bag and handed me a large tissue. 'Here. Mop. And scrape, you might wanna scrape a little.'

'Thanks.' I mopped and, furtively, scraped.

My streaming eyes showed me a misty image of Jack looking sideways at Lissa. 'What is it you want, Liss?'

She perched herself on the edge of the small table under the window, tiny buttocks barely causing it to tip forward. 'Wanted to talk to you about this crazy idea you've got in your head about cutting out. Running for the border.' She opened her bag and fussed with lipstick and a mirror. 'You mentioned it, but are you serious about it? It's not one of your, like, abstract concepts?'

He slumped, leaning his whole body against the wall. 'Sorry, yeah, you're right. We should have talked it through, Liss. Will you get onto the network guys?

They should be fine with Scotty taking over, let's face it, he was doing all the practical stuff during the first series anyway, and you can tell them I'll turn in the scripts I'm contracted for . . .'

I could only stare.

'Mmmmm.' She carefully outlined her mouth in scarlet and began filling in her lips. 'I'll do it, but – why?'

Jack shrugged and gave me a quick look that I didn't think I was supposed to see. 'I need a new life. This was fun when we started out; yeah, it all got a bit lairy when we thought we were being cancelled, but I *liked* all that, the uncertainty and everything, it kept me wired. The big bosses who hired me were loving the stories, the other writers were great and let me muck about with their scripts – it was all *new,* all exciting.' He folded his arms and let his body slide a little lower down the wall. 'Now it's . . .' He shrugged again. 'It's personalities. It's the needs of the few outweighing the needs of the many; it's people using their power and position and their name to get access to things they shouldn't have. It's all crapped up, basically, Liss, and I want out. I want *home.*' His voice lowered, became so quiet I wasn't sure either of us were supposed to hear. 'I want *Peace.*'

She snapped shut the mirror and twisted the lipstick away. 'Gethryn,' was all she said.

'Partly.'

'Even though you've done what you could? Won't be a problem next series.'

'No, but he can still do damage.' He gave me a tiny, sideways glance. 'Look, I've got an editor in Britain hassling me to pick up the novels again. It's a whole different ballgame, writing the books, doing the signings, and it's something I love. I mean, that's how I made my name, after all. Don't get me wrong, I was flattered when the network guys hauled me over here. It was a chance to do something new, and it's been brilliant, the whole thing. Fantastic. But it was only ever going to be temporary, which is why I didn't sell Beck Farm when I came over; this was just another move in the Fame Game, getting my face, my name out there. When it comes down to it, I'm a novelist, Liss, and Yorkshire is my home.'

Lissa turned abruptly to me. 'What's the story with Felix? He brings you over here but you're not a couple. You share a room, a bed, but you're not –' she made little hooks in the air with her fingers – '*sleeping together.* He's heading for destruction-city and you seem to want to drive him there in your own little suicide-wagon . . . what *is* it with you two?'

I finished mopping my face. 'He's my best friend. That's all.'

'Uh huh.' Lissa shot a quick glance at Jack. 'Wow. Don't envy you this one.'

He and Lissa exchanged a look that went on rather longer than I was comfortable with.

'I think I'll go to bed,' I said, not sure that they'd hear me. 'What's happening tomorrow?'

Jack pushed away from the wall. 'They're . . . *we* are announcing the quiz results in the morning. Afternoon is all the practical stuff, setting up the prizes, then in the evening there's another signing session – apparently I'm giving away signed copies of some scripts. And then everyone's getting geared up for the fancy dress ball. Highlight of the event. People like to get together on the evening before it all to discuss costumes and stuff.' He made a face. 'Really it's just an excuse for everyone to get lathered.'

'Do you know who's won the quiz?' I asked quietly.

'Nah. They get some kids trying to boost their college funds to the tune of a couple of dollars an hour to do the marking.' He gave me a stern look. 'And I wouldn't tell you, even if I knew.'

'No. Right.'

Lissa cleared her throat. 'Think we've got some paperwork to cover, Jackie-boy. If you're heading back to good old Blighty, that's the end of my representation, you know that? It's over.'

He nodded. 'I know. And I'm sorry. I know we talked about it, but I never made it clear that I wasn't just chucking ideas about, that it was something I really wanted to do. Should have told you earlier, but . . . I've really only just made up my mind definitely.'

I headed out of the door while they stood looking at each other, but I didn't immediately head for my own room, because just as I pulled the door closed behind me, I heard Lissa say quietly, 'So, Iceman. You really gonna throw this all over, huh?'

I instantly pretended an almost terminal case of untied shoelaces, ear pressed to the slim crack in the doorframe.

'Come on, Liss, you know it's for the best.'

'Networks love you. Ratings love you. Hell, the fucking viewers all want to have your babies.' There was a pause. 'Sorry, Ice. That was cruel of me. Didn't mean . . .'

'I know you didn't. It's okay.'

Heart pounding and holding my breath so that I could hear, I slid my body along the wall to the next doorway, flattened myself against it and tried the handle, to be pitched backwards into a cleaning cupboard just as the door to Jack's room opened. I crouched in the bleach-scented darkness with my face against the door panel and wondered if I was falling into some kind of pattern of listening at half-open doors.

'You really don't have any emotion at all, do you, Jack? All this "Iceman" thing, you really got it down, man.' There was a hint, just the merest whisper, of pain in her voice.

I heard him sigh, and it was a sound that pulled at something instinctive inside me. I wanted to touch him, to hold him, to reassure him that all the pain contained within that single outbreath could be forgotten. But I didn't dare move.

'Yeah.' His voice faded. He'd probably gone back to stand by the window.

'How long have I known you, Iceman, hey? And now – come on, this is me, I *know* you. You've never had any kinda feeling in all this time, even when . . . and now suddenly you're overcome with wanting to go back the UK? Smells of fish, boy. How much of this is down to Geth? I could shoot myself over that one, I never thought . . .'

A sigh. 'It doesn't matter. It wasn't you, Liss, it was . . . I don't know. Me. It's all me. My head is . . . I promise I'll tell you when I get it sorted.'

'Yeah. So. You want me to fetch over the paperwork or not?

'I guess.' I heard him sigh deeply, then a scratchy sort of noise as though he was running his hands over his stubbled face. 'I guess.'

Abandoning the cleaning cupboard as soon as Jack's door closed, I dashed back to my room to hug a pillow and wonder exactly what secrets were being kept by the reticent Mr Whitaker.

CHAPTER 16

The crowd were waiting in the diner to hear the quiz results. The makeshift stage had been reassembled at one end, much to the chagrin of the waitresses, who were stomping about behind the counter with coffee pots, and there were so many people that the big glass doors had been opened to allow the overspill to sit outside on the steps. I could hear Spanish arguments and dog yapping coming from the kitchen, which was almost enough to distract me from the fact that they were announcing in reverse order, and had got to number five. Felix was holding my hand, bobbing like a tethered balloon.

'You must have got *something*,' he kept whispering. 'I mean, you're not *that* crap.'

'Thanks.'

'Ssssshhh.' A small woman wearing jeans far too long for her and a Status Quo T-shirt hissed at us and I cringed, ducking down behind Fe's shoulder.

'Third prize, the pilot's uniform . . . is . . .'

Jared paused for dramatic effect, and Felix breathed in my ear, 'That guy is just the most fantastic man it has ever been my privilege to date,' which put me off and I didn't catch the winner's name. A small group in the corner nearest the doors cheered and whooped, and a lot of shoulder-slapping went on.

'Second prize.' My whole body stopped, even my heart seemed not to beat. I was suspended in the moment, held up by hope.

'Skye?'

Now it was my turn to ssssshhh, craning my head forward.

'A dinner date with Gethryn Tudor-Morgan,' Jared said slowly, as if it was necessary. Behind me, a girl who had her fingers crossed so tightly that her hands were white, was muttering 'please God, please,' and the lady in the Quo shirt crossed herself furtively.

Jared opened an envelope, someone in the crowd shouted, 'Oscar for Best Picture goes to –' and everyone laughed, diffusing some of the tension that had built around us. It was like waiting for a thunderstorm to break. My hands were sweating.

'Jennifer-Lee Warner!'

To my left a girl with long, blonde hair gave a scream. 'That's *me*. Oh, thankyouthankyou . . .' and began spinning around to receive the congratulations coming from everyone standing near. I was ashamed of my sudden relief and managed a 'Well done', accompanied by a smile which probably looked quite scary from the other side of my face.

'Hey, Skye.' Felix squeezed my fingers until I

turned to face him. 'First prize now.' His eyes were very wide, firmly fixed on the slender figure in the tight jeans on the stage. I wasn't sure if it was lust or ambition burning behind them.

'Yeah. First prize. Hooray.'

But he didn't hear, or chose not to.

Jared looked at the crowd from lowered lashes and Felix gave a small moan. 'First prize,' Jared repeated. 'A part in the new series. I've seen the scripts for the two-parter, and, man, is it going to be *exciting*. I think Jay gave some hints yesterday as to what we can expect.' He held out a hand and I noticed Jack for the first time, standing behind some of the other crew members at the edge of the stage. He gave a half-smile and a shrug. 'Whoever wins this prize is gonna get some *huge* surprises, not only a part but the entire series' scripts autographed by the whole cast, a day on set, you name it.'

Felix's lips were moving as though he was praying.

'And the winner.' A rip of paper. 'Skye Threppel!'

Felix sagged. 'You did it,' he whispered. 'You actually *did it*.'

The crowd looked around. I hadn't made a sound, suddenly empty of all feeling, and my fingers crept up to my scar. I'd won a prize I couldn't even use. A mutter rose as everyone wondered where the winner was.

'Here!' Felix held up our joined hands. 'Skye is here!'

And then I was surrounded, hands reaching out to touch me, pat me, as though my luck was a communicable disease, a solid push of bodies crowding me. I began to gasp.

'You did it.' Felix was still whispering. 'I'm on the show. This is *it*, Skye, this is my break.'

My skin prickled with sweat and I felt suddenly sick. My lungs wouldn't work, there was more air going out than getting in, too warm, no oxygen . . . and then the dark, rushing over me, pouring like water behind my eyes, and I was dropping . . .

When I opened my eyes again, I was lying on a bed. The light was muted and soft and the air con was turned down low, so that the temperature was cool but not unpleasantly so.

Jack was standing at the window with his back to me. I half-raised my head, took in my surroundings, and flopped down again. 'I don't know why I don't just move in,' I said. 'All my most embarrassing moments seem to have happened in here.' My mind jumped away to the overheard conversation of the night before, Lissa's quiet sadness at his intransigence. She'd sounded as though she'd expected nothing else from him, as though a lack of concern, a lack of *caring* was normal for him and yet, here he was, rescuing me yet again from an awkward situation. Which was the real Jack Whitaker? The intense writer with the wicked grin, or the man they called the Iceman – emotionally arid? And – my mind held the question up in front of me but didn't dare even to put it into words – where did Gethryn feature in all this?

He turned round and smiled at me. He certainly didn't look like a man without feelings. 'You passed out.'

'I kind of gathered that.'

'I carried you up. Told them I'd do the publicity stuff later, said I was feeling a bit ill myself. They're all down there now drawing up the paperwork in case it means that there's something contagious going around; I think that they're two minutes from putting out a Legionnaire's alert.' He gave a grin that lightened his eyes and sat on the edge of the bed. 'Felix says you'd agreed to give the part to him if you won?'

'Yes, sort of.'

'Sort of.' Jack repeated, shaking his head.

'It was for Faith.' I felt ashamed for some reason, as though I should be explaining myself.

'You think you *owe* Felix something because his sister died?'

'No, I don't owe him. But I can't take the part anyway, Jack. The scars . . .'

He leaned forward and ran a finger over my face. 'There's always something. You could be a Thulos telepath.'

'Yeah. Silent, under fourteen layers of latex. What's that, your perfect woman?'

He smiled again. 'Yowza.' Then the smile faded. 'You went along with it for second prize though, didn't you? I saw your face, waiting for the announcement.'

'I can't act any more, Jack. I can't even remember what it was that made me want to stand up in front of people. I get nervous now just ordering off Amazon. If I ever had any confidence it's gone. I'm useless, hopeless, I'm even bloody *pointless* now, an actress who's so stressed out in crowds that she passes out . . . Felix can have the part. I don't want it.'

Now his expression was very serious, almost grave. 'What's happened to you, Skye? What's made you feel so worthless?'

'*This*.' I pointed at my scar. 'And this.' I parted the hair which had grown back after the operation as an even more unmanageable wiry fuzz of curls than it had been before, to show the fine line of scarring where my skull had been opened up. 'Losing your memory doesn't just mean that you can't remember things. It's not as simple as that. It means you lose all the things that define you – every decision I made in that year before the accident, every conclusion I reached, gone. Anything. Everything. Whatever made me *me* is gone. Okay, yes, I'm glad I'm not dead, on the whole. Glad that, instead of going through the windscreen face first, by sheer fluke I went through backwards, so my face got gashed instead of crushed. I've got a lot to be grateful for. But all that gratitude doesn't help when I can't even remember meeting my own fiancé! Do you see? And then there was *Fallen*

Skies, about people setting up a new world, being allowed to forget what had happened before, in the Shadow War. New lives. And Gethryn . . . Lucas James . . . He'd done terrible things, awful things, but he was allowed to forget and start again, and I loved that, loved the new beginnings, the redemption. The idea that just because the past was gone didn't mean that the future couldn't be great.'

Jack tipped his head forward so I couldn't see his face. 'Skye, Gethryn's just an actor, he does what he's told, says the words he's given. The new beginnings, wanting a new life . . . that was *me*.' Then his head came back and I could see the stress lines around his mouth, deeper now. 'That's some kind of irony, that is. You fancy the guy because he's talking about recovery and rebirth, and it's all *my* words.' A hollow kind of laugh. 'Bit of a Cyrano de Bergerac moment here, I think.'

'What about your whole "Iceman" thing?' I couldn't stop myself, the words just had to come out.

'What? What do you mean?'

'Last night. I overheard you and Lissa . . . she was saying about you being called the Iceman? I thought it was just because you were . . .' I felt myself blushing, but drove on regardless, 'because you were cool. But Lissa said it was something to do with having no emotion?'

'Ha!' Jack let out a long breath, like a sigh, and jumped up from his seat on the bed. 'Shit.' He began a rather fevered rummage through pockets and drawers as though he'd forgotten I was there, finally finding a battered packet unopened behind his laptop. There was a shaky and sweary couple of moments while he tried to find a lighter that worked, but he finally brought it all into conjunction and blew a long string of smoke into the air. 'It's nothing.'

'Right. So that's why it drives you to smoke, because it's nothing.'

He stared at his fingers for a second, turning his hand over to examine the filter tip. 'Yep.'

'Jack, you only smoke when you're wound up. And you're smoking now.' I watched his back view as he placed himself in front of the window again, staring out at the desert and blowing smoke which stuttered across the room before vanishing like lost ghosts.

'Hoist by my own habit,' he muttered, not turning round. 'Skye, when I said it was nothing, I meant it was nothing to you. None of your business. Okay?'

I stared at him, from the tousled dark fall of hair which hung to his shoulders, his defensively straight back, down past his, admittedly tasty, tightly jeaned backside to where his bare feet dug into the carpet as though he was anchoring himself to something. He was intense, like no man I'd seen. I half-hoped that he was about to confess that his accident had destroyed his ability to feel, as mine had stopped me remembering; a moment of wanting that kind of connection with him. 'Is there anything I can do to help?'

'Yeah. Come to the ball with me.' A sudden grinding out of the cigarette in a cup, and he'd turned to face me again, a con-trail of smoke following his movement. He stretched out his arms as though the muscles were sore, and flexed his fingers. 'Please.'

I closed my eyes, pretended a moment of faintness. 'I don't have a costume or anything.'

'Hey, I was just on a panel with our wardrobe girl, I'm sure I can persuade her to release a couple of costumes. What do you fancy, B'Ha? Pilot?' He grinned at me round a tightness in his eyes. 'I can see you as a pilot, in one of those uniforms.' He leered and I had to laugh; his face wasn't meant for anything as insalubrious as letching.

'I'm not sure.'

'I'll get someone to bring some stuff to your room. You can choose what you want to wear and send the rest back to wardrobe. Come on, I'm prepared to do all this, least you can do is agree to come. You must have been to a fancy dress ball before, surely?'

'I don't know.'

'But . . . how bad is this memory loss thing? Presumably you remember your parents, your childhood?'

I let my thoughts go. 'Yes, of course. Only child, doting parents who emigrated when I started drama school. It's all in there, just . . . they're all . . . furry.'

He gave me a half-grin. 'Furry?'

'Well, fuzzy then. When I look back it's like looking through – oh, I don't know, a sheet of tracing paper. Something like that. Not quite opaque but not clear either. I do have one or two vivid memories of those years between teenage and twenty-seven, but not that many. Not enough to be able to pin down, to say "this is what I thought". Everything from the year leading up to the accident, though, is stuff I've been told, memories I've fabricated.' I shrugged. 'But I've remembered every day since I woke up in hospital, with Michael and Faith dead. How about you? Did your accident leave you with any problems, or just the scars?'

I stopped, saw his expression and felt embarrassed. He'd gone goosebumped; I could see the little hairs on his arms standing up as his fingers closed over the leather thong around his neck, even though the room was warm. He fiddled with the necklace under his T-shirt, twisting it back and forth and, although he seemed to be watching me, his eyes were far, far away. Watching something else, something that made his skin chill.

'Jack?' I swung my legs over the edge of the bed, an instinctive move to get closer to him. 'Are you all right?'

A moment with no answer. Then his eyes lifted to mine. 'I'm thirty-five. I've lived nineteen years past the accident, and still I live it every day. Perhaps *that* is the real problem.' His voice was soft. 'Survivor guilt, Skye. You know about that?' A short laugh. 'Maybe you do.' A deep inhalation. 'And I've never said this to anyone else, not even the doctors. Never told them how much it still haunts me, like . . . like I can *feel* Ryan, just there.' He waved a hand vaguely over his shoulder. 'There's people down there . . . dressing up as my characters, discussing them, fucking *analysing* them, can you believe it? And all the while, these pilots, these alien creatures, all my novels, the *Two Turns North* storylines – they're my way of working through what happened.' Now his gaze bored through me, eyes like black holes. 'My whole *life* has been trying to work through what happened. And after that, anything else is just . . .' he threw his hands wide, 'meaningless. I exist for my work, Skye, for writing, for trying to put into words what's happening to me. That makes me, I dunno, careless with people. I can't – oh God, I'm going to use some terrible Americanism here – I can't *relate*.' Now one arm lay loosely at his side, as though he'd even stopped trying to express things through body language, and the other hand hooked back into the necklace. 'And then I met you and . . .'

I stared at him. 'So you think I'm, what, different? Because I know how it feels not to be dead?'

'You're not like . . . you don't . . . I can't explain. You're something else.' He dropped his hand from his throat and shrugged. 'I don't know what I'm trying to say here. I don't know why . . . And, for the record, yes, I can dance.'

'You're really messed up, aren't you?' I asked it softly, half-hoping he wouldn't hear. But he did, and his head went up higher, his eyes slipped from mine to stare at some spot near the ceiling.

'Of course I'm messed up,' he said. 'I'm a writer.'

There was a tap at the door and Felix's voice came through the frame. 'Skye? Jack?'

After a long, weighted pause, Jack opened the door to reveal Felix, wearing the biggest smile I'd ever seen. 'What's up?'

'They've sent me up to ask if you're okay? Only they want you downstairs. For the signing?'

'Shit!' Jack shook his head briefly, as though trying to bring himself back to consciousness. 'Forgot.'

'They've been doing my pictures already, God, it was brilliant – like being Miss World. I explained about you, darling, not being fit to take the part. They might want a little siggy from you, but they can wait until you feel better, they said. And if you're poorly Jack, they'll put it off.'

'No. No, it's okay. I'll go. Get it over with.' He checked his reflection in the mirror which hung opposite the bed, pulled a face, ran a hand over his unshaven cheeks and grimaced again. Both Felix and I were transfixed, watching him move around the room searching for his glasses and then splashing aftershave randomly across his stubble with the expression of someone who knows it's too late to shower and who hopes no-one will notice. When he unbuttoned the front of his shirt and splashed some of the aftershave across his chest, Felix gave a small whine. 'Oh Lord, will you look at him? It shouldn't be walking the streets, it really shouldn't.'

Jack raised his eyebrows and rebuttoned his shirt. 'I'd better put my face in front of them. Get up when you're feeling like it and lock up after you.' He slipped his glasses on. 'Do I look okay?'

'Be still my beating heart,' Felix said.

'Actually I was asking Skye.'

I looked at him for what felt longer than decent. 'Oh yes. You look okay. But, no shoes?'

'Nah. Catch you later.' And, with a flip of his hand, he was gone.

Felix immediately went over to the laptop and switched it on.

'What are you doing?'

'Just looking, lover. He might have something incriminating on there. Or some script, something, anything I can work with. Some insider secrets.' He turned to me, his eyes full of fire and life. 'You *did it*, my darling, you actually *did it*. I'm gonna be on *Fallen Skies*!'

'Might be just a bit part. Walk on.'

'Don't care. Think how great it'll look on my CV. And I'll get a name check on the closing credits; you never know, might jog someone in Hollywood into asking for me.'

'I thought that's why you had an agent?'

'He's useless. Told me to stick to EastEnders auditions. Ah, here we go.'

The screen burst into life. 'It'll be passworded. He's not going to risk someone stealing his ideas.'

'Yeah, but he might have left something running in the background. He'd never suspect you of trying to sneak a look at his Great Work, would he? Silly, silly boy.' A sharp look. 'He seems pretty serious about you, darling. Can't keep his eyes off you. You getting any action in that direction yet?' Felix scrolled down the screen. 'Because I am *seriously* jealous, he is definitely on my things-to-do list. I tell you, he shows the slightest inclination and I am going for it.' A moment's silent reading. 'You, or no you.'

'We've got things in common, Fe, that's all.'

'Huh.' He went quiet, then bounced away from the laptop, shutting off the power and carefully tipping the screen to the exact angle it had been before he touched it. 'Yeah. Useless, but, hey, it was worth a shot. Never mind, tall order really. Right. Okay. You ready to get off your man's bed yet?' Then he sat on the bed and the manic choirboy persona dropped away so quickly that I was derailed. 'Skye, are you really okay with me taking this part? I mean, you can do it if you want to. I won't mind.'

'Yes, you would. And yes, I'm really okay with it. I'd half-hoped for the dinner with Gethryn . . .'

'I *knew it!* I fucking *knew it!*' Felix jumped up, but didn't look annoyed. 'I said to Jack that I reckoned you'd try and throw it, just to get a date with your Welshman. I told him last night. Just the sort of thing you'd do.'

'It's okay, I'd changed my mind. Not even sure I'm going to go to the fancy dress ball, to be honest.' I tried not to think about those searching fingers, the mouth that wouldn't give me space to breathe, that insistence . . .

'So, you've gone off the luscious Gethryn, have you? What, switched allegiance to Mr Dark and Mysterious? That was quick and, if I may say so, rather shallow of you.'

A quick pang of shame speared me. Eighteen months. For eighteen months I'd lusted after Gethryn, so yes, Felix was right, superficially I *was* being petty and two-faced. 'It was . . .' But I couldn't do it. Couldn't even bring myself to mention letting Gethryn kiss me and then chickening out because he got a bit forceful about it. 'Gethryn is a star. There's millions of women clustering around him, he doesn't really want me and my scars, he was just being . . .' *What? Nice?* 'I don't know about Jack. He's not very forthcoming.'

'Maybe he's shy.'

'Maybe I'm not his type. Maybe he's not mine.' I stared at Felix for a moment. 'Was Michael my type?'

Felix turned his head away, running his hands through his hair until it spiked up in random peaks. His shoulders hunched forward. 'You've seen the photos.'

'Yes, but I want to *know*. Not just album loads of shots of faces I can't remember, but to know about *who I* am, do you see, Fe? A year's worth of memory loss is one hell of a lot of things just gone "poof".'

'Existential angst. It's a bastard.' Fe kept his head turned away but his tone was light. 'You know who you are, Skye, you know what you're like. Why does that year matter so much?'

I stared at his back. 'Shouldn't it?'

He turned around then and his face had changed. He looked older, that childish playfulness had gone and been replaced by a pulled-down, almost feral, expression and his yellow-diamond eyes were chilly. 'Yeah. You could be right.' Even his voice was different, deeper and hoarser. 'Maybe we *should* talk about that.'

His intensity scared me. It meant there was something to know, something I didn't suspect and had never seen, despite all those endless frames I'd scoured through, still desperately hoping that some memory had been left to me. 'Is it . . . is it something I should tell Jack?'

There was a momentary wavering, as though Felix hovered between breaking down or running away, but his mood settled out at manic once again. 'Hey, you're very concerned about him all of a sudden! Just how far *have* you got with Mr Moody Stare Whitaker? How many bases have you collectively touched? And no lying to your uncle Felix, because he'll know.'

'He held my hand. Patted my back when I threw up.'

Felix affected disgusted disbelief. 'And that's *all*? Darling, the guy is burning for you, his loins throb in your direction, and you're telling me that all you've done is a little maiden-aunting?'

I lifted the edge of my T-shirt to where the scars criss-crossing my body began. 'How do you think he'd react to this, if we got any further?'

Fe raised his eyebrows. 'But I reckon, if he really likes you, why should he worry? It's only a bit of scarring, like your face. Doesn't stop you doing the dirty, does it?'

'It affects who I am.' I dropped the shirt and stood up. 'The accident made me into a different person, Fe.'

A pause. He cleared his throat and drew down his eyebrows until they nearly touched his lashes. I wondered what he was going to say. 'Yeah, I know,' he said softly. 'I know.'

My heart slid and skidded in my chest. *What was going on?*

CHAPTER 17

Jack forced himself to smile. It wasn't natural, this level of hero-worship. He was just a writer. He had ideas and wrote them down; it wasn't like he turned those words into actions, or directed the show or anything. He was just the ideas-man and this constant call for his attention felt wrong.

'Jay! Jay, over here!' Another girl, jumping up and down and waving an arm to catch his eye. 'Will you sign this?'

'Sure.' Slipping into his writerly persona, approachable but withdrawn, he pushed the glasses up tight to his eyes like a mask. 'Who to?'

'Candy.' Breasts jostled his arm as she bent low beside him. He tried to smile again.

'Lovely name.'

'Yeah. I'm gonna break into writing, y'know. Next year, when I finish college.'

Jack scribbled his name. 'Good luck with that,' he muttered, knowing he sounded sarcastic. Inside he was aching in a way he hadn't for a decade, hating himself for the performance he was putting on. Hating who he was, what he was, just about everything about himself.

'Yeah. Perhaps you could, y'know, give me some tips?'

He looked up at her face now. Tight pink lips in a knowing smile, perfect teeth, perfect skin. Perfect hair, loose and blonde across narrow shoulders, swinging aside now and again to show glimpses of a bustier top and hints of a bra strap. He should be turned on, he knew that. Should be wriggling in his seat, adjusting himself under the table, so as not to let his body's eagerness show. But all he could think of was Skye and the look in her eyes when she'd asked if she could help him. Even without knowing what he'd done, what he might need help *with*, she'd cared enough to offer. More than Lissa ever had. More than anyone ever had, come to that. All they saw were the scars, the superficial damage to his body. Skye had been the first one to look underneath, to see that so much more had been ripped apart than skin and flesh; the first one to see how cut up his soul was. Maybe it was because she had suffered too, or maybe it was just an innate desire to reach out and heal, he didn't know.

'You going to the ball, Jay?'

It took him a second to pull back, to realise that the girl, *Candy*, was still talking to him. 'Maybe.'

'I'll see you there then.' A knowing wink. 'I'm going as a Thulos. You can't get a lot of underwear under that costume, know what I'm saying, Jay?' The breast nudged his arm again and this time he was slightly relieved to feel himself stiffening.

At least his autonomic nervous system was still on-line, whatever else might have packed up.

'Maybe,' he repeated, and watched Candy slither off into the crowd, giving him a tiny wave over her shoulder as she went. *Well, if Skye doesn't want me* . . . he thought. *At least I'll get a dance.*

CHAPTER 18

The velvet clung to me like a removable pelt. Its dark crimson shone against my skin, making my features glow and my hair look a deep, untouchable colour. As I clasped the wristbands around my arms and the collar around my neck, I felt very alien.

'Wow. No, really. Wow.' Felix stood back to let me out of the bathroom. 'That is incredible.'

The Dowager Queen of Skeldar, in all her glory. Or, at least, me in her clothes. Of all the outfits that Jack had sent up, this one revealed the least skin and also gave me a borrowed dignity. The headpiece pulled my hair back from my face, which had given me a few moments of uncertainty until Fe assured me that the scar was mostly covered by the dangling fake-jewels. I had to lace the bodice quite tightly to make the floor-length dress fit my body perfectly, although the shoes supplied with it were too high and slightly too big; the actress who wore it was a shoe size and a dress size larger than I was, but, on the plus side, the heels made me walk more regally.

'Does make you look a bit like a Christmas tree, but apart from that . . .'

I aimed my Shadow rifle at him. 'Shut up. Better a Christmas tree than a pimp.' Felix had begged a costume, and was, in consequence, wearing the get-up of a Shadow Planet refugee, mock-fur coat with big Ugg-type boots and Ray-Bans against the solar glare. 'You look like you're trying to break into rap music.'

'I am going to *boil*.' Fe waved his arms up and down to create a draught. 'How does anyone manage to wear this on a film set?'

'The wardrobe girl told me, when she brought the costumes up, that these are for publicity shots. On set they have to wear stuff they can actually walk in without sweating like carthorses.'

'Figures.' He reached inside his furs and flapped his T-shirt. 'So, I guess dirty dancing is out?'

'Dirty anything. We have to hand these back after the ball, undamaged and unstained. I promised. And, since it looks like anything involving you also involves stains . . .'

Felix looked at me, eyes shining. 'I can't believe I'm going to be doing this for real come next January,' he whispered. '*Fallen Skies.* You are *such* a clever girl, Skye.'

'Yeah.' I didn't feel clever. But then, neither did I feel the sense of dread at attending a gathering of fans which had so paralysed me only a couple of days ago. I wasn't going to be the life and soul of the party, but I could face walking into a room full of people, and the thought of going home to my little terrace in York now filled me with warmth, not the urge to board the next plane back. 'You were pretty clever too, Fe, getting me out here. Forcing me to face up to things.'

Felix had his back to me. 'You think you've faced up to things?' His voice sounded odd. A bit choked.

'Not so much faced-up to, but more . . . I dunno, worked through, perhaps. I was thinking, all those panic attacks that they kept telling me were "stress related", maybe they weren't. Perhaps the doctors got it wrong. I'm starting to think that they were all symptoms of depression.' *Yeah, Skye, you miserable cow.*

'You think you were depressed.' Not a question, I noticed, and an odd stress on the words.

'Maybe not, not proper clinical depression but . . . I wasn't very well. So maybe you forcing me to come here kind of kicked me out of a destructive sort of slump. Made me realise that there is more to life.'

'And, play your cards right, you could get to take home the biggest trophy of all. Mr Whitaker clearly can't wait to have you back on home soil, and I use the term *having you* in all its possible contexts.'

'Jack . . . I *like* Jack.' I adjusted the lie of the skirt. It raked across my hips to fall behind me in a heavy train, body-tight in the front and yet fluidly generous behind. 'I just don't think he's interested in me like that. And, anyway, I don't want to jump in and replace Michael.'

'Don't you?' Felix's voice was oddly high-pitched.

'Michael was my fiancé. We were going to get married. I can't just up and start . . . well, anything with someone else after only eighteen months, it's not right.'

Felix turned and the expression on his face looked misplaced, as though he'd stuck it on the front of his head to cover his real feelings. 'There's always Gethryn.' He gave a grin which also looked out of place.

'That was more of a crush than anything real.'

I waited for Felix to disagree but, disappointingly, he didn't. Instead he sighed and began to strip, until he'd pulled off the coat and boots and was left in his T-shirt and jeans. He poked his feet back into his shoes but kept on the glasses. 'Right. Now I'm going downstairs, get stuck into the Jack Daniels. I'll see you there.'

'Glasses?'

He paused a moment. 'Reckon they make me look mysterious, don't you think, darling? I'll keep them on.'

I sat on the edge of the bed, appreciating the costume. The weight of it hung from my shoulders and stiffened my spine; it swept along the floor with a delicious sound and, as a bonus feature, it made my boobs look pertly luscious. For the first time I knew why so many women have a Cinderella complex. 'See you later, Fe.'

The door closed on his smug expression. Tonight

I was going to relax. Gear myself up for tomorrow. Decide whether to take Jack up on his offer of an escort to the ball.

And what was stopping me? Was it *really* loyalty to Michael? According to Fe my relationship with Michael had been high-octane and frantic. He could never have been accused of intensity or moodiness, only of a desire to live life as fast and as frenetically as possible, dragging me along with him in his rocket-fuelled search for the bigger, the better, the most superlative.

Or was it Jack himself? He was so self-contained, there was something very shut-in about him. He laughed and smiled but all the time I felt there was something else going on behind it all, something he kept tightly confined. Some emotion that he didn't want spotted. And, to be honest with myself, I was afraid. That year of memory loss and the fuzzing-out of preceding years had affected me more deeply than I'd ever thought it could. If I couldn't remember even my own *fiancé*, could I even remember who *I* was? And if I couldn't remember that, then how did I know how to be with someone else? How did I know *who* to be? *And what was it that Felix knew*?

Even so. It was a ball, a fancy dress ball, not an arranged marriage. And I'd look such a dork walking in on my own in this frock-of-frocks. And Jack was undeniably attractive . . .

The phone rang and made me jump. Horribly cautiously – who knew where I was? – I picked it up. 'Skye Threppel, right?' said the voice on the other end. 'Do you have a costume picked out for tomorrow?'

I didn't recognise the voice. Pure American, pure business. 'I'm just trying it on.'

'Great. My name's Erlon, I run The Shadow Planet.'

'Oh,' I said, disconcerted. 'That had better be the online fanzine, because otherwise you ought to get help.' In the series the Shadow Planet was run by the Skeel, and Erlon was most definitely not a Skeel name.

A laugh. 'Yeah. I wonder if I could get a couple shots of you and Gethryn in your outfits? No use trying to do it tomorrow, when everyone will be getting in on the act, so I figured, tonight's my chance. I spoke with Geth earlier, he says to meet him in his trailer at twenty after seven, then I'll get some pictures of the two of you. Post 'em on the 'zine.'

'I suppose so.' I fingered the skirt, feeling the softness. 'Yes. Okay.' Erlon would be there, I wouldn't be left alone with Gethryn and it would be nice to be able to talk to him, to indulge my crush without alcohol intruding and blurring his actions into borderline harassment. To establish that he was a decent human being, and that what had happened out in that car park had been the result of overexcitement and unwise come-ons on my part. Besides, he was hardly going to tear all my clothes off in front of other people, was he?

It was already ten past seven, so I decided to leave immediately. For one thing, in these heels it would probably take me ages to get down to Gethryn's Winnebago, and for another, I didn't dare do anything whilst wearing the dress in case I ended up in another embarrassing situation from which Mr Whitaker had to rescue me. In fact I'd ruled out doing anything at all, apart from standing very still and *never* going to the toilet.

I adjusted my cleavage, hitched up the train and set off down the back stairs. Part way down I had to stop and haul the skirts up over my arm until it looked as though I was carrying a very heavy set of curtains. This outfit was definitely made to be seen, which was ego-boostingly reassuring, and was surprisingly comfortable to walk in, but it did spend a lot of time trying to escape off me. The weight of the velvet train almost pulled it from my shoulders, and it was only the laced-up bodice which kept my boobs from being further uncovered with every step. The whole dress swayed sensuously and rhythmically whilst trying to reveal my body a little bit at a time, as though it was a kind of mobile strip-club. I tottered down the last few stairs and arrived at the side door leading directly out onto the yard, fabric cascading around me but at least managing to prevent public indecency. A couple headed past me into the motel and did a double-take but I kept on walking, head straight, eyes forward. No-one else was about. Everyone was still too busy getting things signed, putting the final touches to their costumes, or mixing it in the bar, at least, that was what I was banking on.

I wafted around the outside of the motel until I reached the Winnebago, whirling through the dust in my draperies like a soft furnishings removal business. About a hundred yards away from the van two men in Security vests were sitting in collapsible chairs under a sunshade, watching a small TV screen. They both looked pretty fed up, arms folded, wearing Day-Glo jackets and sullen expressions, despite the hearty laughter track from the TV. I wondered about saying something to them, giving some kind of excuse for being there, but since neither of them acknowledged my passing, and neither looked as if they were up for taking a bullet for Gethryn, I didn't bother. However, outside the van a harassed-looking girl wearing a headpiece on top of punishingly short hair and carrying a clipboard stopped me.

'Is Mr Tudor-Morgan expecting you?'

But then she had a call on the mobile clipped to her belt and headed off away from me to answer it. I was really *not* about to stand around sweating in velvet, so I tiptoed up the steps and tapped on the metal door. 'Gethryn? It's Skye.'

There was no answer. I knocked again, harder. Then I tried the handle and the door swung outwards, nearly knocking me down. There was no outraged shout so I walked in.

The door led into an enormous living area with

sofas and a central table, which gave onto a kitchen bigger than the one in my house. It contained a vast refrigerator, a microwave you could have stabled a horse in and enough leather seating for about fifty people, but no visible sink or way of preparing anything more than TV dinners. There was no-one else about.

'Hello,' I called as I stared. 'I've come for the photoshoot.'

Still no answer. Maybe I hadn't called loudly enough. Maybe Gethryn was giving Erlon a tour of the mobile home. Maybe they'd snuck off to get away from Her Outside with the prison haircut.

I walked further in. The floor was carpeted a deep grey which made the place look very dark, and there were signs of recent habitation in a shirt dropped over the back of a couch, a half-eaten apple turning slowly brown on the table. I picked up the shirt and self-consciously sniffed it. It smelled of some unknown cologne, something musky and citrusy, like the smell of sex itself, with an undertone of something alcoholic.

As I stood, breathing in the smell of Gethryn, I heard a sound. A low groan, as if coming from the back of a throat. I put down the shirt and moved towards the noise, picking my way down a mirror-lined corridor until it opened out into a vast bedroom. In the middle stood a bed too large to be called king-sized, it had to be emperor-sized, or possibly dictator. Spread-eagled face up across the bed with his hair dangling from one side, lay Gethryn, surrounded by a much stronger smell of alcohol. In fact, if I'd struck a match, the air would have flamed like a Christmas pudding.

'Gethryn?' I approached cautiously, keeping one eye on the distance between me and the door.

Another groan.

'Are you all right?'

A hand waved. It had a bottle in it. So, now I came to look at it, did the other hand. Liquid had poured over the bed sheets, over Gethryn's clothes, and his hair was damply roped with it. I took a step back and put one hand on the wall to steady myself.

'I think I'd better fetch Jack.'

At the sound of the name, Gethryn sat up, still clutching both bottles. 'No! Don' wan' that bastard in he'. Am havin' day off. Entitled to day off, aren't I? For rest and . . .' he sloshed the bottle in his right hand, 'relaxation.' Now he got to his knees, carefully. 'Why you come here, anyway, Skye? You here to keep me company? Man needs company on his day off. Have a drink.' He held out a bottle my way, his whole body bouncing slightly as the bed moved underneath him.

'No, thanks.' My heart was pushing blood into my throat, where I could feel it bashing the walls of my veins and, beneath my feet, the carpet felt dry and full of electricity. 'I ought to . . .' Not wanting to turn my back on him, I began shuffling in reverse towards the doorway with the skirt tangling around behind my legs like an over-affectionate cat. 'The others will be here in a minute anyway,' I said quickly, just in case he decided to make a lunge for me. 'I came for the photoshoot. For the e-zine? Us in our ball costumes?'

'Fuck photoshoot.' Geth walked forward on his knees to come closer. 'They can't make me do it. Only had to appear at the convention to fulfil terms, after the ball I'm free as a bird! More free, in fac'.' He clambered down off the bed to stand in front of me, swaying slightly. 'Tired of filming in bloody cheap places, all sandy and Canadian. I'm goin' to Holwoody.'

Even unfocused those yellow eyes were fascinating. 'You mean Hollywood,' I said, transfixed by his stare.

'Yeah. That.' He leaned in and sour breath bounced off my cheek.

'But you told Erlon that you'd do the shoot for him. He said he'd spoken to you?' I shuffled back a few more steps, the thick carpet snagging at my heels with a crisp sound. The adrenaline flooding me tasted sour and my heart was beating so fast I wondered that I wasn't airborne. Deep in the skirts of the dress I bunched a fist in case of a sudden swoop.

A long pause. Then, 'Fuck. Yes. Did. Bollocks. Mustn't know I've been drinking.'

'Erlon mustn't know you've been drinking?'

A vigorous head shake that made his snakes of hair whip his cheeks. 'No! Not Erlon, Erlon's lovely guy. Lovely. Drinks tequila with the little worm in. An' brandy. Jack. Don' wan' Jack to know I've had a drink. He'll tell people I'm a drunk. I'm no' drunk, he's a bastard. Doesn't like me drinking, but thass bollocks, isn't it, lovely? Just 'cos he's on some Ten-Step programme thing, reckons we should all give up the booze. Bastard,' he repeated.

'Jack doesn't drink?' I found I was fascinated, despite my fear.

Gethryn squinted. 'He's not told you then? Oh, thass good, that is, the Iceman not telling the pretty little girlie allllllll about his lousy habits.' He hiccupped. 'Our Iceman, he's a bit handy with a bottle, *bach.* Didn't *wan'* to give up, oh no. *Had to.* That or lose the show.' He took another shaky step towards me and suddenly wrapped both arms around me. I heard the bottles clang as they made contact behind my back. 'Oh, our Jack's got them secrets just *pilin'* up. You look ve' sexy in that dress. What do you look like out of it?'

A wobbly finger ran along my spine. I felt the slow trickle as the bottle he was holding tipped and spilled drink down my back. This dress was going to smell like a winery. 'Erlon will be here in a few minutes,' I said, scared to move in case it encouraged him. My pulse began to race again, and I checked the distance to the door, not sure how capable he'd be of stopping me getting away. My hands readied themselves to claw, to punch, to fight my way out.

'Shit. Bugger.' Gethryn wobbled dramatically and only managed to steady himself by holding onto my shoulders. More liquid rolled over the dress, beads of it sinking into the soft fabric.

Golden eyes narrowed to take in my face, golden hair wrapping itself against me. I saw the small blond prickles of stubble breaking out on his chin, the little indent under his lower lips that jutted his mouth forward in a permanent half-kiss. He was beautiful. Very, very lovely. *But he wasn't Lucas James.* He was a mixed-up drunken actor, that was all, and I'd made the classic mistake of confusing the actor with the script. All that heart-breakingly wonderful language, all that emotion. It was Jack's. Without knowing it, I'd fallen for Jack, a man who could only express his locked-down feelings by giving the words to someone else to say.

'You can kiss me, though. Come on, girl, gi' us a kiss.' He blinked hard and screwed his eyes up as though trying to bring my face into focus. 'Bet you go like a train, doncha?' A hand rolled down my neck and squeezed at the front of the dress, where boning and corseting protected my breasts and a knee tried to brush aside my skirts. 'Where d'you keep the good stuff then, eh, girlie? 'S got to be under here somewhere . . .' The hand stopped trying to fondle my boobs and groped futilely amid the masses of velvet, trying to locate me underneath it all. 'Gonna show you a goo' time . . .'

And then I realised that I wasn't scared, not any more. Gethryn wasn't a threat, with his posturing and his leery eyes; he was a sad drunk with terrible people skills and absolutely no chat-up lines at all. A single slap to the cheek was all it took to knock him sideways and from there it was ridiculously easy to push him backwards onto the bed with one hand to his solar plexus almost knocking him completely off his feet and sending him sprawling down onto the soaked bedding. 'Stop it, Gethryn.'

'Playin' hard to get, eh?' It was pathetic really, to hear him trying to talk sex when he couldn't even manage to rock himself to his feet. 'Like my girlies to fight a bit, I do. Bit of life, d'you see? No' juss lyin' back and lettin' me . . .'

'So you do it even if they're fighting you off?' I tried to brush the droplets of liquid off the plush fabric with the back of my hand, keeping half an eye on Gethryn's attempts to get up. 'Don't you think it might have meant that they wanted you to stop?'

'Nah. They wanted Lucas James, all of 'em.' He hiccupped loudly again, swore and shook his head, looking at me out of each eye alternately. 'Think I'm gonna be sick,' he muttered.

I looked around. 'Bathroom?'

A hand waved towards a mirrored wall. ''hind there.' A cheesily ominous belch followed, and I dragged him off the bed towards the indicated wall, flinging myself at it until I hit whichever secret button opened the door, and flung Gethryn inside with a strength I hadn't known I'd got until it came to potentially getting vomit on the dress. It was going to be bad enough with the alcohol, but at least I could hang it up outside and pray for that to evaporate – sick was pretty much terminal.

Gethryn began making unpicturesque noises. 'I'll go find you some water,' I said, whisking the dress out of reach.

He raised a bleary face. 'Not gonna offer to hold my hair back for me? Oh, shit . . .'

I looked at him sternly. 'I think you'll manage.'

I was in the kitchen, investigating the potential of the enormous fridge for ice cubes, when there came a hammering on the van door. Not just a gentle knock but a proper, closed-fist banging. Then a voice. 'Skye! Are you in there?'

Jack.

Oh God.

If I let him in, he'd know about Gethryn. That he had been – not just drinking, what Gethryn was went way beyond being merely domestically drunk; he was gloriously shooting out of the far side of sloshed and Gethryn clearly didn't want Jack to know, for whatever reasons of his own. But, if I didn't let Jack in, he'd make assumptions. He might even think that I'd come back to finish what Geth and I had started out in the car park under those merciless stars, and I didn't want Jack to think of me as a girl who went back for seconds of that sort of thing.

'Hold on a second,' I called, flinging a few sad ice-drops into a glass and dashing as best as I could in the long dress back to the bathroom, where Gethryn was now lying on the floor. 'Jack's here,' I said succinctly.

Gethryn just groaned.

'You've got to sober up.' This could mean his career, didn't he *realise*? 'Can you stand?' And there, in that tiny bathroom which was almost flooded with the smell of vomit, I began to strip Gethryn Tudor-Morgan naked.

Oh, how many times had I imagined slowly undressing Geth, gradually revealing the Celtic tattoo which lay along one jutting hip, just asking for a tongue to trace its smooth length? How many ways had I conjured of watching my fingers pass over his taut, muscular stomach, tanned as golden as the rest of his skin? But in none of my daydreams had Gethryn actually peed in his tight, button-fly jeans, or had to be helped to pull his shirt over his head because his balance was too unsteady for him to let go of the wall.

'Just get in the shower.' And I turned it on, viciously, to extreme chill, and gave him a shove. His golden nakedness immediately puckered and pimpled as the cold water hit, and he gave a scream, plunging helplessly directly under the impressive torrent. I half-ran, half-tottered from the room back through the acres of Winnebago and opened the door. Jack, looking customarily furious, stood on the steps with a large, bestubbled man who appeared to have no chin, just an expanse of face sloping gently down into his neck.

'Erlon?' I ignored Jack and held out a hand to shake. 'Gethryn's just . . . ummm . . . He'll be out in a minute.'

'Cool.' Erlon moved past me and began fiddling with the camera in his hand. 'In here's good. On the sofa, maybe?'

Jack stayed in the doorway with a bitten-back expression on his face. 'What took you so long?' he asked me in the sort of furious hiss that mothers use to ask questions to which they already know the answers. Then he sniffed suspiciously. 'What have you been doing with Gethryn?'

I was desperate not to lie to Jack. As I watched his expression alternate between moody and frustrated, I had to work quite hard not to reach out and touch him, to reassure him that he was allowed to lighten up every now and again.

'And stop bloody staring at me! Just tell me, what are you doing over here?'

Keep him talking. 'I came over for the photos. Of course. You know that. Why are *you* here, couldn't Erlon manage to take the pictures on his own?'

'Vanessa told me you've been here for nearly half-an-hour. You stink of booze. And worse.'

I presumed Vanessa was the punitive-haircut girl outside. 'I had a drink while I was waiting for Gethryn. And I'm all sweaty; it took me ages to walk over in this dress.'

‘So where’s Geth?’

‘Having a shower.’ Now I couldn’t miss the look Jack was giving me. It was two-thirds contempt and the rest was made up of scorn. Maybe with half a percent left for pity. ‘And will you stop eyeballing me like that? I’ve not been having rampant sex with him, if that’s what you’re thinking.’

‘Right.’

‘Get a look at this dress, Jack. I doubt I could brush my teeth wearing this, let alone get down and dirty.’ I wafted a hand at myself. His eyes followed the hand.

‘Looks good on you.’ There was a bit of a spark in his eyes now. ‘I’ll just go get Geth . . .’

‘No!’ If he set one foot in that reeking bedroom he’d know that Gethryn had been on a bender. Jack eyeballed me a bit more and the spark died. ‘I’ll go and fetch him.’

As I spoke I tottered out, down the hallway again and into the bedroom, where Gethryn was just emerging, tawny and splendid, from the shower. ‘Hey, girl.’ He sounded steadier. ‘What’s the rush?’

My eyes were transfixed by his chest, which rivulets of water were still navigating, passing between nipples so perfectly brown and round they looked like pennies, and down into uncharted regions, now concealed beneath a fluffy blue towel. Even with all I knew about him now, I *still* felt a little tremor of lust – Felix was right, I *was* shallow. ‘Erlon’s here,’ I started to say, but my voice went all thick at the way his fringe split into fragments, each with its own diamond-tip of water over those treacle-golden eyes. 'And Jack.'

'*Fuck*.' Gethryn muttered something I couldn't hear, but it didn't sound good. 'Better get back out there, *cariad*. Don't let him in here, he'll know something's up. Like a bloody terrier that man is. Just . . .' he swiped a hand over his wet hair and blinked hard, 'just keep him talking. Okay?'

'Right.' Again I tottered down the hallway, arriving just as Jack had started to walk towards the bedroom and we ended up nose-to-nose. I performed a little jig to prevent him from getting past me without pressing me into the opposite wall. From the look on his face, pressing me anywhere at all was a *long* way from being on the agenda.

'What is going on?' We were back to the hiss again and the spark in his eyes now was one of anger.

'I want to go to the ball with you.' I'd meant to lead up to it, to smile and soften his expression first, but it just came out, I don't know why. First thing in my head, probably, pushed out by that smouldering look on Jack's face, the way his eyes burned into me. He was like a cold supernova, a black hole. Dragging me in with his gravitational field.

'*What?*'

'Remember, you asked me? To go to the ball? I want to. Please,' I added. 'You said you could dance.'

He looked curiously behind me, towards the bedroom. 'You're behaving very strangely. What's going on back there – have you left Geth dead on the bed or something?'

'No.'

'Then why are you . . . why choose now to tell me you want to come with me to the ball?'

'What's wrong with now?'

We stared at each other again, until Erlon interrupted, clearing his throat. ''Um, maybe I could just do one or two of you first? Maybe, with Jack?' He waggled his camera under his non-existent chin. 'While we wait.'

'I'm not sure that's a good idea.' Jack spoke with his teeth clenched.

'Aw, go on. Just be natural.' Erlon led me to the velvet couch, onto which the dress snagged like Velcro. 'Look as if you're chatting.' Defeated, Jack slumped beside me, folded his arms and dropped his head down onto his chest. If we were chatting, it could only be about death and despondency. 'Now, put your arm around Skye.' The world's most reluctant hug commenced as Jack slid one arm between my neck and the couch, leaving his hand flopping onto my shoulder. 'Ah, that's great.'

Erlon's digital camera didn't have the decency to go 'click' so we didn't know when it was safe to relax. Jack remained with one hand behind my back, the other loosely in his lap, as though covering up some furtive groinal activity, and both my arms lay lifelessly along the seams of the wine-dark dress.

We looked like a mannequin and a mannequin fetishist.

'Hey, Jack.' Gethryn wandered in, fully dressed in his uniform. He smelled very strongly of after-shave and his eyes were a bit unsettled, but apart from that he looked sober. 'Erlon. So. Pictures then?'

I thought I heard Jack mutter, 'Thank God,' but it might have been something else, as he made way for Gethryn to pose alongside me. Geth looked lip-lickingly tasty in the tight uniform, hair still curling damply down his neck but, when he sat beside me, there was a distinct whiff of sourness on his breath and his pupils were shrunken. Erlon took a few shots, then made us stand up, arms around one another, smiling into the lens. My smile was tight, I could feel tremors running up and down Gethryn's body and there was a faint alcohol-scented sweat breaking out on his neck.

To think, only a few weeks ago I would have eaten my own arm for the chance to stand this close to Gethryn Tudor-Morgan. I'd seen him *naked* for God's sake! And now . . . now that the glamour had broken and I'd seen Gethryn for who and what he truly was, I could still admire that sexy physique and that sculpted face, but I was glad that there were other people with us. Gethryn had clearly been in another room when the self-control was being handed out.

Jack was gazing at us both with a very odd expression on his face.

As soon as Erlon had the last picture satisfactorily in his camera, Jack hustled me out of the van. He almost manhandled me down the steps and around the side of the motel, not letting me stop to hitch up my skirt and I had to settle for letting most of it trail behind me in the dust, where it sent up little flurries of worried sand as I moved.

Finally we reached the yard near the dumpsters, and Jack let go of my arm. 'Well?'

'Well, what?' I reeled in as much of the skirt as I could and tried to brush the worst of the dirt off with my hands.

'Gethryn didn't hurt you, did he?' Jack leaned back against the wall and managed to find a cigarette somewhere about his person. God knows where from, his jeans were skin-tight and the grey shirt had no pockets. 'Just tell me. If he hurt you, I'll . . .'

I looked down at my velvet hem, slightly ragged and dusty. 'No.'

'Are you *sure*?'

'What, you think I might not have noticed him trying to grope my boobs and shove his tongue down my throat? No, I shan't fall for that one again, Jack, whatever you might think, I'm not *that* desperate.'

'Oh for God's sake.' Jack got the cigarette lit and the first puff visibly relaxed him. 'I'm not saying anything like that. But you were very odd when Erlon and I got there. Like something had happened and you were covering it up. Although why you're not yelling sexual assault from the rooftops already I can't fathom.'

Jack smoking. Worried. Perhaps I should tell the truth. 'He was . . . a bit pissed when I arrived.'

'How pissed?'

'How am I supposed to tell?'

'How many bottles did he have?' Jack wasn't looking at me now; his eyes were following the smoke as it trailed lazily into the hot air.

'Two. That I could see. But he could still walk and talk. And anyway, he's a grown man, what was I supposed to do?'

He sighed. 'Nothing. I was worried, that's all. When you opened that door, I was scared that he might have . . . he takes advantage of who he is sometimes. Well, you know that already, I guess. It's okay, Skye, it's not you I'm angry at, it's Geth. He's behaving like a total pillock . . .' A long exhale. 'It'll be the end of him. Professionally, I mean, he'll never work over here again. In fact, given the way reputations travel, he'll be lucky to get a job filming public information videos in Uzbekistan.'

'He said he was going to Hollywood.' I brushed the skirt down once more.

'Yeah. I bet he did.' Jack sounded tired. 'Did I tell you yet that the dress looks fantastic on you? Very *sumptuous*.'

Distracted and pleased I pulled some imaginary fluff from the bodice. 'Thanks.'

'You're welcome.' A sudden turn and he bent to

stub out the cigarette, grinding it into the floor beside his feet as though he had a personal grudge against that particular bit of dirt. 'Okay. Better get back to work. I've scripts to deliver, so –'

'What's the rush?'

He stopped and turned around, looking baffled and switching back hair from his face as though it annoyed him. 'What? I just said, two scripts to finish.'

'I mean, why are you wanting to quit the show and go back to Britain?'

Jack stared at me. He really did have beautiful eyes, I thought, and there was something about the way he stood, the way he *was*, that was inherently attractive. 'What makes you ask that?' He had to clear his throat to speak and his fingers were fiddling, searching for another cigarette.

'Just wondering. If you needed to get home for anything specific.'

A sudden smile, and he'd turned away. 'Nah. Need a change, new challenge. I've done the TV thing now, I'm not a novelty to them any more. And, like I told Liss, my editor wants more novels.' His voice dropped a tone. 'And I miss Yorkshire. You get a bit sick of relentless sunshine and OJ. I'm pining for drizzle and curd tarts.' And then he was walking away, slamming the heavy door that led to the stairs without looking back.

I found my fingers were picking at each other again; Jack wasn't the only one with a habit he indulged when he was stressed. But this time I wasn't thinking about the past, or fretting over the loss of Michael, or Faith. I was thinking about Jack Whitaker. About the weight of longing in his voice when he spoke about Yorkshire, about how looking at him made me think of the dark infinity of the whole of space. Of how I wanted to give myself up to him but didn't know how or whether he even wanted that from me. Of how I could hardly offer him anything when I didn't even know what I had to offer.

He walked to the base of the stairs and punched the motel wall hard enough to make his fist sting. *Buggerbuggerbugger*! 'Sumptuous'! He'd told Skye she looked like a fucking *sofa*! And then she'd caught him out, cut right through to what was at the heart of everything right now, and there'd been nothing he could say or do without telling her she'd hit it spot on. *Home*. He wanted to go home. And, yes, it was specific.

I want to go home with you, Skye. I want to show you where I live, that lovely little white house set on its own in the dale. I want to walk in the air with you, sit and write in the office while you . . . I dunno, do whatever it is that you do. I want to feel that you're close by . . .

He raised his head and stared a challenge at the ceiling. Yeah, he wanted it. But he'd wanted an awful lot of things over the years. Starting with death and working his way up to success, which, now he had it, didn't look like such a great deal any more. Success came with debts to the life he'd had before.

Without thinking, he rolled the leather lace through his fingers and knew he didn't deserve the life he'd got. Didn't deserve Skye. Couldn't have her. *Push it away, Jack. Keep the feelings down. If you don't feel, you don't hurt* . . . And definitely don't let Geth see. If Gethryn knew Jack cared . . . if he knew Jack could hurt, then he'd hurt him.

He'd been totally blasted; even Skye's best efforts hadn't totally sobered him up – what was he playing at? He must know his career was on the line here. Had he stopped caring? *If Geth ever even suspects I feel anything, anything at all for Skye* . . . Jack bit a fingernail, chewed it down to the quick as he stood, using the pain to distract himself from the horrible inevitability of Skye finding out what a bastard he was. Not just a bastard either, he could have dealt with that . . . A sharp jab of adrenaline hit him in the gut, as though he was looking down from a great height, preparing to fall. If this wasn't just a day off's unwinding then . . .

Shit. Everything is blowing up in my face. And Jack remembered the compassion in Skye's eyes when she'd asked him if he needed help, wondered how far that compassion would stretch. Would she have been there for him, if she'd known him in the old days? Would she have talked him down, held him when the demons came calling with their vicious, insinuating claws digging deeper and deeper every day?

He chewed at his forefinger in the absence of another cigarette and contemplated the newly rising emotion that beat away inside him as though he'd swallowed a seagull. *Skye.* She made him feel . . . different. *She makes me feel.* All that passion, all that nerve-scraping stuff that had once made him so alive, all that stuff that he'd locked down so tight that nothing really got through any more. She drew it all to the surface, like the poison in an abscess. *Like all the stuff worth living for.*

Jack shook his head hard, still mouthing around his knuckle. He was letting her get to him, that was all. Skye was like a cat which had been kept indoors all its life suddenly allowed out into the big world, creeping around, almost afraid of each new discovery. *Be afraid, Skye, be very afraid. Most of those things you discover have the potential to turn septic underneath you. Like me. You should stay away from me . . .*

Okay, Jack. Now say it like you mean it . . .

CHAPTER 19

When I came out of the bathroom Felix was sprawled on the bed shirtless with his jeans slightly undone, like a suggestive pin-up. 'Heard you'd been summoned. So, how'd the photo shoot go?' He raised a knee and lounged provocatively, but his words had a strange edge.

'It was, uh, interesting.'

He jumped up and began walking around the room, not meeting my eyes as he talked. 'You vanish off the face of the earth, turn up *covered* in dust, you've got Whitaker slamming doors looking for you, online is alive with speculation about you and Gethryn – I've been checking on my phone and they are *all* talking about you. A girl I had to *drug* just to get across the Atlantic!'

I couldn't tell if he was joking or not. He was talking fast, breathily and using his fingertips to spike up his hair at the same time. 'Fe?'

'I am presuming, because you've got all this going on, you've managed to stage some kind of miraculous recovery? What happened there?'

'Have you been doing coke?' It was the only

reason I could think of for this fast, inflectionless delivery. 'You're being really weird, Fe.'

'Is that a yes?'

I looked at him, at those wide apple-juice eyes and cherubic cheeks. 'I don't know,' I said, honestly. 'I feel like . . . the past, that year . . . maybe I've been concentrating on that too much. Maybe I should think about the memories I *do* have and worry less about what's gone before . . .'

Felix sat on the bed and rested his arms on his thighs, raising an innocent face to look at me. 'So, all it took was a bit of male attention? That's rather shallow, lover, don't you think?'

'I told you, it was like a depression. Maybe my brain chemistry sorted itself out, maybe the change of scenery has shown me that I don't need to let the lack of a bit of memory weigh me down so much. And anyway, do you *want* me to stay home pining?' I met his eyes. His stare was wide, schoolboyish, but there was a sharp set to his lips which tinged his whole expression with cruelty.

'You're right.' Felix swept his legs up onto the bed again, his knees jiggling. 'You really have changed since the accident. You wouldn't have been like this two years ago, you know that?'

I shook my head. 'I don't remember.'

He was picking at the seam of his jeans, twisting a thread. 'And you don't remember the accident itself.'

Was this it? Did he finally want to talk about it all? 'We went off the road, they told me at the hospital. It's not amnesia, Fe, not like memories that are going to come back with time, it's the brain damage from the operation.'

'Y'see, I'm never really sure with you, Skye. Whether it's real, this memory loss thing, or whether you're just pretending, or whether you've blanked out stuff you don't want to remember.'

'Why wouldn't I want to remember? I can't remember meeting Michael, or any of the fun we had together, I can't remember getting engaged or planning the wedding . . . it's all memories I *should* have and I don't. I feel . . . cheated, that's it really. Cheated of my happiness. When I came round from the anaesthetic it was all gone, and it's not *fair!*'

'Ain't that the truth,' Felix muttered, then gave me a direct look. His eyes were hooded. 'You really, honest-to-God don't remember? No pissing me about here, Skye, this is important. You don't even have a flicker?'

I shook my head. 'Nothing. I can't even remember Michael's face, only from the photos. What is it, Fe, what are you trying to tell me here?'

'You and Mike, it wasn't quite the relationship you thought, you know.'

I felt something cold trickle through my blood. 'How do you mean?'

'Just what you were saying before, about not wanting to bounce straight to another man? It wouldn't really be the betrayal of Mike's memory that you think, that's all.' Felix got up and went to the mirror, began examining his face as he talked, checking for stubble and stray hairs. 'You fought a lot. He . . . it even made *me* uncomfortable, and you know I'm the Queen of Confrontation.' He stroked his cheeks, cocking each eyebrow in turn at his reflection. 'I guess a New Year's party was the worst place to be that night.'

'Oh come on, all couples fight now and again, it doesn't mean we didn't love one another, does it?'

Felix turned his back on the mirror. 'Look, I'm going downstairs for a drink with Lissa. Do you want to come? Oh, maybe best not, not if you've got the hots for her ex.'

'I haven't. He's just . . .'

'I am *so* not hanging around for the end of that sentence, darling. See you later.' And he flipped out of the door with an anticipatory grin already spreading across his face.

I lay on the recently vacated bed, with the new knowledge. Michael and I had been fighting. Why had no-one ever told me that earlier, right at the beginning? Everyone who had been at the party had gone to his funeral. Fe had taken my place at the crematorium, limping in his ankle cast, while I'd still been in hospital, weighed down with drips and bandages and sadness. They'd all come in afterwards, offered their condolences, and had behaved as though Michael and I had been the Couple of the Year; no-one had even mentioned that we'd fought.

And then, a week later, Faith's funeral. That stood out clearer in my mind. I'd been on the road to recovery by then and Fe had come to my bedside to describe the whole scene to me. Their parents sobbing in each other's arms. Our drama school friends at their second funeral in as many weeks, all playing the part of friends of the bereaved in their smart black suits and pale make-up.

They'd all known Michael and I had been fighting. And no-one had said anything.

I fell asleep, and woke when Felix blundered in, waving the key card randomly. 'Hey, darling.'

'Fe? It's late . . .'

'Yep. Just came to wash and brush up, then head over to Jared's.' He went into the bathroom and ran water, then began shaving, wandering around the bathroom and bedroom, unable to settle.

'Can't you stay here for a bit? I want . . . I think I really need to talk to you.'

He paused. His eyes were crystalline, as though the irises had turned into pebbles. 'I don't think there's anything to say.'

'All that stuff earlier, me and Mike, Fe . . . I need to know. All this –' I waved my hands around my head in an attempt to show my mental confusion, – 'it's like new information for me. Please, try to understand, it's like everything you tell me is one tiny part of that year coming back, little bits kind of slot into place, as though I'm some kind of jigsaw that's got all broken up and now I'm putting the pieces back in order.' I followed him into the bathroom, standing behind him as he sprayed his face with water. 'And I need you; you're the only one who can help. You're like my picture on the box lid.'

He looked at me, half his face covered in lather. 'Sometimes,' he said slowly, his mouth moving under the foam like an animation, 'sometimes it's better to leave the puzzle undone, Skye.'

'But it's my *past*.'

He smiled, but there were too many teeth on show. 'The present is what matters, darling, trust me on that. Hey, by the way, can I take the Valium with me?'

'Why?'

I got an old-fashioned look. 'Because sometimes the present includes a little recreational pharmaceutical abuse and the Valium will help me calm down afterwards. Or I might just fancy a really good night's sleep.'

'Help yourself.' I threw him the bottle and he poked it down into the pocket of his jeans. 'Just be careful.'

He waved a reckless hand. 'I'm always careful. I'll get changed over there and see you at the ball.'

'But that's not until tomorrow night! Are you not coming back between times?'

Another shaky stroke of the razor and Fe patted his face with a towel. 'Skye, darling, I'm hoping that there aren't going to *be* any "between times". This is the last time I'm going to be able to spend with Jared so I want to make the most of it.'

Another sparkling stare. 'Why don't you get Jack to come keep you company?'

I watched him, moving quickly, restlessly around the room, picking things up and putting them down, shoving things into an overnight bag and then unpacking them back onto the bed. 'Are you ever going to come down on one side or the other?' I asked.

'What? You mean boys or girls? Why should I? They both have things to recommend them, and I don't see that changing any time soon, unless there's some kind of gender-specific mutation in the works. You should try it, lover. Spread your wings a bit, get some experience.'

'But don't you ever want to settle down? Have a family?'

He froze. 'No.'

'Why not?'

'Jesus, Skye, what is it with you? Before the accident you were all short skirts and sharp heels, now you've gone *Good Housekeeping* on me.'

'I just thought . . .'

'I'll tell you, shall I? Why I don't want kids? Ever? Because – and you won't know this, because you dropped out of their lives as soon as you came out of hospital – my parents were *destroyed* when Faith died. Dad had to give up work, and Mum . . . she's never been well since. Her heart, you know.'

'I didn't . . .'

'*Fuck*, Skye, they took you in when your parents

did their “we want our freedom” act, Mum cooked you Sunday lunch every week for six months while you were waiting to get a break! They were the ones all agog for news when you auditioned, they were the ones breaking out the champagne when you got a part! Then you take to locking yourself in your house and not seeing anyone, and they’re left with broken hearts, and a son who spends every spare minute running around with trash of both genders. How do you think they feel, Skye? And I’ll tell you something, I *never* want to feel like that. So, no. I don’t want kids. I’ve seen what they do to you.’

We stared at each other. He dropped his eyes first and went back to trying to stuff his fake-fur into a holdall. ‘I’m sorry,’ I said at last.

‘Yeah.’

‘I couldn’t go and see them. I was so scared.’

‘You were like a second daughter to them, they would have understood, Skye, it would have been enough for them just to have seen you. And now . . . what? You start shaking the boys up again, make a full recovery, go live a life with a guy rich enough to keep you? Well, good luck with that, darling; I’ll just head back to missing my sister, shall I?’

I’d never heard Felix sound so bitter. His words were diamond-edged and he’d got feelings on display that I’d never seen before

‘I’ll go and see them. Your parents. You’re right, I’ve been selfish.’

'You do that.' A moment stationary, then he was back to leaping around. 'Catch you later.'

'Have a good evening.'

I watched him dance out and when the door closed, I gave into the urge to cry. *That* hadn't been the Felix I knew, it had been someone else in his skin, someone brittle and cold. The things he'd said, the pain in his eyes, none of it was my Felix. My Felix was impervious, break proof, a body full of fun and lax morals, a smile, a blown kiss and a slow dance away from who he'd been tonight.

But he had been right. At first I hadn't been able to face seeing his parents because I was afraid of the look that I'd see on their faces. That look that said I reminded them of everything they'd lost; their slow, sad, pitiful acceptance that I had lived while their daughter had died. The look that would have told me they wished it had been the other way around. *Yeah, Skye. You're a waste of space . . .*

And a tiny voice that hid right in the back of my mind whispered guilt to me. The guilt that poked at me whenever I wondered why I'd given up my seat to slump in the back with Felix . . . well, after his outburst I guess I knew now. Michael and I had fought. That was all, some stupid argument about our engagement probably, something so pathetic and disposable had meant that my best friend had taken my passenger seat and died because of it.

The tears dried stiff on my cheeks. Goose pimples rose on my arms and the back of my neck, and I remembered Jack earlier, standing with his arms clamped around himself, obviously fighting his own memory.

Jack. Jack who was giving me only half a story. Felix, who was changing in front of my eyes. I couldn't sit here with my brain spinning, I needed to do . . . something. I opened the door and saw Lissa going into Jack's room down the corridor. She had her hair on sideways and was carrying her shoes, both clear marks of someone who's been in the vicinity of Felix for a while.

I locked my room and followed her. Jack opened the door at my knock. 'Hey. Checking up to see that I'm working, eh? Genius.' He stood back to let me in. Lissa was flopped in a chair, one foot up on her thigh, massaging her toes with an expression of mingled bliss and agony.

'Hi, Skye. Wow, your Felix certainly knows how to party.'

'What did you want, Liss?' Jack folded his arms and stared at her.

'Cool down, Iceman. I came to fix some of the paperwork.' Lissa put both feet back on the floor and then looked from Jack to me, and back again. 'But I guess it can wait, if you two have a prior engagement.' She kept her eyes on Jack.

His expression never flickered.

'Actually, Lissa, I wanted to talk to you,' I said. 'About Felix.'

She held both hands up in the air. 'Whoa, back off girlfriend and let someone else play with the toys.'

'He's all yours. But what I mean was . . . what you said about him the other day. That he was on some kind of destruction course?'

'Yeah,' she said, cautiously. 'What about it?'

'Has he said anything, or . . . He was devastated right after the accident, of course, but it's just not in Fe's nature to be down for long. He was back to partying a few weeks later, and showing up at mine with a takeaway and incredibly tall tales.'

'He cries a lot, you know that?'

I stared at her. 'Felix hardly *ever* cries. He didn't even cry on the anniversary. I was a wreck, but he sat in with me, we watched some crappy TV show where everyone sings "Auld Lang Syne" and drank a bottle of Zinfandel and I cried so much I was sick.'

Jack moved, warily. 'Liss, maybe this isn't really the time for this conversation.'

'D'you know Jack, I think it might be?' She didn't take her eyes off me. 'Felix is . . . ah, I guess even *I* don't know what Felix is. One hell of an actor? Maybe. Destroying himself?' She shrugged. 'Something is with him, and I sure as Christ don't know what it is. But you ever see him on a come-down, you watch his *eyes*, Skye. That boy is ruined.'

I sat down suddenly on the edge of the bed. 'Why? Why is he pretending, why is he falling apart and not letting me know?'

'Maybe he didn't dare.' Jack sat next to me. 'Maybe he felt he had to carry the pain for the both of you.'

'Perhaps there are questions he doesn't want you to ask.' Lissa kicked her high heels back on, shuffling her toes right down into them. 'Okay, guys, time to do business. I've brought papers for you to sign, Jack.' She scuffled in her tote bag and pulled out a sheaf of typewritten A4.

Jack held the stack loosely. 'What will you do now, Liss?'

Lissa waved an arm. 'Sea, fish, plenty more. I got other clients, sweetie, other irons in the fire. The whole agency never revolved around you.'

'I know, but . . .'

'Jackie-boy, the good old U S of A is my territory. Okay, your British agency and mine have affiliations, but you want to head back to the land of teacakes and white cliffs and "gor blimey guvnor", you go alone. Right?' He shrugged. 'It's really okay,' she said, more softly. 'It was never real with us. You were lonely. You still *are* lonely, I get that, but you don't need me any more.'

'Just, after what happened . . .'

Lissa looked sharply towards me. 'Yeah, well. Maybe that was just meant to be, you ever think of that? I'll live, I *am* living. Things are going pretty good, don't waste your tears on me.' Her gaze flicked from me to Jack and back again. 'You save yourself, Brit-boy. I got the feeling that you both got a lot of saving to do, maybe you can save each other, I don't know. But I'm not a part of it any more.'

Jack smiled. It was one of his nice smiles, a genuine expression that softened the whole of his saturnine face.

'Hey, Lissa Zimmerman, you're a really nice lady, do you know that?'

'Don't shout so loud, you'll ruin my rep. Now sign here and give us both our freedom.'

I left them arguing good-naturedly about final terms and settlements and other such technical details, and went back to my room, to bed. Alone, whatever Felix might have suggested.

CHAPTER 20

After Lissa left him, papers tucked under her arm, he turned out the room lights and stood in the darkness, feeling every inch of his skin dance with the need for nicotine. Geth hadn't told Skye anything. That much was obvious from the way she was still speaking to him, still willing to be anywhere near him. His tongue prickled and the roof of his mouth was dry as the craving swept across his nerve endings; masochistically he refused to let his fingers wander towards the pack on the bedside table. Used the unfulfilled need to punish himself for all of it, the sharp needles of want niggling his nerve endings, like a dentist's drill. He should give up smoking, he knew it. Quitting the alcohol had taught him that the pain came early and left late but it still left, eventually, and it left a better, cleaner, more responsible life behind it. Giving up was *easy*, whatever he'd told Skye.

It was what the giving up meant that was difficult.

You didn't just give up the substance; you gave up everything that went with it, the lifestyle, the friends, the *feelings*. And he was very much afraid that he couldn't lose any more of those and still function as a human being.

Okay. So, he was safe a while longer. Just let it *be* a while longer, let him talk to Skye, tell her in his own words, let her make up her own mind what to think about him.

Jack ran a hand through his hair as he stood at the window watching the neon motel lights send their shimmering messages out into the waiting desert. The bright lights that meant nothing, shining into the empty dark. He'd always thought of himself as a bit like that empty darkness, a hollow, infinite space that would never fill with light. But now . . . now Skye was starting to make him see that he didn't have to be like this. That he didn't *want* to be like this, not any more. He wanted to throw himself open to her, let her in, let her brightness illuminate all those dark corners that had festered over the years.

But is wanting it enough? He wanted a new life, but that was easy. Enough money thrown at the situation and it would resolve itself. Back to Britain, back to the little farm on the edge of the moors, back to writing the books and protecting himself from the outside world, that would do it. Just feeling . . . now that was harder. After all, with feeling the good stuff – and with Skye he rather thought there'd be a lot of good stuff – would come the memories of the bad stuff. Memories he lived with by never giving them room to turn round, like caging a savage bull. Keeping them so carefully guarded that he remembered them under controlled conditions. Letting her *in* would mean letting them *out*.

He took half a step towards the dressing table, then stopped, the pain of denial blocking everything else. Would letting everything out be so bad, really? Wouldn't it be better to wipe the slate clean, bring all that darkness from inside himself into the light, where it might lose its power to hag-ride him every night through his dreams?

The urgent desperate need died back as he relaxed. Skye. Yes. Not despite her scars but because of them. Because she would understand.

CHAPTER 21

I hid in the room until the following evening, with the assistance of a kind of ad hoc room service, who brought me, rather oddly, a plate of toast, two hard-boiled eggs and an enormous pan of something which resembled paella. I wasn't about to attempt any outings downstairs, not when I might run into Gethryn, either sober or drunk, and the few times I ventured up the corridor and knocked on his door, Jack hadn't been in his room.

I did my make-up with shaking hands. Gethryn would be there tonight. I'd have to look him in the face, knowing him for what he truly was under the glamour of show business. Knowing him for the drunken letch who used his screen persona as bait, a man for whom the word 'no' was an aphrodisiac. I shivered at how close I might have come to being forced into something I didn't want, wondering how many other girls had fallen for Gethryn's patter and then found themselves trying to gloss over something that hadn't been consensual. Wondered how many had pushed the memories away behind the signed photographs he handed out like boons. Did they tell themselves that they'd wanted it? Because of who he was?

It was almost like a mini panic attack, this sudden flushing of my system with adrenaline, the desire to pee every ten seconds and the great Stomach Rebellion which made me feel alternately sick and as though everything I'd ever eaten was going to fall out of my bottom if I so much as coughed. When I checked my face in the mirror, I saw that I was almost green and my scar stood out like a bone marker under the make-up, thrown into relief by the lighting and the foundation, streaking down my forehead, splitting my eyebrow in two and stuttering to a standstill across my cheekbone. I couldn't go anywhere like this.

I began struggling out of the dress, unlacing the bodice-strapping across my chest with both hands to save time. When I heard the knock at the door, I held the velvet up against me in an attitude of Victorian shock. 'Who is it?'

'Who were you expecting?'

'Oh, Jack . . .' I pulled the door open, still attempting modesty with the flapping bodice, 'I can't go to the ball, I really can't. Don't try to make me. If you go down now I expect Ruth will still be free and she'll . . . accommodate you,' I finished, my mind suddenly flashing unwanted images of Jack being accommodated by another woman.

'Hey.' Jack held out a hand to shut me up. 'Don't worry about it.' He came in and sat on the edge of the bed. 'Take your time.'

I looked at him. He was wearing his pyjama bottoms, tightly fastened around the fly I was glad to see, bare feet and a T-shirt which was more crumple than fabric, and bore the legend 'Sweet . . . maybe. Passionate . . . I suppose. But don't ever mistake that for nice.' 'That's a *Doctor Who* quote.'

He inclined his head, gravely.

'But . . . what the hell were you going as?'

He flipped his glasses from where they were hooked into the neck of the T and pushed them on. 'Isn't it obvious?'

I began to giggle. 'Oh, my God, you're going as yourself! That's brilliant.'

'Glad you think so.' The glasses magnified his eyes and made the little flecks that danced within them look like slices of sunlight.

'Yeah. Cheating, but brilliant.'

The black lace showed against his throat under the baggy neck of the shirt, and I found that I was staring at it. The darkness of it made his skin look very pale. 'What are you staring at now?'

'The thong around your neck. Do you always wear it?'

His hand came up, almost defensively, and a finger traced the leather. 'Pretty much.'

'Even when you're working?'

There was a kind of pause, during which I suddenly realised that the thong was so much more to him than mere decoration. I didn't know what it stood for, why he wore it, but I could see in his eyes that questions about it made him wary.

'Mmm. Look, what's all this about not wanting to go to the ball?'

I sat on the bed, fiddling with the flappy bit of dress where I was still incompletely laced up. 'Jack. Look at me.'

His stare briefly traced my face before settling back into my eyes. 'What am I supposed to be seeing?'

'This!' I poked myself in the scar and stood up again. The weight of the skirt tugged the dress down a few inches and I had to perform a haulage operation in order to get the bodice to cover my chest.

'Okay. Seeing it. Refusing to believe that's what's stopping you from coming to the ball with me. Don't you think it's just a touch solipsistic to think that people will even notice? There're people down there who have spent months on their costumes, getting every detail right . . .' He gave a short, hollow laugh. 'They're really not going to be looking at your scar. And anyway, don't you want to see if I can dance?'

'You said you could.'

'Maybe I was lying.' He tilted his head to one side and gave me an unblinking stare. 'Or is it something else? Some*one* . . . oh, please tell me you're not going to let Gethryn ruin our evening! Skye, I know the guy is a bastard but . . .'

'He scared me,' I said quietly. 'What you saw in the car park, you were right, I didn't want it. He was . . . I mean, I *think* he would have stopped if I'd told him, but . . . I'm not sure, and he's said things . . . just because he's famous he seems to think he can have any woman he wants, can make her do whatever he wants.'

Despite my anxiety, when Jack ran his tongue along his lower lip, thinking, a tingle ran the length of my spine. 'Nobody has ever accused him of anything,' he said slowly. 'But then he does tend to pick girls who . . . sorry . . . have issues. Girls who might be grateful, girls he can manipulate because they think he . . .' A sudden shake of his head sent his glasses askew across his face and he pulled them off, pushed one of the side arms into his mouth. 'I tried to warn you.'

'Yeah, right, for the record, Jack, an *actual* warning might have been more use than your oblique "he's not very nice", you know. If you're going to warn someone, telling them what you're warning them about is generally better than dark, broody hinting. This isn't an episode; you don't have to keep up the tension for the full fifty minutes.' I realised that my bodice was heading floorwards again and gave it a mighty heave.

I got a grin for that. 'Sorry. Force of habit and lack of experience. Now, come on, you're not going to let him deprive you of the chance to watch me strut my funky thing, are you?'

I closed my arms against my body. 'I don't know.'

Gently he pushed me by one shoulder until I turned around. 'Do it up properly and we'll go down. Go on, I'm not looking.'

He wasn't. When I sneaked a quick glance over my shoulder I saw him staring down at his feet, wiggling his long toes against the carpet. His hair hid his face from me. 'So, then.' I began relacing the dress, refusing to let my mind go back to thinking about Gethryn when Jack was there, so darkly alluring. 'You were going to tell me about that thing around your neck?'

He did it again, raising his fingers to toy with the leather. 'It was Ryan's,' he said in such a quiet voice that I wasn't sure I'd heard.

Ryan. His best friend. Who'd been killed in the accident that had given Jack his scars. Whoo. Was there some kind of homoerotic thing going on here?

'I wear it to remind me.' And then his voice strengthened. 'Why don't you wear your engagement ring? I'd have thought it would be something you'd find it hard to be parted from.'

My fingers became clumsy. 'I . . . we . . . I don't have one.'

Why didn't I have a ring? Michael had been loaded, some kind of job in investments, regular bonuses, a collection of cars and his own flat. I'd been told all that much, seen the pictures. So why hadn't he bought me a ring? If I'd thrown it at him during that last fight at the party, why hadn't Felix mentioned it? I pulled the last string through. 'I've finished.'

'You look fabulous.' Jack's eyes gleamed behind his glasses. 'Real Skeldarian Queen. Apart from the strange smell.'

'That was Gethryn. Well, it was his drink. I've had the dress hanging out of the window ever since, but it still smells a bit . . .' I sniffed, 'fruity. Do you think I should change?'

'I really don't think anyone but me is going to notice, Skye. Honestly, it's okay, it doesn't even smell like drink any more.'

'Well, sorry, but colour me still slightly worried.'

He stood up alongside me. His height matched mine now I wore the towering shoes I'd borrowed along with the dress; my gaze was exactly level with his eyes. I could just make out the darker ring of pupil inside the near-black iris. 'Onward then.' After a momentary hesitation, Jack took my hand and looped it through his elbow. 'Come on. Let's make a grand entrance.'

'You're in your pyjamas.'

'And you smell of boiled fruit, but we can still make an entrance, can't we?'

It was, indeed, an entrance. I hadn't realised, but most people were already in the diner and our arrival coincided with a pause between tracks that the band had been playing, accompanied by images from the show projected onto the long back wall. We walked in to chatting, which died away, to be replaced by a round of applause.

I was holding my breath.

'You okay?' Jack murmured to me, over the clapping. 'Sure?'

I let my breath out in a little gasp and nodded. Jack's hold on my arm increased, pulling me hard up against his body. He smelled clean, of ironed linen and coconut shampoo, not a trace of smoke about him, so he must, I reasoned, be fairly relaxed. Which was good, one nervous wreck per couple was quite enough. 'Hey,' he whispered in my ear, 'let's find out if I was lying, shall we?'

With one arm still around me he moved out onto the dance floor which was a posh name for the space surrounding the band, who were playing in a corner of the diner and consisted of two scruffy guitarists, a sweaty drummer and a keyboard player with only one arm. Jack stepped, faultlessly, into the rhythm of the music. He put both hands on my waist until we swayed in unison to the indie rock track, grinning at me as he did so. 'You can dance,' I said into his ear as the music drove us closer together. 'You're pretty good, for a miserable git.'

'Yep.' He stepped around me, sliding his body around mine, with maximum contact, until the velvet of my skirt wound across his skinny hips and drew us even closer. He moved like a snake and actually seemed to be enjoying himself, for once. 'Love dancing. Always have.'

'All right.' The band took the tempo up, driving into a Green Day cover. 'Let's see how good you *really* are.'

I lost myself in the music, in the proximity of Jack's whirling body, in the occasional close moments when he pressed his hot skin against mine and whispered, 'Had enough yet?'

'Not while you're still standing, Whitaker,' I whispered back, and he laughed and threw himself back into the beat.

At last the band took a break and, panting and giggling, Jack and I left the floor. His face had softened; without the lines of stress he usually carried he was more than just good-looking, he was quite breathtaking. Little shivers of enjoyment rippled the surface of my skin. 'Hey, you go and sit over there. I'll get us both a drink.'

I perched on a chair just inside the doors which were open to the yard, in the way of the cooling breeze, and admired the costumes on display. I couldn't see Felix, but there were a lot of Shadow Planet refugees dotted around the room; in their furs and dark glasses they were interchangeable and any one of them could have been him, although I would have taken bets on him being the one weaving furiously closer to the bar which had been erected behind the usual food-counter. A number of beautiful girls wearing pilot costumes were clustering around a sober-looking Gethryn, who, to my relief, hadn't even acknowledged my presence, the Thulos telepaths moved ethereally in character through the crowd and over near the door to the reception area I saw the two lads dressed as the alien Skeel race that I'd noticed before, weighted nearly double by the cylinders on their backs and I wondered how they'd managed to get those through the doors.

For a while I sat, legs stretched out, and watched the rise and fall of groupings. Everyone seemed automatically drawn to those wearing similar costumes, so the crowd rapidly clotted into sets of B'Ha, Shadow Planet residents, Thulos and pilots, with the alien races forming a separate subset on the other side of the room. Two token Klingons and a solitary person inside an inflatable Dalek suit free-floated for a while then latched onto each other and were drawn into the rest of the aliens. Everyone seemed happy, relaxed.

I could see Jack across the room, talking to Jared, who was wearing his full regalia as Prince of Skeldar. They saw me watching. Jared raised his glass and Jack winked, flicking back his sweat-dampened hair, and I smiled back, the smile dying a little when a young man approached me. He was cropped-headed and massively stubbled, as though his hair grew in a consistent ring around his whole skull, and was wearing a crew T-shirt, jeans and an earpiece. 'Hi,' he said in a business-like way. 'You're Skye Threppel, right?' He came and stood in front of me, blocking my view of the diner. 'We need to have a conversation.'

'Why, are you trying to avoid someone?' I looked up at him, unwilling to stand up and risk spiking him on the unfamiliar heels.

'I mean, we need to talk with you.'

'Who's *we*?'

'Just come with me please.' He touched a walkie-talkie device at his belt and spoke into a headset. 'Yeah, she's with me. I'm bringing her in now.'

'What? Bringing me in where?'

'Please. Just come with me.' He reached out a burly arm which, I was slightly comforted to see, bore a tattoo of a Shadow Ship, and hauled me to my feet, where I tottered for a second until I got my balance.

'Brandon? What's up?' Jack arrived back at my side and pushed a bottle of chilled water into my hand. 'What do you want with Skye?'

'Hello, Mr Whitaker.' Was it my imagination or did this official guy look a bit shame-faced? 'Maybe you better come along too.'

'Where?' Jack took his glasses off and hooked them back into his shirt. His eyes had gone chilly. 'What's this about?'

'I've been told to bring Miss Threppel to the office. They'll explain there.'

The three of us walked from the diner. Jack led the way and I followed the security guy, who wove through the crowd as though no-one in the world existed apart from him. I saw a few glances thrown at us, a couple of conversations interrupted to watch us pass through the room, one pilot nudged another and one of the Skeel half-raised his tinted visor. It all made me very uncomfortable, and I was glad when we'd reached the reception area again.

'This way.'

Again, with Jack leading, I was waved through, past the reception desk and into the back offices of the motel, through a small room with a telephone and a TV showing a Fawlty Towers episode, into a tiny square room with only one high window. It was a little bit like a cell, even down to the concrete floor, although it had several plastic chairs and a cast-off looking table sitting directly in the middle. On one of the chairs, elbows on the table, sat a man I'd seen around the place all week. He too wore a crew T-shirt but was older than most of the backstage guys. His hair was a cropped salt-and-pepper mix, but his jaw was square and his face uncompromisingly good-looking. He looked as though he'd walked out of *Law and Order*.

'Hey, Jay.' He stood up to shake Jack's hand. Didn't offer to shake mine.

'Hi, Gary. What's going on?' Jack turned around and I shuffled up closer to him. Although Brandon had gone to stand over near the door, he was still too present for my liking. 'This is all a bit formal, isn't it?'

He looked over at the little fold-up table and I saw his eyebrows lift. On the table sat my quiz answer sheet. I recognised the crossed out answer to the name of Defries's mother, where I'd scratched out the right answer and replaced it with Mary in order to throw first prize. Were they going to accuse me of that? But it hadn't worked, had it?

'Kinda has to be formal, I'm afraid.' Gary had a gruff voice, again straight out of Central Casting. 'Some serious accusations have been made.'

I made a little squeaky sound and Jack looked at me sharply. 'Gethryn?'

Gary smiled. 'No.'

Jack closed his eyes in a long blink. 'Okay, what then?'

Gary turned to me. 'You're Skye Threppel?'

'Yes, I'm Skye.'

'And you won our quiz.' It wasn't a question. He picked up my answers and flipped through the papers. 'Mind telling me how you did that?'

My fingers found each other and twiddled in front of me, fingertips tracing scars. 'I answered more questions right than anyone else.'

'Smart lady, eh?' Gary stood up and I was reassured to see that he was only a couple of inches taller than me. Brandon, the burly man with the tattoo who'd fetched me away from the party, wasn't much taller. Neither of them was physically overwhelming, but I began to feel a little bit intimidated.

'You asked.'

'There's one question here . . . 'Name the pilot who fired the first shot in the Shadow War'.' Again, not framed as a question, but it sounded as though he wanted an answer.

'Jevan Klye.' I couldn't help myself. 'Piloting the Shadow Ship D'Veen.'

'That's the answer you gave here.'

'Because it's the right answer.'

'And how did you know that, Miss Threppel?' He ran both hands over his streaked hair, looking tired.

I put my water bottle down on the table, very carefully. 'Because I watched the episode.' Lots of times, actually. It had been a very early episode in Series One, but hadn't been released on DVD because of some kind of copyright issues. I'd burned it to DVD myself, via my laptop, but I wasn't going to admit that in case it was against the law.

'Look, Gary . . .' Jack began, but was stopped with a raised hand.

'Please, Jay, let her go on.'

'Well, that's it really. I knew the answer.'

'How about here?' Gary pointed at my changed answer. 'How come you altered this?'

'I . . .'

'It wasn't, how shall I say this, because Mr Whitaker here fed you the answers before you even sat down to the quiz and you didn't want to arouse suspicion by getting too many right?'

Jack made a startled noise.

'What? Jack? Why on earth would he do that?' I looked across at him and Jack was looking back at me, his expression as baffled as I'm sure mine was.

'You tell me, Miss Threppel. You tell me.' Gary sat down again. There was a long pause, during which I ran through every conversation Jack and I had had in case he might have given me some clue as to what the quiz contained. 'You see, we've had a lot of complaints.'

'About what?' I wasn't sure whether to feel indignant or not, yet.

'There have been concerns expressed about the fairness of allowing you to participate in what is a very important part of the *Fallen Skies* convention when you have had a . . . err . . . relationship with the main writer.'

‘Oh, come on!’ Jack was bristling. ‘Skye and I have had no kind of relationship.’

‘Okay, you deny that she’s been in your motel room on several occasions?’

‘Well, no.’

‘But that was all just . . . stuff!’ I protested. ‘Personal stuff.’

‘Yeah.’ Jack put a hand on my shoulder; I leaned into him for solidarity. ‘We’re friends. That’s all, Gary. We never met before Wednesday.’

‘Right. But even if that were true, we’ve got people saying . . .’ Gary consulted another piece of paper, ‘that Miss Threppel conducted a meeting with Mr Tudor-Morgan in the car park of this motel, where you sat, and I quote, “in physical proximity” for several minutes?’

‘But that was *after* the quiz!’

‘So you *don’t* deny that. What about an unauthorised attempt to access *Fallen Skies* material from Jay’s laptop? You know anything about that?’

I opened my mouth and closed it again. Bloody Felix and his trying to look for information! There was a sick feeling starting at the base of my throat.

‘All right. Do you deny that you went to Mr Tudor-Morgan’s accommodation yesterday, that you let yourself in, and that some minutes later you were alone with him in the bathroom?’

‘He was in the shower. I wasn’t.’ I sounded sulky but really it was just me trying to avoid hyperventilating. This was a set up.

‘Have you, or have you not, ever been – now

how shall I put this so as not to cause offence? – naked, or partly naked with Mr Tudor-Morgan or Mr Whitaker and have you ever kissed, touched intimately or had sexual congress with Mr Tudor-Morgan or Mr Whitaker, delete where applicable.'

I frowned. 'No! *Delete where applicable*?'

'Sorry. It's a standard lawyers' form.' Gary rubbed his eyes and the man leaning on the wall with his arms folded, shifted position, as though both of them were embarrassed by this. 'Y'see Skye,' he leaned forward and the table rocked, 'it's not about what you've done, or haven't done. It's the fact that you *could have*. There's a lot of young people out there who wanted that part in the series. And, if I might say it, you do look *awful* close with Jay.'

'Gethryn kissed me. That's all that happened,' I muttered. Behind me, Jack swore.

Gary moved his eyes slowly over my face. They lingered on the scar, moved off and came back to it. Twice. 'Yeah. But d'you see it from the organisers' point of view? There's an element of doubt in your winning. I'm real sorry, Skye, but that's how it is.'

'Fuck it.' Jack moved forward to lean on the table. 'She won fair and square, Gary, and you know it. Even if we *had* been sleeping together, you know me well enough to say that I'd never give information out like that.'

'For the record, I don't think you cheated. But it isn't what I think that matters here.' Gary lowered his voice. 'And while *you* would never give anything away, there's Geth in this equation, and can you truly say that he'd never fix the quiz?' The two men stared at one another for a few seconds.

'He never had access to the answers,' Jack almost breathed. 'I made sure.'

'It's not about what *happened*, Jay. It's about what *could have* happened. We have to be seen to be doing it right, or next year our viewing figures get blown outta the water by some Stargate shit.'

Jack straightened up and replaced his glasses. 'Okay,' he said tiredly. 'Okay. Yes, you're right. We have to be seen to be doing it right. Course.' He ran both hands through his hair, raking them down to his shoulders, which he raised in a quick shrug. 'Sorry, Skye.'

'You're taking the prize away from me?' Oh my God, Felix! He was already planning his future LA career; knowing him he'd already picked out his Oscars' outfit. And written the acceptance speech.

Gary shrugged. 'We'll move every winner up a prize category. And don't worry, Jay, we'll say that there was a mistake with the marking system, you won't be implicated.'

Jack gave him a dark look. 'That,' he said tightly, 'is very kind of you, but the least of my worries.'

I thought of Jennifer, second-prize winner, and her face when she learned she'd won the date with Gethryn. I didn't think she would regard being bumped up to being an extra as an improvement, particularly when Gethryn wasn't even going to be in the series any more. And third-prize winner, now Gethryn's date, was a bloke. Probably safer.

I only realised that I was crying when Jack held out a handkerchief. 'Go on. It's clean.'

I blubbed into it for a second, then looked at him. 'Where did you have it? There's no pockets in that.'

'Trouser leg.'

'Oh. Ewwww.'

'Go back to the ball. We won't announce this until tomorrow, give you a chance to get clear, okay?' Gary looked at Jack. 'Best I can do.' Then his eyes rested on me, almost kindly. 'I'm real sorry, Skye. But, you gotta see it from our point of view, and you and him seem real tight, y'know?'

'Yes,' I sniffed. 'But I didn't even know who Jack was when I first met him.'

Gary grinned. 'How's your ego, Iceman?'

'It's good, thanks. Come on, Skye, let's go back. We can try and enjoy ourselves.'

I just shook my head and let Jack lead the way back, squeezing past an eyebrow-raising Antonio on the reception desk to the entry to the diner. Through the doors I could see that some of the Thulos had cast off their restrictive all-enveloping muslin wraps to dance to the band, a Klingon was smoking outside, smoke straining through his pasty forehead looking very peculiar, and the inflatable Dalek was attempting to snog a pilot. I had to find Felix and tell him what had happened, before one of the organisers did.

'Skye.' Jack steered me into a dark corner near

the stairs in the reception area. 'I am truly sorry about this.'

'Not your fault.' I blew my nose again.

'Well, it is. I should have known, should have stayed away from you. But I . . .' He stopped talking suddenly, and his hands began fidgeting. The arm of his glasses made its way back between his teeth.

'Cigarette?' I asked, sympathetically.

'Kill for one,' he agreed. 'But not important. Not now. Come here.' Shoving his glasses resolutely into the neck of his shirt he manoeuvred us further back until we were hidden by the shadows under the deep staircase. 'You've heard the phrase "might as well be hung for a sheep as a lamb"?'

'Well, of course I have. I'm British.'

'Good. Here's my sheep then.' With his eyes boring their way through to my brain, he tilted my chin with a finger and, when my mouth reached the requisite angle, lowered his lips to mine and kissed me.

My mouth opened under his gentle onslaught. Lips parted, I kissed him back, and suddenly we were in a tight clinch; my hands wound into his hair, his fingers ran up my arms and down over my back, making my skin burn where he touched it, and sing with the pressure of the velvet where he stroked the dress.

He was one hot kisser, no doubt about it. He ran his tongue along the underside of my upper lip, sending pulses of warmth through my bloodstream, bit gently on my lower lip until it swelled, grazed his fingertips along my collarbone until I almost fell off my high heels.

'God. Jack,' was all I could say when he eventually stepped back. My mouth tasted of oranges from the juice he'd drunk at the bar, and all my nerve endings were standing to attention, waiting for the next move.

'Yay.' He let out a breath which sounded like he'd been holding it since before we'd gone into that room. 'Genius. I'm a bit impressed myself.'

'That was . . .'

'Yes. It was. I think I need to sit down. Well, maybe in a minute. Bloody hell, what possessed me to wear *these*?' He moved the pyjama trousers around carefully, re-tying the cord that kept them closed. 'Better. Right. Look, hate to abandon you after that . . . little moment, but I really, *really* need a smoke. I'm going to pop up to my room, grab my pack and then I'll meet you outside, okay?'

'Okay,' I half-whispered, running my tongue over my now-pouting lower lip.

'Back in five.' With a last, hair-raising kiss dropped on the base of my neck and a lazy finger traced over my mouth, he was gone.

My heart was still thundering so loudly that I couldn't hear the band playing in the diner, only the other side of the doors, and I found myself touching my lips with a feeling close to disbelief. Jack. Not only sensationally good-looking but a fantastic kisser? My skin felt alive, and the dress was charged with static, giving off little sparks whenever I moved. Wow. I needed to sit down. But I needed to find Felix more.

I slipped out of the shoes and with them hanging from a finger, and my other hand hitching up the skirts of the dress, I stepped out into the subtle lighting effects of the diner. Continuous scenes from the show were still being projected, but people walked through the beams, causing images to be flashed onto skin, making everyone look chameleon-like and unfamiliar.

'Lissa!' I spotted the slim figure, wearing a gold spray-on catsuit and crystal tiara, hanging around by the bar. 'Have you seen Felix?'

She turned slowly, careful not to spill her drink. 'Hello, Skye. He's . . .' an emphatic arm stroked the air, 'somewhere.'

'I really need to talk to him.' Needed to get things straight with him before I could even think about what had happened . . . *was happening* with Jack. I didn't want Felix to think badly of me, was what it came down to.

A slender shrug and I sighed. Much as I was growing to quite like Lissa, I just wished that sometimes she'd give me an absolute, definite answer.

'Just out of curiosity – what did you come as?' I looked at her slender figure, not a misplaced bump or dimple anywhere.

'A diamond ring,' she enunciated slowly.

'Lovely. Very . . . sci-fi.' I looked around the crowd and at last spotted Felix, minus his fur coat, standing in a corner with one arm wrapped around Jared. They were laughing hysterically and I seriously hoped that he wasn't too drunk because I needed him to concentrate. I walked over to them.

'Fe . . . we need to go somewhere quiet.'

Jared laughed louder. 'Man, I don't know whether to love you or despise you. Is there anyone here you *haven't* had?'

Felix tipped his chin up, confrontationally. 'This isn't like that. But Skye, does it have to be now?'

Jared touched his shoulder. 'I'll see you later, babe.'

'Jared!' But Jared was melting into the crowd, a few last-minute autograph hunters at his heels. 'Great. Just great.' Felix turned on me. 'This had better be good, darling.'

'It's not.' I took his arm and drew him into the relative peace of the gap between the two open doors, through which the night breeze was cooling things down a little. There, holding my high heels in one hand and Felix's elbow in the other, I told him about the little scene in the office. About his losing out on the prize.

Felix stood absolutely still. There was no trace of expression on his face, nothing to tell me whether he was devastated or amused by the accusations. No sign that he was on my side either. I finished telling him that Gary hadn't believed that anyone *had* fed me the answers but that they had to be seen to be doing the right thing, and waited.

I didn't have a long wait. Fe shook his head hard, like a horse that's been bitten by a fly, then looked at me with dead eyes. 'You stupid little bitch,' he said.

'Fe, I didn't . . .'

'Didn't *what*, lover? Didn't do it? Oh, maybe not, but you wanted Gethryn Tudor-Morgan, and you've been fooling around with Whitaker for anyone to see. If you'd had any sense you'd have stayed clear of the both of them but, no. Skye sees, Skye wants, Skye takes.'

'That's not fair!'

'But they weren't playing, were they?' Felix had both hands bunched by his sides and his words were coming out in short bursts, like verbal punches. 'They weren't falling for the poor little girl routine. Maybe they saw right through it, saw the *real* you underneath this whole "I'm so damaged" act, maybe they saw you for the manipulative, self-obsessed *whore* that you really are!'

'Hey.' I looked up and Jack was standing beside us, unlit cigarette between his fingers. 'It's a misunderstanding. No need to take it out on Skye, Felix.' In one smooth move he turned away from Fe, caught me by the elbow and half-dragged me out through the doors, my shoes still hanging from my finger. Once in the open air he lit his cigarette. 'Why did you tell him? In the middle of all this? Couldn't it have waited?'

'It had to come from me, Jack. That was only right.'

There was a noise behind us. Felix was standing a few feet away, hands on hips. His T-shirt was sweat-drenched. His hair had flopped from its spikes across his forehead and his eyes were almost dark in his pale face. He came fast, before either of us knew what he intended; his compact body hit Jack in the midriff, shoulder first, sending Jack skewering down onto the dusty ground, then his fists followed up with a poorly aimed double blow to the face. But Felix was drunk and Jack was fitter and taller. He sliced to his feet underneath Felix, pushing him over until Fe thumped onto his back, lying sprawled and breathless with fists still balled. 'Don't,' Jack said, straightening up. 'Really. Don't.' He retrieved his cigarette and blew the dust off the tip. 'Bugger. It's gone out.'

I looked up and saw a small crowd beginning to gather in the doorway, all staring out into the yard, where Felix lay trying to get his breath back while Jack, looking rumpled, frantically tried to relight his cigarette. I wanted to say something, anything to make this all right again, but I couldn't think of a bloody thing.

Lissa rescued us. She arrived at the front of the crowd, looking spectacular and thin and bringing with her two of the burliest security men. 'Okay, nothing to see, guys.' She spoke over the speculative rumblings. 'Just a private matter?' The question was aimed at Jack, over my head. He did the twisted-mouth thing again and blew smoke high into the air, and she marshalled the security team to push everyone back inside the diner. Just before she followed, she hissed at Jack, 'Take your bar-brawl somewhere else, Ice, yeah? Go play out the jealous boyfriend performance where no-one can see. I can't hold this forever.'

Jack jerked his head at me and I followed as he walked further out into the night, stopping when we got past the circle of lights which described the edge of the car park. Felix came with us at a wary distance. This wasn't over.

'Okay.' Jack leaned against the tree under which I'd met Gethryn. 'What's this *really* about?'

I shook my head. 'Felix is angry that I hung around with you and Geth. He thinks it's all my fault that I've been disqualified because I . . . flirted with you both.'

But Jack wasn't looking at me. He was looking at Felix, whose head hung forward as though it was too heavy for his neck. The soaked T-shirt had pulled out of shape and twisted around his body and his carefully trendy jeans were caked with dust. He was crying, lumpy tears streaking down his face and rolling onto his chest. I thought back to what Lissa had said, about watching for the real Felix, behind the drugs and the sex-addiction. Was *that* what I was seeing now – the real man?

'Fe?'

A slow, uneven headshake and a long, sobbing intake of breath. It didn't even look like Felix any more, this leaden, hunched figure. His hair had gone flat, and the old Felix would have been frantic, teasing fingers through it to spike it back. This man just stood, unaware.

'Leave him a minute, Skye.' Jack's voice was surprisingly gentle, considering that Felix had tried to beat his head in. 'Let him settle.'

Felix collapsed forward, landing on his hands and knees then crouching back so that his legs were against his chest and his arms encircled them, pulling himself in. He laid his head on his drawn-up knees and continued to sob, white-knuckled.

I felt sympathetic tears prick my own eyes and gulped past the clogging in my throat so that I could speak. 'Is this drugs?'

Felix spoke then, his voice harsh and torn. 'No. It's you.'

Jack, showing extraordinary courage I thought, crouched beside him. 'Felix,' he said softly, 'losing the quiz prize doesn't have to be the end of it, you know. I'm writing a part, not huge but pivotal, Seran Vye. I think you'd be perfect for it. I'll recommend you.'

'You'd do that, just for this?' I stared at him.

'Hey, it's still my show. I can do what I like until I hand over.' A steady look. 'It's partly my fault you lost out. I should have known. I should have stayed away from everyone. It was just . . .' He lowered his head and hid his expression. 'So, yeah. Making amends.' He reached out and rubbed Felix's back gently. 'But this, this is more.'

Fe looked up then. 'Yes,' he said. 'It's more. It's fucking *everything*.' Jack waited. A few seconds passed and Felix reached out. Grabbed Jack's hand and held it. 'I'm falling apart.'

'You've been holding it together too long. Let us in, Felix. It'll help.'

Their joined hands were white with pressure from Felix's fingers. 'Fe.' I bent down too, letting the dress sweep the dust. 'If it's me, if it's something I did, I'm sorry.'

A muffled laugh. Felix had his mouth pressed against his knees now, as if he was afraid words would leak out without his permission. 'You! It's all been about you, hasn't it?'

Jack moved until he was hugging Felix, arms around the huddled body. 'Felix, you have to tell us. You're going to break down completely if you try to keep everything inside.'

Fe half-raised his head. 'How do you know all this shit?' Then he slumped again, resting his face against Jack's chest. 'It hurts.'

'Then talk.'

A huge breath, like an inverted sigh. 'I know what caused the accident. I've always known. And Skye . . . I'm never sure how much she's really forgotten and how much she's pretending.' He spoke into Jack's shirt, one hand still gripping Jack's, the other wound into the fabric like a child holding his mother's skirts. 'She can't face it, y' see. Her life . . . that perfect life that she thinks she was living . . . a total fucking sham. All of it.'

Suddenly I could taste blood. 'Felix?'

'Hey, easy.' Jack spoke as though Fe was a nervous animal. He carried on rubbing Fe's back, small circular motions like a mother trying to bring up her baby's wind. It smeared the dust and sweat into streaking mud but Felix was beyond caring.

He looked at me. There was nothing cherubic about his face now; in fact it was almost demonic. 'You don't get it, do you? It was never real, you and Mike. You weren't engaged at all, it was just a story you told people. Oh, you told lots of stories, Skye, how you "only just" missed out on being cast in *Being Human*, you were offered *Mamma Mia* but had to turn it down, you were on the shortlist to be the new *Doctor Who* companion . . . all stories. All fucking *fake*. All to make you look better. Mike and Faith were dating, Skye. Seeing each other behind your back.'

Suddenly it was as though Jack didn't exist. All I could see was Felix, head up, defiant. 'How long?' I whispered. 'How long had they . . . ?'

'All the fucking time.' Felix's voice was so cold the air almost vaporised around the words. '*All the fucking time*, Skye. And you know what? They had a good time. Not that destructive, screaming thing you had going on with him.'

'Then why . . . ?'

Even as I said it, I felt the huge plummeting in my stomach. Like my internal organs were in a lift with a snapped cable, like freefall. And a new understanding slammed me between the eyes, like a cashmere-wrapped anvil; the force nearly knocked me to the floor. *All those little whispers, that nasty, snidey voice in the back of my head, telling me how worthless I was all the time . . . I'd thought it was my subconscious. But they'd been memories . . . memories of Michael . . .*

'Now let me think . . .' Fe was still in my face. 'You dated him. He took you out, gave you a good time and suddenly – *WHAM* – you're in love. You wouldn't leave him alone, you stalked him, turned up at his flat all suspenders and high heels . . . he *had* to date Faith without you knowing because we were all afraid of what you might do. To him, to them, to yourself.' Felix raked his eyes up and down me. 'You were mental, Skye. Really mental.'

'Easy.' Jack repeated. He'd stopped rubbing Felix's back now, but was still holding his hand.

Felix raised an eyebrow over a glacial stare. 'I reckon you don't want to know the truth about your girlfriend's past life.'

'We all have things to hide.' Jack was even, but cool.

'Mike was . . . he kind of liked it. He'd lead her on, pretend they still had a relationship, that Skye could save it if she tried hard enough.' Felix shook his head. 'But the night of the accident . . .' Now he looked at me directly. 'You caught them. Found them snogging in the bathroom at the party. I'm not surprised you don't remember, even *I* tried to wipe that little image out of my head. We thought we'd have to call the police. But you passed out.' He looked up at Jack now. 'I put her in the back of the car, but on the way home she came round. Saw them sitting there in the front, with Faith's hand on Mike's cock.' Felix gave me a look that nearly seared the flesh from my skeleton, a look so deep with cold that mammoths could have walked on it. 'What did you think would happen, Skye?'

'I didn't know,' I whispered. 'I didn't know.' My skin was chilled but inside I felt a huge fire flame up. 'I caused the accident?'

'You tried to climb through. Just undid your seatbelt and started trying to get at Mike, going for him with your nails, all flailing and screaming . . . grabbing at the wheel . . . I got hold of you, tried to drag you off but then you went for my face . . . kicked Mike in the head. Your whole life was a fake, Skye. Even your grief is fake. You weren't Mike's real girlfriend, and *you killed my sister.*'

'So all this . . . you used me to win you that part?' Shock had made my voice shake a little. Jack looked at me and his eyes were huge.

'I didn't know what to do.' Felix hid his face again and all the anger seemed to have drained away. 'I *liked* you. Yeah, you were batshit crazy but you . . . you were always nice to me, you know? Before. And I'd got no-one. My parents, oh, they love me all right but all they really want is Faith back, they can't *see* me any more. They used to be interested, involved, wanting to know how the auditions went, how my life was going . . . and now . . .' He held up empty hands. 'I've lost them too, you know? And you were all I had. So I . . .

And then, last year, at the convention they had the quiz. And I got to thinking . . . maybe, if they held it again you would . . . I *need* that part, Skye. I've got nothing else.'

'Skye,' Jack's voice was calm. 'Take it easy. You're shaking. And Felix, you need to calm down. Let's go back to the diner, then I reckon you ought to head to bed.' Those super-nova eyes met mine, crawled inside my head. 'You'd better come, too. We need to talk.'

'I don't know what to say to you.'

He got to his feet, pulling a reluctant Felix along with him, hands still joined. 'Fuck, you smell good.' Fe's voice was stronger; he'd managed to work in a little bit of the old Felix's flirty tone. 'But I don't know about these clothes.'

'I'm a writer. I don't have to *look* good.' With barely a glance at me, Jack began helping Felix across the sand towards the lights of the motel and the noisy flickering that was the ball in full swing.

CHAPTER 22

Skye's face had gone beyond pale and into moonstruck. Jack kept his eyes forward, concentrating on Felix, whose body was shuddering with something like repressed sobs. 'Take it easy,' he muttered, but for a million pounds he couldn't have told anyone which one of them he was saying it to, or was it to himself?

Her face. Her pain. Oh God, her pain. He could see it, feel it and his arms ached with something like the desire to touch her. Was it only minutes ago that he'd kissed her? He felt so much older now, millennia settling in his bones, the weight of experience dragging at his feet as the new implications pulled at the edges of Skye's mouth and made her expression stretch.

'I killed them,' he heard her whisper above the scratch and scrape of sand. 'I killed them. It was me.'

She stumbled and it was all he could do not to drop Felix there on the dirt and catch her, wrap his arms around those frail shoulders and pull her close. Whisper into her hair that the agony would pass. It would never leave her, but it would pass, and life would take on a new sharpness as she realised she was living it not just for herself but for Faith and Michael as well. But Felix leaned in more heavily and he had to let Skye find her own feet, balance herself.

'Take it easy,' he murmured again, for her this time. Was this why he felt the way he did? Had he seen it coming all this time?

'They're dead because of me.'

No, he wanted to say. You might have been instrumental in their deaths, but their careless brutality was their real undoing. Your best friend, seeing the man you were convinced you were in love with, and him, teasing you, torturing you with thoughts of a life you'd never have. What kind of people *were* they? *What did they think would happen?*

But he couldn't say any of it. Felix was holding his hand as if it was his anchor to sanity and it would be callous to disregard his feelings, even if it made her feel better. She was grieving all over again, not for the deaths of her friend and lover but for the death of the life she'd thought she had had.

Jack let his gaze brush over her and the sudden scalding of memory made him drop his eyes. All that emotion, everything he had denied himself, he could see it all on display in Skye. And now he was beginning to realise just how much he'd pushed away all these years, how he'd kept himself isolated just so that he didn't have to feel anything. It was no wonder they called him the Iceman.

He'd always assumed it was some kind of compliment, that the name meant he was on top of it all, his head was cool enough to deal with life; not that they'd seen right through him to the lack of caring, that lack of connection with anyone, that he'd let run him for so long.

And was he better for it? Was Jack Whitaker really a nicer man for never allowing himself to cry? Did never really letting go make you a superior person? Or did it just allow you to feel superior to anyone who suffered? Jack shook his head. *Am I really heartless or am I just empty?*

CHAPTER 23

The party had reached that stage of drunkenness where people were coming and going and falling over all the time, in various permutations of sexuality, so Felix and Jack's hand-in-hand re-entry was largely ignored. I came in behind them. Although I knew it was hot in the diner, I was still chilled, even my stomach felt frozen.

'Right,' Jack kept his voice low and even. 'Think you'd better get upstairs.'

Felix shrugged. 'Need my coat. It's over there.'

I rummaged around until I found the soft fur heaped in a careless pile in a corner. Went to pass it over to Felix but he snatched it from me, groped around inside it for a second then produced a little brown bottle. He grabbed it and upended it into his mouth, then pulled the coat up around his shoulders as though he was cold, too.

'Was that Valium?' My voice sounded hoarse and strained, as though normal questions were just too banal to utter. 'Fe?'

'Yeah. Want to sleep, don't want to think. Don't want all this hanging all night.'

I was about to say something about ODing, but Jack caught my eye and gave his head a tiny shake. 'Right. When those take effect you'd better get yourself into bed, okay? I'll go find Jared and get him to take care of you.'

Felix gave a grin which belied the streaked cheeks and desperate eyes. 'Oh yeah? You up for a threesome, Mr Whitaker?' But there was a fake note in his voice, as though he was acting, badly. 'Think I might just take you up on that.'

It hurt to see him trying to slip back into his old self, the carefree player of games. Now I knew what was running underneath it all, his contempt for me, the loss and grief that he carried. 'Jack,' I whispered, 'I need to talk to Felix alone.'

'I don't know if that's . . .'

'Please.'

'Hey. As long as you know what you're doing. As long as you're prepared for the consequences.' A quick flash of some hidden emotion, not humour. 'And we need to talk too. There are things . . . I think you need to know about me.'

'Because of what Felix said?'

He stared down at his bare feet, now filthy with a mixture of dirt and sand. 'Partly. And partly because of what happened earlier.'

My lips gave a kind of sympathetic throb. 'Oh. That.'

'Yes. That. It's not . . . straightforward.' He stood up. 'Right. I'll catch up with you in a minute.' He slipped back out through the doors. I saw women turn to watch him go and my lips throbbed again.

'Fingers,' Felix said, behind me.

'Sorry.' It was automatic. 'Fe . . . Why? Before . . . before the accident, why was I like that? Why was I so awful to be around?'

He shrugged. 'Background, I guess.'

'And why don't I know what I was like? Why does everything I *can* remember seem . . . I dunno, normal?'

'Because it was normal. For you. That was how you always behaved, how you always were. Why should it stand out as being different? You were needy, difficult, a bitch who acted out . . . It was all just the Skye we knew and lo . . . *knew*.'

'I'm sorry.'

Another shrug. 'You say.'

'I really don't remember. Everything is so . . . scattered. I can't make sense of any of the things I *can* remember, all just scenes and snapshots. You have to believe me.' I went quiet, looking down at my feet. 'After the accident . . . why didn't you tell the police?'

An explosive laugh. 'Is that what you're worried about? That I'll turn you in? Is that *really* what concerns you most at this moment, Skye, whether you're going to get into trouble?' He pushed his face close up against mine so that I could see the narrowness of his pupils and the shiny gleam of denied tears. 'I'll never spend another Christmas with Faith. We'll never go to another audition, we'll never sing happy birthday to our mother, never sit in the little study shooting the crap. I'll never be an uncle. I'll never see her in white on her wedding day. My beautiful, wonderful sister is dead.' A slow tear escaped from under his lashes. 'And all you're worried about is whether I'm going to tell the police.'

'It's not all, not by a long way.'

'Yeah?' Felix stared at me, his eyes tracing the outline of my face. 'You've really changed, Skye, I mean, totally. Like you've been re-written from the inside. But I wonder . . .' he raised a hand and slack fingers held my chin, turning my face from side to side, 'is it enough? Could it ever be enough?'

'I think you should. Tell the police the real reason for the accident. Tell them what I did.'

'Whoa, now *that* would never have come from the Skye I knew! What is it, atonement you're after, lover? You think if I make you suffer it'll make me feel better – well, sweetie, I'm here to tell you that *nothing* will make it better. Nothing will bring her back. So that's what I'm going to do – nothing. Because I want you to remember every day, you smashed something that you could never afford to pay for.'

'She was my friend.' I put my hand up to touch his fingers where he held my face. 'Whatever she and Michael did, she was still my friend, and I wouldn't have had it end like this for anything.'

For a second I saw the façade crack and a

glimpse of the old Felix, *my* Felix, peeping out. 'Oh, Skye . . .' His fingers brushed mine, twined, joined over the screaming ruin that was my heart. Then fell away. 'But are you really different? Can anyone really change themselves that much?'

'The old me is gone. Wiped out by going through a windscreen at sixty miles an hour.' I tried to make a joke of it. 'It's amazing what it does for your personality, having your skull opened up on an operating table.'

He shrugged again and turned away, his shoulders lowering in tired defeat. 'I dunno,' he said, rocking slightly. 'It's just words, Skye. It's just words.'

I watched him ricochet through the crowd like a large-scale bagatelle game, making his way towards the exit. The party was beginning to break up now, the tighter knots were starting to move towards the bar for a night's solid drinking; I watched the Thulos contingent stagger arm-in-arm through the door out into the night, seeing Jack just beyond the circle of light, a shadow watching me.

I needed fresh air. Needed Jack. Surely he must have finished his cigarette by now? I moved towards the open doors to the outside, cannoning off the now somewhat deflated Dalek, whose eyepiece was drooping carpetwards. Saw, over near the band, Felix similarly bouncing off one of the pair of Skeel boys, catching him off balance and sending him toppling backwards under the weight of his 'carbon dioxide' cylinder. It was so heavy that it pulled itself free from the harness that kept it on his back, performed two long bounces and then vanished into a corner. I had just begun to move towards Jack again when the whole place went mad.

First was the noise. A huge, deep sound like a giant sneeze followed so quickly by the blast that I nearly didn't have time to register it. The force was vast, like a hot fist in the chest. It was dark, then white light, then a red-toned blackness, with the silhouettes of chairs rising into the air as I fell backwards, caught and carried by the explosion, tumbling amid the debris. I was bowled along the floor with wood splintering around me; I couldn't breathe, the air was burning, too hot to swallow and my lungs felt like they'd been punched. A noise like rain falling and blows to my head and my back as I carried on rolling; felt something give way and then I was outside being scuffed by sand along the length of my body.

It went on forever and for no time, and then there was silence. My ears felt bulgy, as though the quiet air was full of feathers, and then the crying started. Distant, underwater crying, and the regular flick, flick as flames took hold and grew somewhere behind me. I clambered to my feet and took a step forward but my balance was gone and I fell, catching myself on something soft, which turned out to be one of the fur coats that the Shadow Planet people had been wearing.

It was wet, and when I pulled my hand away I saw the red smearing my palm and the sky above me rocked.

Breathe. I pulled air in and blew it out, concentrating on keeping the rhythm steady, not letting the shakiness get the better of me. All the exercises I'd learned to help manage the stress cut in and took over, *count your breaths, concentrate on something, drop your shoulders, relax your muscles.*

'For God's sake, someone, help me!'

The cry echoed through into the here and now, jolting me into reality. People were hurt.

I turned around slowly so as not to overbalance again.

The diner still stood, bulging into the desert as though the motel had suddenly acquired a pot-belly. The three standing walls were convex, the roof had partially collapsed, and the dusty sand in front now shone with millions of glass fragments. In the far corner a fire flicked lazy tongues from the wreckage of the kitchen, and the ground was littered with people lying or half-sitting amid the ruins of their clothing. *Breathe.*

I fought the urge to be sick with fear and shock and the smell of hot wood and a sweet, unfamiliar gas. Two seconds more and I'd started to run. 'Jack! Felix!' I clambered over the remains of the doorway I'd been blown through, with the velvet dress snagging on nails and splinters, and surveyed the wreckage inside. Called hopelessly into the dark, as around me others began to weave and sway to their feet, holding various parts of their anatomy. Knew that Jack had been outside, was probably behind me somewhere. Safe. But Felix had been inside.

I could smell the blood, the metal-sweet tang underneath the smell of burning wood, and had to fight the urge to run back out into the desert again. I bit my tongue and stumbled into a woman, bleeding from a deep scratch across her forehead. 'Head this way,' I shouted at her, my voice sounding strained and unfamiliar. 'You need to get out! The place is burning.' I grabbed her arm as she circled away from me and shoved her towards where the doors had been. A breeze was coming in from outside, bringing small showers of dust pattering into the shocked quiet. 'Outside!'

Other figures began to follow her, sheeplike. 'This way.' I pushed more of them into line, anyone I came across who was still upright. 'Come on. Follow me.' I began to move around the room, collecting little knots of people who fell into step behind me like a giant, bloodstained game of Grandmother's Footsteps winding through the dark. Some stopped to help others to their feet. Two men formed a cat's cradle with their hands to carry a girl whose leg was so clearly broken that I had to look away. But I wasn't just being noble, leading survivors to safety. I was searching.

Two circuits of the room and the remains of the roof were beginning to swing over our heads. Flames had found their way from the kitchen, where small-scale eruptions indicated cans blowing behind the swing-doors, and mouths of fire were beginning to eat into the dust. I seized the man who'd been behind me. 'Get everyone over that side. Step down through the rubble and get out into the desert. Make sure they all follow you.'

He nodded, a trickle of blood seeping from his nose and dripping down onto a ruined pilot costume. 'This way,' I heard him call, as I stepped back into the ringing darkness closer to the door that led through to reception. This was where I'd last seen Felix. It was now a circus of smashed glass; spilled drink made the place smell like an alcoholic's armpit, but at least there were no bodies slumped in the mess. Felix must have moved just in time to avoid the worst of the blast. So where was he?

'*Felix*,' I breathed. He lay, arms wide as though to push away the explosion, face down on the floor with part of the ruined ceiling on top of him. No reaction. No movement. I couldn't see if he was breathing under his fur coat, but the pelt was suspiciously spiked, as though a liquid was seeping through. I crouched down, ignoring the sudden heat as part of the wall behind us began to smoulder, worked my hand underneath him, found an area near his ribs and rested my palm against the bone.

Two short, shallow movements and I went weak with relief. He was breathing. I began to clear the debris from his shoulders, whilst being constantly knocked into by people, zombie-like, as they made their groping way towards the starlit outdoors, led by those brave enough to re-enter the building. One figure crashed into me, groped forward and grabbed me by the arm. 'Go away, I have to get him free.'

'Skye, it's me.' Jack raised his head and the moon caught his wicked eyes. 'I was looking for you. Heard you shout but . . .' An arm wiped across his face. 'Bloody blast was so bright it knocked my night vision right out.' He glanced down. 'God, it's Felix. Is he . . . you know . . . because he's very quiet.'

'Fuck . . . right off . . . and die, Whitaker.' The voice came from beneath the shards of plaster-board. It sounded slight and wheezy, but definitely Felix. 'Ow. Ribs. What happened?'

Jack sniffed, then he moved his head tracking a scent, like a dog. 'Acetylene. That sweet smell. Where did it come from?'

'I think one of the Skeel boys.' I carried on freeing Felix. 'Fe knocked into one of them, I saw the cylinder fall . . .'

'Leave me . . . alone.' Felix tried to roll away from under my hand.

'Shut up. I have to move this to get you out.' I tried to push the rubble more gently off his body. 'You can't stay here, the place is on fire.'

'Maybe I want to. Die.'

His words made the mild night air chill down to near freezing. 'Fe . . .'

'Can you move him?' Jack put a hand on my arm.

I screwed up my eyes and tried for levity. 'It's Felix. He weighs the same as a small dog.'

'Are you sure?' Somehow his eyes were darker than the darkness. 'Because I need to find out where that smell is coming from.' He helped me move another lump of box-beam from Felix's back. 'If we can smell it, that means there's more.'

Felix took a harsh-sounding breath. 'Go. Find it. We will . . . manage.' Jack gave me a long look and moved off through the darkness, still sniffing, and vanished. 'Now. Your turn to . . . disappear.'

'I am not leaving you.'

'You would have done. Before.'

His words hit me like another explosion. I had been the sort of person who'd leave a friend. The sort of person who lied and deceived herself just to keep from hurting. *That had been me*. 'Not now.' I hauled another beam off his back. Thankfully the diner seemed to have been built on the cheap, all box-beams and boarding rather than solid wood. But this did mean that it was burning a real treat behind us. 'Whatever happened changed all of me. But it's all right, you don't have to believe me, after all, why would you? Just let me do this one thing. Let me get you out of here.'

'Bravery? That's . . . new, too.'

I freed the last beam and pulled him to his feet with my arms around his waist. 'It doesn't matter now what you think of me, Felix. Truly. I know I can never turn back time. All I can do is re-make my life and try not to make the same mistakes again.' I leaned him against me, taking his weight. 'Knowing I killed them.'

Felix sagged in my grasp. 'Still just words,' he murmured, and with a small sigh he passed out, dropping back to the floor again.

I tried to get purchase for another lifting hold, carrying on my rambling theorising, while the smell of burning paint scorched the back of my throat. The adrenaline was beginning to wear off, leaving me free to feel the soreness in my arms and along my spine where my skin had been flayed through the torn dress as I'd been blown along the sandy ground. I tried to get another grip on Felix but my hands wouldn't obey, closing uselessly and feebly around his coat but unable to find enough force to grab him as shock paralysed my muscles and ordered me to freeze. Stay still. Wait for rescue. I gave a choked kind of sob as pain and weakness hit me together but I wouldn't . . . *would not* give up. Would not let this fire win.

The fire had taken full hold in the kitchen now. We had to get all the way across the ruined diner and out into the desert before it overtook us, and, at the rate it was moving, we had to get there *fast*. A whoosh, and I felt my hair begin to frazzle. 'Eighteen months it's taken me to grow that back.' I tried again to clutch at the fur coat. 'Come on, Fe, wake up and help.' The heat had begun to gnaw into my bones now, insistent, unignorable. The metal holes on the dress bodice were heating up like little buttons of pain across my cleavage, and I could smell the scorching material. 'Fe!'

But his head was lolling and his skin was grey. I couldn't carry him, I couldn't drag him, and I could feel my skin starting to blister on the back of my neck as the fire ate its way across the floor towards us. Despite the heat I was starting to shiver and my breath wouldn't catch properly; it felt as though I was only breathing with the top third of my lungs and somewhere behind where the bar used to stand, I could hear an ominous 'tick tick' noise, as though metal was heating up and not liking it very much.

'Fe, we have to get out of here,' I whispered to the inert form slumped at my feet. 'We *have* to.' But he didn't so much as groan or flicker an eyelash, even when a sudden spurt of flame flicked quickly over the top of both of us, retreating but leaving a smell of singed nylon and burning hair. It stung briefly over the backs of my hands and the pain made me clench tight, despite the sagging weakness in my wrists. The clench brought a handful of Felix's coat closer to me and I grabbed it with everything I had, arms into holes where the fabric had split, fingers into pelt, I even pushed a foot through a torn hemline. The pain spurred me on enough to move back, dragging Felix along the floor by his coat like a cat dragging a kitten; one step, two steps with the back of his head bumping along the wrecked floor, and we were away from the flames, three steps and he started to slide along on the rollers formed by the broken chairs and tables. I pulled him, using my body-weight, bent double, dragging him behind me by the tattered material of his coat. Another step and I had to stop. coughing and gasping until I thought I was going to be sick. We were away from the fire now, but it was only a matter of time before it caught up with us; maybe I could get Felix conscious enough to help . . . I collapsed forward. If I could only catch my breath . . .

And then Jack was there beside me. He seized Felix round the waist and tugged him upright.

'Great. Show up now and do the hero bit.' I coughed again, raising only my head. I was totally exhausted.

'I've found the cause of all this. We'd better get out . . .'

Suddenly the 'tick tick' was louder. Jack grabbed my arm, my *injured* arm and pulled me to my feet, then began to run. He ran through the wrecked diner, jumped down through the blown-out glass doors, hit the dirt outside, pulling Felix and me behind him, and accelerated for a few strides, then dived onto the sand, dropping Fe and throwing his own body over mine. I just had time to say 'ow, you're really heavy,' before all words were drowned out by the second, louder, explosion of the night.

CHAPTER 24

When I came back to myself I found I was walking. There was no sign of the motel on any horizon and my feet were bleeding, the dress was torn along the grain of the velvet across my shoulders and back and my arm was stiff and sore. The only light I could see was speckled on distant clouds from the town we'd passed through on our way to the motel. How long ago? Felt like months.

I stopped. How long had I been moving? What had happened after Jack had pulled Felix and me out of the building? I shook my head, feeling the crispy little curls drag at the back of my neck, and all I could remember was noise and panic. People moving around, paramedics arriving. Nothing else, nothing about how I'd come to leave the scene or where I'd thought I was going.

There was a faint golden wire lying behind some distant hills; either a distant town or dawn was coming up. As my eyes traced the far horizon I felt the familiar fluttering wings of panic start to beat alongside my heart. That breaking, bursting feeling that left no space for air or sense, the feeling that told me I was going to die, suffocated by my own fear as it rose up my throat and tightened my windpipe. *Where the hell was I?*

I picked a direction and ran. It was like running through a dream, with the softness of velvet periodically soothing my feet as the dress trailed beneath me and alternated with the rocky viciousness of the desert floor. I think I might have shouted too, calling for help as I ran, my throat and lungs thundering with my breath and my heart a white-hot cable searing through my chest.

A sudden misstep and the ground opened underneath me. I fell in a whirling mass of velvet and scraped skull, landing at the bottom of a small gulley, with my vision blurred and my head ringing. My hands clawed out once, reaching towards a sky that seemed tiny and then a glossy kind of blackness crawled in behind my eyes and I stopped registering anything at all.

The next thing I knew was footsteps crunching on the sand above me. A voice said 'Oh God,' and a figure jumped down to land alongside me, pushing fingers to my throat, groping for a pulse. Another exhaled 'Oh God,' and something was being forced under my head, cushioning it from a rock I'd only just realised was there. 'Oh my God, Skye, never do this to me again.'

'Wha . . . ?' My voice was almost non-existent.

'Take it easy.' The silhouetted shape, backlit by the lightening sky, crouched down beside me. 'You'll be okay. Here, have some water.'

My parched throat wouldn't allow more than the merest swallow, but my thirst forced me to gulp, and I ended up spitting and gagging to avoid drowning. 'Jack?'

'Yep.'

'How did you find me?'

He was laughing, but it was a relieved laugh. 'You left quite a trail. Bits have been falling off that costume all night; it was like Hansel and Gretel with fake jewels. But I'm surprised you managed to cover such a distance, we're a good couple of miles from the motel. And you've still got no shoes on.'

'It would have been easier in stilettos?' I struggled into a half-sit with Jack's assistance. 'What happened last night? The explosion?'

'The boys dressed as Skeel stole their gas canisters from a breaker's yard near Reno; hadn't realised that they were old welding cylinders half-full of oxy-acetylene that had been marked for disposal. Not the most stable of substances, and when our friend Felix went barging into them . . . boom!' He pushed his hair away from his eyes. 'But no-one died. Lots of cuts and bruises and broken bones, but no-one died, Skye.' For a second shock clouded his eyes, as though he was seeing it all again. 'No-one died,' he half-whispered, again, then gave his head a tiny shake and his voice strengthened. 'Even Felix got away with only two broken ribs and a head wound. Oh, and my fags got shredded.' I felt his arm slide behind me.

'The paramedics were treating you, they turned around to check on another casualty, and when they turned back, you'd gone. What was all that about?'

'I don't know. Shock.'

'Figures. It was quite a night.'

I leaned against the wall of the gulley. Jack was so close that I could see the light flicker in his eyes when he blinked. 'Yes.'

'You want me to give you a hand up? We should get back, people are worried.'

'I don't think I can walk.'

'No need. I borrowed Antonio's car. He was too busy having hysterics to stop me.' The smile burst onto his face again. 'He has got *such* a hairdresser's car!'

'I thought you couldn't drive.' I remembered his anxiety when Felix and Lissa had gone off, his desperate impotence at not being able to follow them.

'No. I *don't* drive. Never said I *couldn't*.' And now he was avoiding looking at me, pushing hands into his pockets, coming up with a solitary, dog-eared cigarette. 'Never said I couldn't,' he repeated, as though he'd slid off into a parallel world of thought. His lighter flared and he spent an unnecessary amount of time staring at the flame.

'Can we just sit here a while longer?'

'Okay.' He still wasn't looking at me. 'So, while we're here, want to give me the rest of the story?'

He shook his fringe out of his eyes. A sudden breeze was playing havoc with hair that had no natural settling point.

'You'll hate me.'

A direct look from those dark, dark eyes. 'Will I, now?'

'You heard Felix. I was horrible, Jack. And the only reason I changed is because I got on the wrong side of a windscreen at sixty miles an hour. Not because I realised the error of my ways or because I decided to change, but because I got hit on the head.' I touched the side of his face. 'And I don't know now which is the real me. Am I nice now?'

His gaze deepened. 'Yes. Yes, you are.'

'No, I mean, is *this* who I really am now?' I smacked myself in the chest. '*Really?* Or is it a personality aberration that could switch at any time?'

The wind twitched his hair again but he sat silent and unmoving. 'Do you know what I think?' He pushed his hair back now, impatient. 'I think that the way you were was a defence. It was a learned behaviour, a way of coping with a situation that would have been unbearable otherwise, and I don't know what that situation was but it must have been pretty catastrophic for you to build an entire personality just to keep yourself safe. The real you, the *true* you that was underneath all the time – that's who I'm seeing now. So . . .' A raised hand and a shrug. 'I like you. But then, judge of character I'm not. Writer and creator, well, that's a different matter.'

I looked at him, as he gazed out across the desert, jaw clenched as though underlining his words. 'I like you too,' I almost whispered. I didn't think he'd hear me as the wind was beginning to whip across the dusty ground with a sound like a large brush being diligently applied, until he suddenly dropped his eyes to mine.

'I guess it's time we had that talk.'

There was something in his voice, something deeper and darker than had been there before, a set to his body that changed everything, that moved him over from the 'friend' category into uncharted regions. He was suddenly a stranger, with his defiant hair and decisive stare.

'You don't have to tell me anything, Jack.'

'Skye.' He moved slightly. 'This is important. I've had times in my life . . . things I've done . . . that no-one knows about. I'm telling you so that you'll know – at least I hope you will – that people change. They *can* change, no-one is set in any particular mould, not if they don't want to be, okay?' My expression must have said 'oh yeah?' because he shifted again and a blush crept up his face from his neck and the fingers of the hand not holding his cigarette hooked into that black leather lace around his throat.

I couldn't look him in the eye now, so I focused instead on the ash-tipped end of his cigarette, poised between his fingers like a death-pencil.

A deep breath. 'I'm an alcoholic. Was. Am . . . When the network guys brought me over here to work on *North* . . . before I started up the *Fallen Skies* team . . . I was pretty much out of control.'

I shook my head slowly and watched ash flutter down to the sand like shot birds. 'I don't need to know this, Jack.' Or did I mean that I didn't *want* to know?

Another inhalation. This one stuttered. 'I think you do. Please, Skye, I *want* you to know. I want you to know what I'm like, what I'm capable of, how much of a complete *shit* I am. Y'see, all this *thing* with Geth,' he drew deeply on the cigarette then threw his arms out wide, 'it was all a sham, wasn't it? Maybe because you lack definition for yourself you fell for an image, for the look, for the words, not the real man inside them all. He's a troubled man, Gethryn, and some of that is because of me, and I want you to know that part of me that makes me behave like . . .' He pulled his arms back in towards his body and wrapped one around his waist. 'I don't want you to have those false illusions about me.'

'I don't . . .'

'Oh, I think you do.' The bitterness of his tone made me glance up. 'Gethryn is an illusion. Oh, he'd been good once, won an Emmy, once. But when I first met him he was about ten stone, pretty much selling his soul to anyone who'd got a part for him. When he got Lucas James, he hired a personal trainer to come and sort out the body.' Jack's eyes were darker than usual, a memory playing behind them in shadow. 'His name isn't even real. He's built himself from bits and pieces of others, an accent here, a hairstyle there; he's picked up and used anything from anyone that he thought might help him along.' A sideways glance caught my eye and I found I couldn't look away. 'He's a fabrication, Skye. A literal self-made man.'

I moved my lips but no words would come out. 'What about you?' just about breathed out of my mouth.

A harsh smile. 'Yeah, me too. A fabrication. A walking lie.' A last deep drag that had all the finality of death about it, and he bent to grind the remains of the cigarette almost viciously into the earth. 'Okay. Let's see. Right, when they came over to England wanting to headhunt me for the writing team on *Two Turns North* . . . I was running scared. Shut up in a little office writing – oh yeah, the books were successful but I was half-dead. Came over here full of crap about broadening my writing CV, working in TV to get some serious cash behind me. All bollocks, of course.' He was looking at his feet now, working them down into the desert dirt, digging to hell. 'I was on the run from some nasty memories, that's all. Running like a coward. And then I came up with *Fallen Skies* and they gave it to me. Me. A bloody drunk with no real TV experience – but they said they had "faith". And I *tried*, tried to tell them that I wasn't what they saw.' He worked a small rock loose and bent to pick it up. 'But they'd made me into something by then. I was their great British success and they thought everything I touched turned to sunshine and awards.'

'That's why the show nearly got cancelled after the first year?'

Jack nodded. 'I was terrified. Drunk and terrified. Couldn't handle the crew, couldn't handle the writing team . . . God, it was a wonder we weren't cancelled half-way through . . .' He gave a small outbreath of a laugh. 'Shows what happens when you trust people like me. Even the guy who made the fucking *coffee* had the drop on me.' Long fingers closed around the pebble, tossing it from hand to hand.

'But they carried on giving you the money.'

A shrug and fierce concentration on the rock. 'They liked what I was turning out, sometimes, somehow, some reason it just *worked*. And the fans got behind it, campaigned to keep us on air – that's part of the reason we have these conventions, it's our chance to say "thank you" for keeping us in work.'

'But the fans didn't do it out of selflessness. They did it because they loved the show. Because you're good at what you do.'

For that I got a sudden, amazing smile which softened his eyes. 'Thank you.' His hands were still for a moment. 'Thank you,' he said again, 'for reminding me what I could be.' Then he was back to fidgeting again, staring up out towards the sky while his fingers restlessly twitched over the surface of that stone as though reading Braille.

'But I'm still a fraud. I let myself get sucked in, let the whole of my past define who I was. Let the memories have the run of my head. And things . . . things went wrong.'

'But you got yourself sorted out.'

A small inclination of the head. 'I chose to change myself. Again. You see what I mean? I stopped drinking so that I could keep the show on the air. Not because I *wanted* to give up, not for my health or my relationship or anything, but simply so that I could keep my characters on screen. So you see, Skye, I know how it is to be changed by circumstances.'

He drew his arm back and suddenly sent the little stone flying with a flick of his wrist, the loose sleeves of his T-shirt flipping down with the movement and flapping like crows' wings. 'But you still gave up drinking,' I said.

'Yes. Got a hold of myself, pulled it all back from the brink.' He made a self-deprecating face. 'There you go. That's me.'

'So why are you so . . . ?'

'So, what?' He gazed upwards as though the sky had spoken.

'So . . . cold. As though you'd break if anyone touched you.'

'Only way I can cope, Skye. By never, *never* letting anything touch me enough to cause trouble. It doesn't always work, of course.' His voice broke, rolling over the name, 'Liss and I . . . Lissa isn't . . . She and I were . . . and then

Geth . . .' He stopped talking, bit his lip until his mouth twisted. 'I wanted him on *Skies*.' A little laugh and a shake of his head and he seemed to pull it all back in, any sign that he felt anything other than a mild annoyance. 'He had a bit-part in *North* and he was the best bloody action-actor I'd seen, so I recruited him. Oh, just about everyone warned me, but I thought, second chances, you know the kind of thing. What we are both living, Skye. A second chance.'

Now his hands went into his pockets, his shoulders came up in a prolonged shrug. 'I fired Geth from the show, and I hate myself for the fact that only *part* of the reason was because he's so often drunk that he's completely unreliable.'

My breathing hurt again. 'You fired him.'

'Yeah. He didn't 'quit his contract', we just let that out to save face. His, ours, I'm not sure even now.'

'What's the other part?'

'Sorry?'

'If his drinking is only part of it?'

Jack raised his shoulders again. 'He uses women. I saw it and I hated it, but it's not exactly a sacking offence, is it, being a womaniser? If it were, I don't think there'd be an actor left on screen, but I used the drinking as my excuse and I shouldn't have done it.'

'Are you a womaniser, too? Is that why they call you the Iceman? Love 'em and leave 'em, is that you, Jack?'

The shoulders rose a little more. 'Liss got as close as anyone to getting under the wire but . . . even her, when she left me . . . I felt nothing. Like I don't know how to feel anything real any more. My heart, as they say, remains unengaged.' He trailed a finger over his stubbled chin, scratching thoughtfully. 'Until now.'

'Jack . . .'

'Look . . .' His shoulders relaxed and he touched my face now, 'we're allowed to make mistakes. Life is one great big learning curve, there's no manual, no instructions. We do the best we can and learn from the things that turn out to have been a steaming pile of shit. Okay?' His fingers pinned a wayward strand of my hair back from my eyes. 'What you were doesn't matter. It's what you *are*, what I see, that counts.'

'And what do you see?' I looked into his eyes, held his gaze. It was so dark it stopped my breath in my throat.

'I see someone I desperately want.' His breathing changed, turned ragged around the edges. 'Sorry. Inappropriate thoughts there. Try to pretend you haven't noticed.'

'Maybe I don't want to.'

His eyes went nova. 'Skye, you don't know what I'm like. I won't be any good for you; I told you I'm a liar and a jerk.'

I was still looking into his face, saw his eyes flicker. 'You said yourself, life is a learning curve, Jack.'

A cautious hand touched the skin at the base of my throat with one finger. Its touch set my pulse thundering under my flesh, like my body was a prison it wanted to escape, but I kept my eyes on his, saw his pupils widen with desire, become twin black suns, heard both our breathing rates rise and match. 'Skye.' It was all he said, just my name, but it held such longing that the word almost warped under the weight of it. 'Skye.'

He leaned forward to let his tongue trace my lips, and my mouth lifted to meet his. I felt as though I'd been released from a cage whose glass walls had been invisible, but which had held me, nonetheless. How I had been was no longer important, all that mattered here was who I was now. And this was the real me now. The person Skye Threppel had been was dead and buried; *this* was who I was, crashing to the surface, drawn by Jack's fingers against my skin, his lips on mine.

I reached my hands between us so that I could lift his T-shirt over his head, strip him of his writer's disguise, and run my hands over the scattered hair across his chest, hearing the deep growl that built in his throat as I did it. When I touched his scars, finally letting my finger follow that line that led from his nipple to dip under the corded waist of his pyjamas, the growl rose and exploded from his mouth into mine. Suddenly he was on top of me and I could feel the tension in his muscles, the coiled-spring effect as he held himself up, the weight of his spare frame along my body and the heat of him. My ridiculously undisciplined hair coiled under his touch as he dragged it back from my face, kissing my scar where it broke the skin around my eye, moving his mouth down until he met the other scars, where he hesitated for a second. 'Skye?' Just my name, again.

I returned the favour. 'Jack,' hearing the catch and sob of need in my throat. Pulled down the bodice of the dress so that it flapped like a red velvet tongue against my breasts, lower, until it lapped at my body, passing over my hips like a kiss. '*Yes.*'

His hair traced the scars as he moved over me, losing the rest of his clothes to the scrubby brushland around the gulley. He looked me in the eyes and smiled. 'Think I just gave up smoking,' he said and moved forward, fingers leading the way, until I was gasping, all my nerve endings flaming into nebulae.

'Oh. God. Jack.' Each word held enough meaning for an entire script. And then his skin was against my skin, each stroke was a move nearer freedom for me. He gave me back my self-respect, my pride and then, eventually, he gave me himself. Utterly unreserved, he threw up his head and blew my name into the breeze on a falling note, until he was gasping and reaching for breath and I was a boneless mass, a new person underneath him.

CHAPTER 25

The tension went, exploding into silver filaments, dragged from the base of his spine to leave him bone-heavy. Beneath him, Skye was still trembling, the raised edges of the extra skin layers that marked her body feeling soft and dry against his chest.

He wanted to speak. Wanted to say something profound, something about having found himself. The ice melting. But he couldn't utter a word, couldn't even make a sentence line up inside his head, because his brain still felt as if it had liquidised and was, even now, pooling inside his skull. Even the jealousy he'd briefly entertained towards Geth couldn't stage a comeback with all these good feelings pounding away through his bloodstream. *She doesn't want Geth. She wants me. And, for once, I think I can feel it and return it.*

It was like coming out in the land of the living after years in the underworld – everything was suddenly bright and real. He understood all those songs about love and loss as magically as if someone had taught him a new language; the air seemed warmer and the sky a brighter shade of blue. Life was sharper and it was all because of this lovely woman, now drowsing in his arms with occasional shudders still rippling inside her.

He touched her hair, her mouth, and she looked up at him with a slow smile that, against all logic and laws of biology, made him stiffen again.

'Hey.' That was all she said. Just acknowledging his desire with one word and a little shuffle of her hips until he thought he was going to die of perfection. *This is it. I'm human again.* Moving, feeling that pull and tug of her, the silent friction that built towards the ultimate release.

And then remembering. All the things he *hadn't* told her. What was she going to say when she found out about those? Would she think he'd had sex with her under false pretences? *Will she hate me?* His rhythm slowed and broke. Skye made a small noise, slightly disappointed, but he knew it was for the best as he pulled back and coiled his body away from her, ashamed. Feeling the colour leaching from life again, feeling the ice settling in his blood.

I told her I was no good for her. I'm no good for anyone. Kill the feelings. I'm better off this way.

CHAPTER 26

Jack handled the Audi TT like a pro, swinging it across the desert to reach the trackway which led to the road. Neither of us spoke, hadn't spoken since we'd breathed one another's names into the rising dawn, as if we were ashamed or trying to forget. I looked across at him behind the wheel. Focused, dark, totally sure of everything, his movements were precise and his eyes never left the track for a moment, not even to acknowledge mine in a glance of shared guilt. The only non-driverly thing he did was to hook two fingers into the thong round his neck for a moment, to roll the leather against his skin, and then we were off again, bouncing along towards the motel. I almost couldn't believe this was the same man who'd lain with me in that dusty little trench, stroking my scars, smiling down at me with a new, softer expression that almost completely dispelled the stress lines around his eyes. The man who'd touched me so expertly, whose kiss had injected fire into my veins and whose body . . . I felt the echo of an internal shiver . . . was so bloody *amazing*.

'Jack.' I needed to break the stony silence. 'Are you okay?' He grunted and twisted the wheel to steer the Audi around some low-lying rocks. 'Only, I'm starting to be scared.'

That got a look. 'Scared? What of?'

'You. That you're regretting telling me all that stuff back there. You must have been keeping it quiet for a reason.'

'Not wanting you to know what a bastard I am isn't a big enough reason?'

I gave a half-laugh. 'Come on! The great Jay Whitaker? They'd forgive you just about anything.'

'No. No they won't. Trust me, Skye, I haven't told you *half* of it.'

'Then . . . ?' I waved a hand to indicate the air between us. 'Why all this?'

'Hey. Moody silence is what I *do*.' Still dark. 'I'm a writer, remember?' Then he reached down and pulled hard, the little car slid into an expert turn, spinning 360 degrees with wheels locked. 'Yeah. I'm a fucked-up drunken mess of a writer.' The engine died. 'And whatever you're thinking, don't. Okay, so we had a . . . moment back there. And it was great, don't get me wrong; *you* were great, there's absolutely nothing wrong with your body. At all.' He turned and I was taken aback by the expression in his eyes. He was *furious*. 'But look. This isn't going to be the start of something big, okay? Like I said, I'm no good for you, I shouldn't have started it but I did, and I'm sorry. I just don't want you to think . . . I don't do relationships. I tried, with Liss . . . kept it going for a while but even then I wasn't really *there*. Sex, yeah, I can do that fine, no problem there. But. Nothing else.' He fired up the engine again and gunned it savagely until the tyres began to scream. 'Nothing.' He pushed the lever into 'Drive' and the car shot forward so suddenly that I banged my head against the side window and my vision blurred for a moment.

'You're right,' I said, after a moment. 'You are a bastard.'

'Yes. I know.'

'Why?'

The car rocked over the rutted track. 'Maybe there isn't a reason. Maybe it's just who I am. Perhaps I like hurting people, letting them get close and then telling them it was all a big joke, ha bloody ha, no compassion here, no understanding, no . . .' He seemed to bite the word off to stop it coming, but I heard it echo through the empty space.

'No love? Never? So, you're some kind of masochist who puts himself in the way of emotion but refuses to give an inch for it? That's just sad, Jack. It's not brave, it's not worthy; it's running away.'

He hiccupped a breath. Might have been a laugh, might have been a sob. 'Yes, Skye. I know,' he said, very quietly, turning his head to look at me. 'I know.'

'So why are you so angry?'

He gritted his teeth and turned back to the road. 'It's not you I'm angry at.' His hands were so tight on the wheel that the plastic was groaning. 'It's me.'

I shut up after that.

We arrived back at the motel to find that an impromptu shanty-town had sprung up around the burned-out remains. Locals from the town had brought tents and blankets and most convention-goers had spent their last night camping out rather than leaving. It was as though the whole experience had bonded *Fallen Skies*' fans into one solid unit that they were reluctant to break.

'Jeez, am I glad to see you!' Gary, my interrogator and all-round security organiser, came running up almost before we'd got out of the car. 'We got problems.'

'You'd better believe it,' Jack muttered. 'What's going on?'

Gary turned to me. He looked haggard, completely shot. 'Getting that guy out before the place went up? That was some work, lady, you oughtta get a medal or something.'

'How about my quiz prize back?'

He shrugged. 'Dunno if they'd go for that.'

'I was joking.' A flat look and he turned back to Jack. 'We need you.'

'What, got a writing emergency? Someone need a script, stat?' A little of the bitter sadness my heart was full of had seeped into my voice. 'A sudden call for mouth-to-mouth monologues?'

Gary ignored me. 'Gethryn's on the roof, threatening to jump. Wants to talk to you. You better get over there pronto.'

'*Shit!*' Jack closed his eyes for a second. 'Okay. Has he been drinking?'

A quick look in my direction. 'What do you think?'

'Anything else?'

'Not so far as we know. But it's not looking good, Jay.'

'*Fuck*. Do we have press?'

'Some lads from *SFX* mag, a few that bussed in from the town to cover the explosion and everyone's got cameraphones. It could be all over the networks in an hour.'

Jack leaned forward, hands on thighs, and let his head drop, then he came back up, impatiently hooking his hair back. 'Right. Gary, get the boys out there to move everyone away. Tell them it's a matter of security, tell them . . . tell them this is promo work for Geth's new movie. Tell them he's . . . tell them we're shooting a commercial. Shit, tell them anything, just get everyone out of there.'

'Sure, boss.' Gary pulled the walkie-talkie from his belt.

'Oh, and if someone could find me a packet of cigarettes, I will be forever grateful.' Jack set off across the yard, then stopped. Turned and looked back over his shoulder to where I was hovering, hooking the velvet skirt up over my arm and wincing as my bruised and bloodied feet picked their way over debris. 'I'm going to need you, too.'

'Me? Why?' The partially ruined motel building stood like a broken tooth. I could see a shadowy shape moving against the sky as Gethryn paced across the rooftop. 'I should go and . . .'

'Skye.' Jack's voice was disturbingly calm but with an undertone that made it impossible to walk away from. 'If I go up there alone, Geth will jump. No question. Now, he likes you, you just might be able to give him a reason not to go off that roof, all right?'

'No pressure, then.'

A quick smile that barely touched his eyes. 'Yeah.' He turned and started walking towards the damaged building.

'Do you really think he's going to jump?'

Jack didn't break stride. 'Yep.'

'But *why*? And why does he want to talk to you?'

Jack spun round. 'Okay. This is really not the time. We've got a suicidal drunk on the roof over there, and if we don't do something fast this is going to blow. There'll already be stuff online, the national press can't be far away, everyone over *there* –' he pointed at the collection of shambling figures and makeshift tents beyond the car park – 'will be Tweeting and Facebooking fit to bust, and if I can't bring it all down . . .' he gave a wide shrug, 'then none of us might ever work again. Yes?'

I gave a half-snigger that owed more to shock than humour. 'And you're in your pyjamas.'

An answering smile. 'Yep. So things really can't get any worse, can they? Come on.'

As he led the way around the apocalyptic ruins of the motel I wondered about his switch. Down in that gulley he'd been kind and gentle. He'd touched my scars, kissed them and, okay, even given the fact that he'd been about to have sex with me, he hadn't needed to do that. And now it was like he'd turned that part of his personality off and let the whole Iceman thing come to the fore.

There was something underneath all this. Something so bad that he'd turned this emotional block into his coping mechanism. It was how he dealt with his life; he'd simply switched everything off so that nothing could hurt him. And he didn't know how to turn it back on. My heart squeezed itself tight around the realisation, and the sympathy I felt for this strong, gorgeous, complicated man became something solid and real.

I watched his back view as he strode ahead of me, his feet kicking up little demons in the sand, his shoulders hunched as though his memories were a solid weight upon him. As I followed, I wondered what those memories were, what he was carrying that made denying all emotion the best option, and felt a sudden chill prick between my shoulder blades.

Gethryn was sitting on the edge of the roof around the far side of the main building. It was four storeys high and it made me feel sick just looking up.

When he saw Jack he stood unsteadily and waved the bottle he was drinking from. 'Well, hello there, Mr Show-Runner! And Skye – whatcha doin' with him, Skye? He's a bastard.'

Even given that he was clearly drunk, and the precarious position he was in, he still looked wonderful. The desert breeze lifted his hair from his shoulders and tossed it carelessly, his unshaven and slightly sunken cheeks were made-up with a dusting of sand and a highlight of sun, and even his torn shirt looked artful and designed.

'We've got to get up there,' Jack hissed to me. 'If you go up the staircase, I'll go round the back and up the fire escape. Try and get round behind him. Maybe if there's two of us we can distract him for long enough to persuade him down.'

'I'll try.' I hitched up my skirts again and made for the inside of the motel, hearing Geth's shout of, 'Oh, you leavin', girl? Doncha want to hear what he's done?'

I'd have cried, if I'd had enough moisture in me. The beautiful, golden Gethryn was threatening to kill himself, the sexy, intense Jack was cold-shouldering me, I'd been up for what felt like forever with no sleep, unless unconsciousness counted, and Felix hated me. Maybe I'd have done better staying locked in my little house on the York ring road and ogling my next-door neighbour. It might lack the whole sleeping-with-a-famous-man thing, but it also lacked the glass-cut feet and suicide scenario.

Inside, the motel was blackened from the fire that had swept through from the diner. The outer walls looked sturdy enough, and no-one would have let me go in if the place was in danger of falling down, would they? *Would they?* Maybe Jack just saw it as a good way of getting rid of me, having fifty tonnes of motel land on my head. And why did I get the feeling that there was more to this than Gethryn being fired from the show and wanting revenge?

I found the stairs, and kept going up until, on the topmost corridor, I found the Fire Exit door standing open to a flight of rickety steps which led, when I followed them, to the roof. I arrived about fifty feet behind Gethryn, terrified to speak in case I startled him. He was still perched on the slightly raised edge of the flat roof, still holding a bottle, and still wearing most of Lucas James's dress-uniform from last night's ball.

'Geth?' I whispered. 'What's going on?'

He heard and turned his head. 'Whoa, party time, *bach*.' He stood up and spun round, giving me a few giddy moments when he swayed close to the edge, then came over and handed me the bottle. 'Have a drink. Celebrate.'

'Celebrate what?'

But he ignored me and pulled another bottle from behind what looked like a cooling duct. 'So, has he told you?'

I was so thirsty I took a swig from the bottle he'd put in my hand. It was warm, but liquid was liquid. 'What about?'

'But why would he?' Gethryn appeared to be conducting a one-man conversation and my input was being disregarded. 'I mean, what are you to him, *bach*? Some tidy piece of skirt, ready to part your legs for the Iceman? What, hoping that you're going to be the one to save him, to make him realise that he feels something for you?' The bottle waved again, recklessly. 'Dream on, girlie. You wouldn't be the first one to go that way. Or the hundredth either. That man puts it into anything that'll wriggle for him. Don't you, Ice? What, you thought I wouldn't see you? Told your little girlie to keep me talking, chat chat chat, give you a chance to creep around and come poppin' up at me from nowhere, like some fucking Jack-in-a-box? Yeah, in a box, boy, where you belong.'

His voice raised in a sudden shout and I turned to see Jack up on the roof behind us. I was filled with sudden anger. How *dare* Gethryn assume how I felt about Jack?

'Before you get carried away, Geth, Jack's already told me about the drinking. And, so what? Plenty of people drink too much! He's given up now,' I indicated the bottle in Geth's hand, 'and maybe it wouldn't be so bad if you followed his example.'

Gethryn started to laugh, blond eyebrows raised in comic surprise. 'Wow, this one's got it bad for you, man.' He took a couple of steps back, away from me, towards the edge. 'Better watch it. Don't want another one on the pills after you dump her ass.' Suddenly his accent sounded less Welsh, the vowels were flattening and the whole intonation had changed, as though he were mirroring Jack's own speech to taunt him.

Jack stood rigid. He was still breathing hard from the four-storey ascent and his hands were so tightly fisted that his knuckles were blue. His whole body was rigid. 'Don't go there, Geth.' Even his voice was tight, as though he was squeezing each word out of a constricted throat. 'Just *don't*.'

'Oh, I dunno. Quite fancy picking up the pieces of this one when she finds out what you're really like.'

There must have been a tiny bit of my old personality still lurking underneath the new me, because normally I would never have thought of behaving the way I suddenly did. I stalked across to Gethryn, slapped him hard across the face and said, 'And don't you assume that I'm some weak, pathetic little thing who's going to collapse if a man doesn't want to fall in love with her. I might have scars, but, you know something? When scars heal, what's underneath is stronger.'

Gethryn started to laugh. He swayed backwards across the roof away from me and raised the bottle to me in a toast as he went. 'Oh, so you've not told her about Suicide Sophie then?' Lowering his voice in pretend confidentiality to me, 'He had a girl, Skye. Bloody adored him, she did, but our Jack, our Iceman, oh, he can't possibly love *her* can he? Not with him bein' all cool and unemotional now, be letting the side down, wouldn't it,

Ice? So she ups and tries to top herself.' Another huge swig. 'And our Jack? Hardly even fucking blinks. That's him, that's the man you've got yourself all hot an' bothered over.'

A quick glance showed me Jack had squeezed his eyes shut.

'I don't care.' I surprised myself by having such a level tone. 'Everyone has the chance to start again, Gethryn. Everyone.'

Geth laughed into the neck of the bottle. 'Playing this one different, are you, writer-man?'

'This one *is* different.' Jack edged a little further onto the roof. 'And this isn't about her. It's about you and me, isn't it? That's why you're up here, Geth, after all. Leave her out of it.'

Gethryn sat suddenly, as though his legs had lost strength. 'Oh, but it's such fun to see you squirm. Betcha regretting all those girls you chucked out; Sophie and Mariette and Del and . . . that little one with the big . . .' cupped hands to chest, Geth grinned hugely. 'All of 'em runnin' to me, full of stories about "*howwible nasty wyter man*".' He tilted the bottle to his lips at an angle that indicated it was almost empty then, in a move that was at odds with his cheerful drunk persona, he drew his arm back and threw the bottle off the edge of the roof, giving it a vicious spin.

We waited a moment, then heard it shatter.

'And anyway,' Gethryn again carried on his one-man conversation, 'if you thought this was only about you and me, why'd you send her up? Eh? Or is she the cover, something disposable?'

'*Skye. Is not. Disposable.*' When I looked at Jack his face was so pale that his eyes and hair seemed to hang unsupported. He had his hands clenched so tightly that his nails must have been hurting his palms.

I crouched down beside Geth, who'd sprawled his legs and leaned up against the air-conditioning funnel. 'What is all this about?'

A sigh. 'Now, let me see. How long have you got?'

I looked out across the 360° panorama of Nevada visible from the roof. To our left the encampment was beginning to pack up as the sun rose and the temperature climbed. A number of people still stood, phones raised as they captured our high-rise drama, but most of them had lost interest as soon as Geth had stepped back from the edge, and were concentrating on the last dregs of convention-spirit flying around. To our right and stretching behind us was a cordon of security, masterminded by the probably increasingly frantic Gary and his huge henchmen. Everyone stood at a distance. No-one could hear a word we said up here. It was probably the ultimate privacy.

'Gethryn.' I copied Jack's technique when he'd been talking to Felix. Made my voice go low and gentle. 'Tell me.'

When I looked across to see how Jack was taking all this I saw that his eyes, burning deep and dark in that haunted face, were fixed on me.

'No,' he said. 'Skye, don't.'

Gethryn laughed. 'She doesn't know the worst of you yet, does she? You given her the edited version of your shit, have you?' His face darkened. 'Told her about the "tortured writer, struggling to keep his show on the road"? Done the whole "but I had the strength to get over it, not like poor old Gethryn who can't stop drinking and had to be fired to stop him ruining the filming"? Christ, man, you really take the fucking biscuit, you know that?' Another new bottle tipped to his lips. He seemed to have an inexhaustible supply, which meant he'd been hiding them up here systematically. Planning this? I couldn't guess.

'I'll tell her.' Jack had come closer while I'd been paying such close attention to Geth. He now stood only a handful of inches away, close enough for me to smell the coconut scent of his hair and the sharp, salty smell of his skin. 'Let me do this, Geth.'

Geth's face had fallen in, become lined and old as though opening that last bottle had released centuries. 'You ask him . . .' he spoke slowly, deliberately, keeping his eyes on my face, 'about that leather lace around his neck. That's what's at the heart of him, if he's even still *got* a fucking heart.' The neck of the bottle pointed at me. 'You ask him about that, girlie.'

'*Geth.*' Jack's voice was heavy with pleading.

Gethryn leaned in closer, lowered his voice to little more than a breath. 'Ask him about Lissa. Ask him about the baby.' Then he leaned back, spread his hands. 'She's all yours, man. Be my guest. I'm looking forward to her slapping you around; she's got one hell of a right hook, your girl.'

Jack reached out a hand and tugged at my elbow. He pulled me across the roof until we stood in the shadow of a cooling tower, our backs to Gethryn. 'I would have told you, you must believe that. *I would have told you*. But I thought it best . . . I wanted . . . ah, shit.' He ran both hands through his hair until it stayed away from his face. 'I wanted you to see me as I wanted to be. I wanted to keep it all going, as though by making you believe it, it could all become a little bit more real.'

I looked steadily at him. 'And that is why you backpedalled on me? After we . . . after the gulley?'

'Everything I've ever touched has ended badly,' he said simply. 'Everything. And I don't want to start something new, something with you, only to watch it all crash and burn When I do something, say something, stupid or when the drink comes back to haunt me or when . . .' A hand reached up to roll the leather against his skin. 'When the memories get too much.'

I put my hand up and covered his to still the restless motion of his fingers on the thong. 'Tell me. Let me make my own decisions, Jack. Please. I can't help you if I don't know.'

Despite the heat from the rapidly ascending sun, Jack's hands were icy. 'I don't want . . .' His voice came at an odd pitch, as though it was fighting to get out of his throat, 'I don't want you to hate me. Not you, Skye, with your kindness and your innocence, wanting to help me – I don't want to see all that die right in front of me when you find out what a useless fuckwit I really am.' His voice lowered still further, hissing out between his teeth. 'I want you to like me. I want to pretend that I'm still someone good enough to like.'

I took both his hands in mine, trying to will some warmth into them. Jack just stood, head hanging so that his hair obscured his face. 'I need to know,' I said, steadily. 'I need to know *you*. If you only tell me the good stuff and I only like you because I think you're . . . well, it won't be real, will it? Like with Gethryn, it'd only be superficial. Jack, *I need to know*.'

One hand released itself so that he could make a half-hearted attempt to clear the hair from his face, but it simply slumped back down again, leaving me staring at a curtain of black. 'I don't know where to start, Skye. That's the truth of it. I've been carrying it all for so long I . . .' A huge, indrawn breath made his shoulders rise. 'Okay. Take it from the top. The car crash where Ryan died.' Seemingly unconscious of what he was doing he looped a finger underneath the lace. I could see his hand shaking. 'I'd stolen the car earlier that night; we were out of our brains on crack, doing ninety down a dual carriageway and I hit a bollard.' He sucked in air as though it wasn't touching his lungs. 'I had a record. Possession of Class As, car theft. They locked me up, Skye. I'd killed the best friend I ever had, and they locked me away.'

He glanced up now; his eyes were desperate, willing me to understand. 'I was a crack-smoking lowlife and I killed my best friend; Ryan died because I was high and thought I could handle a performance car.' It was only when I felt the hot, wet weight hit my hand that I realised he was crying. His expression hadn't changed, but tears were gathering and falling steadily. 'And I didn't learn my lesson.' Without acknowledging the tears he swiped the back of his wrist across his eyes. 'You'd think, wouldn't you, killing someone would do it? But not for me, Skye, for me *that wasn't enough*.'

Gethryn was watching us over the lip of the bottle. He raised an eyebrow when he saw me looking at him, and gave me a little wave. He seemed to be enjoying Jack's misery.

'When I got out of prison I reinvented myself. Used my mother's maiden name, went on courses, started writing. Had to tell the network heads when they brought me over to the US, had to tell immigration and all, but I'd been a minor when I was convicted and they were desperate to get me over here so it all got . . . swept away. Pushed underground. No-one knew about the real me, the old me. I felt such a fucking *fraud*, is it any wonder I stayed hidden? Lied to anyone who asked, "Yeah, I'm just this guy from Leeds, nothing to see here, keep moving." It made me feel crap. And people were digging, y'know, press, other writers, looking for that little titbit they could use against me, get me fired, get me off the show, fucking Brit boy coming over here, taking their jobs . . .' He held a finger against his mouth as if to stop himself pouring the horror out over the gritty roof. 'I needed help, needed someone, and one night I got blasted and I told Lissa. She helped me keep the lie, mostly to save her own skin, or at least the agency's. Don't think people would have liked to deal with an agency that had a convicted criminal who's lying about his identity as a client.'

'It was her choice, Jack.' I touched his arm, but he didn't react. 'And how does it affect Geth? Why does he hate you so much?'

Jack's whole body stilled. 'I thought it was fate, you know? Finding Geth . . . persuading him to come back into acting for *Fallen Skies*, because, even with everything, even with all this –' an arm swept around, – 'he's still a terrific actor. That Emmy wasn't a fluke, Geth.' He raised his voice slightly, but it was met with a shrug and another raised bottle. 'But I didn't know about him. I should have checked up, looked into it all but . . . too drunk. Too desperate to get the show made while they still liked me.'

'So his drinking was a problem?'

That got me an impatient shake of the head.

'Geth's family came over here when he was fifteen. Running from their own ruined lives – what the hell *is* it with the States, that we all end up here when we can't bear it at home any more? Sorry. Rhetorical. Can't help myself sometimes.' Another tear caught on the stubble on his cheek, one single bead of misery, unacknowledged. 'They moved from Leeds. He's Ryan's brother. I never even knew Ry *had* a brother – course, we weren't exactly dropping round to each other's houses for tea or anything but . . . you'd have thought I'd have *known*. But. Yeah. He was eleven when Ryan died . . .' Another indrawn breath, as though he was trying to pull all the misery back inside. 'I didn't find out until he told me. The English accent he used on *Skies*, that's his real one. It's the Welsh that's a put on.'

My eyes went back to Gethryn. He was still sprawled as though lying on this sunny rooftop was the only thing he had to do all day, relaxed and at ease. But now I could see underneath to the bones of unhappiness. '*Geth*,' I whispered.

'Y'see?' Jack's voice sounded as though it came from years away. 'It shouldn't have come as a surprise that we found each other, the TV world isn't that huge. But I'd changed my name and I'd never known he existed, so . . . and we worked together. It all worked.'

'But he found out who you were.'

Jack bunched the hem of his T-shirt and scrubbed it over his face. The scar over his ribcage flickered in and out of vision for a moment, like a flip-book animation, as though two alternate lives rode one over the other. 'It was Lissa. She got pregnant. My baby, Skye. My child. And I thought . . . I honestly thought that it would save me. That I'd finally be able to care for something, that I'd be able to leave the past behind and start to love someone.'

'*Jack.*'

I couldn't stop myself from looking away from him, tearing my eyes from his hunched shoulders and glancing over at Gethryn. The expression of triumph on his face made me feel sick.

'But by then I'd crapped it all up with Liss – and I don't blame her for it. Having a baby by a guy with my background, a drunken bastard who didn't love her, *couldn't* love her – who said I'd even be able to love the child? And she ran.'

Gethryn was nodding now, smirking at me and raising his eyebrows.

'She ran to *him*?'

Jack's eyes were closed and new lines of strain creased around them. 'Yeah. She said she loved me. He was all body and brawn, she said. Until . . . well, he *understood*. That's his real gift, Skye. He took all of them after that, all the girls I . . . every one I couldn't love, they all ran to Geth in the end. I damaged them and he *understood*.' Jack rested his forehead against my shoulder and just stood silently. I knew he was still crying because of the spreading dampness of the velvet across my skin, but he made no sound and no movement at all, until I put my arms around him, when he let out the single word, 'Sorry.'

The Iceman had shattered.

'She told him all about me and he's used it against me every day since.' He spoke into my skin. 'Every day. Whispering Ryan's name, telling me what a lousy, fucked-up father I would have made . . .'

'The baby . . . ?' I felt his tears against my neck, felt his shoulders give one last, huge heave.

'She lost it. Stress, they said, when Geth cheated on her. Geth cheated on all of them, in the end.' The words sounded as though they came from between clenched teeth. 'No baby. No Lissa. No love.' A violent shudder. '*No salvation.*'

Gethryn had lost all pretence of gazing at the view or concentrating on the bottle. Those golden eyes were watching us and I noticed, for the first time, how predatory they looked. 'You still think it was coincidence, don't you, Ice? You finding me, me getting that part on *North*, you bringing me onto *Skies*? No, I knew who to talk to, who to put pressure on, to get in. You stupid, fucked-up bastard, I knew who you were all along. People talk, you know that? Everyone back home in Leeds, in the old neighbourhood, they all knew when you came out of prison, all knew you'd changed your name and ponced off to live in York like nothing had ever happened – people don't like that sort of thing, see. They like men who stand up and take responsibility, not men who run off and try to pretend to be someone else. Must have had thirty letters that week, my family. Leeds might be a big city, but you get a name for things like you did, a name that carries with you, whatever you call yourself. No, I knew who you were; I was just biding my time.'

'So you let me blame Lissa?' Jack's words were muffled against my skin.

Gethryn's laughter made my skin creep.

CHAPTER 27

The pain was indescribable. Jack felt it take the strength from his legs and the will from his mind as it swept through, riding the train of memory. But Skye stood steadily, letting him embrace the agony and wash it out in tears on her skin. She was even holding him, murmuring words he couldn't hear into his hair, putting her cheek to his as if to share some of the pain.

'You see what kind of man I am? Now, do you *see*? When I got out . . . I locked it all up tight, all the feelings and the guilt, all in a little box marked "alcohol". I drank so that I could feel drunk. To reassure myself that I could at least feel *something*; even altered states of consciousness are better than nothing.'

He didn't tell her that nineteen years hadn't dulled any of the memories. That he could still hear Ryan's scream as the car hit, still hear the tearing, grinding sound of the car being peeled apart like an orange. Could still hear himself laughing, that stupid, piercing laugh of the recklessly high, blindly incomprehensive of just what he'd done.

Remorse stabbed at his gut and twisted. For the first time in nineteen years, he let it. 'I leaned on alcohol and then I leaned on Lissa. Never really stood alone and faced what I'd done, just buried it all, the emotion, the guilt. So, you see, I'm not much use,' he said. Skye smelled of hot velvet and he wondered if he'd ever be able to pass an uncut moquette sofa on a warm day without thinking of her, and then frowned. That was the second time he'd compared this lovely, willowy, *tragically* sexy girl to a three-piece suite. 'Really, not much use at all,' he repeated to himself.

'But you've got potential.' Skye gave him a half-smile, which was more than he deserved, he reckoned. His heart gave a peculiar double beat which at first he mistook for lust, but then realised was hope.

A few muscles uncoiled from their rigid stance and he passed a hand over the back of his neck, almost surprised to feel the heat of his own skin. *Still alive. Bleeding inside, but still alive. And with her . . . with Skye, I might even recover.*

He raised his head, knowing that his cheeks were smeared with desert dust, knowing that his eyes probably looked like hellpits. 'I can get you help, Geth . . . *Tyler*, you know I can. Shit, I can even help you myself, if that's what you want.' Using Gethryn's real name for the first time, here like this, gave him back some of his certainty. He felt stronger now, as though some of her strength had transferred to him in that smile. 'Get off the booze, clean up your act. Maybe do a stint in a clinic or something, yeah? Get yourself straight and maybe I can write you another part. I'll go and see your family . . . I'll do anything. I just want to make amends.'

Gethryn clambered to his feet. With his heart sinking Jack saw the giveaway signs: the lack of co-ordination, the shrunken pupils. Geth was beyond listening to whatever he had to say. He wanted revenge, pure and simple.

'Fuck off. Leave me here. I'm gonna throw myself off, end it all. You've told them all about me, that I'm . . . what was it you said? "Unreliable, unprofessional and unencumbered by morals", wasn't it? Fine piece of word-play that, I'd almost admire you for it, if it didn't mean that I'd be lucky to get a bit part in *Days of our Lives.* You've ruined my life, Jack.'

'That's not true.' Jack knew it probably was, but that wouldn't help here. 'Come back to Britain. We'll come up with something together, Ty.'

'You just don't want me to tell them, do you? Kept it quiet, never breathed a word about Ryan, let Liss think it was all news to me – I didn't tell no-one, see. Get me Lucas James back and I might just manage to keep it all down a bit longer, might be able to see my way to 'forgetting' what you did to my brother. What do you say, Jack?' Geth held his arms wide. 'You overlook my little habits and I'll overlook you being a murdering son of a bitch. Okay?'

Jack felt the hope well up inside him. He could get out of this clean, get away; no-one need ever know what he'd done. All he had to do was bend a little. Make excuses. Tell everyone that Geth was re-hired and . . .

Her eyes. She was watching him as though she stood a million miles away, afraid to reach out because of the distance. Her dress was still stained with his tears. This woman, who'd overcome her own fears, who was building herself a new present on a shaky history. A woman whose past scarred her inside and out and yet was brave enough to be content to forget. No compromise, just moving on.

'No,' he said aloud, startling himself. 'No, Tyler. You go ahead, you tell them all about me. I've spent nineteen years denying myself everything I should have felt back then. I pushed it all down, the guilt, the fear, even the love; I wouldn't let any of it out in case it hurt, but now? Now I'm *sick* of running scared.' He tilted his chin towards the other man. 'Sick of living in fear. I *want* it out in the open. Go ahead.'

'Skye.' Geth's voice was slow, like something was taking effect. Jack cursed himself for having let himself take his eye off the man. 'Come here a second. I want to tell you something.'

'Geth . . .' Jack started forward, but Skye touched his shoulder, her simple, easy gesture paralysing him.

'It's okay. I'm assuming I know the worst now?'

Her eyes were so wonderful. Why had he never

noticed how lovely they were? *Iceman, you've not just melted, you've puddled.* 'Yeah. That was it.' He even managed a smile. 'And I've always been kind to kittens.'

'If I find *that* was a lie, I'll be very upset.' She crossed the roof, stopping just short of where Gethryn was standing. 'What is it? What do you want, Geth? I'll listen, whatever. Just . . . just stop this.'

Gethryn took half a step forward, towards her. 'I'll tell you what I want,' he said. Another step. 'I want this over.'

And before Jack could move, react, *breathe*, Gethryn had seized her around the waist, thrown himself backwards, and taken them both off the edge of the roof.

CHAPTER 28

He sat alone in the white room on a chair that squeaked. From somewhere he'd found an old biro which jutted from between his teeth as he sucked and bit on it to keep the cravings at bay, cravings which crept up his spine like insects and threatened his brain. A cup of very elderly coffee occupied his hands, occasional whispers of its smell making his stomach churn.

'Mr Whitaker?' The nurse put her head around the door. Jack shot to his feet, the coffee sprawling out across the tiles, the biro falling from his lips. 'Yes. What's happening? How is . . . I mean, how is she?' His stomach turned over again, but it wasn't at the smell of the coffee now. Cold, hard dread burned a hole through his gut, aided and abetted by hot fury.

The nurse shook her head. 'I'm sorry, I just came to let you know that there's not going to be any news for a while, you might as well go home.' Her eyes flickered over the pooling coffee. 'If there's anything, we can call you.'

Jack embraced the fury. It ran through his blood

now, overflowing and flooding every organ, rushing his brain like a tsunami. *Nineteen years. Nineteen years of feeling nothing, of keeping it all shut away like a mad dog. I'm out of practice . . .* 'Look.' He tried to keep the worst of the anger from his voice but he knew it was shining from his eyes by the way the nurse took a step back and held the door half-closed between them. 'I'm staying here. I will not leave until there is something that you can tell me, all right? So, if I were you, I'd get back to that *fucking* Emergency Room and not leave it until you can tell me what the *fuck* is going on.'

His whole body was vibrating with it. The terror that had taken over his brain when he saw Skye fall hadn't moved an inch, even though he knew she was alive, knew she was in good hands, knew all the right things were being done. It had simply changed form.

Jack went back to the squeaky chair and sat, elbows on knees, head in hands. He let himself sink just for a second into the sleep his body so desperately wanted, but the dreams were queuing up already; nineteen years of denial had built up a huge backlog of nightmares he was very afraid he was going to have to work his way through before he reached any sense of resolution. *Like having to read the whole series to find out whodunit. Except, in this case, I know who.* It was me.

A sad-eyed orderly came in and began sluicing a desultory mop over the coffee spill. Jack let his eyes follow the movement, its hypnotic rhythm easing more thoughts from his brain. Why did Skye touch him in a way that no-one else had? Did he have a huge case of white-knight syndrome, wanting to ride in and rescue her from her lack of a past and an uncertain future? He rocked the chair back on two legs, the plastic squealing and flexing like a heretic under torture by the Inquisition and remembered her quiet acceptance of him as he was. Remembered the touch of that velvet dress. The scent of her skin. The way she'd let him cry . . .

His mouth let out a sharp sound as a backwash from the anger hit and then a hand touched his knee and made him jump.

'Skye?'

Another chair squealed in protest at a sitting body. 'Hi, Jackie-boy. Looking like shit, if I might say so.'

Jack sank back. 'What are you doing here, Liss?' He didn't want to admit that he'd thought Skye might have died and visited him as some kind of farewell. Even as a writer, *that* kind of imagination was frowned on.

Lissa sighed. 'Here for Geth. You might hate him and wish him to hell but . . . he's a good man, underneath it all. He's confused, is all. And I'm . . . hey, I'm quite fond of him, y'know? He's had a rough time.' She gave another sigh and rubbed the back of a dirty hand over her cheek. 'I want him to make it,' she whispered.

'Yeah.'

'You waiting to hear about Skye?'

'No, I'm hoping Elvis might stage a come-back tour.' His head sank lower until all he could see was a circle of tiled floor between his feet. 'It's the memories, Liss.' He spoke to a cracked tile. 'I can't lose them. They've ruined my life, and I can't lose them. How am I supposed to do anything, live a normal life with . . . with anyone, when I've got these *things* following me?'

He smelled a sudden billow of perfume as Lissa moved her chair closer. 'Memories make us what we are, Jackie. Ask your Skye, poor little chick's scared to death that she's not real because her memory's all mixed up. And here's you, scared that you're too real, too tied to what's gone before.' Another hand brushed his shoulder. 'It gets easier, y'know. When you turn around and face it. I found that when I had to look at you knowing who you were, *what* you were, and then after when . . . when I lost the baby.' She touched his cheek with a cool hand. 'Learn to deal, Ice. That's all I got. Learn to deal.'

Jack felt a slow uncoiling in his chest, as though an overwound spring was losing tension. He put a hand to his throat where the leather lace felt slimy against his slick skin. 'I'm holding it all like it defines me.' The quiet words weren't for Lissa, who was staring at a poster about sexually transmitted diseases. 'I'm *letting* it define me.'

Without looking at him, Lissa shrugged. 'Life, huh?'

Yes. Life. We're pitched into it, expected to know what to do, how to cope. How to manage those situations where everything spirals down. And sometimes we just can't adapt fast enough, it sucks us down with it and the weight of what we've done keeps us there. But sometimes . . . he traced the curve of his throat, where the lace marked a line, echoed a scar . . . *sometimes life spirals upwards. And maybe the trick is knowing which is which . . .*

CHAPTER 29

When I woke up, I thought I'd gone back in time. Above my head arched a drip unit, the bag swelling down into a tube I could feel somewhere in the back of my hand. Underneath me was a hard bed, my head and chest hurt and I could feel the various stings and weights of needles and bandages around my body.

When I turned my head, Felix was sitting in a chair beside me, feet up on the bed, doing a crossword. He was shirtless, wearing a neck-brace and one arm in a removable plastic cast. When I said 'hi,' he jumped, whipped his feet off the bed, winced, and dropped the pen.

'Fuck, you scared me!'

Despite the various medical interventions surrounding him, he looked good, although, to be fair, he would have had to go some to have looked worse than the last time I saw him. His hair was spiked, he was clean-shaven, and he smelled of some delicious cologne. Although there were bruises along his side, they were losing their immediate puffiness and flaring into black and red.

'How long have I been here?'

'Look, I'm just sitting duty. Jack's the guy you need to talk to, hang on a sec.' Fumbling one-handed, Felix drew a mobile phone out of his grey joggers pocket and pushed a single button. It seemed to be answered almost immediately. 'Hey. She's awake.' He listened for a minute. 'No. Nothing. That's your job, Whitaker. Two minutes.' He hung up.

'That's not your phone.' My voice sounded hoarse, crackly with disuse. My throat was dry and ached slightly and my mouth was all sticky.

'No.' Felix leaned forward as close as he could get with the brace and the cast. 'It's Jared's.'

I blinked. 'We're still in America?'

'Well, darling, this sure as hell isn't the NHS, is it?' Felix waved a hand to indicate the gleaming room with the impeccably tasteful wall art and the enormous plasma-screen TV in the corner. He flipped open the phone again. 'Not unless you've been unconscious through several changes of government. Although I do think you should congratulate me for my farsightedness in taking out the medical insurance – have to admit I thought it might be *me* having to use it, but, hey, there you go.' He waggled his eyebrows.

'I didn't think you were allowed to phone in hospitals,' I croaked.

'Yeah, 'cos it's going to interfere with your pace-maker,' Felix said, dialling.

'I've got a *pacemaker*!' The croak changed to

squeak and my voice broke like a fourteen-year-old boy's.

'Joke. Now, shut up, this is serious. Hey, Jared. It's me. She's awake, I'm free. Come pick me up?' He flipped the phone shut and got to his feet. 'Right. Catch you later, lover.'

'Fe.' I managed to motion with one hand to stop him leaving. 'How's Gethryn?'

He avoided my eye. 'Jack's on his way over. You need to talk to him.'

'I need to talk to *you*.'

Felix looked at me sideways. 'It was true, you know. Everything I said about Mike and Faith. They were laughing at you.' He sighed and his mouth twisted. 'I hardly knew my own sister sometimes,' he whispered. 'So determined to hurt, to get what she wanted.' A sudden smile and a lightening in his eyes. 'But I guess that's actors for you, isn't it?'

'From what you said I deserved it. No excuses, and it's too late now to be sorry. If I was one tenth as bad as you said I'm not surprised that they got together; the only thing I'm surprised about is that you and faith ever wanted to know me.'

'Yeah, well.' Felix shuffled his feet. 'It wasn't really your fault, Skye. Your parents weren't . . . even when I first knew you they never really cared much about you. We always wondered about your dad, I mean he had one heck of a temper but . . . you never said anything. They were another one of those things that you made up stories about – they doted on you, adored you, brought you flash presents – we never saw the evidence, of course. And maybe there was some kind of other reason that your grandma left you the house? And then they flew over to see you in hospital, what? Once? You nearly *died* and they didn't even stay long enough to drive you home. You'd had to make yourself into someone that could cope with that kind of neglect.'

I looked up at the metal ceiling grill where the recessed lights reminded me of Gethryn's eyes, fixing me, holding me tight as we plunged towards the ground. I gave a little shake to stop myself thinking about the landing and felt a few, weak tears spill towards the bedcover. 'It was never that bad,' my voice sounded weak. 'They loved me in their own way, as best they could, they were just wrapped up in each other. I . . . I wanted it to be different, and I thought if I wanted it hard enough, then maybe . . .'

Felix steepled his fingers underneath his chin and gave me a level look. 'I'm sorry for what I said, Skye. I mean, yes, you were pretty horrible but . . . you could be very sweet, too. You and I always got on, well, yeah, you could tell some pretty tall tales sometimes but I took them for what they were – a scared little girl trying to make herself look bigger so that no-one would realise how frightened you were inside. And I didn't just bring you over here to get you to win the part for me. Okay, maybe that was a part of it, in the back of my mind but . . . only in the *very* back, where I keep all those other things I'm ashamed of.'

'Like your Mamma Mia CD and your David Tennant life-sized cut-out?'

A grin. 'Hush. I'm not ashamed of those. Just *reticent* about them.' He took a sudden step closer to the bed and I could see the twinkle back in those hazel eyes again. 'And, while we're here –' his voice dropped – 'the accident . . . it wasn't entirely your fault. Oh yes, you fought, Skye, punched me *right* in the gonads that night but . . . Mike was driving like a lunatic, and, come on . . . letting Faith, well, *handle* him while he was driving? But Mike always thought he was in control of everything – there you were, fighting and trying to get to him; he should have stopped, pulled over, but he was too arrogant. Girl in the back raising hell? Girlfriend dealing out the hand jobs? Nah, Mike thought he could do sixty through all of that. And *that* was what killed them.' Felix leaned in closer. 'I much prefer the new, improved Skye and her new taste in men. You can never accuse Jack of arrogance, can you? I mean, the guy doesn't have *any idea* just how tasty he is . . . oh, how I hope you're going to put him right on that score. For the good of all of us, I mean.'

'We've got so much to talk about now, haven't we? Now you've started telling me the truth.'

Felix grinned. 'Maybe you're ready to hear it now. This last year-and-a-half it's been like you were turning Mike into some kind of saint, some kind of perfect boyfriend, and I had to bite my tongue to stop blurting out the truth. He led you along, Skye. He could have told you it was over, but he kept picking you up and putting you down, messing with your head and all the while he was sleeping with your best friend, but since the accident you wanted . . . no, sorry, you *needed* to think of him as having been the love of your life. So I let you. And I'm sorry about that, really I am but . . .'

A shrug and he started to stare at the floor with a pink tinge rising up his neck to engulf his cheeks. A silent hand raised and squeezed mine which made both of us wince. 'Ow. And then you saved my life. I'd just destroyed yours and you saved mine.' A sound outside and his head whipped up to stare thankfully at the door. 'Right then, lover, better be off. Despite these –' he indicated the brace and the cast – 'my darling Jared is raring to go.' With a blown kiss he walked out of the room, limping slightly and giving me a full view of his back, which was covered in newer bruises than the ones on his side. He looked like he'd been beaten, and not in a pervy-sexy-game way.

As soon as he'd gone out, Jack came in. He was pale, there were shadows under his eyes and he had, if it were possible, lost weight. He looked like a gauntly beautiful zombie. He walked into the room, closed the door carefully behind him and held onto it, as though he needed its support.

'Hey.' Then he shut his eyes and breathed a long breath in and out.

My heart hurt. 'Hey, Jack.' I tried to move but was held in place by the needle in the back of my hand. 'What happened? How's Gethryn?'

The eyes stayed shut. 'He tried to kill you.'

'I know. I was there.'

Now the eyes snapped open. There was something hellish in them and his voice was savage. 'He's recovering, Skye. He could have been killed falling off that roof, but he wasn't. I wish he had been. He tried to kill you,' he repeated, as though I might be in some doubt.

'He's okay?' The gorgeous, ruined Gethryn Tudor-Morgan. But . . . 'What happened? How come we survived?' I wouldn't think about the falling, wouldn't think about that fantastic tawny body, those greenish amber eyes staring into mine, falling . . . falling . . .

Jack took a deep breath in again. 'In a huge twist of ironic fate, you landed on Felix.' His mouth creased. 'He'd just got out of the hospital, got dropped off by taxi round the back of the motel, therefore neatly missing all the Security teams I had lined up at the front, and came to find out what was going on on the roof.'

'Is that why . . . ?'

'You dislocated his neck, broke two bones in his arm and rebroke his ribs for him. You, incidentally, got away with a broken ankle and concussion. I think Felix has a massive complex about that.'

'Why the drip?'

'It's just to rehydrate you. You'd been wandering in the desert for quite a while before I found you, and then, with the accident . . . they had to put you out to set your ankle.'

'But what about Gethryn?'

'Two broken legs, broken pelvis, spinal trauma, and I hope it drove his cock out through his eye-sockets.' Now he let go of the door and came over to the bed. He was wearing his white shirt, sleeves rolled up to the elbows, and his tight black jeans, but his feet were bare again. 'But he's going to be all right. Eventually. He's going to get a lot of treatment, but it's all for the best, because the public loves a tortured star. He's even got bloody *Lissa* sitting at his bedside. By the time he's recovered he'll probably be a national fucking hero, everything will be forgiven. But not by me, Skye. He tried to kill you. Because of me, because he knew . . . he wanted to take you.' He put his head in his hands with his voice cracking. 'You could have died, because of me.'

'Jack . . .'

'I *told* you, I told all of them, I'm useless. I can't love, I can't *feel*, I cause more pain just by existing than anyone should have a right to, every single thing I touch turns to shit and ashes!'

I wriggled up the bed. The needle dragged at my skin. It hurt. Everything hurt. 'That's not true, though, is it? Look at *Two Turns North* for example – classic sci-fi TV. People will still be watching that in fifty years and enjoying it.'

'*North* wasn't mine, though. I was just one of the team.'

'And doesn't that tell you something?'

He raised his head slowly and stared at me. 'Is it meant to?'

His skin was paler than I'd ever seen a human look. Like paper, with his eyes drawn in pain over the top. 'Sometimes you need other people to make things truly work,' I whispered. 'And, look at it this way, if bad things come in threes, well, I ought to be immune for . . . oooh, the next fifty years or so.'

The bedside chair rasped against the floor as he dropped into it and slumped forward as though even his bones were tired. 'I told you I was no good for you.' Jack's voice was muffled. 'I *told* you.' And when he dragged his head up to look at me, his eyes were wet and clouded. 'I should have told you why . . .' He looked quickly at me, then away. 'I shouldn't have sent you up there; I shouldn't have let you get within a mile of Gethryn when he was in that state. I'm no good for anyone, that's what it comes down to.'

'You've been good for me.'

He stared at me then, with a kind of disbelief. 'What? How have I been "good for you"? Have you looked at yourself lately?'

I held his stare. 'Yes, I have, actually. And compared to the Skye that flew over here only a few days ago, I think I'm pretty much of an improvement.'

'Maybe I shouldn't have . . . I should have kept my distance.'

'You can't keep your distance forever, Jack.' If I really strained the drip line I could just touch him. Should I? Those eyes . . .

'But if I hadn't got involved, you wouldn't be lying here, all bruised and . . .' He tailed off.

'Yeah, and if you hadn't got involved, you would never have followed me after the explosion. None of that would have happened.'

'You'd have been fine. Someone would have found you, or you'd have made your way back to the motel.'

I wiggled my way further up the bed. It hurt like buggery, but now I could sit properly, meet his eye. 'I wasn't talking about that. I meant . . . after.' Kept my eyes on his.

'Oh.'

'You were good for me then too, Jack. That was the first time since the accident.'

A tiny flash of smile. 'I'm glad it was good for you.' His eyes had softened a little; his mouth wasn't that tight line any more. 'For the record, I enjoyed it, too.'

'No, you don't understand. Sex is . . . well, let's face it, unless it's pretty spectacular it's not the kind of thing you remember forever, is it? It all kind of blurs.' My cheeks were heating up, I could feel it, and just hoped that it wasn't making my scar glow like a beacon, then realised that Jack probably wouldn't care even if it was. 'At least, for me it has, with all the memory woo-woo that's gone on.'

'Oh,' he said again, but there was almost a hint of a smile behind his eyes now. 'You mean –'

'My body knows I'm not a virgin, but my brain hasn't quite caught on yet. That was the first sex I can remember, properly, in full, glorious detail.' I gave him a slightly shy smile. 'And it was all pretty glorious. You are one hell of a sexy guy, Mr Whitaker.'

That got him. He laughed and his face relaxed. 'Well, likewise, Miss Threppel, you are one hell of a sexy woman.'

'But you're afraid of getting involved.' I whispered it, so that he had to move his head closer to hear me, the laugh fading into a new, darker expression.

'I'm afraid of a lot of things, Skye,' he whispered back. 'I started screwing up my life before I was even old enough to vote, and I haven't let up since. The only things that have gone well have been the things I've done alone – it doesn't exactly fill me with confidence that I will . . . *would* make a good partner.'

'That's not true though, is it? You've only remembered the things that you've done alone as being successful because that's how you've needed to think of yourself. You are more than capable of being part of a team.' My heart was squashing itself in behind my lungs, but this wasn't stress, wasn't some kind of panic attack, I knew now. This was love.

'I locked myself up in ice to stop me feeling, because I'm so scared of what happens when I do, I'm scared of all the bad stuff that comes crashing down on me when I . . . All I can do is write, that is the only thing that works.'

'The only thing you could control.' Now his forehead was almost touching mine. 'Loss of control, Jack. Isn't that what this has all been about?'

He moved away so sharply that we almost cracked heads, and cleared his throat. 'Felix is coming back to the States,' he said. 'Did you know? He's flying back to the UK to sort stuff out and apply for his visas, but he's got three months before filming starts so it should be fine. He and Jared are moving in together, don't tell him I said so, but I think it's the real thing. He'll get his Green Card on the strength of working on the new series of *Fallen Skies*, and I think he'll take off; he's got that kind of innocent evil look that they're loving right now. And the British accent, of course.'

'Oh.' I tried to keep pace with his mental switch, stop thinking about all those emotionally complicated things that he clearly couldn't deal with. Tears bulged behind my eyes – he'd been so close to realising, so close to reaching inside that frozen exterior and finding the true core of himself. But obviously he'd find it easier to keep going as he was. Never dealing with it. Functioning, rather than living. And I'd thought he was stronger than that. 'Right, yes, okay.'

Bugger. They wouldn't let me fly home yet. And I doubted Felix would hang around and wait for me, so I'd have to fly back alone . . . Oh, sod it, after this week crowds and airports would be a *picnic*. At least they didn't explode, or try to kill me. In fact, after everything that had happened here, I didn't think I'd ever be scared of anything as simple as the outdoors or people again.

'You'll have to stay over here for a while longer without him. Will you be all right?'

I thought for a second. 'I expect so. I'm learning more about myself all the time now; I don't need to lean on Felix for old memories any more. It's who I am now that matters, after all.'

Jack made a jerky movement, as though he'd jumped. 'God,' he said suddenly.

'What? Are you all right?' I stared at him. His head had come up and he'd stopped looking so hunched, but his eyes were wide.

'Oh, yes, Skye. I am beginning to think I might be. What you said then, "it's who I am now that matters." It's something I've been trying to get my head around. Something I've been trying to articulate to myself, but I'd overcomplicated it. Overthought it.'

'Jack,' I said gently, 'you are rambling again.'

'Yes'. But he wasn't agreeing with me, he was agreeing with the person he was arguing with in his head. 'Yes. Of course. It's that simple.' He leaned back in the chair, which put us level. The open collar of the white shirt hung loose, with at

least the top three buttons undone and he slid his fingers inside it, fiddled for a moment and then brought his hand out with something dangling from his palm.

'You've taken off the lace,' I whispered. 'Ryan's lace.'

'Er. Yep.' Almost reverently he laid it on top of the bedside cupboard.

'Why?'

'Can we talk about it when I'm allowed to smoke again? I'm running out of legal things to shove in my mouth.'

'No. Try. Concentrate.'

'"It's who I am now that matters." You said it Skye. And this is who I am now. Me. Not dragging the memories of Ryan, all the bad stuff. Me.' He moved in closer again. 'Look. They reckon you'll be fit to leave hospital by tomorrow, but you're going to need to mend that ankle, no walking, that kind of thing, so you'll need someone with you. Fly back with me. I'll get your ticket changed, buy one myself . . . come up to my place, up on the moors, just for a break, a holiday. I can work up there on these scripts. I'll need to come back over to tie up the loose ends but . . . ?'

'Have you just done a complete 180, or wasn't I listening properly?'

'When Geth . . . when he jumped and I thought I'd lost you . . . God, I really need a cigarette . . . it made me think, reappraise, you know? But I was scared. Pinned down by what had happened

in the past. But I have just decided I need to do what you did when you flew out here with Felix.'

'What, take a stupendous amount of Valium?'

'Step outside. Do it. As those godawful new-agey things would have it, "feel the fear and do it anyway". I'm going to come clean. Do a couple of interviews, tell them about my past, about what I did to Ryan. Get in touch with his parents, talk to them, lance this horrible boil of dread that I've been living on top of all these years, but I need . . . I need *you* to help me. I'm terrified, Skye, terrified of not being able to love you, about trying to live without that ice block round my heart. I'm not good at pain; I run, I hide rather than face up to things, and you're going to have screaming nightmares about falling off that roof for years but . . . hey.' His eyes were so deep that looking into them was like falling all over again. 'We could try.'

'Me and you? You think it would work?'

'They could probably write psychology text books about the pair of us but, yeah. Stranger things have happened.' He pushed both hands through his hair, making it fall back from his face, so I could see his eyes properly. 'Do you want to?' 'I want to help you, yes.' 'And the rest?' 'I'd . . . like to, I think.'

A sudden, fleeting smile. 'Memories . . . they're all about what's gone, they don't have to have anything to do with what we *become*. They don't have to define us. And I'm going to ask

you again, now. Do you want to make yourself again with *me*?'

There was a pale line around his throat where the lace had blocked the light for so many years. My eyes kept going to it as my mind wrapped itself around what it meant. 'A new life?' The words eased over my sore throat and past my cracked lips. 'With you?'

Another smile. This one seemed lighter. 'Yeah.'

'But we hardly know each other.' The words came out slowly, as though I was already disregarding them.

'Skye, we hardly even know *ourselves*. Come for a while, a week, a month. No commitment; see how it goes when we've got space to breathe away from all this.'

I found I was shivering, but not from cold. Jack ran his finger along the line of goosebumps which broke out on my arms, followed them up to my shoulder and under the neckline of the hospital gown I was wearing. His touch made me shiver even more, and I hadn't even *thought* about how my hair must look. I remembered his kiss, his kindness and I was suddenly looking to a clear future. 'I think I'd like that, Jack.'

Long, cool fingers brushed against my creased skin. 'Have you got a private bathroom?'

'I think so. At least, I'm assuming that's what's behind that door there. Why?'

God, he was gorgeous when he looked at me like that. 'Just wanted to check that what happened in that gulley wasn't a fluke.'

'I've got a broken ankle and an IV drip, you weirdo.' But I was smiling.

'Course. Yes. Sorry.' Now he was grinning too. 'Plenty of time for all that.'

'Yes. Plenty. All the time in the world, in fact.'

He leaned closer and his lips brushed mine, more of a promise than a kiss. 'I shall remember you said that.'

This time the shiver was a shudder. 'Just one thing, Jack Whitaker. When we fly home, you will wear shoes, won't you?'

'Darling Skye, I'll wear a Laura Ashley frock if that's what it takes.'

Then he kissed me properly. And the skies fell.